The Second Leonaur Christmas Book of Great Ghost Stories

The Second Leonaur Christmas Book of Great Ghost Stories

Twenty-Two Short Stories of the Strange and Unusual Including 'John Charrington's Wedding', 'The Ghost at the Rath', 'The Shadow of a Shade', 'The Old Nurse's Story', and 'The Botathen Ghost'

Eunice Hetherington

LEONAUR

The Second Leonaur Christmas Book of Great Ghost Stories
Twenty-Two Short Stories of the Strange and Unusual Including 'John Charrington's Wedding', 'The Ghost at the Rath', 'The Shadow of a Shade', 'The Old Nurse's Story', and 'The Botathen Ghost'

by Eunice Hetherington

FIRST EDITION

Leonaur is an imprint of Oakpast Ltd

ISBN: 978-1-78282-696-5 (hardcover)
ISBN: 978-1-78282-697-2 (softcover)

http://www.leonaur.com

Publisher's Notes

Contents

Was it an Illusion? A Parson's Story

Amelia Edwards

The facts which I am about to relate happened to myself some sixteen or eighteen years ago, at which time I served Her Majesty as an Inspector of Schools. Now, the Provincial Inspector is perpetually on the move; and I was still young enough to enjoy a life of constant travelling.

There are, indeed, many less agreeable ways in which an unbeneficed parson may contrive to scorn delights and live laborious days. In remote places where strangers are scarce, his annual visit is an important event; and though at the close of a long day's work he would sometimes prefer the quiet of a country inn, he generally finds himself the destined guest of the rector or the squire. It rests with himself to turn these opportunities to account. If he makes himself pleasant, he forms agreeable friendships and sees English home-life under one of its most attractive aspects; and sometimes, even in these days of universal common-placeness, he may have the luck to meet with an adventure.

My first appointment was to a West of England district largely peopled with my personal friends and connections. It was, therefore, much to my annoyance that I found myself, after a couple of years of very pleasant work, transferred to what a policeman would call 'a new beat,' up in the North.

Unfortunately for me, my new beat—a rambling, thinly populated area of something under 1,800 square miles—was three times as large as the old one, and more than proportionately unmanageable. Intersected at right angles by two ranges of barren hills and cut off to a large extent from the main lines of railway, it united about every inconvenience that a district could possess. The villages lay wide apart, often separated by long tracts of moorland; and in place of the well-warmed railway compartment and the frequent manor-house, I now spent half my time in hired vehicles and lonely country inns.

I had been in possession of this district for some three months or so, and winter was near at hand, when I paid my first visit of inspection to Pit End, an outlying hamlet in the most northerly corner of my county, just twenty-two miles from the nearest station. Haying slept overnight at a place called Drumley, and inspected Drumley schools in the morning, I started for Pit End, with fourteen miles of railway and twenty-two of hilly cross-roads between myself and my journey's end.

I made, of course, all the enquiries I could think of before leaving; but neither the Drumley schoolmaster nor the landlord of the Drumley 'Feathers' knew much more of Pit End than its name. My predecessor, it seemed, had been in the habit of taking Pit End 'from the other side', the roads, though longer, being less hilly that way. That the place boasted some kind of inn was certain; but it was an inn unknown to fame, and to mine host of the 'Feathers'. Be it good or bad, however, I should have to put up at it.

Upon this scant information I started. My fourteen miles of railway journey soon ended at a place called Bramsford Road, whence an omnibus conveyed passengers to a dull little town called Bramsford Market. Here I found a horse and 'trap' to carry me on to my destination; the horse being a rawboned grey with a profile like a camel, and the trap a rickety high gig which had probably done commercial travelling in the days of its youth. From Bramsford Market the way lay over a succession of long hills, rising to a barren, high-level plateau. It was a dull, raw afternoon of mid-November, growing duller and more raw as the day waned and the east wind blew keener.' How much further now, driver?' I asked, as we alighted at the foot of a longer and a stiffer hill than any we had yet passed over.

He turned a straw in his mouth, and grunted something about 'fewer or foive mile by the rooad'.

And then I learned that by turning off at a point which he described as 't'owld tollus', and taking a certain footpath across the fields, this distance might be considerably shortened. I decided, therefore, to walk the rest of the way; and, setting off at a good pace, I soon left driver and trap behind. At the top of the hill I lost sight of them, and coming presently to a little road-side ruin which I at once recognised as the old toll-house, I found the footpath without difficulty.

It led me across a barren slope divided by stone fences, with here and there a group of shattered sheds, a tall chimney, and a blackened cinder-mound, marking the site of a deserted mine. A light fog, meanwhile, was creeping up from the east, and the dusk was gathering fast.

Now, to lose one's way in such a place and at such an hour would be disagreeable enough, and the footpath—a trodden track already half obliterated—would be indistinguishable in the course of another ten minutes. Looking anxiously ahead, therefore, in the hope of seeing some sign of habitation, I hastened on, scaling one stone stile after another, till I all at once found myself skirting a line of park-palings. following these, with bare boughs branching out overhead and dead leaves rustling underfoot, I came presently to a point where the path divided; here continuing to skirt the enclosure, and striking off yonder across a space of open meadow.

Which should I take?

By following the fence, I should be sure to arrive at a lodge where I could enquire my way to Pit End; but then the park might be of any extent, and I might have a long distance to go before I came to the nearest lodge. Again, the meadow-path, instead of leading to Pit End, might take me in a totally opposite direction. But there was no time to be lost in hesitation; so I chose the meadow, the further end of which was lost to sight in a fleecy bank of fog.

Up to this moment I had not met a living soul of whom to ask my way; it was, therefore, with no little sense of relief that I saw a man emerging from the fog and coming along the path. As we neared each other—I advancing rapidly; he slowly—I observed that he dragged the left foot, limping as he walked. It was, however, so dark and so misty, that not till we were within half a dozen yards of each other could I see that he wore a dark suit and an Anglican felt hat, and looked something like a dissenting minister. As soon as we were within speaking distance, I addressed him.

'Can you tell me', I said, 'if I am right for Pit End, and how far I have to go?'

He came on, looking straight before him; taking no notice of my question; apparently not hearing it.

'I beg your pardon,' I said, raising my voice; 'but will this path take me to Pit End, and if so'—He had passed on without pausing; without looking at me; I could almost have believed, without seeing me!

I stopped, with the words on my lips; then turned to look after—perhaps, to follow—him.

But instead of following, I stood bewildered.

What had become of him? And what lad was that going up the

path by which I had just come—that tall lad, half-running, half-walking, with a fishing-rod over his shoulder? I could have taken my oath that I had neither met nor passed him. Where then had he come from? And where was the man to whom I had spoken not three seconds ago, and who, at his limping pace, could not have made more than a couple of yards in the time? My stupefaction was such that I stood quite still, looking after the lad with the fishing-rod till he disappeared in the gloom under the park-palings.

Was I dreaming?

Darkness, meanwhile, had closed in apace, and, dreaming or not dreaming, I must push on, or find myself benighted. So I hurried forward, turning my back on the last gleam of daylight, and plunging deeper into the fog at every step. I was, however, close upon my journey's end. The path ended at a turnstile; the turnstile opened upon a steep lane; and at the bottom of the lane, down which I stumbled among stones and ruts, I came in sight of the welcome glare of a blacksmith's forge.

Here, then, was Pit End. I found my trap standing at the door of the village inn; the rawboned grey stabled for the night; the landlord watching for my arrival.

The 'Greyhound' was a hostelry of modest pretensions, and I shared its little parlour with a couple of small farmers and a young man who informed me that he 'travelled in' Thorley's Food for Cattle. Here I dined, wrote my letters, chatted awhile with the landlord, and picked up such scraps of local news as fell in my way.

There was, it seemed, no resident parson at Pit End; the incumbent being a pluralist with three small livings, the duties of which, by the help of a rotatory curate, he discharged in a somewhat easy fashion. Pit End, as the smallest and furthest off, came in for but one service each Sunday, and was almost wholly relegated to the curate. The squire was a more confirmed absentee than even the vicar. He lived chiefly in Paris, spending abroad the wealth of his Pit End coal-fields.

He happened to be at home just now, the landlord said, after five years' absence; but he would be off again next week, and another five years might probably elapse before they should again see him at Blackwater Chase.

Blackwater Chase!—the name was not new to me; yet I could not remember where I had heard it. When, however, mine host went on to say that, despite his absenteeism, Mr Wolstenholme was 'a pleasant gentleman and a good landlord', and that, after all, Blackwater Chase was 'a lonesome sort of world-end place for a young man to bury himself in', then I at once remembered Phil Wolstenholme of Balliol, who, in his grand way, had once upon a time given me a general invitation to the shooting at Blackwater Chase. That was twelve years ago, when I was reading hard at Wadham, and Wolstenholme-the idol of a clique to which I did not belong-was boating, betting, writing poetry, and giving wine parties at Balliol.

Yes; I remembered all about him—his handsome face, his luxurious rooms, his boyish prodigality, his utter indolence, and the blind faith of his worshippers, who believed that he had only 'to pull himself together' in order to carry off every honour which the University had to bestow. He did take the Newdigate; but it was his first and last achievement, and he left college with the reputation of having narrowly escaped a plucking.

How vividly it all came back upon my memory—the old college life, the college friendships, the pleasant time that could never come again! It was but twelve years ago; yet it seemed like half a century. And now, after these twelve years, here were Wolstenholme and I as near neighbours as in our Oxford days! I wondered if he was much changed, and whether, if changed, it were for the better or the worse.

Had his generous impulses developed into sterling virtues, or had his follies hardened into vices?

Should I let him know where I was, and so judge for myself? Nothing would be easier than to pencil a line upon a card tomorrow morning, and send it up to the big house. Yet, merely to satisfy a purposeless curiosity, was it worthwhile to reopen the acquaintanceship? Thus musing, I sat late over the fire, and by the time I went to bed, I had well nigh forgotten my adventure with the man who vanished so mysteriously and the boy who seemed to come from nowhere.

Next morning, finding I had abundant time at my disposal, I did pencil that line upon my card—a mere line, saving that I believed we had known each other at Oxford, and that I should be inspecting the National Schools from nine till about eleven. And then, having dispatched it by one of my landlord's sons, I went off to my work. The day was brilliantly fine. The wind had shifted round to the north, the sun shone clear and cold, and the smoke-grimed hamlet, and the gaunt buildings clustered at the mouths of the coal pits round about, looked as bright as they could look at any time of the year.

The village was built up a long hillside; the church and schools being at the top, and the 'Greyhound' at the bottom. Looking vainly for the lane by which I had come the night before, I climbed the one rambling street, followed a path that skirted the churchyard, and found myself at the schools. These, with the teachers' dwellings, formed three sides of a quadrangle; the fourth side consisting of an iron railing and a gate. An inscribed tablet over the main entrance-door recorded how 'These school-houses were rebuilt by Philip Wolstenholme, Esquire: *a.d.* 18—.'

Mr Wolstenholme, sir, is the Lord of the Manor,' said a soft, obsequious voice.

I turned, and found the speaker at my elbow, a square-built, sallow man, all in black, with a bundle of copy-books under his arm.

'You are the—the schoolmaster?' I said; unable to remember his name, and puzzled by a vague recollection of his face.

'Just so, sir. I conclude I have the honour of addressing Mr Frazer?'

It was a singular face, very pallid and anxious-looking. The eyes, too, had a watchful, almost a startled, look in them, which struck me as peculiarly unpleasant.

'Yes,' I replied, still wondering where and when I had seen him. 'My name is Frazer. Yours, I believe, is—is—,' and I put my hand into my pocket for my examination papers.

'Skelton-Ebenezer Skelton. Will you please to take the boys first, sir?'

The words were commonplace enough, but the man's manner was studiously, disagreeably deferential; his very name being given, as it were, under protest, as if too insignificant to be mentioned.

I said I would begin with the boys; and so moved on. Then, for we had stood still till now, I saw that the schoolmaster was lame. In that moment I remembered him. He was the man I met in the fog.

'I met you yesterday afternoon, Mr Skelton,' I said, as we went into the school-room.

'Yesterday afternoon, sir?' he repeated.

'You did not seem to observe me,' I said, carelessly. 'I spoke to you, in fact; but you did not reply to me.'

'But—indeed, I beg your pardon, sir—it must have been someone else,' said the schoolmaster, 'I did not go out yesterday afternoon.'

How could this be anything but a falsehood? I might have been mistaken as to the man's face; though it was such a singular face, and I had seen it quite plainly. But how could I be mistaken as to his lameness? Besides, that curious trailing of the right foot, as if the ankle was broken, was not an ordinary lameness.

I suppose I looked incredulous, for he added, hastily: 'Even if I had not been preparing the boys for inspection, sir, I should not have gone out yesterday afternoon. It was too damp and foggy. I am obliged to be careful—I have a very delicate chest.'

My dislike to the man increased with every word he uttered. I did not ask myself with what motive he went on heaping lie upon lie; it was enough that, to serve his own ends, whatever those ends might be, he did lie with unparalleled audacity.

'We will proceed to the examination, Mr Skelton,' I said, contemptuously.

He turned, if possible, a shade paler than before, bent his head silently, and called up the scholars in their order.

I soon found that, whatever his shortcomings as to veracity, Mr Ebenezer Skelton was a capital schoolmaster. His boys were uncommonly well taught, and as regarded attendance, good conduct, and the like, left nothing to be desired. When, therefore, at the end of the examination, he said he hoped I would recommend the Pit End Boys' School for the government grant, I at once assented. And now I thought I had done with Mr Skelton for, at all events, the space of one year. Not so, however. When I came out from the Girls' School, I found him waiting at the door.

Profusely apologizing, he begged leave to occupy five minutes of my valuable time. He wished, under correction, to suggest a little improvement. The boys, he said, were allowed to play in the quadrangle, which was too small, and in various ways inconvenient; but round at the back there was a piece of waste land, half an acre of which, if enclosed, would admirably answer the purpose. So saying, he led the way to the back of the building, and I followed him.

'To whom does this ground belong?' I asked.

'To Mr Wolstenholme, sir.'

'Then why not apply to Mr Wolstenholme? He gave the schools, and I dare say he would be equally willing to give the ground.'

'I beg your pardon, sir. Mr Wolstenholme has not been over here since his return, and it is quite possible that he may leave Pit End without honouring us with a visit. I could not take the liberty of writing to him, sir.'

'Neither could I in my report suggest that the Government should offer to purchase a portion of Mr Wolstenholme's land for a playground to schools of Mr Wolstenholme's own building.' I replied. 'Under other circumstances'.

I stopped and looked round.

The schoolmaster repeated my last words.

'You were saying, sir—under other circumstances?'

I looked round again.

'It seemed to me that there was someone here,' I said; 'some third person, not a moment ago.'

'I beg your pardon, sir—a third person?'

'I saw his shadow on the ground, between yours and mine.'

The schools faced due north, and we were standing immediately behind the buildings, with our backs to the sun. The place was bare, and open, and high; and our shadows, sharply defined, lay stretched before our feet.

'A—a shadow?' he faltered. 'Impossible.'

There was not a bush or a tree within half a mile. There was not a cloud in the sky. There was nothing, absolutely nothing, that could have cast a shadow.

I admitted that it was impossible, and that I must have fancied it; and so went back to the matter of the playground.' Should you see Mr Wolstenholme,' I said, 'you are at liberty to say that I thought it a desirable improvement.'

'I am much obliged to you, sir. Thank you—thank you very much,' he said, cringing at every word. 'But—but I had hoped that you might perhaps use your influence—'

'Look there!' I interrupted. 'Is that fancy?'

We were now close under the blank wall of the boys' schoolroom. On this wall, lying to the full sunlight, our shadows—mine and the schoolmaster's—were projected. And there, too—no longer between his and mine, but a little way apart, as if the intruder were standing back-there, as sharply defined as if cast by lime-light on a prepared background, I again distinctly saw, though but for a moment, that third shadow. As I spoke, as I looked round, it was gone!

'Did you not see it?' I asked.

He shook his head.

'I—I saw nothing,' he said, faintly. 'What was it?'

His lips were white. He seemed scarcely able to stand.

'But you must have seen it!' I exclaimed. 'It fell just there—where that bit of ivy grows. There must be some boy hiding—it was a boy's shadow, I am confident.'

'A boy's shadow!' he echoed, looking round in a wild, frightened way. 'There is no place—for a boy—to hide.'

'Place or no place,' I said, angrily, 'if I catch him, he shall feel the weight of my cane!'

I searched backwards and forwards in event direction, the schoolmaster, with his scared face, limping at my heels; but, rough and irregular as the ground was, there was not a hole in it big enough to shelter a rabbit.

'But what was it?' I said, impatiently.

'An—an illusion. Begging your pardon, sir—an illusion.'

He looked so like a beaten hound, so frightened, so fawning, that I felt I could with lively satisfaction have transferred the threatened caning to his own shoulders.

'But you saw it?' I said again.

'No, sir. Upon my honour, no, sir. I saw nothing—nothing whatever.'

His looks belied his words. I felt positive that he had not only seen the shadow, but that he knew more about it than he chose to tell. I was by this time really angry. To be made the object of a boyish trick, and to be hoodwinked by the connivance of the schoolmaster, was too much. It was an insult to myself and my office.

I scarcely knew what I said; something short and stern at all events. Then, having said it, I turned my back upon Mr Skelton and the schools, and walked rapidly back to the village.

As I neared the bottom of the hill, a dog-cart drawn by a high-stepping chestnut dashed up to the door of the 'Greyhound', and the next moment I was shaking hands with Wolstenholme, of Balliol. Wolstenholme, of Balliol, as handsome as ever, dressed with the same careless dandyism, looking not a day older than when I last saw him at Oxford! He gripped me by both hands, vowed that I was his guest for the next three days, and insisted on carrying me off at once to Backwater Chase.

In vain I urged that I had two schools to inspect tomorrow ten miles the other side of Drumley; that I had a horse and trap waiting; and that my room was ordered at the 'Feathers'. Wolstenholme laughed away my objections.

'My dear fellow,' he said, 'you will simply send your horse and trap back with a message to the "Feathers", and a couple of telegrams to be dispatched to the two schools from Drumley station.

Unforeseen circumstances compel you to defer those inspections till next week!'. And with this, in his masterful way, he shouted to the landlord to send my portmanteau up to the manor-house, pushed me up before him into the dog-cart, gave the chestnut his head, and rattled me off to Backwater Chase.

It was a gloomy old barrack of a place, standing high in the midst of a sombre deer-park some six or seven miles in circumference. An avenue of oaks, now leafless, led up to the house; and a mournful heron-haunted tarn in the loneliest part of the park gave to the estate its name of Blackwater Chase. The place, in fact, was more like a border fastness than an English north-country mansion. Wolstenholme took me through the picture gallery and reception rooms after luncheon, and then for a canter round the park; and in the evening we dined at the upper end of a great oak hall hung with antlers, and armour, and antiquated weapons of warfare and sport.

'Now, tomorrow,' said my host, as we sat over our claret in front of a blazing log-fire; 'tomorrow, if we have decent weather, you shall have a day's shooting on the moors; and on Friday, if you will but be persuaded to stay a day longer, I will drive you over to Broomhead and give you a run with the duke's hounds. Not hunt? My dear fellow, what nonsense! All our parsons hunt in this part of the world. By the way, have you ever been down a coal pit? No?

Then a new experience awaits you. I'll take you down Carshalton shaft, and show you the home of the gnomes and trolls.'

'Is Carshalton one of your own mines?' I asked.

'All these pits are mine,' he replied. 'I am king of Hades, and rule the underworld as well as the upper. There is coal everywhere underlying these moors. The whole place is honeycombed with shafts and galleries. One of our richest seams runs under this house, and there are upwards of forty men at work in it a quarter of a mile below our feet here every day. Another leads right away under the park, heaven only knows how far! My father began working it five-and-twenty years ago, and we have gone on working it ever since; yet it shows no sign of failing.'

'You must be as rich as a prince with a fairy godmother!'

He shrugged his shoulders.

'Well,' he said, lightly, 'I am rich enough to commit what follies I please; and that is saying a good deal. But then, to be always squandering money—always rambling about the world—always gratifying the impulse of the moment—is that happiness? I have been trying the experiment for the last ten years; and with what result? Would you like to see?'

He snatched up a lamp and led the way through a long suite of unfurnished rooms, the floors of which were piled high with packing cases of all sizes and shapes, labelled with the names of various foreign ports and the addresses of foreign agents innumerable. What did they contain?

Precious marbles from Italy and Greece and Asia Minor; priceless paintings by old and modern masters; antiquities from the Nile, the Tigris, and the Euphrates; enamels from Persia, porcelain from China, bronzes from Japan, strange sculptures from Peru; arms, mosaics, ivories, wood-carvings, skins, tapestries, old Italian cabinets, painted bride-chests, Etruscan terracottas; treasures of all countries, of all ages, never even unpacked since they crossed that threshold which the master's foot had crossed but twice during the ten years it had taken to buy them!

Should he ever open them, ever arrange them, ever enjoy them? Perhaps—if he became weary of wandering—if he married—if he built a gallery to receive them. If not—well, he might found and endow a museum; or leave the things to the nation. What did it matter? Collecting was like fox-hunting; the pleasure was in the pursuit, and ended with it!

We sat up late that first night, I can hardly say conversing, for Wolstenholme did the talking, while I, willing to be amused, led him on to tell me something of his wanderings by land and sea.

So the time passed in stories of adventure, of perilous peaks ascended, of deserts traversed, of unknown ruins explored, of 'hair-breadth 'scapes' from icebergs and earthquakes and storms; and when at last he flung the end of his cigar into the fire and discovered that it was time to go to bed, the clock on the mantelshelf pointed far on among the small hours of the morning.

Next day, according to the programme made out for my entertainment, we did some seven hours' partridge-shooting on the moors; and the day next following I was to go down Carshalton shaft before breakfast, and after breakfast ride over to a place some fifteen miles distant called Picts' Camp, there to see a stone circle and the ruins of a prehistoric fort.

Unused to field sports, I slept heavily after those seven hours with the guns, and was slow to wake when Wolstenholme's valet came next morning to my bedside with the waterproof suit in which I was to effect my descent into Hades.

'Mr Wolstenholme says, sir, that you had better not take your bath till you come back,' said this gentlemanly vassal, disposing the ungainly garments across the back of a chair as artistically as if he were laying out my best evening suit. 'And you will be pleased to dress warmly underneath the waterproofs, for it is very chilly in the mine.'

I surveyed the garments with reluctance. The morning was frosty, and the prospect of being lowered into the bowels of the earth, cold, tasting, and unwashed, was anything but attractive.

Should I send word that I would rather not go? I hesitated; but while I was hesitating, the gentlemanly valet vanished, and my opportunity was lost. Grumbling and shivering, I got up, donned the cold and shiny suit, and went downstairs.

A murmur of voices met my ear as I drew near the breakfast-room. Going in, I found some ten or a dozen stalwart colliers grouped near the door, and Wolstenholme, looking somewhat serious, standing with his back to the fire.

'Look here, Frazer,' he said, with a short laugh, 'here's a pleasant piece of news. A fissure has opened in the bed of Blackwater tarn; the lake has disappeared in the night; and the mine is flooded! No Carshalton shaft for you today!'

'Seven foot o' wayter in Jukes's seam, an' eight in th' owd north and south galleries,' growled a huge red-headed fellow, who seemed to be the spokesman.

'An' it's the Lord's own marcy a' happened o' noight-time, or we'd be dead men all,' added another.

'That's true, my man,' said Wolstenholme, answering the last speaker. 'It might have drowned you like rats in a trap; so we may thank our stars it's no worse. And now, to work with the pumps! Lucky for us that we know what to do, and how to do it.'

So saying, he dismissed the men with a good-humoured nod, and an order for unlimited ale.

I listened in blank amazement. The tarn vanished! I could not believe it. Wolstenholme assured me, however, that it was by no means a solitary phenomenon. Rivers had been known to disappear before now, in mining districts; and sometimes, instead of merely cracking, the ground would cave in, burying not merely houses, but whole hamlets in one common ruin. The foundations of such houses were, however, generally known to be insecure long enough before the crash came; and these accidents were not therefore often followed by loss of life.

'And now,' he said, lightly, 'you may doff your fancy costume; for I shall have time this morning for nothing but business. It is not every day that one loses a lake, and has to pump it up again!'

Breakfast over, we went round to the mouth of the pit, and saw the men fixing the pumps.

Later on, when the work was fairly in train, we started off across the park to view the scene of the catastrophe. Our way lay far from the house across a wooded upland, beyond which we followed a broad glade leading to the tarn. Just as we entered this glade—Wolstenholme rattling on and turning the whole affair into jest—a tall, slender lad, with a fishing-rod across his shoulder, came out from one of the side paths to the right, crossed the open at a long slant, and disappeared among the tree-trunks on the opposite side. I recognized him instantly. It was the boy whom I saw the other day, just after meeting the schoolmaster in the meadow.

'If that boy thinks he is going to fish in your tarn,' I said, 'he will find out his mistake.'

'What boy?' asked Wolstenholme, looking back.

'That boy who crossed over yonder, a minute ago.'

'Yonder!—in front of us?'

'Certainly. You must have seen him?'

'Not I.'

'You did not see him?—a tall, thin boy, in a grey suit, with a fishing-rod over his shoulder. He disappeared behind those Scotch firs.'

Wolstenholme looked at me with surprise.

'You are dreaming!' he said. 'No living thing—not even a rabbit—has crossed our path since we entered the park gates.'

'I am not in the habit of dreaming with my eyes open,' I replied, quickly.

He laughed, and put his arm through mine.

'Eyes or no eyes,' he said, 'you are under an illusion this time!'

An illusion—the very word made use of by the schoolmaster! What did it mean? Could I, in truth, no longer rely upon the testimony of my senses? A thousand half-formed apprehensions flashed across me in a moment. I remembered the illusions of Nicolini, the bookseller, and other similar cases of visual hallucination, and I asked myself if I had suddenly become afflicted in like manner.

'By Jove! this is a queer sight!' exclaimed Wolstenholme. And then I found that we had emerged from the glade, and were looking down upon the bed of what yesterday was Blackwater Tarn.

It was indeed a queer sight—an oblong, irregular basin of blackest slime, with here and there a sullen pool, and round the margin an irregular fringe of bulrushes. At some little distance along the bank—

less than a quarter of a mile from where we were standing—a gaping crowd had gathered. All Pit End, except the men at the pumps, seemed to have turned out to stare at the bed of the vanished tarn.

Hats were pulled off and curtsies dropped at Wolstenholme's approach. He, meanwhile, came up smiling, with a pleasant word for everyone.

'Well,' he said, 'are you looking for the lake, my friends? You'll have in go down Carshalton shaft to find it! It's an ugly sight you've come to see, anyhow!'

"Tes an ugly soight, squoire,' replied a stalwart blacksmith in a leathern apron; 'but thar's summat uglier, mebbe, than the mud, ow'r yonder.'

'Something uglier than the mud?' Wolstenholme repeated.

'Wull yo be pleased to stan' this way, squoire, an' look strite across at yon little tump o' bulrashes—doan't yo see nothin'?'

I see a log of rotten timber sticking half in and half out of the mud,' said Wolstenholme; 'and something—a long reed, apparently. . . by love! I believe it's a fishing rod!'

'It is a fishin' rod, squoire,' said the blacksmith with rough carnesmess; 'an' if yon rotten timber bayn't an unburied corpse, mun I never stroike hammer on anvil agin!'

There was a buzz of acquiescence from the bystanders. 'Twas an unburied corpse, sure enough. Nobody doubted it. Wolstenholme made a funnel with his hands, and looked through it long and steadfastly.

'It must come out, whatever it is,' he said presently. 'Five feet of mud, do you say? Then here's a sovereign apiece for the first two fellows who wade through it and bring that object to land!'

The blacksmith and another pulled off their shoes and stockings, turned up their trousers, and went in at once.

They were over their ankles at the first plunge, and, sounding their way with sticks, went deeper at every tread. As they sank, our excitement rose. Presently they were visible from only the waist upwards. We could see their chests heaving, and the muscular efforts by which each step was gained. They were yet full twenty yards from the goal when the mud mounted to their armpits. . . a few feet more, and only their heads would remain above the surface!

An uneasy movement ran through the crowd.

'Call 'em back, for God's sake!' cried a woman's voice.

But at this moment—having reached a point where the ground

gradually sloped upwards—they began to rise above the mud as rapidly as they had sunk into it. And now, black with clotted slime, they emerge waist-high . . . now they are within three or four yards of the spot. . . and now. . . now they are there!

They part the reeds—they stoop low above the shapeless object on which all eyes are turned—they half-lift it from its bed of mud—they hesitate—lay it down again—decide, apparently, to leave it there; and turn their faces shorewards. Having come a few paces, the blacksmith remembers the fishing-rod; turns back; disengages the tangled line with some difficulty, and brings it over his shoulder.

They had not much to tell—standing, all mud from head to heel, on dry land again—but that little was conclusive. It was, in truth, an unburied corpse; part of the trunk only above the surface. They tried to lift it; but it had been so long under water, and was in so advanced a stage of decomposition, that to bring it to shore without a shutter was impossible. Being cross-questioned, they thought, from the slenderness of the form, that it must be the body of a boy.

'Thar's the poor chap's rod, anyhow,' said the blacksmith, laying it gently down upon the turf.

I have thus far related events as I witnessed them. Here, however, my responsibility ceases. I give the rest of my story at second-hand, briefly, as I received it some weeks later, in the following letter from Philip Wolstenholme:

Blackwater Chase, Dec. 20th, 18—.

Dear Frazer, My promised letter has been a long time on the road, but I did not see the use of writing till I had something definite to tell you. I think, however, we have now found out all that we are ever likely to know about the tragedy in the tarn; and it seems that—but, no; I will begin at the beginning. That is to say, with the day you left the Chase, which was the day following the discovery of the body.

You were but just gone when a police inspector arrived from Drumley (you will remember that I had immediately sent a man over to the sitting magistrate); but neither the inspector nor anyone else could do anything till the remains were brought to shore, and it took us the best part of a week to accomplish this difficult operation. We had to sink no end of big stones in order to make a rough and ready causeway across the mud. This done, the body was brought over decently upon a shutter. It proved to be the corpse of a boy of perhaps fourteen or fifteen years of age.

There was a fracture three inches long at the back of the skull, evidently fatal. This might, of course, have been an accidental injury; but when the body came to be raised from where it lay, it was found to be pinned down by a pitchfork, the handle of which had been afterwards whittled off, so as not to show above the water, a discovery tantamount to evidence of murder. The features of the victim were decomposed beyond recognition; but enough of the hair remained to show that it had been short and sandy As for the clothing, it was a mere mass of rotten shreds; but on being subjected to some chemical process, proved to have once been a suit of lightish grey cloth.

A crowd of witnesses came forward at this stage of the inquiry—for I am now giving you the main facts as they came out at the coroner's inquest—to prove that about a year or thirteen months ago, Skelton the schoolmaster had staying with him a lad whom he called his nephew, and to whom it was supposed that he was not particularly kind. This lad was described as tall, thin, mud sandy-haired. He habitually wore a suit corresponding in colour and texture to the shreds of clothing discovered on the body in the tarn; and he was much addicted to angling about the pools and streams, wherever he might have the chance of a nibble.

And now one thing led quickly on to another. Our Pit End shoemaker identified the boy's boots as being a pair of his own making and selling. Other witnesses testified to angry scenes between the uncle and nephew. Finally, Skelton gave himself up to justice, confessed the deed, and was duly committed to Drumley gaol for wilful murder.

And the motive? Well, the motive is the strangest part of my story. The wretched lad was, after all, not Skelton's nephew, but Skelton's own illegitimate son. The mother was dead, and the boy lived with his maternal grandmother in a remote part of Cumberland. The old woman was poor, and the schoolmaster made her an annual allowance for his son's keep and clothing. He had not seen the boy for some years, when he sent for him to come over on a visit to Pit End. Perhaps he was weary of the tax upon his purse. Perhaps, as he himself puts it in his confession, he was disappointed to find the boy, if not actually half-witted, stupid, wilful, and ill brought-up. He at all events took a dislike to the poor brute, which dislike by and by developed into positive hatred.

Some amount of provocation there would seem to have been. The boy was as backward as a child of five years old. That Skelton put him into the Boys' School, and could do nothing with him; that he defied discipline, had a passion for fishing, and was continually wandering about the country with his rod and line, are facts borne out by the independent testimony of various witnesses. Having hidden his fishing-tackle, he was in the habit of slipping away at school-hours, and showed himself the more cunning and obstinate the more he was punished.

At last there came a day when Skelton tracked him to the place where his rod was concealed, and thence across the meadows into the park, and as far as the tarn. His (Skelton's) account of what followed is wandering and confused. He owns to having beaten the miserable lad about the head and arms with a heavy stick that he had brought with him for the purpose; but denies that he intended to murder him.

When his son fell insensible and ceased to breathe, he for the first time realized the force of the blows he had dealt. He admits that his first impulse was one, not of remorse for the deed, but of fear for his own safety. He dragged the body in among the bulrushes by the water's edge, and there concealed it as well as he could. At night, when the neighbours were in bed and asleep, he stole out by starlight, taking with him a pitchfork, a coil of rope, a couple of old iron-bars, and a knife.

Thus laden, he struck out across the moor, and entered the park by a stile and footpath on the Stoneleigh side; so making a circuit of between three and four miles.

A rotten old punt used at that time to be kept on the tarn. He loosed this punt from its moorings, brought it round, hauled in the body, and paddled his ghastly burden out into the middle of the lake as far as a certain clump of reeds which he had noted as a likely spot for his purpose. Here he weighted and sunk the corpse, and pinned it down by the neck with his pitchfork. He then cut away the handle of the fork; hid the fishing-rod among the reeds; and believed, as murderers always believe, that discovery was impossible. As regarded the Pit End folk, he simply gave out that his nephew had gone back to Cumberland; and no one doubted it.

Now, however, he says that accident has only anticipated him; and that he was on the point of voluntarily confessing his crime. His dreadful secret had of late become intolerable. He was haunted by an invisible Presence. That Presence sat with him at table, followed him in his walks stood behind him in the school-room, and watched by his bedside. He never saw it; but he felt that it was always there. Sometimes he raves of a shadow on the wall of his cell. The gaol authorities are of opinion that he is of unsound mind.

I have now told you all that there is at present to tell. The trial will not take place till the spring assizes. In the meanwhile I am off tomorrow to Paris, and thence, in about ten days, on to Nice, where letters will find me at the Hotel des Empereurs.

Always, dear Frazer,

Yours, e.t.c.,

P.W.

P.S-Since writing the above, I have received a telegram from Drumley to say that Skelton has committed suicide. No particulars given. So ends this strange eventful history.

By the way, that was a curious illusion of yours the other day when we were crossing the park; and I have thought of it many times. Was it an illusion?—that is the question.'

Ay, indeed! that is the question; and it is a question which I have never yet been able to answer.

Certain things I undoubtedly saw—with my mind's eye, perhaps—and as I saw them, I have described them; withholding nothing, adding nothing, explaining nothing. Let those solve the mystery who can. For myself, I but echo Wolstenholme's question: Was it an illusion?

Pichon & Sons, of the Croix Rousse

Anon

Giraudier, *pharmacien, première classe*, is the legend, recorded in huge, ill-proportioned letters, which directs the attention of the stranger to the most prosperous-looking shop in the grand *place* of La Croix Rousse, a well-known suburb of the beautiful city of Lyons, which has its share of the shabby gentility and poor pretence common to the suburban commerce of great towns.

Giraudier is not only *pharmacien* but *propriétaire*, though not by inheritance; his possession of one of the prettiest and most prolific of the small vineyards in the beautiful suburb, and a charming inconvenient house, with low ceilings, Lilliputian bedrooms, and a profusion of *persiennes, jalousies*, and *contrevents*, comes by purchase. This enviable little *terre* was sold by the nation, when that terrible abstraction transacted the public business of France; and it was bought very cheaply by the strong-minded father of the Giraudier of the present, who was not disturbed by the evil reputation which the place had gained, at a time the peasants of France, having been bullied into a renunciation of religion, eagerly cherished superstition.

The Giraudier of the present cherishes the particular superstition in question affectionately; it reminds him of an uncommonly good bargain made in his favour, which is always a pleasant association of ideas, especially to a Frenchman, still more especially to a Lyonnais; and it attracts strangers to his *pharmacie*, and leads to transactions in *Grand Chartreuse* and *Créme de Roses*, ensuing naturally on the narration of the history of Pichon & Sons. Giraudier is not of aristocratic principles and sympathies; on the contrary, he has decided republican leanings, and considers *Le Progrès* a masterpiece of journalistic literature; but, as he says simply and strongly, "it is not because a man is a *marquis* that one is not to keep faith with him; a bad action is not good because it harms a good-for-nothing of a noble; the more when that good-for-nothing is no longer a noble, but *pour rire*." At the easy price of acquiescence in these sentiments, the stranger hears one of the most authentic, best-remembered, most popular of the many traditions of the bad old times "before General Bonaparte," as Giraudier, who has no sympathy with any later designation of *le grand homme*, calls the emperor, whose statue one can perceive—a speck in the distance—from the threshold of the *pharmacie*.

The Marquis de Sénanges, in the days of the triumph of the great Revolution, was fortunate enough to be out of France, and wise enough to remain away from that country, though he persisted, long after the old *regime* was as dead as the Ptolemies, in believing it merely suspended, and the Revolution a lamentable accident of vulgar complexion, but happily temporary duration. The Marquis de Sénanges, who affected the *style régence*, and was the politest of *infidels* and the most refined of voluptuaries, got on indifferently in unappreciative foreign parts; but the members of his family—his brother and sisters, two of whom were guillotined, while the third escaped to Savoy and found refuge there in a convent of her order—got on exceedingly ill in France.

If the *ci-devant marquis* had had plenty of money to expend in such feeble imitations of his accustomed pleasures as were to be had out of Paris, he would not have been much affected by the fate of his relatives. But money became exceedingly scarce; the *marquis* had actually beheld many of his peers reduced to the necessity of earning the despicable but indispensable article after many ludicrous fashions. And the duration of this absurd upsetting of law, order, privilege, and property began to assume unexpected and very unpleasant proportions.

The Château de Sénanges, with its surrounding lands, was confiscated to the Nation, during the third year of the "emigration" of the Marquis de Sénanges; and the greater part of the estate was purchased by a thrifty, industrious, and rich *avocat*, named Prosper Alix, a widower with an only daughter. Prosper Alix enjoyed the esteem of the entire neighbourhood. First, he was rich; secondly, he was of a taciturn disposition, and of a neutral tint in politics. He had done well under the old *regime* and, he was doing well under the new—thank God, or the Supreme Being, or the First Cause, or the goddess Reason herself, for all;—he would have invoked Dagon, Moloch, or Kali, quite as readily as the Saints and the Madonna, who has gone so utterly out of fashion of late. Nobody was afraid to speak out before Prosper Alix; he was not a spy; and though a cold-hearted man, except in the instance of his only daughter, he never harmed anybody.

Very likely it was because he was the last person in the vicinity whom anybody would have suspected of being applied to by the dispossessed family, that the son of the *marquis'* brother, a young man of promise, of courage, of intellect, and of morals of decidedly a higher calibre than those actually and traditionally imputed to the family, sought the aid of the new possessor of the Château de Sénanges, which had changed its old title for that of the Maison Alix. The father of M. Paul de Sénanges had perished in the September massacres; his mother had been guillotined at Lyons; and he—who had been saved by the interposition of a young comrade, whose father had, in the wonderful rotations of the wheel of Fate, acquired authority in the place where he had once esteemed the notice of the nephew of the *marquis* a crowning honour for his son—had passed through the common vicissitudes of that dreadful time, which would take a volume for their recital in each individual instance.

Paul de Sénanges was a handsome young fellow, frank, high-spirited, and of a brisk and happy temperament; which, however, modified by the many misfortunes he had undergone, was not permanently changed. He had plenty of capacity for enjoyment in him still; and as his position was very isolated, and his mind had become enlightened on social and political matters to an extent in which the men of his family would have discovered utter degradation and the women diabolical possession, he would not have been very unhappy if, under the new condition of things, he could have lived in his native country and gained an honest livelihood. But he could not do that, he was too thoroughly "suspect;" the antecedents of his family were too powerful against him: his only chance would have been to have gone into the popular camp as an extreme, violent partisan, to have out-Heroded the revolutionary Herods; and that Paul de Sénanges was too honest to do. So he was reduced to being thankful that he had escaped with his life, and to watching for an opportunity of leaving France and gaining some country where the reign of liberty, fraternity, and equality was not quite so oppressive.

The long-looked-for opportunity at length offered itself, and Paul de Sénanges was instructed by his uncle the *marquis* that he must contrive to reach Marseilles, whence he should be transported to Spain—in which country the illustrious emigrant was then residing—by a certain named date. His uncle's communication arrived safely, and the plan proposed seemed a secure and eligible one. Only in two respects was it calculated to make Paul de Sénanges thoughtful. The first was, that his uncle should take any interest in the matter of his safety; the second, what could be the nature of a certain deposit which the *marquis*'s letter directed him to procure, if possible, from the Château de Sénanges.

The fact of this injunction explained, in some measure, the first of the two difficulties. It was plain that whatever were the contents of this packet which he was to seek for, according to the indications marked on a ground-plan drawn by his uncle and enclosed in the letter, the *marquis* wanted them, and could not procure them except by the agency of his nephew. That the *marquis* should venture to direct Paul de Sénanges to put himself in communication with Prosper Alix, would have been surprising to any one acquainted only with the external and generally understood features of the character of the new proprietor of the Château de Sénanges. But a few people knew Prosper Alix thoroughly, and the *marquis* was one of the number; he was keen enough to know in theory that, in the case of a man with only one weakness, that is likely to be a very weak weakness indeed, and to apply the theory to the *avocat*.

The beautiful, pious, and aristocratic mother of Paul de Sénanges—a lady to whose superiority the *marquis* had rendered the distinguished testimony of his dislike, not hesitating to avow that she was "much too good for *his* taste"—had been very fond of, and very kind to, the motherless daughter of Prosper Alix, and he held her memory in reverence which he accorded to nothing beside, human or divine, and taught his daughter the matchless worth of the friend she had lost. The *marquis* knew this, and though he had little sympathy with the sentiment, he believed he might use it in the present instance to his own profit, with safety. The event proved that he was right.

Private negotiations, with the manner of whose transaction we are not concerned, passed between the *avocet* and the *ci-devant marquis*; and the young man, then leading a life in which skulking had a large share, in the vicinity of Dijon, was instructed to present himself at the Maison Alix, under the designation of Henri Glaire, and in the character of an artist in house-decoration. The circumstances of his life in childhood and boyhood had led to his being almost safe from recognition as a man at Lyons; and, indeed, all the people on the *ci-devant* visiting-list of the *château* had been pretty nearly killed off, in the noble and patriotic ardour of the revolutionary times.

The ancient Château de Sénanges was proudly placed near the

summit of the "Holy Hill," and had suffered terrible depredations when the church at Fourvières was sacked, and the shrine desecrated with that ingenious impiety which is characteristic of the French; but it still retained somewhat of its former heavy grandeur. The château was much too large for the needs, tastes, or ambition of its present owner, who was too wise, if even he had been of an ostentatious disposition, not to have sedulously resisted its promptings. The jealousy of the nation of brothers was easily excited, and departure from simplicity and frugality was apt to be commented upon by domiciliary visits, and the eager imposition of fanciful fines.

That portion of the vast building occupied by Prosper Alix and the *citoyenne* Berthe, his daughter, presented an appearance of well-to-do comfort and modest ease, which contrasted with the grandiose proportions and the elaborate decorations of the wide corridors, huge flat staircases, and lofty panelled apartments. The *avocet* and his daughter lived quietly in the old place, hoping, after a general fashion, for better times, but not finding the present very bad; the father becoming day by day more pleasant with his bargain, the daughter growing fonder of the great house, and the noble *bocages*, of the scrappy little vineyards, struggling for existence on the sunny hill-side, and the place where the famous shrine had been.

They had done it much damage; they had parted its riches among them; the once ever-open doors were shut, and the worn flags were untrodden; but nothing could degrade it, nothing could destroy what had been, in the mind of Berthe Alix, who was as devout as her father was unconcernedly unbelieving. Berthe was wonderfully well educated for a Frenchwoman of that period, and surprisingly handsome for a Frenchwoman of any. Not too tall to offend the taste of her compatriots, and not too short to be dignified and graceful, she had a symmetrical figure, and a small, well-poised head, whose profuse, shining, silken dark-brown hair she wore as nature intended, in a shower of curls, never touched by the hand of the coiffeur,—curls which clustered over her brow, and fell far down on her shapely neck.

Her features were fine; the eyes very dark, and the mouth very red; the complexion clear and rather pale, and the style of the face and its expression lofty. When Berthe Alix was a child, people were accustomed to say she was pretty and refined enough to belong to the aristocracy; nobody would have dared to say so now, prettiness and refinement, together with all the other virtues admitted to a place on the patriotic roll, having become national property.

Berthe loved her father dearly. She was deeply impressed with the sense of her supreme importance to him, and fully comprehended that he would be influenced by and through her when all other persuasion or argument would be unavailing. When Prosper Alix wished and intended to do anything rather mean or selfish, he did it without letting Berthe know; and when he wished to leave undone something which he knew his daughter would decide ought to be done, he carefully concealed from her the existence of the dilemma. Nevertheless, this system did not prevent the father and daughter being very good and even confidential friends.

Prosper Alix loved his daughter immeasurably, and respected her more than he respected any one in the world. With regard to her persevering religiousness, when such things were not only out of fashion and date, but illegal as well, he was very tolerant. Of course it was weak, and an absurdity; but every woman, even his beautiful, incomparable Berthe, was weak and absurd on some point or other; and, after all, he had come to the conclusion that the safest weakness with which a woman can be afflicted is that romantic and ridiculous *faiblesse* called piety. So these two lived a happy life together, Berthe's share of it being very secluded, and were wonderfully little troubled by the turbulence with which society was making its tumultuous way to the virtuous serenity of republican perfection.

The communication announcing the project of the *ci-devant marquis* for the secure exportation of his nephew, and containing the skilful appeal before mentioned, grievously disturbed the tranquillity of Prosper, and was precisely one of those incidents which he would especially have liked to conceal from his daughter. But he could not do so; the appeal was too cleverly made; and utter indifference to it, utter neglect of the letter, which naturally suggested itself as the easiest means of getting rid of a difficulty, would have involved an act of direct and uncompromising dishonesty to which Prosper, though of sufficiently elastic conscience within the limit of professional gains, could not contemplate.

The Château de Sénanges was indeed his own lawful property; his without prejudice to the former owners, dispossessed by no act of his. But the *ci-devant marquis*—confiding in him to an extent which was quite astonishing, except on the *pis-aller* theory, which is so unflattering as to be seldom accepted—announced to him the existence of a certain packet, hidden in the *château*, acknowledging its value, and urging the need of its safe transmission. This was not his property. He heartily wished he had never learned its existence, but wishing that was clearly of no use; then he wished the nephew of the *ci-devant* might come soon, and take himself and the hidden wealth away with all possible speed.

This latter was a more realisable desire, and Prosper settled his mind with it, communicated the interesting but decidedly dangerous secret to Berthe, received her warm sanction, and transmitted to the *marquis*, by the appointed means, an assurance that his wishes should be punctually carried out. The absence of an interdiction of his visit before a certain date was to be the signal to M. Paul de Sénanges that he was to proceed to act upon his uncle's instructions; he waited the proper time, the reassuring silence was maintained unbroken, and he ultimately set forth on his journey, and accomplished it in safety.

Preparations had been made at the Maison Alix for the reception of M. Glaire, and his supposed occupation had been announced. The apartments were decorated in a heavy, gloomy style, and those of the *citoyenne* in particular (they had been occupied by a lady who had once been designated as *feue Madame la Marquise*, but who was referred to now as *la mère du ci-devant*) were much in need of renovation. The alcove, for instance, was all that was least gay and most far from simple. The *citoyenne* would have all that changed. On the morning of the day of the expected arrival, Berthe said to her father:

"It would seem as if the *marquis* did not know the exact spot in which the packet is deposited. M. Paul's assumed character implies the necessity for a search."

M. Henri Glaire arrived at the Maison Alix, was fraternally received, and made acquainted with the sphere of his operations. The young man had a good deal of both ability and taste in the line he had assumed, and the part was not difficult to play. Some days were judiciously allowed to pass before the real object of the masquerade was pursued, and during that time cordial relations established themselves between the *avocet* and his guest. The young man was handsome, elegant, engaging, with all the external advantages, and devoid of the vices, errors, and hopeless infatuated unscrupulousness, of his class; he had naturally quick intelligence, and some real knowledge and comprehension of life had been knocked into him by the hard-hitting blows of Fate.

His face was like his mother's, Prosper Alix thought, and his mind and tastes were of the very pattern which, in theory, Berthe approved. Berthe, a very unconventional French girl—who thought the new era of purity, love, virtue, and disinterestedness ought to do away with marriage by barter as one of its most notable reforms, and had been disenchanted by discovering that the abolition of marriage altogether suited the taste of the incorruptible Republic better—might like, might even love, this young man. She saw so few men, and had no fancy for patriots; she would certainly be obstinate about it if she did chance to love him. This would be a nice state of affairs. This would be a pleasant consequence of the confiding request of the *ci-devant*. Prosper wished with all his heart for the arrival of the concerted signal, which should tell Henri Glaire that he might fulfil the purpose of his sojourn at the Maison Alix, and set forth for Marseilles.

But the signal did not come, and the days—long, beautiful, sunny, soothing summer-days—went on. The painting of the panels of the *citoyenne's* apartment, which she vacated for that purpose, progressed slowly; and M. Paul de Sénanges, guided by the ground-plan, and aided by Berthe, had discovered the spot in which the jewels of price, almost the last remnants of the princely wealth of the Sénanges, had been hidden by the *femme-de-chambre* who had perished with her mistress, having confided a general statement of the fact to a priest, for transmission to the *marquis*. This spot had been ingeniously chosen. The sleeping-apartment of the late *marquis* was extensive, lofty, and provided with an alcove of sufficiently large dimensions to have formed in itself a handsome room. This space, containing a splendid but gloomy bed, on an *estrade*, and hung with rich faded brocade, was divided from the general extent of the apartment by a low railing of black oak, elaborately carved, opening in the centre, and with a flat wide bar along the top, covered with crimson velvet.

The curtains were contrived to hang from the ceiling, and, when let down inside the screen of railing, they matched the draperies which closed before the great stone balcony at the opposite end of the room. Since the *avocat's* daughter had occupied this palatial chamber, the curtains of the alcove had never been drawn, and she had substituted for them a high folding screen of black-and-gold Japanese pattern, also a relic of the grand old times, which stood about six feet on the outside of the rails that shut in her bed. The floor was of shining oak, testifying to the conscientious and successful labours of successive generations of *frotteurs*; and on the spot where the railing of the alcove opened by a pretty quaint device sundering the intertwined arms of a pair of very chubby cherubs, a square space in the floor was also richly carved.

The seekers soon reached the end of their search. A little effort removed the square of carved oak, and underneath they found a casket, evidently of old workmanship, richly wrought in silver, much tarnished but quite intact. It was agreed that this precious deposit should be replaced, and the carved square laid down over it, until the signal for his departure should reach Paul. The little baggage which under any circumstances he could have ventured to allow himself in the dangerous journey he was to undertake, must be reduced, so as to admit of his carrying the casket without exciting suspicion.

The finding of the hidden treasure was not the first joint discovery made by the daughter of the *avocet* and the son of the *ci-devant.* The cogitations of Prosper Alix were very wise, very reasonable; but they were a little tardy. Before he had admitted the possibility of mischief, the mischief was done. Each had found out that the love of the other was indispensable to the happiness of life; and they had exchanged confidences, assurances, protestations, and promises, as freely, as fervently, and as hopefully, as if no such thing as a Republic, one and indivisible, with a keen scent and an unappeasable thirst for the blood of aristocrats, existed.

They forgot all about "Liberty, Fraternity, and Equality"—these egotistical, narrow-minded young people;—they also forgot the characteristic alternative to those unparaleled blessings—"Death." But Prosper Alix did not forget any of these things; and his consternation, his provision of suffering for his beloved daughter, were terrible, when she told him, with a simple noble frankness which the *grandes dames* of the dead-and-gone time of great ladies had rarely had a chance of exhibiting, that she loved M. Paul de Sénanges, and intended to marry him when the better times should come. Perhaps she meant when that alternative of *death* should be struck off the sacred formula;—of course she meant to marry him with the sanction of her father, which she made no doubt she should receive.

Prosper Alix was in pitiable perplexity. He could not bear to terrify his daughter by a full explanation of the danger she was incurring; he could not bear to delude her with false hope. If this young man could be got away at once safely, there was not much likelihood that he would ever be able to return to France. Would Berthe pine for him, or would she forget him, and make a rational, sensible, rich, republican marriage, which would not imperil either her reputation for pure patriotism or her father's? The latter would be the very best thing that could possibly happen, and therefore it was decidedly unwise to calculate upon it; but, after all, it was possible; and Prosper had not the courage, in such a strait, to resist the hopeful promptings of a possibility. How ardently he regretted that he had complied with the prayer of the *ci-devant*! When would the signal for Mr. Paul's departure come?

Prosper Alix had made many sacrifices, had exercised much self-control for his daughter's sake; but he had never sustained a more severe trial than this, never suffered more than he did now, under the strong necessity for hiding from her his absolute conviction of the impossibility of a happy result for this attachment, in that future to which the lovers looked so fearlessly. He could not even make his anxiety and apprehension known to Paul de Sénanges; for he did not believe the young man had sufficient strength of will to conceal anything so important from the keen and determined observation of Berthe.

The expected signal was not given, and the lovers were incautious. The seclusion of the Maison Alix had all the danger, as well as all the delight, of solitude, and Paul dropped his disguise too much and too often. The servants, few in number, were of the truest patriotic principles, and to some of them the denunciation of the *citoyen*, whom they condescended to serve because the sacred Revolution had not yet made them as rich as he, would have been a delightful duty, a sweet-smelling sacrifice to be laid on the altar of the country. They heard certain names and places mentioned; they perceived many things which led them to believe that Henri Glaire was not an industrial artist and pure patriot, worthy of respect, but a wretched *ci-devant*, resorting to the dignity of labour to make up for the righteous destruction of every other kind of dignity.

One day a gardener, of less stoical virtue than his fellows, gave Prosper Alix a warning that the presence of a *ci-devant* upon his premises was suspected, and that he might be certain a domiciliary visit, attended with dangerous results to himself, would soon take place. Of course the *avocet* did not commit himself by any avowal to this lukewarm patriot; but he casually mentioned that Henri Glaire was about to take his leave. What was to be done? He must not leave the neighbourhood without receiving the instructions he was awaiting; but he must leave the house, and be supposed to have gone quite away. Without any delay or hesitation, Prosper explained the facts to Berthe and her lover, and insisted on the necessity for an instant parting. Then the courage and the readiness of the girl told. There was no crying, and very little trembling; she was strong and helpful.

"He must go to Pichon's, father," she said, "and remain there until the signal is given.—Pichon is a master-mason, Paul," she continued, turning to her lover, "and his wife was my nurse. They are avaricious people; but they are fond of me in their way, and they will shelter you faithfully enough, when they know that my father will pay them handsomely. You must go at once, unseen by the servants; they are at supper. Fetch your valise, and bring it to my room. We will put the casket in it, and such of your things as you must take out to make room for it, we can hide under the plank. My father will go with you to Pichon's, and we will communicate with you there as soon as it is safe."

Paul followed her to the large gloomy room where the treasure lay, and they took the casket from its hiding-place. It was heavy, though not large, and an awkward thing to pack away among linen in a small valise. They managed it, however, and, the brief preparation completed, the moment of parting arrived. Firmly and eloquently, though in haste, Berthe assured Paul of her changeless love and faith, and promised him to wait for him for any length of time in France, if better days should be slow of coming, or to join him in some foreign land, if they were never to come. Her father was present, full of compassion and misgiving. At length he said:

"Come, Paul, you must leave her; every moment is of importance."

The young man and his betrothed were standing on the spot whence they had taken the casket; the carved rail with the heavy curtains might have been the outer sanctuary of an altar, and they bride and bridegroom before it, with earnest, loving faces, and clasped hands.

"Farewell, Paul," said Berthe; "promise me once more, in this the moment of our parting, that you will come to me again, if you are alive, when the danger is past."

"Whether I am living or dead, Berthe," said Paul de Sénanges, strongly moved by some sudden inexplicable instinct, "I will come to you again."

In a few more minutes, Prosper Alix and his guest, who carried, not without difficulty, the small but heavy leather valise, had disappeared in the distance, and Berthe was on her knees before the *prie-dieu* of the *ci-devant marquise*, her face turned toward the "Holy Hill" of Fourvières.

Pichon, *mâitre*, and his sons, *garçons-maçons*, were well-to-do people, rather morose, exceedingly avaricious, and of taciturn dispositions; but they were not ill spoken of by their neighbours. They had amassed a good deal of money in their time, and were just then engaged on a very lucrative job. This was the construction of several of the steep descents, by means of stairs, straight and winding, cut in the face of the *côteaux*, by which pedestrians are enabled to descend into the town. Pichon *père* was a *propriétaire*as well; his property was that which is now in the possession of Giraudier, *pharmacien, première classe*, and which was destined to attain a sinister celebrity during his proprietorship. One of the straightest and steepest of the stairways had been cut close to the *terre* which the mason owned, and a massive wall, destined to bound the high-road at the foot of the declivity, was in course of construction.

When Prosper Alix and Paul de Sénanges reached the abode of Pichon, the master-mason, with his sons and workmen, had just completed their day's work, and were preparing to eat the supper served by the wife and mother, a tall, gaunt woman, who looked as if a more liberal scale of housekeeping would have done her good, but on whose features the stamp of that devouring and degrading avarice which is the commonest vice of the French peasantry, was set as plainly as on the hard faces of her husband and her sons. The *avocet* explained his business and introduced his companion briefly, and awaited the reply of Pichon *père* without any appearance of inquietude.

"You don't run any risk," he said; "at least, you don't run any risk which I cannot make it worth your while to incur. It is not the first time you have received a temporary guest on my recommendation. You know nothing about the citizen Glaire, except that he is recommended to you by me. I am responsible; you can, on occasion, make me so. The citizen may remain with you a short time; can hardly remain long. Say, citizen, is it agreed? I have no time to spare."

It was agreed, and Prosper Alix departed, leaving M. Paul de Sénanges, convinced that the right, indeed the only, thing had been done, and yet much troubled and depressed.

Pichon *père* was a short, squat, powerfully built man, verging on sixty, whose thick, dark grizzled hair, sturdy limbs, and hard hands, on which the muscles showed like cords, spoke of endurance and strength; he was, indeed, noted in the neighbourhood for those qualities. His sons resembled him slightly, and each other closely, as was natural, for they were twins. They were heavy, lumpish fellows, and they made but an ungracious return to the attempted civilities of the stranger, to whom the offer of their mother to show him his room was a decided relief. As he rose to follow the woman, Paul de Sénanges lifted his small valise with difficulty from the floor, on which he had placed it on entering the house, and carried it out of the room in both his arms. The brothers followed these movements with curiosity, and, when the door closed behind their mother and the stranger, their eyes met.

★★★★★★

Twenty-four hours had passed away, and nothing new had occurred at the Maison Alix. The servants had not expressed any curiosity respecting the departure of the citizen Glaire, no domiciliary visit had taken place, and Berthe and her father were discussing the propriety of Prosper's venturing, on the pretext of an excursion in another direction, a visit to the isolated and quiet dwelling of the master-mason. No signal had yet arrived. It was agreed that after the lapse of another day, if their tranquillity remained undisturbed, Prosper Alix should visit Paul de Sénanges. Berthe, who was silent and preoccupied, retired to her own room early, and her father, who was uneasy and apprehensive, desperately anxious for the promised communication from the *marquis*, was relieved by her absence.

The moon was high in the dark sky, and her beams were flung across the polished oak floor of Berthe's bedroom, through the great window with the stone balcony, when the girl, who had gone to sleep with her lover's name upon her lips in prayer, awoke with a sudden start, and sat up in her bed. An unbearable dread was upon her; and yet she was unable to utter a cry, she was unable to make another movement. Had she heard a voice? No, no one had spoken, nor did she fancy that she heard any sound. But within her, somewhere inside her heaving bosom, something said, "Berthe!"

And she listened, and knew what it was. And it spoke, and said:

"I promised you that, living or dead, I would come to you again. And I have come to you; but not living."

She was quite awake. Even in the agony of her fear she looked around, and tried to move her hands, to feel her dress and the bedclothes, and to fix her eyes on some familiar object, that she might satisfy herself, before this racing and beating, this whirling and yet icy chilliness of her blood should kill her outright, that she was really awake.

"I have come to you; but not living."

What an awful thing that voice speaking within her was! She tried to raise her head and to look toward the place where the moonbeams marked bright lines upon the polished floor, which lost themselves at the foot of the Japanese screen. She forced herself to this effort, and lifted her eyes, wild and haggard with fear, and there, the moonbeams at his feet, the tall black screen behind him, she saw Paul de Sénanges. She saw him; she looked at him quite steadily; she rose, slowly, with a mechanical movement, and stood upright beside her bed, clasping her forehead with her hands, and gazing at him. He stood motionless, in the dress he had worn when he took leave of her, the light-coloured riding-coat of the period, with a short cape, and a large white cravat tucked into the double breast. The white muslin was flecked, and the front of the riding-coat was deeply stained, with blood. He looked at her, and she took a step forward—another—then, with a desperate effort, she dashed open the railing and flung herself on her knees before him, with her arms stretched out as if to clasp him. But he was no longer there; the moonbeams fell clear and cold upon the polished floor, and lost themselves where Berthe lay, at the foot of the screen, her head upon the ground, and every sign of life gone from her.

★★★★★★

"Where is the citizen Glaire?" asked Prosper Alix of the *citoyenne* Pichon, entering the house of the master-mason abruptly, and with a stern and threatening countenance. "I have a message for him; I must see him."

"I know nothing about him," replied the *citoyenne*, without turning in his direction, or relaxing her culinary labours. "He went away from here the next morning, and I did not trouble myself to ask where; that is his affair."

"He went away? Without letting me know! Be careful, *citoyenne*; this is a serious matter."

"So they tell me," said the woman with a grin, which was not altogether free from pain and fear; "for you! A serious thing to have a *suspect* in your house, and palm him off on honest people. However, he went away peaceably enough when he knew we had found him out, and that we had no desire to go to prison, or worse, on his account, or yours."

She was strangely insolent, this woman, and the listener felt his helplessness; he had brought the young man there with such secrecy, he had so carefully provided for the success of concealment.

"Who carried his valise?" Prosper Alix asked her suddenly.

"How should I know?" she replied; but her hands lost their steadiness, and she upset a stew-pan; "he carried it here, didn't he? and I suppose he carried it away again."

Prosper Alix looked at her steadily—she shunned his gaze, but she showed no other sign of confusion; then horror and disgust of the woman came over him.

"I must see Pichon," he said; "where is he?"

"Where should he be but at the wall? he and the boys are working there, as always. The citizen can see them; but he will remember not to detain them; in a little quarter of an hour the soup will be ready."

The citizen did see the master-mason and his sons, and after an interview of some duration he left the place in a state of violent agitation and complete discomfiture. The master-mason had addressed to him these words at parting:

"I assert that the man went away at his own free will; but if you do not keep very quiet, I shall deny that he came here at all—you cannot prove he did—and I will denounce you for harbouring a *suspect* and *ci-devant* under a false name. I know a De Sénanges when I see him as well as you, Citizen Alix; and, wishing M. Paul a good journey, I hope you will consider about this matter, for truly, my friend, I think you will sneeze in the sack before I shall."

******

"We must bear it, Berthe, my child," said Prosper Alix to his daughter many weeks later, when the fever had left her, and she was able to talk with her father of the mysterious and frightful events which had occurred. "We are utterly helpless. There is no proof, only the word of these wretches against mine, and certain destruction to me if I speak. We will go to Spain, and tell the *marquis* all the truth, and never return, if you would rather not. But, for the rest, we must bear it."

"Yes, my father," said Berthe submissively, "I know we must; but God need not, and I don't believe He will."

The father and the daughter left France unmolested, and Berthe "bore it" as well as she could. When better times come they returned, Prosper Alix an old man, and Berthe a stern, silent, handsome woman, with whom no one associated any notions of love or marriage. But long before their return the traditions of the *Croix Rousse* were enriched by circumstances which led to that before-mentioned capital bargain made by the father of the Giraudier of the present. These circumstances were the violent death of Pichon and his two sons, who were killed by the fall of a portion of the great boundary-wall on the very day of its completion, and the discovery, close to its foundation, at the extremity of Pichon's *terre*, of the corpse of a young man attired in a light-coloured riding-coat, who had been stabbed through the heart.

Berthe Alix lived alone in the Château de Sénanges, under its restored name, until she was a very old woman. She lived long enough to see the golden figure on the summit of the "Holy Hill," long enough to forget the bad old times, but not long enough to forget or cease to mourn the lover who had kept his promise, and come back to her; the lover who rested in the earth which once covered the bones of the martyrs, and who kept a place for her by his side. She has filled that place for many years. You may see it, when you look down from the second gallery of the bell-tower at Fourvières, following the bend of the outstretched golden arm of Notre Dame.

The *château* was pulled down some years ago, and there is no trace of its former existence among the vines.

Good times, and bad times, and again good times have come for the *Croix Rousse*, for Lyons, and for France, since then; but the remembrance of the treachery of Pichon & Sons, and of the retribution which at once exposed and punished their crime, outlives all changes. And once, every year, on a certain summer night, three ghostly figures are seen, by any who have courage and patience to watch for them, gliding along by the foot of the boundary-wall, two of them carrying a dangling corpse, and the other, implements for mason's work and a small leather valise. Giraudier, *pharmacien*, has never seen these ghostly figures, but he describes them with much minuteness; and only the *esprits forts* of the *Croix Rousse* deny that the ghosts of Pichon & Sons are not yet laid.

The Old Nurse's Story

Elizabeth Gaskell

You know, my dears, that your mother was an orphan, and an only child; and I daresay you have heard that your grandfather was a clergyman up in Westmoreland, where I come from. I was just a girl in the village school, when, one day, your grandmother came in to ask the mistress if there was any scholar there who would do for a nursemaid; and mighty proud I was, I can tell ye, when the mistress called me up, and spoke of me being a good girl at my needle, and a steady, honest girl, and one whose parents were very respectable, though they might be poor. I thought I should like nothing better than to serve the pretty young lady, who was blushing as deep as I was, as she spoke of the coming baby, and what I should have to do with it.

However, I see you don't care so much for this part of my story, as for what you think is to come, so I'll tell you at once. I was engaged and settled at the parsonage before Miss Rosamond (that was the baby, who is now your mother) was born. To be sure, I had little enough to do with her when she came, for she was never out of her mother's arms, and slept by her all night long; and proud enough was I sometimes when missis trusted her to me. There never was such a baby before or since, though you've all of you been fine enough in your turns; but for sweet, winning ways, you've none of you come up to your mother. She took after her mother, who was a real lady born; a Miss Furnivall, a grand-daughter of Lord Furnivall's, in Northumberland.

I believe she had neither brother nor sister, and had been brought up in my lord's family till she had married your grandfather, who was just a curate, son to a shopkeeper in Carlisle—but a clever, fine gentleman as ever was—and one who was a right-down hard worker in his parish, which was very wide, and scattered all abroad over the Westmoreland Fells.

When your mother, little Miss Rosamond, was about four or five years old, both her parents died in a fortnight—one after the other. Ah! that was a sad time. My pretty young mistress and me was looking for another baby, when my master came home from one of his long rides, wet and tired, and took the fever he died of; and then she never held up her head again, but just lived to see her dead baby, and have it laid on her breast, before she sighed away her life. My mistress had asked me, on her death-bed, never to leave Miss Rosamond; but if she had never spoken a word, I would have gone with the little child to the end of the world.

The next thing, and before we had well stilled our sobs, the executors and guardians came to settle the affairs. They were my poor young mistress's own cousin, Lord Furnivall, and Mr. Esthwaite, my master's brother, a shopkeeper in Manchester; not so well to do then as he was afterwards, and with a large family rising about him. Well! I don't know if it were their settling, or because of a letter my mistress wrote on her death-bed to her cousin, my lord; but somehow it was settled that Miss Rosamond and me were to go to Furnivall Manor House, in Northumberland, and my lord spoke as if it had been her mother's wish that she should live with his family, and as if he had no objections, for that one or two more or less could make no difference in so grand a household.

So, though that was not the way in which I should have wished the coming of my bright and pretty pet to have been looked at—who was like a sunbeam in any family, be it never so grand—I was well pleased that all the folks in the Dale should stare and admire, when they heard I was going to be young lady's maid at my Lord Furnivall's at Furnivall Manor.

But I made a mistake in thinking we were to go and live where my lord did. It turned out that the family had left Furnivall Manor House fifty years or more. I could not hear that my poor young mistress had never been there, though she had been brought up in the family; and I was sorry for that, for I should have liked Miss Rosamond's youth to have passed where her mother's had been.

My lord's gentleman, from whom I asked as many questions as I durst, said that the Manor House was at the foot of the Cumberland Fells, and a very grand place; that an old Miss Furnivall, a great-aunt of my lord's, lived there, with only a few servants; but that it was a very healthy place, and my lord had thought that it would suit Miss Rosamond very well for a few years, and that her being there might perhaps amuse his old aunt.

I was bidden by my lord to have Miss Rosamond's things ready by a certain day. He was a stern, proud man, as they say all the Lords Furnivall were; and he never spoke a word more than was necessary. Folk did say he had loved my young mistress; but that, because she knew that his father would object, she would never listen to him, and married Mr. Esthwaite; but I don't know. He never married, at any rate. But he never took much notice of Miss Rosamond; which I thought he might have done if he had cared for her dead mother. He sent his gentleman with us to the Manor House, telling him to join him at Newcastle that same evening; so there was no great length of time for him to make us known to all the strangers before he, too, shook us off; and we were left, two lonely young things (I was not eighteen) in the great old Manor House.

It seems like yesterday that we drove there. We had left our own dear parsonage very early, and we had both cried as if our hearts would break, though we were travelling in my lord's carriage, which I thought so much of once.

And now it was long past noon on a September day, and we stopped to change horses for the last time at a little smoky town, all full of colliers and miners. Miss Rosamond had fallen asleep, but Mr. Henry told me to waken her, that she might see the park and the Manor House as we drove up. I thought it rather a pity; but I did what he bade me, for fear he should complain of me to my lord. We had left all signs of a town, or even a village, and were then inside the gates of a large wild park—not like the parks here in the south, but with rocks, and the noise of running water, and gnarled thorn-trees, and old oaks, all white and peeled with age.

The road went up about two miles, and then we saw a great and stately house, with many trees close around it, so close that in some places their branches dragged against the walls when the wind blew; and some hung broken down; for no one seemed to take much charge of the place;—to lop the wood, or to keep the moss-covered carriage-way in order. Only in front of the house all was clear. The great oval drive was without a weed; and neither tree nor creeper was allowed to grow over the long, many-windowed front; at both sides of which a wing protected, which were each the ends of other side fronts; for the house, although it was so desolate, was even grander than I expected.

Behind it rose the Fells; which seemed unenclosed and bare enough; and on the left hand of the house, as you stood facing it, was a little, old-fashioned flower-garden, as I found out afterwards. A door opened out upon it from the west front; it had been scooped out of the thick, dark wood for some old Lady Furnivall; but the branches of the great forest-trees had grown and overshadowed it again, and there were very few flowers that would live there at that time.

When we drove up to the great front entrance, and went into the hall, I thought we would be lost—it was so large, and vast and grand. There was a chandelier all of bronze, hung down from the middle of the ceiling; and I had never seen one before, and looked at it all in amaze. Then, at one end of the hall, was a great fire-place, as large as the sides of the houses in my country, with massy andirons and dogs to hold the wood; and by it were heavy, old-fashioned sofas. At the opposite end of the hall, to the left as you went in—on the western side—was an organ built into the wall, and so large that it filled up the best part of that end. Beyond it, on the same side, was a door; and opposite, on each side of the fire-place, were also doors leading to the east front; but those I never went through as long as I stayed in the house, so I can't tell you what lay beyond.

The afternoon was closing in, and the hall, which had no fire lighted in it, looked dark and gloomy, but we did not stay there a moment. The old servant, who had opened the door for us, bowed to Mr. Henry, and took us in through the door at the further side of the great organ, and led us through several smaller halls and passages into the west drawing-room, where he said that Miss Furnivall was sitting. Poor little Miss Rosamond held very tight to me, as if she were scared and lost in that great place; and as for myself, I was not much better.

The west drawing-room was very cheerful-looking, with a warm fire in it, and plenty of good, comfortable furniture about. Miss Furnivall was an old lady not far from eighty, I should think, but I do not know. She was thin and tall, and had a face as full of fine wrinkles as if they had been drawn all over it with a needle's point. Her eyes were very watchful, to make up, I suppose, for her being so deaf as to be obliged to use a trumpet.

Sitting with her, working at the same great piece of tapestry, was Mrs. Stark, her maid and companion, and almost as old as she was. She had lived with Miss Furnivall ever since they both were young, and now she seemed more like a friend than a servant; she looked so cold, and grey, and stony, as if she had never loved or cared for anyone; and I don't suppose she did care for any one, except her mistress; and, owing to the great deafness of the latter, Mrs. Stark treated her very much as if she were a child. Mr. Henry gave some message from my lord, and then he bowed good-by to us all,—taking no notice of my sweet little Miss Rosamond's outstretched hand—and left us standing there, being looked at by the two old ladies through their spectacles.

I was right glad when they rung for the old footman who had shown us in at first, and told him to take us to our rooms. So we went out of that great drawing-room and into another sitting-room, and out of that, and then up a great flight of stairs, and along a broad gallery—which was something like a library, having books all down one side, and windows and writing-tables all down the other—till we came to our rooms, which I was not sorry to hear were just over the kitchens; for I began to think I should be lost in that wilderness of a house.

There was an old nursery, that had been used for all the little lords and ladies long ago, with a pleasant fire burning in the grate, and the kettle boiling on the hob, and tea-things spread out on the table; and out of that room was the night-nursery, with a little crib for Miss Rosamond close to my bed. And old James called up Dorothy, his wife, to bid us welcome; and both he and she were so hospitable and kind, that by-and-by Miss Rosamond and me felt quite at home; and by the time tea was over, she was sitting on Dorothy's knee, and chattering away as fast as her little tongue could go.

I soon found out that Dorothy was from Westmoreland, and that bound her and me together, as it were; and I would never wish to meet with kinder people than were old James and his wife. James had lived pretty nearly all his life in my lord's family, and thought there was no one so grand as they. He even looked down a little on his wife; because, till he had married her, she had never lived in any but a farmer's household. But he was very fond of her, as well he might be.

They had one servant under them, to do all the rough work. Agnes they called her; and she and me, and James and Dorothy, with Miss Furnivall and Mrs. Stark, made up the family; always remembering my sweet little Miss Rosamond! I used to wonder what they had done before she came, they thought so much of her now. Kitchen and drawing-room, it was all the same. The hard, sad Miss Furnivall, and the cold Mrs. Stark, looked pleased when she came fluttering in like a bird, playing and pranking hither and thither, with a continual murmur, and pretty prattle of gladness.

I am sure, they were sorry many a time when she flitted away into the kitchen, though they were too proud to ask her to stay with them, and were a little surprised at her taste; though to be sure, as Mrs. Stark said, it was not to be wondered at, remembering what stock her father had come of. The great, old rambling house was a famous place for little Miss Rosamond. She made expeditions all over it, with me at her heels; all, except the east wing, which was never opened, and whither we never thought of going. But in the western and northern part was many a pleasant room; full of things that were curiosities to us, though they might not have been to people who had seen more. The windows were darkened by the sweeping boughs of the trees, and the ivy which had overgrown them; but, in the green gloom, we could manage to see old china jars and carved ivory boxes, and great heavy books, and, above all, the old pictures!

Once, I remember, my darling would have Dorothy go with us to tell us who they all were; for they were all portraits of some of my lord's family, though Dorothy could not tell us the names of every one. We had gone through most of the rooms, when we came to the old state drawing-room over the hall, and there was a picture of Miss Furnivall; or, as she was called in those days, Miss Grace, for she was the younger sister. Such a beauty she must have been! but with such a set, proud look, and such scorn looking out of her handsome eyes, with her eyebrows just a little raised, as if she wondered how anyone could have the impertinence to look at her, and her lip curled at us, as we stood there gazing. She had a dress on, the like of which I had never seen before, but it was all the fashion when she was young; a hat of some soft white stuff like beaver, pulled a little over her brows, and a beautiful plume of feathers sweeping round it on one side; and her gown of blue satin was open in front to a quilted white stomacher.

'Well, to be sure!' said I, when I had gazed my fill. 'Flesh is grass, they do say; but who would have thought that Miss Furnivall had been such an out-and-out beauty, to see her now.'

'Yes,' said Dorothy. 'Folks change sadly. But if what my master's father used to say was true, Miss Furnivall, the elder sister, was handsomer than Miss Grace. Her picture is here somewhere; but, if I show it you, you must never let on, even to James, that you have seen it. Can the little lady hold her tongue, think you?' asked she.

I was not so sure, for she was such a little sweet, bold, open-spoken child, so I set her to hide herself; and then I helped Dorothy to turn a great picture, that leaned with its face towards the wall, and was not hung up as the others were. To be sure, it beat Miss Grace for beauty; and, I think, for scornful pride, too, though in that matter it might be hard to choose. I could have looked at it an hour, but Dorothy seemed half frightened at having shown it to me, and hurried it back again, and bade me run and find Miss Rosamond, for that there were some ugly places about the house, where she should like ill for the child to go. I was a brave, high-spirited girl, and thought little of what the old woman said, for I liked hide-and-seek as well as any child in the parish; so off I ran to find my little one.

As winter drew on, and the days grew shorter, I was sometimes almost certain that I heard a noise as if someone was playing on the great organ in the hall. I did not hear it every evening; but, certainly, I did very often, usually when I was sitting with Miss Rosamond, after I had put her to bed, and keeping quite still and silent in the bedroom. Then I used to hear it booming and swelling away in the distance. The first night, when I went down to my supper, I asked Dorothy who had been playing music, and James said very shortly that I was a gowk to take the wind soughing among the trees for music; but I saw Dorothy look at him very fearfully, and Bessy, the kitchen-maid, said something beneath her breath, and went quite white. I saw they did not like my question, so I held my peace till I was with Dorothy alone, when I knew I could get a good deal out of her. So, the next day, I watched my time, and I coaxed and asked her who it was that played the organ; for I knew that it was the organ and not the wind well enough, for all I had kept silence before James.

But Dorothy had had her lesson, I'll warrant, and never a word could I get from her. So then I tried Bessy, though I had always held my head rather above her, as I was evened to James and Dorothy, and she was little better than their servant. So she said I must never, never tell; and if ever I told, I was never to say *she* had told me; but it was a very strange noise, and she had heard it many a time, but most of all on winter nights, and before storms; and folks did say it was the old lord playing on the great organ in the hall, just as he used to do when he was alive; but who the old lord was, or why he played, and why he played on stormy winter evenings in particular, she either could not or would not tell me. Well! I told you I had a brave heart; and I thought it was rather pleasant to have that grand music rolling about the house, let who would be the player; for now it rose above the great gusts of wind, and wailed and triumphed just like a living creature, and then it fell to a softness most complete, only it was always music, and tunes, so it was nonsense to call it the wind.

I thought at first, that it might be Miss Furnivall who played, unknown to Bessy; but one day, when I was in the hall by myself, I opened the organ and peeped all about it and around it, as I had done to the organ in Crosthwaite church once before, and I saw it was all broken and destroyed inside, though it looked so brave and fine; and then, though it was noon-day, my flesh began to creep a little, and I shut it up, and run away pretty quickly to my own bright nursery; and I did not like hearing the music for some time after that, any more than James and Dorothy did. All this time Miss Rosamond was making herself more and more beloved. The old ladies liked her to dine with them at their early dinner.

James stood behind Miss Furnivall's chair, and I behind Miss Rosamond's all in state; and after dinner, she would play about in a corner of the great drawing-room as still as any mouse, while Miss Furnivall slept, and I had my dinner in the kitchen. But she was glad enough to come to me in the nursery afterwards; for, as she said, Miss Furnivall was so sad, and Mrs. Stark so dull; but she and I were merry enough; and by-and-by, I got not to care for that weird rolling music, which did one no harm, if we did not know where it came from.

That winter was very cold. In the middle of October the frosts began, and lasted many, many weeks. I remember one day, at dinner, Miss Furnivall lifted up her sad, heavy eyes, and said to Mrs. Stark, 'I am afraid we shall have a terrible winter,' in a strange kind of meaning way. But Mrs. Stark pretended not to hear, and talked very loud of something else. My little lady and I did not care for the frost; not we! As long as it was dry, we climbed up the steep brows behind the house, and went up on the Fells, which were bleak and bare enough, and there we ran races in the fresh, sharp air; and once we came down by a new path, that took us past the two old gnarled holly-trees, which grew about half-way down by the east side of the house. But the days grew shorter and shorter, and the old lord, if it was he, played away, more and more stormily and sadly, on the great organ.

One Sunday afternoon—it must have been towards the end of November—I asked Dorothy to take charge of little missy when she came out of the drawing-room, after Miss Furnivall had had her nap; for it was too cold to take her with me to church, and yet I wanted to go. And Dorothy was glad enough to promise, and was so fond of the child, that all seemed well; and Bessy and I set off very briskly, though the sky hung heavy and black over the white earth, as if the night had never fully gone away, and the air, though still, was very biting and keen.

'We shall have a fall of snow,' said Bessy to me. And sure enough, even while we were in church, it came down thick, in great large flakes,—so thick, it almost darkened the windows. It had stopped snowing before we came out, but it lay soft, thick and deep beneath our feet, as we tramped home. Before we got to the hall, the moon rose, and I think it was lighter then—what with the moon, and what with the white dazzling snow—than it had been when we went to church, between two and three o'clock. I have not told you that Miss Furnivall and Mrs. Stark never went to church; they used to read the prayers together, in their quiet, gloomy way; they seemed to feel the Sunday very long without their tapestry-work to be busy at.

So when I went to Dorothy in the kitchen, to fetch Miss Rosamond and take her upstairs with me, I did not much wonder when the old woman told me that the ladies had kept the child with them, and that she had never come to the kitchen, as I had bidden her, when she was tired of behaving pretty in the drawing-room. So I took off my things and went to find her, and bring her to her supper in the nursery.

But when I went into the best drawing-room, there sat the two old ladies, very still and quiet, dropping out a word now and then, but looking as if nothing so bright and merry as Miss Rosamond had ever been near them. Still I thought she might be hiding from me; it was one of her pretty ways,—and that she had persuaded them to look as if they knew nothing about her; so I went softly peeping under this sofa, and behind that chair, making believe I was sadly frightened at not finding her.

'What's the matter, Hester?' said Mrs. Stark, sharply. I don't know if Miss Furnivall had seen me, for, as I told you, she was very deaf, and she sat quite still, idly staring into the fire, with her hopeless face.

'I'm only looking for my little Rosy Posy,' replied I, still thinking that the child was there, and near me, though I could not see her.

'Miss Rosamond is not here,' said Mrs. Stark. 'She went away, more than an hour ago, to find Dorothy.' And she, too, turned and went on looking into the fire.

My heart sank at this, and I began to wish I had never left my darling. I went back to Dorothy and told her. James was gone out for the day, but she, and me, and Bessy took lights, and went up into the nursery first; and then we roamed over the great, large house, calling and entreating Miss Rosamond to come out of her hiding-place, and not frighten us to death in that way. But there was no answer; no sound.

'Oh!' said I, at last, 'can she have got into the east wing and hidden there?'

But Dorothy said it was not possible, for that she herself had never been in there; that the doors were always locked, and my lord's steward had the keys, she believed; at any rate, neither she nor James had ever seen them: so I said I would go back, and see if, after all, she was not hidden in the drawing-room, unknown to the old ladies; and if I found her there, I said, I would whip her well for the fright she had given me; but I never meant to do it. Well, I went back to the west drawing-room, and I told Mrs. Stark we could not find her anywhere, and asked for leave to look all about the furniture there, for I thought now that she might have fallen asleep in some warm, hidden corner; but no! we looked—Miss Furnivall got up and looked, trembling all over—and she was nowhere there; then we set off again, everyone in the house, and looked in all the places we had searched before, but we could not find her.

Miss Furnivall shivered and shook so much, that Mrs. Stark took her back into the warm drawing-room; but not before they had made me promise to bring her to them when she was found. Well-a-day! I began to think she never would be found, when I bethought me to look into the great front court, all covered with snow. I was upstairs when I looked out; but, it was such clear moonlight, I could see, quite plain, two little footprints, which might be traced from the hall-door and round the corner of the east wing. I don't know how I got down, but I tugged open the great stiff hall-door, and, throwing the skirt of my gown over my head for a cloak, I ran out. I turned the east corner, and there a black shadow fell on the snow; but when I came again into the moonlight, there were the little foot-marks going up—up to the Fells. It was bitter cold; so cold, that the air almost took the skin off my face as I ran; but I ran on crying to think how my poor little darling must be perished and frightened.

I was within sight of the holly-trees, when I saw a shepherd coming down the hill, bearing something in his arms wrapped in his maud. He shouted to me, and asked me if I had lost a bairn; and, when I could not speak for crying, he bore towards me, and I saw my wee bairnie, lying still, and white, and stiff in his arms, as if she had been dead. He told me he had been up the Fells to gather in his sheep, before the deep cold of night came on, and that under the holly-trees (black marks on the hill-side, where no other bush was for miles around) he had found my little lady—my lamb—my queen—my darling—stiff and cold in the terrible sleep which is frost-begotten. Oh! the joy and the tears of having her in my arms once again! for I would not let him carry her; but took her, maud and all, into my own arms, and held her near my own warm neck and heart, and felt the life stealing slowly back again into her little gentle limbs. But she was still insensible when we reached the hall, and I had no breath for speech. We went in by the kitchen-door.

'Bring me the warming-pan,' said I; and I carried her upstairs and began undressing her by the nursery fire, which Bessy had kept up. I called my little lammie all the sweet and playful names I could think of,—even while my eyes were blinded by my tears; and at last, oh! at length she opened her large blue eyes. Then I put her into her warm bed, and sent Dorothy down to tell Miss Furnivall that all was well; and I made up my mind to sit by my darling's bedside the live-long night. She fell away into a soft sleep as soon as her pretty head had touched the pillow, and I watched by her till morning light; when she wakened up bright and clear—or so I thought at first—and, my dears, so I think now.

She said, that she had fancied that she should like to go to Dorothy, for that both the old ladies were asleep, and it was very dull in the drawing-room; and that, as she was going through the west lobby, she saw the snow through the high window falling—falling—soft and steady; but she wanted to see it lying pretty and white on the ground; so she made her way into the great hall; and then, going to the window, she saw it bright and soft upon the drive; but while she stood there, she saw a little girl, not so old as she was, 'but so pretty,' said my darling, 'and this little girl beckoned to me to come out; and oh, she was so pretty and so sweet, I could not choose but go.' And then this other little girl had taken her by the hand, and side by side the two had gone round the east corner.

'Now you are a naughty little girl, and telling stories,' said I. 'What would your good mamma, that is in heaven, and never told a story in her life, say to her little Rosamond, if she heard her—and I daresay she does—telling stories!'

'Indeed, Hester,' sobbed out my child, 'I'm telling you true. Indeed I am.'

'Don't tell me!' said I, very stern. 'I tracked you by your foot-marks through the snow; there were only yours to be seen: and if you had had a little girl to go hand-in-hand with you up the hill, don't you think the footprints would have gone along with yours?'

'I can't help it, dear, dear Hester,' said she, crying, 'if they did not; I never looked at her feet, but she held my hand fast and tight in her little one, and it was very, very cold. She took me up the Fell-path, up to the holly-trees; and there I saw a lady weeping and crying; but when she saw me, she hushed her weeping, and smiled very proud and grand, and took me on her knee, and began to lull me to sleep; and that's all, Hester—but that is true; and my dear mamma knows it is,' said she, crying. So I thought the child was in a fever, and pretended to believe her, as she went over her story—over and over again, and always the same. At last Dorothy knocked at the door with Miss Rosamond's breakfast; and she told me the old ladies were down in the eating parlour, and that they wanted to speak to me. They had both been into the night-nursery the evening before, but it was after Miss Rosamond was asleep; so they had only looked at her—not asked me any questions.

'I shall catch it,' thought I to myself, as I went along the north gallery. 'And yet,' I thought, taking courage, 'it was in their charge I left her; and it's they that's to blame for letting her steal away unknown and unwatched.' So I went in boldly, and told my story. I told it all to Miss Furnivall, shouting it close to her ear; but when I came to the mention of the other little girl out in the snow, coaxing and tempting her out, and willing her up to the grand and beautiful lady by the holly-tree, she threw her arms up—her old and withered arms—and cried aloud, 'Oh! Heaven forgive! Have mercy!'

Mrs. Stark took hold of her; roughly enough, I thought; but she was past Mrs. Stark's management, and spoke to me, in a kind of wild warning and authority.

'Hester! keep her from that child! It will lure her to her death! That evil child! Tell her it is a wicked, naughty child.' Then, Mrs. Stark hurried me out of the room; where, indeed, I was glad enough to go; but Miss Furnivall kept shrieking out, 'Oh, have mercy! Wilt Thou never forgive! It is many a long year ago——'

I was very uneasy in my mind after that. I durst never leave Miss Rosamond, night or day, for fear lest she might slip off again, after some fancy or other; and all the more, because I thought I could make out that Miss Furnivall was crazy, from their odd ways about her; and I was afraid lest something of the same kind (which might be in the family, you know) hung over my darling. And the great frost never ceased all this time; and, whenever it was a more stormy night than usual, between the gusts, and through the wind, we heard the old lord playing on the great organ.

But, old lord, or not, wherever Miss Rosamond went, there I followed; for my love for her, pretty, helpless orphan, was stronger than my fear for the grand and terrible sound. Besides, it rested with me to keep her cheerful and merry, as beseemed her age. So we played together, and wandered together, here and there, and everywhere; for I never dared to lose sight of her again in that large and rambling house. And so it happened, that one afternoon, not long before Christmas-day, we were playing together on the billiard-table in the great hall (not that we knew the right way of playing, but she liked to roll the smooth ivory balls with her pretty hands, and I liked to do whatever she did); and, by-and-by, without our noticing it, it grew dusk indoors, though it was still light in the open air, and I was thinking of taking her back into the nursery, when, all of a sudden, she cried out,

'Look, Hester! look! there is my poor little girl out in the snow!'

I turned towards the long narrow windows, and there, sure enough, I saw a little girl, less than my Miss Rosamond—dressed all unfit to be out-of-doors such a bitter night—crying, and beating against the window-panes, as if she wanted to be let in. She seemed to sob and wail, till Miss Rosamond could bear it no longer, and was flying to the door to open it, when, all of a sudden, and close upon us, the great organ pealed out so loud and thundering, it fairly made me tremble; and all the more, when I remembered me that, even in the stillness of that dead-cold weather, I had heard no sound of little battering hands upon the window-glass, although the phantom child had seemed to put forth all its force; and, although I had seen it wail and cry, no faintest touch of sound had fallen upon my ears.

Whether I remembered all this at the very moment, I do not know; the great organ sound had so stunned me into terror; but this I know, I caught up Miss Rosamond before she got the hall-door opened, and clutched her, and carried her away, kicking and screaming, into the large, bright kitchen, where Dorothy and Agnes were busy with their mince-pies.

'What is the matter with my sweet one?' cried Dorothy, as I bore in Miss Rosamond, who was sobbing as if her heart would break.

'She won't let me open the door for my little girl to come in; and she'll die if she is out on the Fells all night. Cruel, naughty Hester,' she said, slapping me; but she might have struck harder, for I had seen a look of ghastly terror on Dorothy's face, which made my very blood run cold.

'Shut the back-kitchen door fast, and bolt it well,' said she to Agnes. She said no more; she gave me raisins and almonds to quiet Miss Rosamond; but she sobbed about the little girl in the snow, and would not touch any of the good things. I was thankful when she cried herself to sleep in bed. Then I stole down to the kitchen, and told Dorothy I had made up my mind. I would carry my darling back to my father's house in Applethwaite; where, if we lived humbly, we lived at peace. I said I had been frightened enough with the old lord's organ-playing; but now that I had seen for myself this little moaning child, all decked out as no child in the neighbourhood could be, beating and battering to get in, yet always without any sound or noise—with the dark wound on its right shoulder; and that Miss Rosamond had known it again for the phantom that had nearly lured her to her death (which Dorothy knew was true); I would stand it no longer.

I saw Dorothy change colour once or twice. When I had done, she told me she did not think I could take Miss Rosamond with me, for that she was my lord's ward, and I had no right over her; and she asked me would I leave the child that I was so fond of just for sounds and sights that could do me no harm; and that they had all had to get used to in their turns? I was all in a hot, trembling passion; and I said it was very well for her to talk; that knew what these sights and noises betokened, and that had, perhaps, had something to do with the spectre child while it was alive. And I taunted her so, that she told me all she knew at last; and then I wished I had never been told, for it only made me more afraid than ever.

She said she had heard the tale from old neighbours that were alive when she was first married; when folks used to come to the hall sometimes, before it had got such a bad name on the country side: it might not be true, or it might, what she had been told.

The old lord was Miss Furnivall's father—Miss Grace, as Dorothy called her, for Miss Maude was the elder, and Miss Furnivall by rights. The old lord was eaten up with pride. Such a proud man was never seen or heard of; and his daughters were like him. No one was good enough to wed them, although they had choice enough; for they were the great beauties of their day, as I had seen by their portraits, where they hung in the state drawing-room. But, as the old saying is, 'Pride will have a fall;' and these two haughty beauties fell in love with the same man, and he no better than a foreign musician, whom their father had down from London to play music with him at the Manor House. For, above all things, next to his pride, the old lord loved music.

He could play on nearly every instrument that ever was heard of, and it was a strange thing it did not soften him; but he was a fierce dour old man, and had broken his poor wife's heart with his cruelty, they said.

He was mad after music, and would pay any money for it. So he got this foreigner to come; who made such beautiful music, that they said the very birds on the trees stopped their singing to listen. And, by degrees, this foreign gentleman got such a hold over the old lord, that nothing would serve him but that he must come every year; and it was he that had the great organ brought from Holland, and built up in the hall, where it stood now. He taught the old lord to play on it; but many and many a time, when Lord Furnivall was thinking of nothing but his fine organ, and his finer music, the dark foreigner was walking abroad in the woods with one of the young ladies; now Miss Maude, and then Miss Grace.

Miss Maude won the day and carried off the prize, such as it was; and he and she were married, all unknown to any one; and before he made his next yearly visit, she had been confined of a little girl at a farmhouse on the Moors, while her father and Miss Grace thought she was away at Doncaster Races. But though she was a wife and a mother, she was not a bit softened, but as haughty and as passionate as ever; and perhaps more so, for she was jealous of Miss Grace, to whom her foreign husband paid a deal of court—by way of blinding her—as he told his wife.

But Miss Grace triumphed over Miss Maude, and Miss Maude grew fiercer and fiercer, both with her husband and with her sister; and the former—who could easily shake off what was disagreeable, and hide himself in foreign countries—went away a month before his usual time that summer, and half-threatened that he would never come back again. Meanwhile, the little girl was left at the farm-house, and her mother used to have her horse saddled and gallop wildly over the hills to see her once every week, at the very least; for where she loved she loved, and where she hated she hated.

And the old lord went on playing—playing on his organ; and the servants thought the sweet music he made had soothed down his awful temper, of which (Dorothy said) some terrible tales could be told. He grew infirm too, and had to walk with a crutch; and his son—that was the present Lord Furnivall's father—was with the army in America, and the other son at sea; so Miss Maude had it pretty much her own way, and she and Miss Grace grew colder and bitterer to each other every day; till at last they hardly ever spoke, except when the old lord was by.

The foreign musician came again the next summer, but it was for the last time; for they led him such a life with their jealousy and their passions, that he grew weary, and went away, and never was heard of again. And Miss Maude, who had always meant to have her marriage acknowledged when her father should be dead, was left now a deserted wife, whom nobody knew to have been married, with a child that she dared not own, although she loved it to distraction; living with a father whom she feared, and a sister whom she hated.

When the next summer passed over, and the dark foreigner never came, both Miss Maude and Miss Grace grew gloomy and sad; they had a haggard look about them, though they looked handsome as ever. But, by-and-by, Maude brightened; for her father grew more and more infirm, and more than ever carried away by his music; and she and Miss Grace lived almost entirely apart, having separate rooms, the one on the west side, Miss Maude on the east—those very rooms which were now shut up. So she thought she might have her little girl with her, and no one need ever know except those who dared not speak about it, and were bound to believe that it was, as she said, a cottager's child she had taken a fancy to.

All this, Dorothy said, was pretty well known; but what came afterwards no one knew, except Miss Grace and Mrs. Stark, who was even then her maid, and much more of a friend to her than ever her sister had been. But the servants supposed, from words that were dropped, that Miss Maude had triumphed over Miss Grace, and told her that all the time the dark foreigner had been mocking her with pretended love—he was her own husband. The colour left Miss Grace's cheek and lips that very day for ever, and she was heard to say many a time that sooner or later she would have her revenge; and Mrs. Stark was forever spying about the east rooms.

One fearful night, just after the New Year had come in, when the snow was lying thick and deep; and the flakes were still falling—fast enough to blind anyone who might be out and abroad—there was a great and violent noise heard, and the old lord's voice above all, cursing and swearing awfully, and the cries of a little child, and the proud defiance of a fierce woman, and the sound of a blow, and a dead stillness, and moans and wailings dying away on the hillside!

Then the old lord summoned all his servants, and told them, with terrible oaths, and words more terrible, that his daughter had disgraced herself, and that he had turned her out of doors—her, and her child—and that if ever they gave her help, or food, or shelter, he prayed that they might never enter heaven. And, all the while, Miss Grace stood by him, white and still as any stone; and, when he had ended, she heaved a great sigh, as much as to say her work was done, and her end was accomplished.

But the old lord never touched his organ again, and died within the year; and no wonder! for, on the morrow of that wild and fearful night, the shepherds, coming down the Fell side, found Miss Maude sitting, all crazy and smiling, under the holly-trees, nursing a dead child, with a terrible mark on its right shoulder. 'But that was not what killed it,' said Dorothy: 'it was the frost and the cold. Every wild creature was in its hole, and every beast in its fold, while the child and its mother were turned out to wander on the Fells! And now you know all! and I wonder if you are less frightened now?'

I was more frightened than ever; but I said I was not. I wished Miss Rosamond and myself well out of that dreadful house for ever; but I would not leave her, and I dared not take her away. But oh, how I watched her, and guarded her! We bolted the doors, and shut the window-shutters fast, an hour or more before dark, rather than leave them open five minutes too late. But my little lady still heard the weird child crying and mourning; and not all we could do or say could keep her from wanting to go to her, and let her in from the cruel wind and the snow. All this time I kept away from Miss Furnivall and Mrs. Stark, as much as ever I could; for I feared them—I knew no good could be about them, with their grey, hard faces, and their dreamy eyes, looking back into the ghastly years that were gone.

But, even in my fear, I had a kind of pity for Miss Furnivall, at least. Those gone down to the pit can hardly have a more hopeless look than that which was ever on her face. At last I even got so sorry for her—who never said a word but what was quite forced from her—that I prayed for her; and I taught Miss Rosamond to pray for one who had done a deadly sin; but often when she came to those words, she would listen, and start up from her knees, and say, 'I hear my little girl plaining and crying very sad—oh, let her in, or she will die!'

One night—just after New Year's Day had come at last, and the long winter had taken a turn, as I hoped—I heard the west drawing-room bell ring three times, which was the signal for me. I would not leave Miss Rosamond alone, for all she was asleep—for the old lord had been playing wilder than ever—and I feared lest my darling should waken to hear the spectre child; see her, I knew she could not. I had fastened the windows too well for that. So I took her out of her bed, and wrapped her up in such outer clothes as were most handy, and carried her down to the drawing-room, where the old ladies sat at their tapestry-work as usual. They looked up when I came in, and Mrs. Stark asked, quite astounded, 'Why did I bring Miss Rosamond there, out of her warm bed?'

I had begun to whisper, 'Because I was afraid of her being tempted out while I was away, by the wild child in the snow,' when she stopped me short (with a glance at Miss Furnivall), and said Miss Furnivall wanted me to undo some work she had done wrong, and which neither of them could see to unpick. So I laid my pretty dear on the sofa, and sat down on a stool by them, and hardened my heart against them, as I heard the wind rising and howling.

Miss Rosamond slept on sound, for all the wind blew so Miss Furnivall said never a word, nor looked round when the gusts shook the windows. All at once she started up to her full height, and put up one hand, as if to bid us to listen.

'I hear voices!' said she. 'I hear terrible screams—I hear my father's voice!'

Just at that moment my darling wakened with a sudden start: 'My little girl is crying, oh, how she is crying!' and she tried to get up and go to her, but she got her feet entangled in the blanket, and I caught her up; for my flesh had begun to creep at these noises, which they heard while we could catch no sound. In a minute or two the noises came, and gathered fast, and filled our ears; we, too, heard voices and screams, and no longer heard the winter's wind that raged abroad. Mrs. Stark looked at me, and I at her, but we dared not speak. Suddenly Miss Furnivall went towards the door, out into the ante-room, through the west lobby, and opened the door into the great hall.

Mrs. Stark followed, and I durst not be left, though my heart almost stopped beating for fear. I wrapped my darling tight in my arms, and went out with them. In the hall the screams were louder than ever; they seemed to come from the east wing—nearer and nearer—close on the other side of the locked-up doors—close behind them. Then I noticed that the great bronze chandelier seemed all alight, though the hall was dim, and that a fire was blazing in the vast hearth-place, though it gave no heat; and I shuddered up with terror, and folded my darling closer to me. But as I did so the east door shook, and she, suddenly struggling to get free from me, cried, 'Hester! I must go. My little girl is there! I hear her; she is coming! Hester, I must go!'

I held her tight with all my strength; with a set will, I held her. If I had died, my hands would have grasped her still, I was so resolved in my mind. Miss Furnivall stood listening, and paid no regard to my darling, who had got down to the ground, and whom I, upon my knees now, was holding with both my arms clasped round her neck; she still striving and crying to get free.

All at once, the east door gave way with a thundering crash, as if torn open in a violent passion, and there came into that broad and mysterious light, the figure of a tall old man, with grey hair and gleaming eyes. He drove before him, with many a relentless gesture of abhorrence, a stern and beautiful woman, with a little child clinging to her dress.

'Oh, Hester! Hester!' cried Miss Rosamond; 'it's the lady! the lady below the holly-trees; and my little girl is with her. Hester! Hester! let me go to her; they are drawing me to them. I feel them—I feel them. I must go!'

Again she was almost convulsed by her efforts to get away; but I held her tighter and tighter, till I feared I should do her a hurt; but rather that than let her go towards those terrible phantoms. They passed along towards the great hall-door, where the winds howled and ravened for their prey; but before they reached that, the lady turned; and I could see that she defied the old man with a fierce and proud defiance; but then she quailed—and then she threw up her arms wildly and piteously to save her child—her little child—from a blow from his uplifted crutch.

And Miss Rosamond was torn as by a power stronger than mine and writhed in my arms, and sobbed (for by this time the poor darling was growing faint).

'They want me to go with them on to the Fells—they are drawing me to them. Oh, my little girl! I would come, but cruel, wicked Hester holds me very tight.' But when she saw the uplifted crutch, she swooned away, and I thanked God for it. Just at this moment—when the tall old man, his hair streaming as in the blast of a furnace, was going to strike the little shrinking child—Miss Furnivall, the old woman by my side, cried out, 'Oh father! father! spare the little innocent child!'

But just then I saw—we all saw—another phantom shape itself, and grow clear out of the blue and misty light that filled the hall; we had not seen her till now, for it was another lady who stood by the old man, with a look of relentless hate and triumphant scorn. That figure was very beautiful to look upon, with a soft, white hat drawn down over the proud brows, and a red and curling lip. It was dressed in an open robe of blue satin. I had seen that figure before. It was the likeness of Miss Furnivall in her youth; and the terrible phantoms moved on, regardless of old Miss Furnivall's wild entreaty,—and the uplifted crutch fell on the right shoulder of the little child, and the younger sister looked on, stony, and deadly serene. But at that moment, the dim lights, and the fire that gave no heat, went out of themselves, and Miss Furnivall lay at our feet stricken down by the palsy—death-stricken.

Yes! she was carried to her bed that night never to rise again. She lay with her face to the wall, muttering low, but muttering always: 'Alas! alas! what is done in youth can never be undone in age! What is done in youth can never be undone in age!'

Bewitched

Edith Wharton

1

The snow was still falling thickly when Orrin Bosworth, who farmed the land south of Lone-top, drove up in his cutter to Saul Rutledge's gate. He was surprised to see two other cutters ahead of him. From them descended two muffled figures. Bosworth, with increasing surprise, recognised Deacon Hibben, from North Ashmore, and Sylvester Brand, the widower, from the old Bearcliff farm on the way to Lonetop.

It was not often that anybody in Hemlock County entered Saul Rutledge's gate; least of all in the dead of winter, and summoned (as Bosworth, at any rate, had been) by Mrs. Rutledge, who passed, even in that unsocial region, for a woman of cold manners and solitary character. The situation was enough to excite the curiosity of a less imaginative man than Orrin Bosworth.

As he drove in between the broken-down white gate-posts topped by fluted urns the two men ahead of him were leading their horses to the adjoining shed. Bosworth followed, and hitched his horse to a post. Then the three tossed off the snow from their shoulders, clapped their numb hands together, and greeted each other.

"Hallo, Deacon."

"Well, well, Orrin—." They shook hands.

"'Day, Bosworth," said Sylvester Brand, with a brief nod. He seldom put any cordiality into his manner, and on this occasion he was still busy about his horse's bridle and blanket.

Orrin Bosworth, the youngest and most communicative of the three, turned back to Deacon Hibben, whose long face, queerly blotched and mouldy-looking, with blinking peering eyes, was yet less forbidding than Brand's heavily-hewn countenance.

"Queer, our all meeting here this way. Mrs. Rutledge sent me a message to come," Bosworth volunteered.

The deacon nodded. "I got a word from her too—Andy Pond come with it yesterday noon. I hope there's no trouble here—"

He glanced through the thickening fall of snow at the desolate front of the Rutledge house, the more melancholy in its present neglected state because, like the gate-posts, it kept traces of former elegance. Bosworth had often wondered how such a house had come to be built in that lonely stretch between North Ashmore and Cold Corners. People said there had once been other houses like it, forming a little township called Ashmore, a sort of mountain colony created by the caprice of an English Royalist officer, one Colonel Ashmore, who had been murdered by the Indians, with all his family, long before the Revolution.

This tale was confirmed by the fact that the ruined cellars of several smaller houses were still to be discovered under the wild growth of the adjoining slopes, and that the Communion plate of the moribund Episcopal church of Cold Corners was engraved with the name of Colonel Ashmore, who had given it to the church of Ashmore in the year 1723. Of the church itself no traces remained. Doubtless it had been a modest wooden edifice, built on piles, and the conflagration which had burnt the other houses to the ground's edge had reduced it utterly to ashes. The whole place, even in summer, wore a mournful solitary air, and people wondered why Saul Rutledge's father had gone there to settle.

"I never knew a place," Deacon Hibben said, "as seemed as far away from humanity. And yet it ain't so in miles."

"Miles ain't the only distance," Orrin Bosworth answered; and the two men, followed by Sylvester Brand, walked across the drive to the front door. People in Hemlock County did not usually come and go by their front doors, but all three men seemed to feel that, on an occasion which appeared to be so exceptional, the usual and more familiar approach by the kitchen would not be suitable.

They had judged rightly; the deacon had hardly lifted the knocker when the door opened and Mrs. Rutledge stood before them.

"Walk right in," she said in her usual dead-level tone; and Bosworth, as he followed the others, thought to himself; "Whatever's happened, she's not going to let it show in her face."

It was doubtful, indeed, if anything unwonted could be made to show in Prudence Rutledge's face, so limited was its scope, so fixed were its features. She was dressed for the occasion in a black calico with white spots, a collar of crochet-lace fastened by a gold brooch, and a grey woollen shawl crossed under her arms and tied at the back. In her small narrow head the only marked prominence was that of the brow projecting roundly over pale spectacled eyes. Her dark hair, parted above this prominence, passed tight and flat over the tips of her ears into a small braided coil at the nape; and her contracted head looked still narrower from being perched on a long hollow neck with cord-like throat-muscles. Her eyes were of a pale cold grey, her complexion was an even white. Her age might have been anywhere from thirty-five to sixty.

The room into which she led the three men had probably been the dining-room of the Ashmore house. It was now used as a front parlour, and a black stove planted on a sheet of zinc stuck out from the delicately fluted panels of an old wooden mantel. A newly-lit fire smouldered reluctantly, and the room was at once close and bitterly cold.

"Andy Pond," Mrs. Rutledge cried to someone at the back of the house, "step out and call Mr. Rutledge. You'll likely find him in the wood-shed, or round the barn somewheres." She rejoined her visitors. "Please suit yourselves to seats," she said.

The three men, with an increasing air of constraint, took the chairs she pointed out, and Mrs. Rutledge sat stiffly down upon a fourth, behind a rickety bead-work table. She glanced from one to the other of her visitors.

"I presume you folks are wondering what it is I asked you to come here for," she said in her dead-level voice. Orrin Bosworth and Deacon Hibben murmured an assent; Sylvester Brand sat silent, his eyes, under their great thicket of eyebrows, fixed on the huge boot-tip swinging before him.

"Well, I allow you didn't expect it was for a party," continued Mrs. Rutledge.

No one ventured to respond to this chill pleasantry, and she continued: "We're in trouble here, and that's the fact. And we need advice—Mr. Rutledge and myself do." She cleared her throat, and added in a lower tone, her pitilessly clear eyes looking straight before her: "There's a spell been cast over Mr. Rutledge."

The deacon looked up sharply, an incredulous smile pinching his thin lips. "A spell?"

"That's what I said: he's bewitched."

Again the three visitors were silent; then Bosworth, more at ease or less tongue-tied than the others, asked with an attempt at humour: "Do you use the word in the strict Scripture sense, Mrs. Rutledge?"

She glanced at him before replying: "That's how *he* uses it."

The deacon coughed and cleared his long rattling throat. "Do you care to give us more particulars before your husband joins us?"

Mrs. Rutledge looked down at her clasped hands, as if considering the question. Bosworth noticed that the inner fold of her lids was of the same uniform white as the rest of her skin, so that when she dropped them her rather prominent eyes looked like the sightless orbs of a marble statue. The impression was unpleasing, and he glanced away at the text over the mantelpiece, which read:

The Soul That Sinneth It Shall Die.

"No," she said at length, "I'll wait."

At this moment Sylvester Brand suddenly stood up and pushed back his chair. "I don't know," he said, in his rough bass voice, "as I've got any particular lights on Bible mysteries; and this happens to be the day I was to go down to Starkfield to close a deal with a man."

Mrs. Rutledge lifted one of her long thin hands. Withered and wrinkled by hard work and cold, it was nevertheless of the same leaden white as her face. "You won't be kept long," she said. "Won't you be seated?"

Farmer Brand stood irresolute, his purplish underlip twitching. "The deacon here—-such things is more in his line. . . . ."

"I want you should stay," said Mrs. Rutledge quietly; and Brand sat down again.

A silence fell, during which the four persons present seemed all to be listening for the sound of a step; but none was heard, and after a minute or two Mrs. Rutledge began to speak again.

"It's down by that old shack on Lamer's pond; that's where they meet," she said suddenly.

Bosworth, whose eyes were on Sylvester Brand's face, fancied he saw a sort of inner flush darken the farmer's heavy leathern skin. Deacon Hibben leaned forward, a glitter of curiosity in his eyes.

"They—*who*, Mrs. Rutledge?"

"My husband, Saul Rutledge. . . . .and her. . . ."

Sylvester Brand again stirred in his seat. "Who do you mean by *her?*" he asked abruptly, as if roused out of some far-off musing.

Mrs. Rutledge's body did not move; she simply revolved her head on her long neck and looked at him.

"Your daughter, Sylvester Brand."

The man staggered to his feet with an explosion of inarticulate sounds. "My—my daughter? What the hell are you talking about? My daughter? It's a damned lie. . . . it's. . . . it's. . . ."

"Your daughter *Ora*, Mr. Brand," said Mrs. Rutledge slowly.

Bosworth felt an icy chill down his spine. Instinctively he turned his eyes away from Brand, and, they rested on the mildewed countenance of Deacon Hibben. Between the blotches it had become as white as Mrs. Rutledge's, and the deacon's eyes burned in the whiteness like live embers among ashes.

Brand gave a laugh: the rusty creaking laugh of one whose springs of mirth are never moved by gaiety. "My daughter *Ora?*" he repeated.

"Yes."

"My *dead* daughter?"

"That's what he says."

"Your husband?"

"That's what Mr. Rutledge says."

Orrin Bosworth listened with a sense of suffocation; he felt as if he were wrestling with long-armed horrors in a dream. He could no longer resist letting his eyes return to Sylvester Brand's face. To his surprise it had resumed a natural imperturbable expression. Brand rose to his feet. "Is that all?" he queried contemptuously.

"All? Ain't it enough? How long is it since you folks seen Saul Rutledge, any of you?" Mrs. Rutledge flew out at them.

Bosworth, it appeared, had not seen him for nearly a year; the deacon had only run across him once, for a minute, at the North Ashmore post office, the previous autumn, and acknowledged that he wasn't looking any too good then. Brand said nothing, but stood irresolute.

"Well, if you wait a minute you'll see with your own eyes; and he'll tell you with his own words. That's what I've got you here for—to see for yourselves what's come over him. Then you'll talk different," she added, twisting her head abruptly toward Sylvester Brand.

The deacon raised a lean hand of interrogation.

"Does your husband know we've been sent for on this business, Mrs. Rutledge?" Mrs. Rutledge signed assent.

"It was with his consent, then—?"

She looked coldly at her questioner. "I guess it had to be," she said. Again Bosworth felt the chill down his spine. He tried to dissipate the sensation by speaking with an affectation of energy.

"Can you tell us, Mrs. Rutledge, how this trouble you speak of shows itself. . . . .what makes you think. . . . .?"

She looked at him for a moment; then she leaned forward across the rickety bead-work table. A thin smile of disdain narrowed her colourless lips. "I don't think—I know."

"Well—but how?"

She leaned closer, both elbows on the table, her voice dropping. "I seen 'em."

In the ashen light from the veiling of snow beyond the windows the deacon's little screwed-up eyes seemed to give out red sparks. "Him and the dead?"

"Him and the dead."

"Saul Rutledge and—and Ora Brand?"

"That's so."

Sylvester Brand's chair fell backward with a crash. He was on his feet again, crimson and cursing. "It's a God-damned fiend-begotten lie. . . . ."

"Friend Brand. . . . .friend Brand. . . . ." the deacon protested.

"Here, let me get out of this. I want to see Saul Rutledge himself, and tell him—"

"Well, here he is," said Mrs. Rutledge.

The outer door had opened; they heard the familiar stamping and shaking of a man who rids his garments of their last snowflakes before penetrating to the sacred precincts of the best parlour. Then Saul Rutledge entered.

2

As he came in he faced the light from the north window, and Bosworth's first thought was that he looked like a drowned man fished out from under the ice—"self-drowned," he added. But the snow-light plays cruel tricks with a man's colour, and even with the shape of his features; it must have been partly that, Bosworth reflected, which transformed Saul Rutledge from the straight muscular fellow he had been a year before into the haggard wretch now before them.

The deacon sought for a word to ease the horror. "Well, now, Saul—you look's if you'd ought to set right up to the stove. Had a touch of ague, maybe?"

The feeble attempt was unavailing. Rutledge neither moved nor answered. He stood among them silent, incommunicable, like one risen from the dead.

Brand grasped him roughly by the shoulder. "See here, Saul Rutledge, what's this dirty lie your wife tells us you've been putting about?"

Still Rutledge did not move. "It's no lie," he said.

Brand's hand dropped from his shoulder. In spite of the man's rough bullying power he seemed to be undefinably awed by Rutledge's look and tone.

"No lie? You've gone plumb crazy, then, have you?"

Mrs. Rutledge spoke. "My husband's not lying, nor he ain't gone crazy. Don't I tell you I seen 'em?"

Brand laughed again. "Him and the dead?"

"Yes."

"Down by the Lamer pond, you say?"

"Yes."

"And when was that, if I might ask?"

"Day before yesterday."

A silence fell on the strangely assembled group. The deacon at length broke it to say to Mr. Brand: "Brand, in my opinion we've got to see this thing through."

Brand stood for a moment in speechless contemplation: there was something animal and primitive about him, Bosworth thought, as he hung thus, lowering and dumb, a little foam beading the corners of that heavy purplish underlip. He let himself slowly down into his chair. "I'll see it through."

The two other men and Mrs. Rutledge had remained seated. Saul Rutledge stood before them, like a prisoner at the bar, or rather like a sick man before the physicians who were to heal him. As Bosworth scrutinized that hollow face, so wan under the dark sunburn, so sucked inward and consumed by some hidden fever, there stole over the sound healthy man the thought that perhaps, after all, husband and wife spoke the truth, and that they were all at that moment really standing on the edge of some forbidden mystery. Things that the rational mind would reject without a thought seemed no longer so easy to dispose of as one looked at the actual Saul Rutledge and remembered the man he had been a year before. Yes; as the deacon said, they would have to see it through...

"Sit down then, Saul; draw up to us, won't you?" the deacon suggested, trying again for a natural tone.

Mrs. Rutledge pushed a chair forward, and her husband sat down on it. He stretched out his arms and grasped his knees in his brown bony fingers; in that attitude he remained, turning neither his head nor his eyes.

"Well, Saul," the deacon continued, "your wife says you thought mebbe we could do something to help you through this trouble, whatever it is."

Rutledge's grey eyes widened a little. "No; I didn't think that. It was her idea to try what could be done."

"I presume, though, since you've agreed to our coming, that you don't object to our putting a few questions?"

Rutledge was silent for a moment; then he said with a visible effort: "No; I don't object."

"Well—you've heard what your wife says?"

Rutledge made a slight motion of assent. "And—what have you got to answer? How do you explain. . . . .?"

Mrs. Rutledge intervened. "How can he explain? I seen 'em."

There was a silence; then Bosworth, trying to speak in an easy reassuring tone, queried: "That so, Saul?"

"That's so."

Brand lifted up his brooding head. "You mean to say you. . . . .you sit here before us all and say..."

The deacon's hand again checked him. "Hold on, friend Brand. We're all of us trying for the facts, ain't we?" He turned to Rutledge. "We've heard what Mrs. Rutledge says. What's your answer?"

"I don't know as there's any answer. She found us."

"And you mean to tell me the person with you was...was what you took to be. . . . . " the deacon's thin voice grew thinner: "Ora Brand?"

Saul Rutledge nodded.

"You knew.. . . . or thought you knew. . . . you were meeting with the dead?"

Rutledge bent his head again. The snow continued to fall in a steady unwavering sheet against the window, and Bosworth felt as if a winding-sheet were descending from the sky to envelop them all in a common grave.

"Think what you're saying! It's against our religion! Ora. . . . .poor child! . . . . .died over a year ago. I saw you at her funeral, Saul. How can you make such a statement?"

"What else can he do?" thrust in Mrs. Rutledge.

There was another pause. Bosworth's resources had failed him, and Brand once more sat plunged in dark meditation. The deacon laid his quivering finger-tips together, and moistened his lips.

"Was the day before yesterday the first time?" he asked.

The movement of Rutledge's head was negative.

"Not the first? Then when. . . . ."

"Nigh on a year ago, I reckon."

"God! And you mean to tell us that ever since—?"

"Well. . . . . look at him," said his wife. The three men lowered their eyes.

After a moment Bosworth, trying to collect himself, glanced at the deacon. "Why not ask Saul to make his own statement, if that's what we're here for?"

"That's so," the deacon assented. He turned to Rutledge. "Will you try and give us your idea . . . .of . . . .of how it began?"

There was another silence. Then Rutledge tightened his grasp on his gaunt knees, and still looking straight ahead, with his curiously clear unseeing gaze: "Well," he said, "I guess it begun away back, afore even I was married to Mrs. Rutledge. . . . ." He spoke in a low automatic tone, as if some invisible agent were dictating his words, or even uttering them for him. "You know," he added, "Ora and me was to have been married."

Sylvester Brand lifted his, head. "Straighten that statement out first, please," he interjected.

"What I mean is, we kept company. But Ora she was very young. Mr. Brand here he sent her away. She was gone nigh to three years, I guess. When she come back I was married."

"That's right," Brand said, relapsing once more into his sunken attitude.

"And after she came back did you meet her again?" the deacon continued.

"Alive?" Rutledge questioned.

A perceptible shudder ran through the room.

"Well—of course," said the deacon nervously.

Rutledge seemed to consider. "Once I did—only once. There was a lot of other people round. At Cold Corners fair it was."

"Did you talk with her then?"

"Only a minute."

"What did she say?"

His voice dropped. "She said she was sick and knew she was going to die, and when she was dead she'd come back to me."

"And what did you answer?"

"Nothing."

"Did you think anything of it at the time?"

"Well, no. Not till I heard she was dead I didn't. After that I thought of it—and I guess she drew me." He moistened his lips.

"Drew you down to that abandoned house by the pond?"

Rutledge made a faint motion of assent, and the deacon added: "How did you know it was there she wanted you to come?"

"She. . . . .just drew me. . . . ."

There was a long pause. Bosworth felt, on himself and the other two men, the oppressive weight of the next question to be asked. Mrs. Rutledge opened and closed her narrow lips once or twice, like some beached shell-fish gasping for the tide. Rutledge waited.

"Well, now, Saul, won't you go on with what you was telling us?" the deacon at length suggested.

"That's all. There's nothing else."

The deacon lowered his voice. "She just draws you?"

"Yes."

"Often?"

"That's as it happens. . . . ."

"But if it's always there she draws you, man, haven't you the strength to keep away from the place?"

For the first time, Rutledge wearily turned his head toward his questioner. A spectral smile narrowed his colourless lips. "Ain't any use. She follers after me . . . ."

There was another silence. What more could they ask, then and there? Mrs. Rutledge's presence checked the next question. The deacon seemed hopelessly to revolve the matter. At length he spoke in a more authoritative tone. "These are forbidden things. You know that, Saul. Have you tried prayer?"

Rutledge shook his head.

"Will you pray with us now?"

Rutledge cast a glance of freezing indifference on his spiritual adviser. "If you folks want to pray, I'm agreeable," he said. But Mrs. Rutledge intervened.

"Prayer ain't any good. In this kind of thing it ain't no manner of use; you know it ain't. I called you here, deacon, because you remember the last case in this parish. Thirty years ago it was, I guess; but you remember. Lefferts Nash—did praying help him? I was a little girl then, but I used to hear my folks talk of it winter nights. Lefferts Nash and Hannah Cory. They drove a stake through her breast. That's what cured him."

"Oh—" Orrin Bosworth exclaimed.

Sylvester Brand raised his head. "You're speaking of that old story as if this was the same sort of thing?"

"Ain't it? Ain't my husband pining away the same as Lefferts Nash did? The deacon here knows—"

The deacon stirred anxiously in his chair. "These are forbidden things," he repeated. "Supposing your husband is quite sincere in thinking himself haunted, as you might say. Well, even then, what proof have we that the.....the dead woman.....is the spectre of that poor girl?"

"Proof? Don't he say so? Didn't she tell him? Ain't I seen 'em?" Mrs. Rutledge almost screamed.

The three men sat silent, and suddenly the wife burst out: "A stake through the breast That's the old way; and it's the only way. The deacon knows it!"

"It's against our religion to disturb the dead."

"Ain't it against your religion to let the living perish as my husband is perishing?" She sprang up with one of her abrupt movements and took the family Bible from the what-not in a corner of the parlour. Putting the book on the table, and moistening a livid finger-tip, she turned the pages rapidly, till she came to one on which she laid her hand like a stony paper-weight. "See here," she said, and read out in her level chanting voice:

"'*Thou shalt not suffer a witch to live.*'

"That's in Exodus, that's where it is," she added, leaving the book open as if to confirm the statement.

Bosworth continued to glance anxiously from one to the other of the four people about the table. He was younger than any of them, and had had more contact with the modern world; down in Starkfield, in the bar of the Fielding House, he could hear himself laughing with the rest of the men at such old wives' tales. But it was not for nothing that he had been born under the icy shadow of Lonetop, and had shivered and hungered as a lad through the bitter Hemlock County winters. After his parents died, and he had taken hold of the farm himself, he had got more out of it by using improved methods, and by supplying the increasing throng of summer-boarders over Stotesbury way with milk and vegetables.

He had been made a selectman of North Ashmore; for so young a man he had a standing in the county. But the roots of the old life were still in him. He could remember, as a little boy, going twice a year with his mother to that bleak hill-farm out beyond Sylvester Brand's, where Mrs. Bosworth's aunt, Cressidora Cheney, had been shut up for years in a cold clean room with iron bars in the windows. When little Orrin first saw Aunt Cressidora she was a small white old woman, whom her sisters used to "make decent" for visitors the day that Orrin and his mother were expected. The child wondered why there were bars to the window. "Like a canary-bird," he said to his mother. The phrase made Mrs. Bosworth reflect. "I do believe they keep Aunt Cressidora too lonesome," she said; and the next time she went up the mountain with the little boy he carried to his great-aunt a canary in a little wooden cage. It was a great excitement; he knew it would make her happy.

The old woman's motionless face lit up when she saw the bird, and her eyes began to glitter. "It belongs to me," she said instantly, stretching her soft bony hand over the cage.

"Of course it does, Aunt Cressy," said Mrs. Bosworth, her eyes filling.

But the bird, startled by the shadow of the old woman's hand, began to flutter and beat its wings distractedly. At the sight, Aunt Cressidora's calm face suddenly became a coil of twitching features. "You she-devil, you!" she cried in a high squealing voice; and thrusting her hand into the cage she dragged out the terrified bird and wrung its neck. She was plucking the hot body, and squealing "she-devil, she-devil!" as they drew little Orrin from the room. On the way down the mountain his mother wept a great deal, and said: "You must never tell anybody that poor Auntie's crazy, or the men would come and take her down to the asylum at Starkfield, and the shame of it would kill us all. Now promise." The child promised.

He remembered the scene now, with its deep fringe of mystery, secrecy and rumour. It seemed related to a great many other things below the surface of his thoughts, things which stole up anew, making him feel that all the old people he had known, and who "believed in these things," might after all be right. Hadn't a witch been burned at North Ashmore? Didn't the summer folk still drive over in jolly buckboard loads to see the meeting-house where the trial had been held, the pond where they had ducked her and she had floated? . . . . .Deacon Hibben believed; Bosworth was sure of it. If he didn't, why did people from all over the place come to him when their animals had queer sicknesses, or when there was a child in the family that had to be kept shut up because it fell down flat and foamed? Yes, in spite of his religion, Deacon Hibben *knew*. . .

And Brand? Well, it came to Bosworth in a flash: that North Ashmore woman who was burned had the name of Brand. The same stock, no doubt; there had been Brands in Hemlock County ever since the white men had come there. And Orrin, when he was a child, remembered hearing his parents say that Sylvester Brand hadn't ever oughter married his own cousin, because of the blood. Yet the couple had had two healthy girls, and when Mrs. Brand pined away and died nobody suggested that anything had been wrong with her mind. And Vanessa and Ora were the handsomest girls anywhere round.

Brand knew it, and scrimped and saved all he could to send Ora, the eldest, down to Starkfield to learn book-keeping. "When she's married I'll send you," he used to say to little Venny, who was his favourite.

But Ora never married. She was away three years, during which Venny ran wild on the slopes of Lonetop; and when Ora came back she sickened and died—poor girl! Since then Brand had grown more savage and morose. He was a hard-working farmer, but there wasn't much to be got out of those barren Bearcliff acres. He was said to have taken to drink since his wife's death; now and then men ran across him in the "dives" of Stotesbury. But not often.

And between times he laboured hard on his stony acres and did his best for his daughters. In the neglected graveyard of Cold Corners there was a slanting headstone marked with his wife's name; near it, a year since, he had laid his eldest daughter. And sometimes, at dusk, in the autumn, the village people saw him walk slowly by, turn in between the graves, and stand looking down on the two stones. But he never brought a flower there, or planted a bush; nor Venny either. She was too wild and ignorant. . . . .

Mrs. Rutledge repeated: "That's in Exodus."

The three visitors remained silent, turning about their hats in reluctant hands. Rutledge faced them, still with that empty pellucid gaze which frightened Bosworth. What was he seeing?

"Ain't any of you folks got the grit—?" his wife burst out again, half hysterically.

Deacon Hibben held up his hand. "That's no way, Mrs. Rutledge. This ain't a question of having grit. What we want first of all is. . . . .proof. . . . ."

"That's so," said Bosworth, with an explosion of relief, as if the words had lifted something black and crouching from his breast. Involuntarily the eyes of both men had turned to Brand. He stood there smiling grimly, but did not speak.

"Ain't it so, Brand?" the deacon prompted him.

"Proof that spooks walk?" the other sneered.

"Well—I presume you want this business settled too?"

The old farmer squared his shoulders. "Yes—I do. But I ain't a sperritualist. How the hell are you going to settle it?"

Deacon Hibben hesitated; then he said, in a low incisive tone: "I don't see but one way—Mrs. Rutledge's."

There was a silence.

"What?" Brand sneered again. "Spying?"

The deacon's voice sank lower. "If the poor girl *does* walk. . . . .her that's your child. . . . .wouldn't you be the first to want her laid quiet? We all know there've been such cases. . . . .mysterious visitations. . . . Can any one of us here deny it?"

"I seen 'em," Mrs. Rutledge interjected.

There was another heavy pause. Suddenly Brand fixed his gaze on Rutledge. "See here, Saul Rutledge, you've got to clear up this damned calumny, or I'll know why. You say my dead girl comes to you." He laboured with his breath, and then jerked out: "When? You tell me that, and I'll be there."

Rutledge's head drooped a little, and his eyes wandered to the window. "Round about sunset, mostly."

"You know beforehand?"

Rutledge made a sign of assent.

"Well, then—tomorrow, will it be?" Rutledge made the same sign.

Brand turned to the door. "I'll be there." That was all he said. He strode out between them without another glance or word. Deacon Hibben looked at Mrs. Rutledge. "We'll be there too," he said, as if she had asked him; but she had not spoken, and Bosworth saw that her thin body was trembling all over. He was glad when he and Hibben were out again in the snow.

3

They thought that Brand wanted to be left to himself, and to give him time to unhitch his horse they made a pretence of hanging about in the doorway while Bosworth searched his pockets for a pipe he had no mind to light.

But Brand turned back to them as they lingered. "You'll meet me down by Lamer's pond tomorrow?" he suggested. "I want witnesses. Round about sunset."

They nodded their acquiescence, and he got into his sleigh, gave the horse a cut across the flanks, and drove off under the snow-smothered hemlocks. The other two men went to the shed.

"What do you make of this business, deacon?" Bosworth asked, to break the silence.

The deacon shook his head. "The man's a sick man—that's sure. Something's sucking the life clean out of him."

But already, in the biting outer air, Bosworth was getting himself under better control. "Looks to me like a bad case of the ague, as you said."

"Well—ague of the mind, then. It's his brain that's sick."

Bosworth shrugged. "He ain't the first in Hemlock County."

"That's so," the deacon agreed. "It's a worm in the brain, solitude is."

"Well, we'll know this time tomorrow, maybe," said Bosworth. He scrambled into his sleigh, and was driving off in his turn when he heard his companion calling after him. The deacon explained that his horse had cast a shoe; would Bosworth drive him down to the forge near North Ashmore, if it wasn't too much out of his way? He didn't want the mare slipping about on the freezing snow, and he could probably get the blacksmith to drive him back and shoe her in Rutledge's shed. Bosworth made room for him under the bearskin, and the two men drove off, pursued by a puzzled whinny from the deacon's old mare.

The road they took was not the one that Bosworth would have followed to reach his own home. But he did not mind that. The shortest way to the forge passed close by Lamer's pond, and Bosworth, since he was in for the business, was not sorry to look the ground over. They drove on in silence.

The snow had ceased, and a green sunset was spreading upward into the crystal sky. A stinging wind barbed with ice-flakes caught them in the face on the open ridges, but when they dropped down into the hollow by Lamer's pond the air was as soundless and empty as an unswung bell. They jogged along slowly, each thinking his own thoughts.

"That's the house. . . . .that tumble-down shack over there, I suppose?" the deacon said, as the road drew near the edge of the frozen pond.

"Yes: that's the house. A queer hermit-fellow built it years ago, my father used to tell me. Since then I don't believe it's ever been used but by the gipsies."

Bosworth had reined in his horse, and sat looking through pine-trunks purpled by the sunset at the crumbling structure. Twilight already lay under the trees, though day lingered in the open. Between two sharply-patterned pine-boughs he saw the evening star, like a white boat in a sea of green.

His gaze dropped from that fathomless sky and followed the blue-white undulations of the snow. It gave him a curious agitated feeling to think that here, in this icy solitude, in the tumble-down house he had so often passed without heeding it, a dark mystery, too deep for thought, was being enacted. Down that very slope, coming from the graveyard at Cold Corners, the being they called "Ora" must pass toward the pond. His heart began to beat stiflingly. Suddenly he gave an exclamation: "Look!"

He had jumped out of the cutter and was stumbling up the bank toward the slope of snow. On it, turned in the direction of the house by the pond, he had detected a woman's foot-prints; two; then three; then more. The deacon scrambled out after him, and they stood and stared.

"God—barefoot!" Hibben gasped. "Then it *is*. . . . .the dead. . . . ."

Bosworth said nothing. But he knew that no live woman would travel with naked feet across that freezing wilderness. Here, then, was the proof the deacon had asked for—they held it. What should they do with it?

"Supposing we was to drive up nearer—round the turn of the pond, till we get close to the house," the deacon proposed in a colourless voice. "Mebbe then. . . . ."

Postponement was a relief. They got into the sleigh and drove on. Two or three hundred yards farther the road, a mere lane under steep bushy banks, turned sharply to the right, following the bend of the pond. As they rounded the turn they saw Brand's cutter ahead of them. It was empty, the horse tied to a tree-trunk. The two men looked at each other again. This was not Brand's nearest way home.

Evidently he had been actuated by the same impulse which had made them rein in their horse by the pond-side, and then hasten on to the deserted hovel. Had he too discovered those spectral foot-prints? Perhaps it was for that very reason that he had left his cutter and vanished in the direction of the house. Bosworth found himself shivering all over under his bearskin. "I wish to God the dark wasn't coming on," he muttered. He tethered his own horse near Brand's, and without a word he and the deacon ploughed through the snow, in the track of Brand's huge feet. They had only a few yards to walk to overtake him. He did not hear them following him, and when Bosworth spoke his name, and he stopped short and turned, his heavy face was dim and confused, like a darker blot on the dusk. He looked at them dully, but without surprise.

"I wanted to see the place," he merely said.

The deacon cleared his throat. "Just take a look. . . . .yes. . . . .We thought so...But I guess there won't be anything to *see*. . . . ." He attempted a chuckle.

The other did not seem to hear him, but laboured on ahead through the pines. The three men came out together in the cleared space before the house. As they emerged from beneath the trees they seemed to have left night behind. The evening star shed a lustre on the speckless snow, and Brand, in that lucid circle, stopped with a jerk, and pointed to the same light foot-prints turned toward the house—the track of a woman in the snow. He stood still, his face working. "Bare feet. . . . ." he said.

The deacon piped up in a quavering voice: "The feet of the dead."

Brand remained motionless. "The feet of the dead," he echoed.

Deacon Hibben laid a frightened hand on his arm. "Come away now, Brand; for the love of God come away."

The father hung there, gazing down at those light tracks on the snow—light as fox or squirrel trails they seemed, on the white immensity. Bosworth thought to himself "The living couldn't walk so light—not even Ora Brand couldn't have, when she lived. . . . ." The cold seemed to have entered into his very marrow. His teeth were chattering.

Brand swung about on them abruptly. "*Now!*" he said, moving on as if to an assault, his head bowed forward on his bull neck.

"Now—now? Not in there?" gasped the deacon. "What's the use? It was tomorrow he said—." He shook like a leaf.

"It's now," said Brand. He went up to the door of the crazy house, pushed it inward, and meeting with an unexpected resistance, thrust his heavy shoulder against the panel. The door collapsed like a playing-card, and Brand stumbled after it into the darkness of the hut. The others, after a moment's hesitation, followed.

Bosworth was never quite sure in what order the events that succeeded took place. Coming in out of the snow-dazzle, he seemed to be plunging into total blackness. He groped his way across the threshold, caught a sharp splinter of the fallen door in his palm, seemed to see something white and wraithlike surge up out of the darkest corner of the hut, and then heard a revolver shot at his elbow, and a cry—

Brand had turned back, and was staggering past him out into the lingering daylight. The sunset, suddenly flushing through the trees, crimsoned his face like blood. He held a revolver in his hand and looked about him in his stupid way.

"They *do* walk, then," he said and began to laugh. He bent his head to examine his weapon. "Better here than in the churchyard. They shan't dig her up *now*," he shouted out. The two men caught him by the arms, and Bosworth got the revolver away from him.

4

The next day Bosworth's sister Loretta, who kept house for him, asked him, when he came in for his midday dinner, if he had heard the news.

Bosworth had been sawing wood all the morning, and in spite of the cold and the driving snow, which had begun again in the night, he was covered with an icy sweat, like a man getting over a fever.

"What news?"

"Venny Brand's down sick with pneumonia. The deacon's been there. I guess she's dying."

Bosworth looked at her with listless eyes. She seemed far off from him, miles away. "Venny Brand?" he echoed.

"You never liked her, Orrin."

"She's a child. I never knew much about her."

"Well," repeated his sister, with the guileless relish of the unimaginative for bad news, "I guess she's dying." After a pause she added: "It'll kill Sylvester Brand, all alone up there."

Bosworth got up and said: "I've got to see to poulticing the grey's fetlock." He walked out into the steadily falling snow.

Venny Brand was buried three days later. The deacon read the service; Bosworth was one of the pall-bearers. The whole countryside turned out, for the snow had stopped falling, and at any season a funeral offered an opportunity for an outing that was not to be missed. Besides, Venny Brand was young and handsome—at least some people thought her handsome, though she was so swarthy—and her dying like that, so suddenly, had the fascination of tragedy.

"They say her lungs filled right up. . . . . Seems she'd had bronchial troubles before. . . . . I always said both them girls was frail. . . . . Look at Ora, how she took and wasted away! And it's colder'n all outdoors up there to Brand's. . . . . Their mother, too, *she* pined away just the same.

They don't ever make old bones on the mother's side of the family. . . . There's that young Bedlow over there; they say Venny was engaged to him . . . . Oh, Mrs. Rutledge, excuse *me*. . . . . Step right into the pew; there's a seat for you alongside of grandma. . . . ."

Mrs. Rutledge was advancing with deliberate step down the narrow aisle of the bleak wooden church. She had on her best bonnet, a monumental structure which no one had seen out of her trunk since old Mrs. Silsee's funeral, three years before. All the women remembered it. Under its perpendicular pile her narrow face, swaying on the long thin neck, seemed whiter than ever; but her air of fretfulness had been composed into a suitable expression of mournful immobility.

"Looks as if the stone-mason had carved her to put atop of Venny's grave," Bosworth thought as she glided past him; and then shivered at his own sepulchral fancy. When she bent over her hymn book her lowered lids reminded him again of marble eye-balls; the bony hands clasping the book were bloodless. Bosworth had never seen such hands since he had seen old Aunt Cressidora Cheney strangle the canary-bird because it fluttered.

The service was over, the coffin of Venny Brand had been lowered into her sister's grave, and the neighbours were slowly dispersing. Bosworth, as pall-bearer, felt obliged to linger and say a word to the stricken father. He waited till Brand had turned from the grave with the deacon at his side. The three men stood together for a moment; but not one of them spoke. Brand's face was the closed door of a vault, barred with wrinkles like bands of iron.

Finally, the deacon took his hand and said: "The Lord gave—"

Brand nodded and turned away toward the shed where the horses were hitched. Bosworth followed him. "Let me drive along home with you," he suggested.

Brand did not so much as turn his head. "Home? What home?" he said; and the other fell back.

Loretta Bosworth was talking with the other women while the men unblanketed their horses and backed the cutters out into the heavy snow. As Bosworth waited for her, a few feet off, he saw Mrs. Rutledge's tall bonnet lording it above the group. Andy Pond, the Rutledge farm-hand, was backing out the sleigh.

"Saul ain't here today, Mrs. Rutledge, is he?" one of the village elders piped, turning a benevolent old tortoise-head about on a loose neck, and blinking up into Mrs. Rutledge's marble face.

Bosworth heard her measure out her answer in slow incisive words.

"No. Mr. Rutledge he ain't here. He would 'a' come for certain, but his aunt Minorca Cummins is being buried down to Stotesbury this very day and he had to go down there. Don't it sometimes seem zif we was all walking right in the Shadow of Death?"

As she walked toward the cutter, in which Andy Pond was already seated, the deacon went up to her with visible hesitation. Involuntarily Bosworth also moved nearer. He heard the deacon say: "I'm glad to hear that Saul is able to be up and around."

She turned her small head on her rigid neck, and lifted the lids of marble.

"Yes, I guess he'll sleep quieter now.—And her too, maybe, now she don't lay there alone any longer," she added in a low voice, with a sudden twist of her chin toward the fresh black stain in the grave-yard snow. She got into the cutter, and said in a clear tone to Andy Pond: "'S long as we're down here I don't know but what I'll just call round and get a box of soap at Hiram Pringle's."

The Romance of Certain Old Clothes

Henry James

1

Towards the middle of the eighteenth century there lived in the Province of Massachusetts a widowed gentlewoman, the mother of three children, by name Mrs. Veronica Wingrave. She had lost her husband early in life, and had devoted herself to the care of her progeny. These young persons grew up in a manner to reward her tenderness and to gratify her highest hopes. The first-born was a son, whom she had called Bernard, in remembrance of his father. The others were daughters—born at an interval of three years apart. Good looks were traditional in the family, and this youthful trio were not likely to allow the tradition to perish.

The boy was of that fair and ruddy complexion and that athletic structure which in those days (as in these) were the sign of good English descent—a frank, affectionate young fellow, a deferential son, a patronising brother, a steadfast friend. Clever, however, he was not; the wit of the family had been apportioned chiefly to his sisters. The late Mr. William Wingrave had been a great reader of Shakespeare, at a time when this pursuit implied more freedom of thought than at the present day, and in a community where it required much courage to patronise the drama even in the closet; and he had wished to call attention to his admiration of the great poet by calling his daughters out of his favourite plays. Upon the elder he had bestowed the romantic name of Rosalind, and the younger he had called Perdita, in memory of a little girl born between them, who had lived but a few weeks.

When Bernard Wingrave came to his sixteenth year his mother put a brave face upon it and prepared to execute her husband's last injunction. This had been a formal command that, at the proper age, his son should be sent out to England, to complete his education at the university of Oxford, where he himself had acquired his taste for elegant literature. It was Mrs. Wingrave's belief that the lad's equal was not to be found in the two hemispheres, but she had the old traditions of literal obedience. She swallowed her sobs, and made up her boy's trunk and his simple provincial outfit, and sent him on his way across the seas. Bernard presented himself at his father's college, and spent five years in England, without great honour, indeed, but with a vast deal of pleasure and no discredit.

On leaving the university he made the journey to France. In his twenty-fourth year he took ship for home, prepared to find poor little New England (New England was very small in those days) a very dull, unfashionable residence. But there had been changes at home, as well as in Mr. Bernard's opinions. He found his mother's house quite habitable, and his sisters grown into two very charming young ladies, with all the accomplishments and graces of the young women of Britain, and a certain native-grown originality and wildness, which, if it was not an accomplishment, was certainly a grace the more. Bernard privately assured his mother that his sisters were fully a match for the most genteel young women in the old country; whereupon poor Mrs. Wingrave, you may be sure, bade them hold up their heads.

Such was Bernard's opinion, and such, in a tenfold higher degree, was the opinion of Mr. Arthur Lloyd. This gentleman was a college-mate of Mr. Bernard, a young man of reputable family, of a good person and a handsome inheritance; which latter appurtenance he proposed to invest in trade in the flourishing colony. He and Bernard were sworn friends; they had crossed the ocean together, and the young American had lost no time in presenting him at his mother's house, where he had made quite as good an impression as that which he had received and of which I have just given a hint.

The two sisters were at this time in all the freshness of their youthful bloom; each wearing, of course, this natural brilliancy in the manner that became her best. They were equally dissimilar in appearance and character. Rosalind, the elder—now in her twenty-second year—was tall and white, with calm gray eyes and auburn tresses; a very faint likeness to the Rosalind of Shakespeare's comedy, whom I imagine a brunette (if you will), but a slender, airy creature, full of the softest, quickest impulses. Miss Wingrave, with her slightly lymphatic fairness, her fine arms, her majestic height, her slow utterance, was not cut out for adventures. She would never have put on a man's jacket and hose; and, indeed, being a very plump beauty, she may have had reasons apart from her natural dignity.

Perdita, too, might very well have exchanged the sweet melancholy of her name against something more in consonance with her aspect and disposition. She had the cheek of a gipsy and the eye of an eager child, as well as the smallest waist and lightest foot in all the country of the Puritans. When you spoke to her she never made you wait, as her handsome sister was wont to do (while she looked at you with a cold fine eye), but gave you your choice of a dozen answers before you had uttered half your thought.

The young girls were very glad to see their brother once more; but they found themselves quite able to spare part of their attention for their brother's friend. Among the young men their friends and neighbours, the *belle jeunesse* of the Colony, there were many excellent fellows, several devoted swains, and some two or three who enjoyed the reputation of universal charmers and conquerors. But the homebred arts and somewhat boisterous gallantry of these honest colonists were completely eclipsed by the good looks, the fine clothes, the punctilious courtesy, the perfect elegance, the immense information, of Mr. Arthur Lloyd.

He was in reality no paragon; he was a capable, honourable, civil youth, rich in pounds sterling, in his health and complacency and his little capital of uninvested affections. But he was a gentleman; he had a handsome person; he had studied and travelled; he spoke French, he played on the flute, and he read verses aloud with very great taste. There were a dozen reasons why Miss Wingrave and her sister should have thought their other male acquaintance made but a poor figure before such a perfect man of the world. Mr. Lloyd's anecdotes told our little New England maidens a great deal more of the ways and means of people of fashion in European capitals than he had any idea of doing.

It was delightful to sit by and hear him and Bernard talk about the fine people and fine things they had seen. They would all gather round the fire after tea, in the little wainscoted parlour, and the two young men would remind each other, across the rug, of this, that and the other adventure. Rosalind and Perdita would often have given their ears to know exactly what adventure it was, and where it happened, and who was there, and what the ladies had on; but in those days a well-bred young woman was not expected to break into the conversation of her elders, or to ask too many questions; and the poor girls used therefore to sit fluttering behind the more languid—or more discreet—curiosity of their mother.

2

That they were both very fine girls Arthur Lloyd was not slow to discover; but it took him some time to make up his mind whether he liked the big sister or the little sister best. He had a strong presentiment—an emotion of a nature entirely too cheerful to be called a foreboding—that he was destined to stand up before the parson with one of them; yet he was unable to arrive at a preference, and for such a consummation a preference was certainly necessary, for Lloyd had too much young blood in his veins to make a choice by lot and be cheated of the satisfaction of falling in love. He resolved to take things as they came—to let his heart speak.

Meanwhile he was on a very pleasant footing. Mrs. Wingrave showed a dignified indifference to his 'intentions', equally remote from a carelessness of her daughter's honour and from that sharp alacrity to make him come to the point, which, in his quality of a young man of property, he had too often encountered in the worldly matrons of his native islands. As for Bernard, all that he asked was that his friend should treat his sisters as his own; and as for the poor girls themselves, however each may have secretly longed that their visitor should do or say something 'marked', they kept a very modest and contented demeanour.

Towards each other, however, they were somewhat more on the offensive. They were good friends enough, and accommodating bedfellows (they shared the same four-poster), betwixt whom it would take more than a day for the seeds of jealousy to sprout and bear fruit; but they felt that the seeds had been sown on the day that Mr. Lloyd came into the house. Each made up her mind that, if she should be slighted, she would bear her grief in silence, and that no one should be any the wiser; for if they had a great deal of ambition, they had also a large share of pride. But each prayed in secret, nevertheless, that upon *her* the selection, the distinction, might fall.

They had need of a vast deal of patience, of self-control, of dissimulation. In those days a young girl of decent breeding could make no advances whatever, and barely respond, indeed, to those that were made. She was expected to sit still in her chair, with her eyes on the carpet, watching the spot where the mystic handkerchief should fall. Poor Arthur Lloyd was obliged to carry on his wooing in the little wainscoted parlour, before the eyes of Mrs. Wingrave, her son, and his prospective sister-in-law. But youth and love are so cunning that a hundred signs and tokens might travel to and fro, and not one of these three pairs of eyes detect them in their passage.

The two maidens were almost always together, and had plenty of chances to betray themselves. That each knew she was being watched, however, made not a grain of difference in the little offices they mutually rendered, or in the various household tasks they performed in common. Neither flinched nor fluttered beneath the silent battery of her sister's eyes. The only apparent change in their habits was that they had less to say to each other. It was impossible to talk about Mr. Lloyd, and it was ridiculous to talk about anything else. By tacit agreement they began to wear all their choice finery, and to devise such little implements of conquest, in the way of ribbons and top-knots and kerchiefs, as were sanctioned by indubitable modesty.

They executed in the same inarticulate fashion a contract of fair play in this exciting game. "Is it better so?" Rosalind would ask, tying a bunch of ribbons on her bosom, and turning about from her glass to her sister. Perdita would look up gravely from her work and examine the decoration. "I think you had better give it another loop," she would say, with great solemnity, looking hard at her sister with eyes that added, 'upon my honour!' So they were forever stitching and trimming their petticoats, and pressing out their muslins, and contriving washes and ointments and cosmetics, like the ladies in the household of the vicar of Wakefield. Some three or four months went by; it grew to be midwinter, and as yet Rosalind knew that if Perdita had nothing more to boast of than she, there was not much to be feared from her rivalry. But Perdita by this time—the charming Perdita—felt that her secret had grown to be tenfold more precious than her sister's.

One afternoon Miss Wingrave sat alone—that was a rare accident—before her toilet-glass, combing out her long hair. It was getting too dark to see; she lit the two candles in their sockets, on the frame of her mirror, and then went to the window to draw her curtains. It was a gray December evening; the landscape was bare and bleak, and the sky heavy with snow-clouds. At the end of the large garden into which her window looked was a wall with a little postern door, opening into a lane. The door stood ajar, as she could vaguely see in the gathering darkness, and moved slowly to and fro, as if someone were swaying it from the lane without.

It was doubtless a servant-maid who had been having a tryst with her sweetheart. But as she was about to drop her curtain Rosalind saw her sister step into the garden and hurry along the path which led to the house. She dropped the curtain, all save a little crevice for her eyes. As Perdita came up the path she seemed to be examining something in her hand, holding it close to her eyes. When she reached the house she stopped a moment, looked intently at the object, and pressed it to her lips.

Poor Rosalind slowly came back to her chair and sat down before her glass, where, if she had looked at it less abstractedly, she would have seen her handsome features sadly disfigured by jealousy. A moment afterwards the door opened behind her and her sister came into the room, out of breath, and her cheeks aglow with the chilly air.

Perdita started. "Ah," said she, "I thought you were with our mother." The ladies were to go to a tea-party, and on such occasions it was the habit of one of the young girls to help their mother to dress. Instead of coming in, Perdita lingered at the door.

"Come in, come in," said Rosalind. "We have more than an hour yet. I should like you very much to give a few strokes to my hair." She knew that her sister wished to retreat, and that she could see in the glass all her movements in the room. "Nay, just help me with my hair," she said, "and I will go to mamma."

Perdita came reluctantly, and took the brush. She saw her sister's eyes, in the glass, fastened hard upon her hands. She had not made three passes when Rosalind clapped her own right hand upon her sister's left, and started out of her chair. "Whose ring is that?" she cried, passionately, drawing her towards the light.

On the young girl's third finger glistened a little gold ring, adorned with a very small sapphire. Perdita felt that she need no longer keep her secret, yet that she must put a bold face on her avowal. "It's mine," she said proudly.

"Who gave it to you?" cried the other.

Perdita hesitated a moment. "Mr. Lloyd."

"Mr. Lloyd is generous, all of a sudden."

"Ah no," cried Perdita, with spirit, "not all of a sudden! He offered it to me a month ago."

"And you needed a month's begging to take it?" said Rosalind, looking at the little trinket, which indeed was not especially elegant, although it was the best that the jeweller of the Province could furnish. "I wouldn't have taken it in less than two."

"It isn't the ring," Perdita answered, "it's what it means!"

"It means that you are not a modest girl!" cried Rosalind. "Pray, does your mother know of your intrigue? does Bernard?"

"My mother has approved my 'intrigue', as you call it. Mr. Lloyd has asked for my hand, and mamma has given it. Would you have had him apply to you, dearest sister?"

Rosalind gave her companion a long look, full of passionate envy and sorrow. Then she dropped her lashes on her pale cheeks and turned away. Perdita felt that it had not been a pretty scene; but it was her sister's fault. However, the elder girl rapidly called back her pride, and turned herself about again. "You have my very best wishes," she said, with a low curtsey. "I wish you every happiness, and a very long life."

Perdita gave a bitter laugh. "Don't speak in that tone!" she cried. "I would rather you should curse me outright. Come, Rosy," she added, "he couldn't marry both of us."

"I wish you very great joy," Rosalind repeated, mechanically, sitting down to her glass again, "and a very long life, and plenty of children."

There was something in the sound of these words not at all to Perdita's taste. "Will you give me a year to live at least?" she said. "In a year I can have one little boy—or one little girl at least. If you will give me your brush again I will do your hair."

"Thank you," said Rosalind. "You had better go to mamma. It isn't becoming that a young lady with a promised husband should wait on a girl with none."

"Nay," said Perdita, good-humouredly, "I have Arthur to wait upon me. You need my service more than I need yours."

But her sister motioned her away, and she left the room. When she had gone poor Rosalind fell on her knees before her dressing-table, buried her head in her arms, and poured out a flood of tears and sobs. She felt very much the better for this effusion of sorrow. When her sister came back she insisted upon helping her to dress—on her wearing her prettiest things. She forced upon her acceptance a bit of lace of her own, and declared that now that she was to be married she should do her best to appear worthy of her lover's choice. She discharged these offices in stern silence; but, such as they were, they had to do duty as an apology and an atonement; she never made any other.

Now that Lloyd was received by the family as an accepted suitor nothing remained but to fix the wedding-day. It was appointed for the following April, and in the interval preparations were diligently made for the marriage. Lloyd, on his side, was busy with his commercial arrangements, and with establishing a correspondence with the great mercantile house to which he had attached himself in England. He was therefore not so frequent a visitor at Mrs. Wingrave's as during the months of his diffidence and irresolution, and poor Rosalind had less to suffer than she had feared from the sight of the mutual endearments of the young lovers.

Touching his future sister-in-law Lloyd had a perfectly clear conscience. There had not been a particle of love-making between them, and he had not the slightest suspicion that he had dealt her a terrible blow. He was quite at his ease; life promised so well, both domestically and financially. The great revolt of the Colonies was not yet in the air, and that his connubial felicity should take a tragic turn it was absurd, it was blasphemous, to apprehend. Meanwhile, at Mrs. Wingrave's, there was a greater rustling of silks, a more rapid clicking of scissors and flying of needles, than ever. The good lady had determined that her daughter should carry from home the genteelest outfit that her money could buy or that the country could furnish.

All the sage women in the Province were convened, and their united taste was brought to bear on Perdita's wardrobe. Rosalind's situation, at this moment, was assuredly not to be envied. The poor girl had an inordinate love of dress, and the very best taste in the world, as her sister perfectly well knew. Rosalind was tall, she was stately and sweeping, she was made to carry stiff brocade and masses of heavy lace, such as belong to the toilet of a rich man's wife. But Rosalind sat aloof, with her beautiful arms folded and her head averted, while her mother and sister and the venerable women aforesaid worried and wondered over their materials, oppressed by the multitude of their resources.

One day there came in a beautiful piece of white silk, brocaded with heavenly blue and silver, sent by the bridegroom himself—it not being thought amiss in those days that the husband-elect should contribute to the bride's *trousseau*. Perdita could think of no form or fashion which would do sufficient honour to the splendour of the material.

"Blue's your colour, sister, more than mine," she said, with appealing eyes. "It's a pity it's not for you. You would know what to do with it."

Rosalind got up from her place and looked at the great shining fabric, as it lay spread over the back of a chair. Then she took it up in her hands and felt it—lovingly, as Perdita could see—and turned about toward the mirror with it. She let it roll down to her feet, and flung the other end over her shoulder, gathering it in about her waist with her white arm, which was bare to the elbow. She threw back her head, and looked at her image, and a hanging tress of her auburn hair fell upon the gorgeous surface of the silk.

It made a dazzling picture. The women standing about uttered a little "Look, look!" of admiration. "Yes, indeed," said Rosalind, quietly, "blue is my colour." But Perdita could see that her fancy had been stirred, and that she would now fall to work and solve all their silken riddles. And indeed she behaved very well, as Perdita, knowing her insatiable love of millinery, was quite ready to declare. Innumerable yards of lustrous silk and satin, of muslin, velvet and lace, passed through her cunning hands, without a jealous word coming from her lips. Thanks to her industry, when the wedding-day came Perdita was prepared to espouse more of the vanities of life than any fluttering young bride who had yet received the sacramental blessing of a New England divine.

It had been arranged that the young couple should go out and spend the first days of their wedded life at the country-house of an English gentleman—a man of rank and a very kind friend to Arthur Lloyd. He was a bachelor; he declared he should be delighted to give up the place to the influence of Hymen. After the ceremony at church—it had been performed by an English clergyman—young Mrs. Lloyd hastened back to her mother's house to change her nuptial robes for a riding-dress. Rosalind helped her to effect the change, in the little homely room in which they had spent their undivided younger years. Perdita then hurried off to bid farewell to her mother, leaving Rosalind to follow.

The parting was short; the horses were at the door, and Arthur was impatient to start. But Rosalind had not followed, and Perdita hastened back to her room, opening the door abruptly. Rosalind, as usual, was before the glass, but in a position which caused the other to stand still, amazed. She had dressed herself in Perdita's cast-off wedding veil and wreath, and on her neck she had hung the full string of pearls which the young girl had received from her husband as a wedding-gift. These things had been hastily laid aside, to await their possessor's disposal on her return from the country. Bedizened in this unnatural garb Rosalind stood before the mirror, plunging a long look into its depths and reading heaven knows what audacious visions. Perdita was horrified. It was a hideous image of their old rivalry come to life again. She made a step toward her sister, as if to pull off the veil and the flowers. But catching her eyes in the glass, she stopped.

"Farewell, sweetheart," she said. "You might at least have waited till I had got out of the house!" And she hurried away from the room.

Mr. Lloyd had purchased in Boston a house which to the taste of those days appeared as elegant as it was commodious; and here he very soon established himself with his young wife. He was thus separated by a distance of twenty miles from the residence of his mother-in-law. Twenty miles, in that primitive era of roads and conveyances, were as serious a matter as a hundred at the present day, and Mrs. Wingrave saw but little of her daughter during the first twelvemonth of her marriage. She suffered in no small degree from Perdita's absence; and her affliction was not diminished by the fact that Rosalind had fallen into terribly low spirits and was not to be roused or cheered but by change of air and company.

The real cause of the young lady's dejection the reader will not be slow to suspect. Mrs. Wingrave and her gossips, however, deemed her complaint a mere bodily ill, and doubted not that she would obtain relief from the remedy just mentioned. Her mother accordingly proposed, on her behalf, a visit to certain relatives on the paternal side, established in New York, who had long complained that they were able to see so little of their New England cousins. Rosalind was despatched to these good people, under a suitable escort, and remained with them for several months. In the interval her brother Bernard, who had begun the practice of the law, made up his mind to take a wife.

Rosalind came home to the wedding, apparently cured of her heartache, with bright roses and lilies in her face and a proud smile on her lips. Arthur Lloyd came over from Boston to see his brother-in-law married, but without his wife, who was expecting very soon to present him with an heir. It was nearly a year since Rosalind had seen him. She was glad—she hardly knew why—that Perdita had stayed at home. Arthur looked happy, but he was more grave and important than before his marriage. She thought he looked 'interesting'—for although the word, in its modern sense, was not then invented, we may be sure that the idea was.

The truth is, he was simply anxious about his wife and her coming ordeal. Nevertheless, he by no means failed to observe Rosalind's beauty and splendour, and to note how she effaced the poor little bride. The allowance that Perdita had enjoyed for her dress had now been transferred to her sister, who turned it to wonderful account. On the morning after the wedding he had a lady's saddle put on the horse of the servant who had come with him from town, and went out with the young girl for a ride. It was a keen, clear morning in January; the ground was bare and hard, and the horses in good condition—to say nothing of Rosalind, who was charming in her hat and plume, and her dark blue riding coat, trimmed with fur. They rode all the morning, they lost their way, and were obliged to stop for dinner at a farmhouse.

The early winter dusk had fallen when they got home. Mrs. Wingrave met them with a long face. A messenger had arrived at noon from Mrs. Lloyd; she was beginning to be ill, she desired her husband's immediate return. The young man, at the thought that he had lost several hours, and that by hard riding he might already have been with his wife, uttered a passionate oath. He barely consented to stop for a mouthful of supper, but mounted the messenger's horse and started off at a gallop.

He reached home at midnight. His wife had been delivered of a little girl. "Ah, why weren't you with me?" she said, as he came to her bedside.

"I was out of the house when the man came. I was with Rosalind," said Lloyd, innocently.

Mrs. Lloyd made a little moan, and turned away. But she continued to do very well, and for a week her improvement was uninterrupted. Finally, however, through some indiscretion in the way of diet or exposure, it was checked, and the poor lady grew rapidly worse. Lloyd was in despair. It very soon became evident that she was breathing her last. Mrs. Lloyd came to a sense of her approaching end, and declared that she was reconciled with death.

On the third evening after the change took place she told her husband that she felt she should not get through the night. She dismissed her servants, and also requested her mother to withdraw—Mrs. Wingrave having arrived on the preceding day. She had had her infant placed on the bed beside her, and she lay on her side, with the child against her breast, holding her husband's hands. The night-lamp was hidden behind the heavy curtains of the bed, but the room was illumined with a red glow from the immense fire of logs on the hearth.

"It seems strange not to be warmed into life by such a fire as that," the young woman said, feebly trying to smile. "If I had but a little of it in my veins! But I have given all *my* fire to this little spark of mortality." And she dropped her eyes on her child. Then raising them she looked at her husband with a long, penetrating gaze. The last feeling which lingered in her heart was one of suspicion. She had not recovered from the shock which Arthur had given her by telling her that in the hour of her agony he had been with Rosalind. She trusted her husband very nearly as well as she loved him; but now that she was called away forever she felt a cold horror of her sister. She felt in her soul that Rosalind had never ceased to be jealous of her good fortune; and a year of happy security had not effaced the young girl's image, dressed in her wedding-garments, and smiling with simulated triumph.

Now that Arthur was to be alone, what might not Rosalind attempt? She was beautiful, she was engaging; what arts might she not use, what impression might she not make upon the young man's saddened heart? Mrs. Lloyd looked at her husband in silence. It seemed hard, after all, to doubt of his constancy. His fine eyes were filled with tears; his face was convulsed with weeping; the clasp of his hands was warm and passionate. How noble he looked, how tender, how faithful and devoted! 'Nay,' thought Perdita, 'he's not for such a one as Rosalind. He'll never forget me. Nor does Rosalind truly care for him; she cares only for vanities and finery and jewels.' And she lowered her eyes on her white hands, which her husband's liberality had covered with rings, and on the lace ruffles which trimmed the edge of her night-dress. 'She covets my rings and my laces more than she covets my husband.'

At this moment the thought of her sister's rapacity seemed to cast a dark shadow between her and the helpless figure of her little girl. "Arthur," she said, "you must take off my rings. I shall not be buried in them. One of these days my daughter shall wear them—my rings and my laces and silks. I had them all brought out and shown me today. It's a great wardrobe—there's not such another in the Province; I can say it without vanity, now that I have done with it. It will be a great inheritance for my daughter when she grows into a young woman. There are things there that a man never buys twice, and if they are lost you will never again see the like. So you will watch them well. Some dozen things I have left to Rosalind; I have named them to my mother. I have given her that blue and silver; it was meant for her; I wore it only once, I looked ill in it.

"But the rest are to be sacredly kept for this little innocent. It's such a providence that she should be my colour; she can wear my gowns; she has her mother's eyes. You know the same fashions come back every twenty years. She can wear my gowns as they are. They will lie there quietly waiting till she grows into them—wrapped in camphor and rose-leaves, and keeping their colours in the sweet-scented darkness. She shall have black hair, she shall wear my carnation satin. Do you promise me, Arthur?"

"Promise you what, dearest?"

"Promise me to keep your poor little wife's old gowns."

"Are you afraid I shall sell them?"

"No, but that they may get scattered. My mother will have them properly wrapped up, and you shall lay them away under a double-lock. Do you know the great chest in the attic, with the iron bands? There is no end to what it will hold. You can put them all there. My mother and the housekeeper will do it, and give you the key. And you will keep the key in your secretary, and never give it to anyone but your child. Do you promise me?"

"Ah, yes, I promise you," said Lloyd, puzzled at the intensity with which his wife appeared to cling to this idea.

"Will you swear?" repeated Perdita.

"Yes, I swear."

"Well—I trust you—I trust you," said the poor lady, looking into his eyes with eyes in which, if he had suspected her vague apprehensions, he might have read an appeal quite as much as an assurance.

Lloyd bore his bereavement rationally and manfully. A month after his wife's death, in the course of business, circumstances arose which offered him an opportunity of going to England. He took advantage of it, to change the current of his thoughts. He was absent nearly a year, during which his little girl was tenderly nursed and guarded by her grandmother. On his return he had his house again thrown open, and announced his intention of keeping the same state as during his wife's lifetime.

It very soon came to be predicted that he would marry again, and there were at least a dozen young women of whom one may say that it was by no fault of theirs that, for six months after his return, the prediction did not come true. During this interval he still left his little daughter in Mrs. Wingrave's hands, the latter assuring him that a change of residence at so tender an age would be full of danger for her health. Finally, however, he declared that his heart longed for his daughter's presence and that she must be brought up to town. He sent his coach and his housekeeper to fetch her home.

Mrs. Wingrave was in terror lest something should befall her on the road; and, in accordance with this feeling, Rosalind offered to accompany her. She could return the next day. So she went up to town with her little niece, and Mr. Lloyd met her on the threshold of his house, overcome with her kindness and with paternal joy. Instead of returning the next day Rosalind stayed out the week; and when at last she reappeared, she had only come for her clothes. Arthur would not hear of her coming home, nor would the baby. That little person cried and choked if Rosalind left her; and at the sight of her grief Arthur lost his wits, and swore that she was going to die. In fine, nothing would suit them but that the aunt should remain until the little niece had grown used to strange faces.

It took two months to bring this consummation about; for it was not until this period had elapsed that Rosalind took leave of her brother-in-law. Mrs. Wingrave had shaken her head over her daughter's absence; she had declared that it was not becoming, that it was the talk of the whole country. She had reconciled herself to it only because, during the girl's visit, the household enjoyed an unwonted term of peace. Bernard Wingrave had brought his wife home to live, between whom and her sister-in-law there was as little love as you please. Rosalind was perhaps no angel; but in the daily practice of life she was a sufficiently good-natured girl, and if she quarrelled with Mrs. Bernard, it was not without provocation.

Quarrel, however, she did, to the great annoyance not only of her antagonist, but of the two spectators of these constant altercations. Her stay in the household of her brother-in-law, therefore, would have been delightful, if only because it removed her from contact with the object of her antipathy at home. It was doubly—it was ten times—delightful, in that it kept her near the object of her early passion. Mrs. Lloyd's sharp suspicions had fallen very far short of the truth. Rosalind's sentiment had been a passion at first, and a passion it remained—a passion of whose radiant heat, tempered to the delicate state of his feelings, Mr. Lloyd very soon felt the influence. Lloyd, as I have hinted, was not a modern Petrarch; it was not in his nature to practise an ideal constancy.

He had not been many days in the house with his sister-in-law before he began to assure himself that she was, in the language of that day, a devilish fine woman. Whether Rosalind really practised those insidious arts that her sister had been tempted to impute to her it is needless to inquire. It is enough to say that she found means to appear to the very best advantage. She used to seat herself every morning before the big fireplace in the dining-room, at work upon a piece of tapestry, with her little niece disporting herself on the carpet at her feet, or on the train of her dress, and playing with her woollen balls.

Lloyd would have been a very stupid fellow if he had remained insensible to the rich suggestions of this charming picture. He was exceedingly fond of his little girl, and was never weary of taking her in his arms and tossing her up and down, and making her crow with delight. Very often, however, he would venture upon greater liberties than the young lady was yet prepared to allow, and then she would suddenly vociferate her displeasure. Rosalind, at this, would drop her tapestry, and put out her handsome hands with the serious smile of the young girl whose virgin fancy has revealed to her all a mother's healing arts. Lloyd would give up the child, their eyes would meet, their hands would touch, and Rosalind would extinguish the little girl's sobs upon the snowy folds of the kerchief that crossed her bosom. Her dignity was perfect, and nothing could be more discreet than the manner in which she accepted her brother-in-law's hospitality. It may almost be said, perhaps, that there was something harsh in her reserve.

Lloyd had a provoking feeling that she was in the house and yet was unapproachable. Half-an-hour after supper, at the very outset of the long winter evenings, she would light her candle, make the young man a most respectful curtsey, and march off to bed. If these were arts, Rosalind was a great artist. But their effect was so gentle, so gradual, they were calculated to work upon the young widower's fancy with a *crescendo* so finely shaded, that, as the reader has seen, several weeks elapsed before Rosalind began to feel sure that her returns would cover her outlay. When this became morally certain she packed up her trunk and returned to her mother's house.

For three days she waited; on the fourth Mr. Lloyd made his appearance—a respectful but pressing suitor. Rosalind heard him to the end, with great humility, and accepted him with infinite modesty. It is hard to imagine that Mrs. Lloyd would have forgiven her husband; but if anything might have disarmed her resentment it would have been the ceremonious continence of this interview. Rosalind imposed upon her lover but a short probation. They were married, as was becoming, with great privacy—almost with secrecy—in the hope perhaps, as was waggishly remarked at the time, that the late Mrs. Lloyd wouldn't hear of it.

The marriage was to all appearance a happy one, and each party obtained what each had desired—Lloyd 'a devilish fine woman', and Rosalind—but Rosalind's desires, as the reader will have observed, had remained a good deal of a mystery. There were, indeed, two blots upon their felicity, but time would perhaps efface them. During the first three years of her marriage Mrs. Lloyd failed to become a mother, and her husband on his side suffered heavy losses of money. This latter circumstance compelled a material retrenchment in his expenditure, and Rosalind was perforce less of a fine lady than her sister had been. She contrived, however, to carry it like a woman of considerable fashion.

She had long since ascertained that her sister's copious wardrobe had been sequestrated for the benefit of her daughter, and that it lay languishing in thankless gloom in the dusty attic. It was a revolting thought that these exquisite fabrics should await the good pleasure of a little girl who sat in a high chair and ate bread-and-milk with a wooden spoon. Rosalind had the good taste, however, to say nothing about the matter until several months had expired. Then, at last, she timidly broached it to her husband. Was it not a pity that so much finery should be lost?—for lost it would be, what with colours fading, and moths eating it up, and the change of fashions.

But Lloyd gave her so abrupt and peremptory a refusal, that she saw, for the present, her attempt was vain. Six months went by, however, and brought with them new needs and new visions. Rosalind's thoughts hovered lovingly about her sister's relics. She went up and looked at the chest in which they lay imprisoned. There was a sullen defiance in its three great padlocks and its iron bands which only quickened her cupidity. There was something exasperating in its incorruptible immobility. It was like a grim and grizzled old household servant, who locks his jaws over a family secret.

And then there was a look of capacity in its vast extent, and a sound as of dense fullness, when Rosalind knocked its side with the toe of her little shoe, which caused her to flush with baffled longing. "It's absurd," she cried; "it's improper, it's wicked"; and she forthwith resolved upon another attack upon her husband. On the following day, after dinner, when he had had his wine, she boldly began it. But he cut her short with great sternness.

"Once for all, Rosalind," said he, "it's out of the question. I shall be gravely displeased if you return to the matter."

"Very good," said Rosalind. "I am glad to learn the esteem in which I am held. Gracious heaven," she cried, "I am a very happy woman! It's an agreeable thing to feel one's self sacrificed to a caprice!" And her eyes filled with tears of anger and disappointment.

Lloyd had a good-natured man's horror of a woman's sobs, and he attempted—I may say he condescended—to explain. "It's not a caprice, dear, it's a promise," he said—"an oath."

"An oath? It's a pretty matter for oaths! and to whom, pray?"

"To Perdita," said the young man, raising his eyes for an instant, but immediately dropping them.

"Perdita—ah, Perdita!" and Rosalind's tears broke forth. Her bosom heaved with stormy sobs—sobs which were the long-deferred sequel of the violent fit of weeping in which she had indulged herself on the night when she discovered her sister's betrothal. She had hoped, in her better moments, that she had done with her jealousy; but her temper, on that occasion, had taken an ineffaceable fold. "And pray, what right had Perdita to dispose of my future?" she cried. "What right had she to bind you to meanness and cruelty? Ah, I occupy a dignified place, and I make a very fine figure! I am welcome to what Perdita has left! And what has she left? I never knew till now how little! Nothing, nothing, nothing."

This was very poor logic, but it was very good as a 'scene'. Lloyd put his arm around his wife's waist and tried to kiss her, but she shook him off with magnificent scorn. Poor fellow! he had coveted a 'devilish fine woman', and he had got one. Her scorn was intolerable. He walked away with his ears tingling—irresolute, distracted. Before him was his secretary, and in it the sacred key which with his own hand he had turned in the triple lock. He marched up and opened it, and took the key from a secret drawer, wrapped in a little packet which he had sealed with his own honest bit of blazonry. *Je garde*, said the motto—*I keep*. But he was ashamed to put it back. He flung it upon the table beside his wife.

"Put it back!" she cried. "I want it not. I hate it!"

"I wash my hands of it," cried her husband. "God forgive me!"

Mrs. Lloyd gave an indignant shrug of her shoulders, and swept out of the room, while the young man retreated by another door. Ten minutes later Mrs. Lloyd returned, and found the room occupied by her little step-daughter and the nursery-maid. The key was not on the table. She glanced at the child. Her little niece was perched on a chair, with the packet in her hands. She had broken the seal with her own small fingers. Mrs. Lloyd hastily took possession of the key.

At the habitual supper-hour Arthur Lloyd came back from his counting-room. It was the month of June, and supper was served by daylight. The meal was placed on the table, but Mrs. Lloyd failed to make her appearance. The servant whom his master sent to call her came back with the assurance that her room was empty, and that the women informed him that she had not been seen since dinner. They had, in truth, observed her to have been in tears, and, supposing her to be shut up in her chamber, had not disturbed her. Her husband called her name in various parts of the house, but without response.

At last it occurred to him that he might find her by taking the way to the attic. The thought gave him a strange feeling of discomfort, and he bade his servants remain behind, wishing no witness in his quest. He reached the foot of the staircase leading to the topmost flat, and stood with his hand on the banisters, pronouncing his wife's name. His voice trembled. He called again louder and more firmly. The only sound which disturbed the absolute silence was a faint echo of his own tones, repeating his question under the great eaves. He nevertheless felt irresistibly moved to ascend the staircase. It opened upon a wide hall, lined with wooden closets, and terminating in a window which looked westward, and admitted the last rays of the sun. Before the window stood the great chest.

Before the chest, on her knees, the young man saw with amazement and horror the figure of his wife. In an instant he crossed the interval between them, bereft of utterance. The lid of the chest stood open, exposing, amid their perfumed napkins, its treasure of stuffs and jewels. Rosalind had fallen backward from a kneeling posture, with one hand supporting her on the floor and the other pressed to her heart. On her limbs was the stiffness of death, and on her face, in the fading light of the sun, the terror of something more than death. Her lips were parted in entreaty, in dismay, in agony; and on her blanched brow and cheeks there glowed the marks of ten hideous wounds from two vengeful ghostly hands.

John Charrington's Wedding

Edith Nesbit

No one ever thought that May Forster would marry John Charrington; but he thought differently, and things which John Charrington intended had a queer way of coming to pass. He asked her to marry him before he went up to Oxford. She laughed and refused him. He asked her again next time he came home. Again she laughed, tossed her dainty blonde head and again refused. A third time he asked her; she said it was becoming a confirmed bad habit, and laughed at him more than ever.

John was not the only man who wanted to marry her: she was the belle of our village coterie, and we were all in love with her more or less; it was a sort of fashion, like masher collars or Inverness capes. Therefore we were as much annoyed as surprised when John Charrington walked into our little local Club—we held it in a loft over the saddler's, I remember—and invited us all to his wedding.

'Your wedding?'

'You don't mean it?'

'Who's the happy pair? When's it to be?'

John Charrington filled his pipe and lighted it before he replied. Then he said:

'I'm sorry to deprive you fellows of your only joke—but Miss Forster and I are to be married in September.'

'You don't mean it?'

'He's got the mitten again, and it's turned his head.'

'No,' I said, rising, 'I see it's true. Lend me a pistol, someone—or a first-class fare to the other end of Nowhere. Charrington has bewitched the only pretty girl in our twenty-mile radius. Was it mesmerism, or a love-potion, Jack?'

'Neither, sir, but a gift you'll never have—perseverance—and the best luck a man ever had in this world.'

There was something in his voice that silenced me, and all chaff of the other fellows failed to draw him further.

The queer thing about it was that when we congratulated Miss Forster, she blushed and smiled and dimpled, for all the world as though she were in love with him, and had been in love with him all the time. Upon my word, I think she had. Women are strange creatures.

We were all asked to the wedding. In Brixham everyone who was anybody knew everybody else who was anyone. My sisters were, I truly believe, more interested in the trousseau than the bride herself, and I was to be best man. The coming marriage was much canvassed at afternoon tea-tables, and at our little Club over the saddler's, and the question was always asked, 'Does she care for him?'

I used to ask that question myself in the early days of their engagement, but after a certain evening in August I never asked it again. I was coming home from the Club through the churchyard. Our church is on a thyme-grown hill, and the turf about it is so thick and soft that one's footsteps are noiseless.

I made no sound as I vaulted the low lichened wall, and threaded my way between the tombstones. It was at the same instant that I heard John Charrington's voice, and saw her. May was sitting on a low flat gravestone, her face turned towards the full splendour of the western sun. Its expression ended, at once and for ever, any question of love for him; it was transfigured to a beauty I should not have believed possible, even to that beautiful little face.

John lay at her feet, and it was his voice that broke the stillness of the golden August evening.

'My dear, my dear, I believe I should come back from the dead if you wanted me!'

I coughed at once to indicate my presence, and passed on into the shadow fully enlightened.

The wedding was to be early in September. Two days before I had to run up to town on business. The train was late, of course, for we are on the South-Eastern, and as I stood grumbling with my watch in my hand, whom should I see but John Charrington and May Forster. They were walking up and down the unfrequented end of the platform, arm in arm, looking into each other's eyes, careless of the sympathetic interest of the porters.

Of course I knew better than to hesitate a moment before burying myself in the booking-office, and it was not till the train drew up at the platform, that I obtrusively passed the pair with my Gladstone, and took the corner in a first-class smoking-carriage. I did this with as good an air of not seeing them as I could assume. I pride myself on my discretion, but if John were travelling alone I wanted his company. I had it.

'Hullo, old man,' came his cheery voice as he swung his bag into my carriage; 'here's luck; I was expecting a dull journey!'

'Where are you off to?' I asked, discretion still bidding me turn my eyes away, though I saw, without looking, that hers were red-rimmed.

'To old Branbridge's,' he answered, shutting the door and leaning out for a last word with his sweetheart.

'Oh, I wish you wouldn't go, John,' she was saying in a low, earnest voice. 'I feel certain something will happen.'

'Do you think I should let anything happen to keep me, and the day after tomorrow our wedding day?'

'Don't go,' she answered, with a pleading intensity which would have sent my Gladstone onto the platform and me after it. But she wasn't speaking to me. John Charrington was made differently: he rarely changed his opinions, never his resolutions.

He only stroked the little ungloved hands that lay on the carriage door.

'I must, May. The old boy's been awfully good to me, and now he's dying I must go and see him, but I shall come home in time for ----' the rest of the parting was lost in a whisper and in the rattling lurch of the starting train.

'You're sure to come?' she spoke as the train moved.

'Nothing shall keep me,' he answered; and we steamed out. After he had seen the last of the little figure on the platform he leaned back in his corner and kept silence for a minute.

When he spoke it was to explain to me that his godfather, whose heir he was, lay dying at Peasmarsh Place, some fifty miles away, and had sent for John, and John had felt bound to go.

'I shall be surely back tomorrow,' he said, 'or, if not, the day after, in heaps of time. Thank heaven, one hasn't to get up in the middle of the night to get married nowadays!'

'And suppose Mr Branbridge dies?'

'Alive or dead I mean to be married on Thursday!' John answered, lighting a cigar and unfolding The Times.

At Peasmarsh station we said 'goodbye', and he got out, and I saw him ride off; I went on to London, where I stayed the night.

When I got home the next afternoon, a very wet one, by the way, my sister greeted me with:

'Where's Mr Charrington?'

'Goodness knows,' I answered testily. Every man, since Cain, has resented that kind of question.

'I thought you might have heard from him,' she went on, 'as you're to give him away tomorrow.'

'Isn't he back?' I asked, for I had confidently expected to find him at home.

'No, Geoffrey,' my sister Fanny always had a way of jumping to conclusions, especially such conclusions as were least favourable to her fellow-creatures—'he has not returned, and, what is more, you may depend upon it he won't. You mark my words, there'll be no wedding tomorrow.'

My sister Fanny has a power of annoying me which no other human being possesses.

'You mark my words,' I retorted with asperity, 'you had better give up making such a thundering idiot of yourself. There'll be more wedding tomorrow than ever you'll take the first part in.' A prophecy which, by the way, came true.

But though I could snarl confidently to my sister, I did not feel so comfortable when late that night, I, standing on the doorstep of John's house, heard that he had not returned. I went home gloomily through the rain. Next morning brought a brilliant blue sky, gold sun, and all such softness of air and beauty of cloud as go to make up a perfect day. I woke with a vague feeling of having gone to bed anxious, and of being rather averse to facing that anxiety in the light of full wakefulness.

But with my shaving-water came a note from John which relieved my mind and sent me up to the Forsters with a light heart.

May was in the garden. I saw her blue gown through the hollyhocks as the lodge gates swung to behind me. So I did not go up to the house, but turned aside down the turfed path.

'He's written to you too,' she said, without preliminary greeting, when I reached her side.

'Yes, I'm to meet him at the station at three, and come straight on to the church.'

Her face looked pale, but there was a brightness in her eyes, and a tender quiver about the mouth that spoke of renewed happiness.

'Mr Branbridge begged him so to stay another night that he had not the heart to refuse,' she went on. 'He is so kind, but I wish he hadn't stayed.'

I was at the station at half past two. I felt rather annoyed with John. It seemed a sort of slight to the beautiful girl who loved him, that he should come as it were out of breath, and with the dust of travel upon him, to take her hand, which some of us would have given the best years of our lives to take.

But when the three o'clock train glided in, and glided out again having brought no passengers to our little station, I was more than annoyed. There was no other train for thirty-five minutes; I calculated that, with much hurry, we might just get to the church in time for the ceremony; but, oh, what a fool to miss that first train! What other man could have done it?

That thirty-five minutes seemed a year, as I wandered round the station reading the advertisements and the timetables, and the company's bye-laws, and getting more and more angry with John Charrington. This confidence in his own power of getting everything he wanted the minute he wanted it was leading him too far. I hate waiting. Everyone does, but I believe I hate it more than anyone else. The three thirty-five was late, of course.

I ground my pipe between my teeth and stamped with impatience as I watched the signals. Click. The signal went down. Five minutes later I flung myself into the carriage that I had brought for John.

'Drive to the church!' I said, as someone shut the door. 'Mr Charrington hasn't come by this train.'

Anxiety now replaced anger. What had become of the man? Could he have been taken suddenly ill? I had never known him have a day's illness in his life. And even so he might have telegraphed. Some awful accident must have happened to him. The thought that he had played her false never—no, not for a moment—entered my head. Yes, some thing terrible had happened to him, and on me lay the task of telling his bride. I almost wished the carriage would upset and break my head so that someone else might tell her, not I, who—but that's nothing to do with this story.

It was five minutes to four as we drew up at the churchyard gate. A double row of eager onlookers lined the path from lychgate to porch. I sprang from the carriage and passed up between them. Our gardener had a good front place near the door. I stopped.

'Are they waiting still, Byles?' I asked, simply to gain time, for of course I knew they were by the waiting crowd's attentive attitude.

'Waiting, sir? No, no, sir; why, it must be over by now.'

'Over! Then Mr Charrington's come?'

To the minute, sir; must have missed you somehow, and I say, sir,' lowering his voice, 'I never see Mr John the least bit so afore, but my opinion is he's been drinking pretty free. His clothes was all dusty and his face like a sheet. I tell you I didn't like the looks of him at all, and the folks inside are saying all sorts of things. You'll see, something's gone very wrong with Mr John, and he's tried liquor. He looked like a ghost, and in he went with his eyes straight before him, with never a look or a word for none of us: him that was always such a gentleman!'

I had never heard Byles make so long a speech. The crowd in the churchyard were talking in whispers and getting ready rice and slippers to throw at the bride and bridegroom. The ringers were ready with their hands on the ropes to ring out the merry peal as the bride and bridegroom should come out.

A murmur from the church announced them; out they came. Byles was right. John Charrington did not look himself. There was dust on his coat, his hair was disarranged. He seemed to have been in some row, for there was a black mark above his eyebrow. He was deathly pale. But his pallor was not greater than that of the bride, who might have been carved in ivory—dress, veil, orange blossoms, face and all.

As they passed out the ringers stooped—there were six of them—and then, on the ears expecting the gay wedding peal, came the slow tolling of the passing bell.

A thrill of horror at so foolish a jest from the ringers passed through us all. But the ringers themselves dropped the ropes and fled like rabbits out into the sunlight. The bride shuddered, and grey shadows came about her mouth, but the bridegroom led her on down the path where the people stood with the handfuls of rice; but the handfuls were never thrown, and the wedding bells never rang. In vain the ringers were urged to remedy their mistake: they protested with many whispered expletives that they would see themselves further first.

In a hush like the hush in the chamber of death the bridal pair passed into their carriage and its door slammed behind them.

Then the tongues were loosed. A babel of anger, wonder, conjecture from the guests and the spectators.

'If I'd seen his condition, sir,' said old Forster to me as we drove off, 'I would have stretched him on the floor of the church, sir, by heaven I would, before I'd have let him marry my daughter!'

Then he put his head out of the window.

'Drive like hell,' he cried to the coachman; 'don't spare the horses.'

He was obeyed. We passed the bride's carriage. I forbore to look at it, and old Forster turned his head away and swore. We reached home before it.

We stood in the doorway, in the blazing afternoon sun, and in about half a minute we heard wheels crunching the gravel. When the carriage stopped in front of the steps old Forster and I ran down.

'Great heaven, the carriage is empty! And yet ----'

I had the door open in a minute, and this is what I saw . . .

No sign of John Charrington; and of May, his wife, only a huddled heap of white satin lying half on the floor of the carriage and half on the seat.

'I drove straight here, sir,' said the coachman, as the bride's father lifted her out; 'and I'll swear no one got out of the carriage.'

We carried her into the house in her bridal dress and drew back her veil. I saw her face. Shall I ever forget it? White, white and drawn with agony and horror, bearing such a look of terror as I have never seen since except in dreams. And her hair, her radiant blonde hair, I tell you it was white like snow.

As we stood, her father and I, half mad with the horror and mystery of it, a boy came up the avenue—a telegraph boy. They brought the orange envelope to me. I tore it open.

Mr Charrington was thrown from the dogcart on his way to the station at half past one. Killed on the spot!

And he was married to May Forster in our parish church at half past three, in presence of half the parish.

'I shall be married, dead, or alive!'

What had passed in that carriage on the homeward drive? No one knows—no one will ever know. Oh, May! oh, my dear!

Before a week was over they laid her beside her husband in our little churchyard on the thyme-covered hill—the churchyard where they had kept their love-trysts.

Thus was accomplished John Charrington's wedding.

At Chrighton Abbey

Mary Braddon

The Chrightons were very great people in that part of the country where my childhood and youth were spent. To speak of Squire Chrighton was to speak of a power in that remote western region of England. Chrighton Abbey had belonged to the family ever since the reign of Stephen, and there was a curious old wing and a cloistered quadrangle still remaining of the original edifice, and in excellent preservation. The rooms at this end of the house were low, and somewhat darksome and gloomy, it is true; but, though rarely used, they were perfectly habitable, and were of service on great occasions when the Abbey was crowded with guests.

The central portion of the Abbey had been rebuilt in the reign of Elizabeth, and was of noble and palatial proportions. The southern wing, and a long music-room with eight tall narrow windows added on to it, were as modem as the time of Anne. Altogether, the Abbey was a very splendid mansion, and one of the chief glories of our County.

All the land in Chrighton parish, and for a long way beyond its boundaries, belonged to the great Squire. The parish church was within the park walls, and the living in the Squire's gift□not a very valuable benefice, but a useful thing to bestow upon a younger son's younger son, once in a way, or sometimes on a tutor or dependent of the wealthy house.

I was a Chrighton, and my father, a distant cousin of the reigning Squire, had been rector of Chrighton parish. His death left me utterly unprovided for, and I was fain to go out into the bleak unknown world, and earn my living in a position of dependence—a dreadful thing for a Chrighton to be obliged to do.

Out of respect for the traditions and prejudices of my race, I made it my business to seek employment abroad, where the degradation of one Chrighton was not so likely to inflict shame upon the ancient house to which I belonged. Happily for myself, I had been carefully educated, and had industriously cultivated the usual modern accomplishments in the calm retirement of the Vicarage. I was so fortunate as to obtain a situation at Vienna, in a German family of high rank; and here I remained seven years, laying aside year by year a considerable portion of my liberal salary. When my pupils had grown up, my kind mistress procured me a still more profitable position at St Petersburg, where I remained five more years, at the end of which time I yielded to a yearning that had been long growing upon me—an ardent desire to see my dear old country home once more.

I had no very near relations in England. My mother had died some years before my father; my only brother was far away, in the Indian Civil Service; sister I had none. But I was a Chrighton, and I loved the soil from which I had sprung. I was sure, moreover, of a warm welcome from friends who had loved and honoured my father and mother, and I was still further encouraged to treat myself to this holiday by the very cordial letters I had from time to time received from the Squire's wife, a noble warm-hearted woman, who fully approved the independent course I had taken, and who had ever shown herself my friend.

In all her letters for some time past Mrs Chrighton begged that, whenever I felt myself justified in coming home, I would pay a long visit to the Abbey.

'I wish you could come at Christmas,' she wrote, in the autumn of the year of which I am speaking. 'We shall be very gay, and I expect all kinds of pleasant people at the Abbey. Edward is to be married early in the spring—much to his father's satisfaction, for the match is a good and appropriate one. His fiancé is to be among our guests. She is a very beautiful girl; perhaps I should say handsome rather than beautiful. Julia Tremaine, one of the Tremaines of Old Court, near Hayswell—a very old family, as I daresay you remember. She has several brothers and sisters, and will have little, perhaps nothing, from her father; but she has a considerable fortune left her by an aunt, and is thought quite an heiress in the county—not, of course, that this latter fact had any influence with Edward. He fell in love with her at an assize ball in his usual impulsive fashion, and proposed to her in something less than a fortnight. It is, I hope and believe, a thorough love-match on both sides.'

After this followed a cordial repetition of the invitation to myself. I was to go straight to the Abbey when I went to England, and was to take up my abode there as long as ever I pleased.

This letter decided me. The wish to look on the dear scenes of my happy childhood had grown almost into a pain. I was free to take a holiday, without detriment to my prospects. So, early in December, regardless of the bleak dreary weather, I turned my face homewards, and made the long journey from St Petersburg to London, under the kind escort of Major Manson, a Queen's Messenger, who was a friend of my late employer, the Baron Fruydorff, and whose courtesy had been enlisted for me by that gentleman.

I was three-and-thirty years of age. Youth was quite gone; beauty I had never possessed; and I was content to think of myself as a confirmed old maid, a quiet spectator of life's great drama, disturbed by no feverish desire for an active part in the play. I had a disposition to which this kind of passive existence is easy. There was no wasting fire in my veins. Simple duties, rare and simple pleasures, filled up my sum of life. The dear ones who had given a special charm and brightness to my existence were gone. Nothing could recall them, and without them actual happiness seemed impossible to me. Everything had a subdued and neutral tint; life at its best was calm and colourless, like a grey sunless day in early autumn, serene but joyless.

The old Abbey was in its glory when I arrived there, at about nine o'clock on a clear starlit night. A light frost whitened the broad sweep of grass that stretched away from the long stone terrace in front of the house to a semicircle of grand old oaks and beeches. From the music-room at the end of the southern wing, to the heavily framed gothic windows of the old rooms on the north, there shone one blaze of light. The scene reminded me of some weird palace in a German legend; and I half expected to see the lights fade out all in a moment, and the long stone façade wrapped in sudden darkness.

The old butler, whom I remembered from my very infancy, and who did not seem to have grown a day older during my twelve years' exile, came out of the dining-room as the footman opened the hall-door for me, and gave me cordial welcome, nay insisted upon helping to bring in my portmanteau with his own hands, an act of unusual condescension, the full force of which was felt by his subordinates.

'It's a real treat to see your pleasant face once more, Miss Sarah,' said this faithful retainer, as he assisted me to take off my travelling-cloak, and took my dressing-bag from my hand 'You look a trifle older than when you used to live at the Vicarage twelve year ago, but you're looking uncommon well for all that; and, Lord love your heart, miss, how pleased they all will be to see you! Missus told me with her own lips about your coming. You'd like to take off your bonnet before you go to the drawing-room, I daresay. The house is full of company. Call Mrs Marjorum, James, will you?'

The footman disappeared into the back regions, and presently re-appeared with Mrs Marjorum, a portly dame, who, like Truefold the huller, had been a fixture at the Abbey in the time of the present Squire's father. From her I received the same cordial greeting, and by her I was led off up staircases and along corridors, till I wondered where I was being taken.

We arrived at last at a very comfortable room—a square tapes-tried chamber, with a low ceiling supported by a great oaken beam. The room looked cheery enough, with a bright fire roaring in the wide chimney; but it had a somewhat ancient aspect, which the superstitiously inclined might have associated with possible ghosts.

I was fortunately of a matter-of-fact disposition, utterly sceptical upon the ghost subject; and the old-fashioned appearance of the room took my fancy.

'We are in King Stephen's wing, are we not, Mrs Marjorum?' I asked; 'this room seems quite strange to me. I doubt if I have ever been in it before.'

'Very likely not, miss. Yes, this is the old wing. Your window looks out into the old stable-yard, where the kennel used to be in the time of our Squire's grandfather, when the Abbey was even a finer place than it is now, I've heard say. We are so full of company this winter, you see, miss, that we are obliged to make use of all these rooms. You'll have no need to feel lonesome.

There's Captain and Mrs Cranwick in the next room to this, and the two Miss Newports in the blue room opposite.'

'My dear good Marjorum, I like my quarters excessively; and I quite enjoy the idea of sleeping in a room that was extant in the time of Stephen, when the Abbey really was an abbey. I daresay some grave old monk has worn these boards with his devout knees.'

The old woman stared dubiously, with the air of a person who had small sympathy with monkish times, and begged to be excused for leaving me, she had so much on her hands just now.

There was coffee to be sent in; and she doubted if the still-room maid would manage matters properly, if she, Mrs Marjorum, were not at hand to see that things were right.

'You've only to ring your bell, miss, and Susan will attend to you. She's used to help waiting on our young ladies sometimes, and she's very handy. Missus has given particular orders that she should be always at your service.'

'Mrs Chrighton is very kind; but I assure you, Marjorum, I don't require the help of a maid once in a month. I am accustomed to do everything for myself. There, run along, Mrs Marjorum, and see after your coffee; and I'll be down in the drawing-mom in ten minutes. Are there many people there, by the bye?'

'A good many. There's Miss Tremaine, and her mamma and younger sister; of course you've heard all about the marriage□such a handsome young lady—rather too proud for my liking; but the Tremaines always were a proud family, and this one's an heiress. Mr Edward is so fond of her—thinks the ground is scarcely good enough for her to walk upon, I do believe; and somehow I can't help wishing he'd chosen someone else—someone who would have thought more of him, and who would not take all his attentions in such a cool offhand way. But of course it isn't my business to say such things, and I wouldn't venture upon it to anyone but you, Miss Sarah.'

She told me that I would find dinner ready for me in the breakfast-room, and then bustled off, leaving me to my toilet.

This ceremony I performed as rapidly as I could, admiring the perfect comfort of my chamber as I dressed. Every modern appliance had been added to the sombre and ponderous furniture of an age gone by, and the combination produced a very pleasant effect. Perfume-bottles of ruby-coloured Bohemian glass, china brush-trays and ring-stands brightened the massive oak dressing-table; a low luxurious chintz-covered easy-chair of the Victorian era stood before the hearth; a dear little writing-table of polished maple was placed conveniently near it; and in the background the tapestried walls loomed duskily, as they had done hundreds of years before my time.

I had no leisure for dreamy musings on the past, however, provocative though the chamber might be of such thoughts. I arranged my hair in its usual simple fashion, and put on a dark-grey silk dress, trimmed with some fine old black lace that had been given to me by the Baroness—an unobtrusive *demi-toilette*, adapted to any occasion. I tied a massive gold cross, an ornament that had belonged to my dear mother, round my neck with a scarlet ribbon; and my costume was complete. One glance at the looking-glass convinced me that there was nothing dowdy in my appearance; and then I hurried along the corridor and down the staircase to the hall, where Truefold received me and conducted me to the breakfast-room, in which an excellent dinner awaited me.

I did not waste much time over this repast, although I had eaten nothing all day; for I was anxious to make my way to the drawing-room. Just as I had finished, the door opened, and Mrs Chrighton sailed in, looking superb in a dark-green velvet dress richly trimmed with old point lace. She had been a beauty in her youth, and, as a matron, was still remarkably handsome. She had, above all, a charm of expression which to me was rarer and more delightful than her beauty of feature and complexion.

She put her arms round me, and kissed me affectionately.

'I have only this moment been told of your arrival, my dear Sarah,' she said; 'and I find you have been in the house half an hour. What must you have thought of me!'

'What can I think of you, except that you are all goodness, my dear Fanny? I did not expect you to leave your guests to receive me, and am really sorry that you have done so. I need no ceremony to convince me of your kindness.'

'But, my dear child, it is not a question of ceremony. I have been looking forward so anxiously to your coming, and I should not have liked to see you for the first time before all those people.

Give me another kiss, that's a darling. Welcome to Chrighton. Remember, Sarah, this house is always to be your home, whenever you have need of one.

'My dear kind cousin! And you are not ashamed of me, who have eaten the bread of strangers?'

'Ashamed of you! No, my love; I admire your industry and spirit. And now come to the drawing-room. The girls will be so pleased to see you.'

'And I to see them. They were quite little things when I went away, romping in the hay-fields in their short white frocks; and now, I suppose, they are handsome young women.

'They are very nice-looking; not as handsome as their brother. Edward is really a magnificent young man. I do not think my' maternal pride is guilty of any gross exaggeration when I say that.'

'And Miss Tremaine?' I said. 'I am very curious to see her.'

I fancied a faint shadow came over my cousin's face as I mentioned this name.

'Miss Tremaine—yes—you cannot fail to admire her,' she said, rather thoughtfully.

She drew my hand through her arm and led me to the drawing-room: a very large room, with a fireplace at each end, brilliantly lighted tonight, and containing about twenty people, scattered about in little groups, and all seeming to be talking and laughing merrily. Mrs Chrighton took me straight to one of the fireplaces, beside which two girls were sitting on a low sofa, while a young man of something more than six feet high stood near them, with his arm resting on the broad marble slab of the mantelpiece. A glance told me that this young man with the dark eyes and crisp waving brown hair was Edward Chrighton. His likeness to his mother was in itself enough to tell me who he was; but I remembered the boyish face and bright eyes which had so often looked up to mine in the days when the heir of the Abbey was one of the most juvenile scholars at Eton.

The lads seated nearest Edward Chrighton attracted my chief attention; for I felt sure that this lady was Miss Tremaine. She was tall and slim, and carried her head and neck with a stately air, which struck me more than anything in that first glance. Yes, she was handsome, undeniably handsome; and my cousin had been right when she said I could not fail to admire her; but to me the dazzlingly fair face with its perfect features, the marked aquiline nose, the short upper lip expressive of unmitigated pride, the full cold blue eyes, pencilled brows, and aureole of pale golden hair, were the very reverse of sympathetic. That Miss Tremaine must needs be universally admired, it was impossible to doubt; but I could not understand how any man could hill in love with such a woman.

She was dressed in white muslin, and her only ornament was a superb diamond locket, heart-shaped, tied round her long white throat with a broad black ribbon. Her hair, of which she seemed to have a great quantity, was arranged in a massive coronet of plaits, which surmounted the small head as proudly as an imperial crown.

To this young lady Mrs Chrighton introduced me.

'I have another cousin to present to you, Julia,' she said smiling—'Miss Sarah Chrighton, just arrived from St Petersburg.'

'From St Petersburg? What an awful journey! How do you do, Miss Chrighton? It was really very courageous of you to come so far. Did you travel alone?'

'No; I had a companion as far as London, and a very kind one. I came on to the Abbey by myself.'

The young lady had given me her hand with rather a languid air, I thought. I saw the cold blue eyes surveying me curiously from head to foot, and it seemed to me as if I could read the condemnatory summing-up—'A frump, and a poor relation'—in Miss Tremaine's face.

I had not much time to think about her just now; for Edward Chrighton suddenly seized both my hands, and gave me so hearty and loving a welcome, that he almost brought the tears up from my heart into my eyes'.

Two pretty girls in blue crape came running forward from different parts of the room, and gaily saluted me as 'Cousin Sarah'; and the three surrounded me in a little cluster, and assailed me with a string of questions—whether I remembered this, and whether I had forgotten duo, the battle in the hayfield, the charity-school tea-party in the vicarage orchard, our picnics in Hawsley Combe, our botanical and entomological excursions on Chorwell Common, and all the simple pleasures of their childhood and my youth. While this catechism was going on, Miss Tremaine watched us with a disdainful expression, which she evidently did not care to hide.

'I should not have thought you capable of such Arcadian simplicity, Mr Chrighton,' she said at last. 'Pray continue your recollections. These juvenile experiences are most interesting.'

'I don't expect you to be interested in them, Julia,' Edward answered, with a one that sounded rather too bitter for a lover. 'I know what a contempt you have for trifling rustic pleasures. Were you ever a child yourself, I wonder, by the way? I don't believe you ever ran after a butterfly in your life.'

Her speech put an end to our talk of the past, somehow. I saw that Edward was vexed, and that all the pleasant memories of his boyhood had fled before that cold scornful face. A young lady in pink, who had been sitting next Julia Tremaine, vacated the sofa, and Edward slipped into her place, and devoted himself for the rest of the evening to his betrothed. I glanced at his bright expressive face now and then as he talked to her, and could not help wondering what charm he could discover in one who seemed to me so unworthy of him.

It was midnight when I went back to my room in the north wing, thoroughly happy in the cordial welcome that had been given me. I rose early next morning—for early rising had long been habitual to me—and, drawing back the damask-curtain that sheltered my window, looked out at the scene below.

I saw a stable-yard, a spacious quadrangle, surrounded by the closed doors of stables and dog-kennels: low massive buildings of grey stone, with the ivy creeping over them here and there, and with an ancient moss-grown look, that gave them a weird kind of interest in my eyes. ‘this range of stabling must have been disused for a long time, I fancied. The stables now in use were a pile of handsome red-brick buildings at the other extremity of the house, to the rear of the music-room, and forming a striking feature in the back view of the Abbey.

I had often heard how the present Squire’s grandfather had kept a pack of hounds, which had been sold immediately after his death; and I knew that my cousin, the present Mr Chrighton, had been more than once requested to follow his ancestor’s good example; for there were no hounds now within twenty miles of the Abbey, though it was a fine country for fox-hunting.

George Chrighton, however—the reigning lord of the Abbey—was not a hunting man. He had, indeed, a secret horror of the sport; for more than one scion of the house had perished untimely in the hunting-field,The family had not been altogether a lucky one, in spite of its wealth and prosperity. It was not often that the goodly heritage had descended to the eldest son. Death in some form or other—on too many occasions a violent death—had come between the heir and his inheritance. And when I pondered on the dark pages in the story of the house, I used to wonder whether my cousin Fanny was ever troubled by morbid forebodings about her only and fondly loved son, Was there a ghost at Chrighton—that spectral visitant without which the state and splendour of a grand old house seem scarcely complete? Yes, I had heard vague hints of some shadowy presence that had been seen on rare occasions within the precincts of the Abbey; but I had never been able to ascertain what shape it bore.

Those whom I questioned were prompt to assure me that they had seen nothing. They had heard stories of the past□foolish legends, most likely, not worth listening to. Once, when I had spoken of the subject to my cousin George, he told me angrily never again to let him hear any allusion to that folly from my lips.

That December passed merrily. The old house was full of really pleasant people, and the brief winter days were spent in one unbroken round of amusement and gaiety. To me the old familiar English country-house life was a perpetual delight—to feel myself amongst kindred an unceasing pleasure. I could not have believed myself capable of being so completely happy.

I saw a great deal of my cousin Edward, and I think he contrived to make Miss Tremaine understand that, to please him, she must be gracious to me. She certainly took some pains to make herself agreeable to me; and I discovered that, in spite of that proud disdainful temper, which she so rarely took the trouble to conceal, she was really anxious to gratify her lover.

Their courtship was not altogether a halcyon period. They had frequent quarrels, the details of which Edward's sisters Sophy and Agnes delighted to discuss with me. It was the struggle of two proud spirits for mastery; but my cousin Edward's pride was of the nobler kind—the lofty scorn of all things mean—a pride that does not ill-become a generous nature. To me he seemed all that was admirable, and I was never tired of hearing his mother praise him. I think my cousin Fanny knew this, and that she used to confide in me as fully as if I had been her sister.

'I daresay you can see I am not quite so fond as I should wish to be of Julia Tremaine,' she said to me one day; 'but I am very glad that my son is going to marry. My husband's has not been a fortunate family, you know, Sarah. The eldest sons have been wild and unlucky for generations past; and when Edward was a boy I used to have many a bitter hour, dreading what the future might bring forth. Thank God he has been, and is, all that I can wish. He has never given me an hour's anxiety by any act of his. Yet I am not the less glad of his marriage. The heirs of Chrighton who have come to an untimely end have all died unmarried. There was Hugh Chrighton, in the reign of George the Second, who was killed in a duel; John, who broke his back in the hunting-field thirty years later; Theodore, shot accidentally by a schoolfellow at Eton; Jasper, whose yacht went down in the Mediterranean forty years ago. An awful list, is it not, Sarah? I shall fret as if my son were safer somehow when he is married. It will seem as if he has escaped the ban that has fallen on so many of our house. He will have greater reason to be careful of his life when he is a married man.'

I agreed with Mrs Chrighton; but could not help wishing that Edward had chosen any other woman than the cold handsome Julia. I could not fancy his future life happy with such a mate.

Christmas came by and by—a real old English Christmas□frost and snow without, warmth and revelry within; skating on the great pond in the park, and sledging on the ice-bound high-roads, by day; private theatricals, charades, and amateur concerts, by night. I was surprised to find that Miss Tremaine refused to take any active part in these evening amusements. She preferred to sit among the elders as a spectator, and had the air and bearing of a princess for whose diversion all our entertainments had been planned. She seemed to think that she fulfilled her mission by sitting still and looking handsome. No desire to show off appeared to enter her mind. Her intense pride left no room for vanity. Yet I knew that she could have distinguished herself as a musician if she had chosen to do so; for I had heard her sing and play in Mrs Chrighton's morning-room, when only Edward, his sisters, and myself were present; and I knew that both as a vocalist and a pianist she excelled all our guests.

The two girls and I had many a happy morning and afternoon, going from cottage to cottage in a pony-carriage laden with Mrs Chrighton's gifts to the poor of her parish. There was no public formal distribution of blanketing and coals, but the wants of all were amply provided for in a quiet friendly way. Agnes and Sophy, aided by an indefatigable maid, the Rector's daughter, and one or two other young ladies, had been at work for the last three months making smart warm frocks and useful undergarments for the children of the cottagers; so that on Christmas morning every child in the parish was arrayed in a complete set of new garments. Mrs Chrighton had an admirable faculty of knowing precisely what was most wanted in every household; and our pony-carriage used to convey a varied collection of goods, every parcel directed in the firm free hand of the chatelaine of the Abbey.

Edward used sometimes to drive us on these expeditions, and I found that he was eminently popular among the poor of Chrighton parish. He had such an airy pleasant way of talking to them, a manner which set them at their ease at once. He never forgot their names or relationships, or wants or ailments; had a packet of exactly the kind of tobacco each man liked best always ready in his coat-pockets; and was kill of jokes, which may not have been particularly witty, but which used to make the small low-roofed chambers ring with hearty laughter.

Miss Tremaine coolly declined any share in these pleasant duties.

'I don't like poor people,' she said. I daresay it sounds very dreadful, but it's just as well to confess my iniquity at once. I never can get on with them, or they with me. I am not simpatica, I suppose And then I cannot endure their stifling rooms. The close faint odour of their houses gives me a fever. And again, what is the use of visiting them? It is only an inducement to them to become hypocrites. Surely it is better to arrange on a sheet of paper what it is just and fair for them in have—blankets, and coals, and groceries, and money, and wine, and so on—and let them receive the things from some trustworthy servant. In that case, there need be no cringing on one side, and no endurance in the other.'

'But, you see, Julia, there are some kinds of people to whom that sort of thing is not a question of endurance,' Edward answered, his face flushing indignantly. 'People who like to share in the pleasure they give—who like to see the poor careworn faces lighted up with sudden joy—who like to make these sons of the soil feel that there is some friendly link between themselves and their masters—some point of union between the cottage and the great house. There is my mother, for instance: all these duties which you think so tiresome are to her an unfailing delight. There will be a change, I'm afraid, Julia, when you are mistress of the Abbey.'

'You have not made me that yet,' she answered; 'and there is plenty of time for you to change your mind, if you do not think me suited for the position. I do not pretend to be like your mother. It is better that I should not affect any feminine virtues which I do not possess.'

After this Edward insisted on driving our pony-carriage almost every day, leaving Miss Tremaine to find her own amusement; and I think this conversation was the beginning of an estrangement between them, which became more serious than any of their previous quarrels had been.

Miss Tremaine did not care for sledging, or skating, or billiard-playing. She had none of the 'fast' tendencies which have become so common lately. She used to sit in one particular bow-window of the drawing-room all the morning, working a screen in berlin-wool and beads, assisted and attended by her younger sister Laura, who was a kind of slave to her—a very colourless young lady in mind, capable of no such thing as an original opinion, and in person a pale replica of her sister.

Had there been less company in the house, the breach between Edward Chrighton and his betrothed must have become notorious; but with a house so full of people, all bent on enjoying themselves, I doubt if it was noticed. On all public occasions my cousin showed himself attentive and apparently devoted to Miss Tremaine. It was only I and his sisters who knew the real state of affairs.

I was surprised, after the young lady's total repudiation of all benevolent sentiments, when she beckoned me aside one morning, and slipped a little purse of gold—twenty sovereigns—into my hand.

'I shall be very much obliged if you will distribute that among your cottagers today, Miss Chrighton,' she said. 'Of course I should like to give them something; it's only the trouble of talking to them that I shrink from; and you are just the person for an almoner. Don't mention my little commission to any one, please.'

'Of course I may tell Edward,' I said; for I was anxious that he should know his betrothed was not as hard-hearted as she had appeared.

'To him least of all,' she answered eagerly. 'You know that our ideas vary on that point, he would think I gave the money to please him. Not a word, pray, Miss Chrighton.' I submitted, and distributed my sovereigns quietly, with the most careful exercise of my judgement.

So Christmas came and passed. It was the day after the great anniversary—a very quiet day for the guests and family at the Abbey, but a grand occasion for the servants, who were to have their annual ball in the evening—a ball to which all the humbler class of tenantry were invited. The frost had broken up suddenly, and it was a thorough wet day—a depressing kind of day for any one whose spirits are liable to be affected by the weather, as mine are. I felt out of spirits for the first time since my arrival at the Abbey.

No one else appeared to feel the same influence. The elder ladies sat in a wide semicircle round one of the fireplaces in the drawing-room; a group of merry girls and dashing young men chatted gaily before the other. From the billiard-room there came the frequent clash of balls, and cheery peals of stentorian laughter. I sat in one of the deep windows, half hidden by the curtains, reading a novel—one of a boxful that came from town every month.

If the picture within was bright and cheerful, the prospect was dreary enough without. The fairy forest of snow-wreathed trees, the white valleys and undulating banks of snow, had vanished, and the rain dripped slowly and sullenly upon a darksome expanse of sodden grass, and a dismal background of leafless timber. The merry sound of the sledge-bells no longer enlivened the air; all was silence and gloom.

Edward Chrighton was not amongst the billiard-players; he was pacing the drawing-room to and fro from end to end, with an air that was at once moody and restless.

'Thank heaven, the frost has broken up at last!' he exclaimed, stopping in front of the window where I sat.

He had spoken to himself, quite unaware of my close neighbourhood. Unpromising as his aspect was just then, I ventured to accost him.

'What bad taste, to prefer such weather as this to frost and snow!' I answered. 'The park looked enchanting yesterday—a real scene from fairyland. And only look at it today!'

'O yes, of course, from an artistic point of view, the snow was better. The place does look something like the great dismal swamp today; but I am thinking of hunting, and that confounded frost made a day's sport impossible. We are in for a spell of mild weather now, I think.'

'But you are not going to hunt, are you, Edward?'

'Indeed I am, my gentle cousin, in spite of that frightened look in your amiable countenance.'

'I thought there were no hounds hereabouts.'

'Nor are there; but there is as fine a pack as any in the country—the Daleborough hounds—five-and-twenty miles away.'

'And you are going five-and-twenty miles for the sake of a day's run?'

'I would travel forty, fifty, a hundred miles for that same diversion. But I am not going for a single day this time; I am going over to Sir Francis Wycherly's place—young Frank Wycherly and I were sworn chums at Christchurch—for three or four days. I am due today, but I scarcely dared to travel by cross-country roads in such rain as this. However, if the floodgates of the sky are loosened for a new deluge, I must go tomorrow.'

'What a headstrong young man!' I exclaimed. 'And what will Miss Tremaine say to this desertion?' I asked in a lower voice.

'Miss Tremaine can say whatever she pleases. She had it in her power to make me forget the pleasures of the chase, if she had chosen, though we had been in the heart of the shires, and the welkin ringing with the baying of hounds.'

'O, I begin to understand. This hunting engagement is not of long standing.'

'No; I began to find myself bored here a few days ago, and wrote to Frank to offer myself for two or three days at Wycherly. I received a most cordial answer by return, and am booked till the end of this week.'

'You have not forgotten the ball on the first?'

'O, no; to do that would be to vex my mother, and to offer a slight to our guests. I shall be here for the first, come what may.'

Come what may! so lightly spoken. The time came when I had bitter occasion to remember those words.

'I'm afraid you will vex your mother by going at all,' I said. 'You know what a horror both she and your father have of hunting.'

'A most un-country-gentleman-like aversion on my father's part. But he is a dear old book-worm, seldom happy out of his library. Yes, I admit they both have a dislike to hunting in the abstract; but they know I am a pretty good rider, and that it would need a bigger country than I shall find about Wycherly to floor me. You need not feel nervous, my dear Sarah; I am not going to give papa and mamma the smallest ground for uneasiness.'

'You will take your own horses, I suppose?'

'That goes without saying. No man who has cattle of his own cares to mount another man's horses. I shall take Pepperbox and the Druid.'

'Pepperbox has a queer temper, I have heard your sisters say.'

'My sisters expect a horse to be a kind of overgrown baa-lamb. Everything splendid in horseflesh and womankind is prone to that slight defect, an ugly temper. There is Miss Tremaine, for instance.'

'I shall take Miss Tremaine's part. I believe it is you who are in the wrong in the matter of this estrangement, Edward.'

'Do you? Well, wrong or right, my cousin, until the fair Julia comes to me with sweet looks and gentle words, we can never be what we have been.'

'You will return from your hunting expedition in a softer mood,' I answered; 'that is to say, if you persist in going. But I hope and believe you will change your mind.'

'Such a change is not within the limits of possibility, Sarah. I am fixed as Fate.'

He strolled away, humming some gay hunting-song as he went. I was alone with Mrs Chrighton later in the afternoon, and she spoke to me about this intended visit to Wycherly.

'Edward has set his heart upon it evidently,' she said regretfully, and his father and I have always made a point of avoiding anything that could seem like domestic tyranny. Our dear boy is such a good son, that it would be very hard if we came between him and his pleasures. You know what a morbid horror my husband has of the dangers of the hunting-field, and perhaps I am almost as weak-minded. But in spite of this we have never interfered with Edward's enjoyment of a sport which he is passionately fond of; and hitherto, thank God! he has escaped without a scratch. Yet I have had many a bitter hour, I can assure you, my dear, when my son has been away in Leicestershire hunting four days a week.'

'He rides well, I suppose.'

'Superbly. He has a great reputation among the sportsmen of our neighbourhood. I daresay when he is master of the Abbey he will start a pack of hounds, and revive the old days of his great-grandfather, Meredith Chrighton.'

'I fancy the hounds were kennelled in the stable-yard below my bedroom window in those days, were they not, Fanny?'

'Yes,' Mrs Chrighton answered gravely; and I wondered at the sudden shadow that fell upon her face.

I went up to my room earlier than usual that afternoon, and I had clear hour to spare before it would be time to dress for the seven o'clock dinner. This leisure hour I intended to devote to letter-writing; but on arriving in my room I found myself in a very idle frame of mind; and instead of opening my desk, I seated myself in the low easy-chair before the fire, and fell into a reverie.

How long I had been sitting there I scarcely know; I had been half meditating, half dozing, mixing broken snatches of thought with brief glimpses of dreaming, when I was startled into wakefulness by a sound that was strange to me.

It was a huntsman's horn—a few low plaintive notes on a huntsman's horn—notes which had a strange far-away sound, that was more unearthly than anything my ears had ever heard. I thought of the music in *Der Freischutz*; but the weirdest snatch of melody Weber ever wrote was not so ghastly a sound as these few simple notes conveyed to my ear.

I stood transfixed, listening to that awful music. It had grown dusk, my fire was almost out, and the room in shadow. As I listened, a light flashed suddenly on the wall before me. The light was as unearthly as the sound—a light that never shone from earth or sky.

I ran to the window; for this ghastly shimmer flashed through the window upon the opposite wall. The great gates of the stable-yard were open, and men in scarlet coats were riding in, a pack of hounds crowding in before them, obedient to the huntsman's whip. The whole scene was dimly visible by the declining light of the winter evening and the weird gleams of a lantern carried by one of the men. It was this lantern which had shone upon the tapestried wall. I saw the stable-doors opened one after another; gentlemen and grooms alighting from their horses; the dogs driven into their kennel; the helpers hurrying to and fro; and that strange wan lantern-light glimmering here and there is the gathering dusk. But there was no sound of horse's hoof or of human voices—not one yelp or cry from the hounds. Since those faint far-away sounds of the horn had died out in the distance, the ghastly silence had been unbroken.

I stood at my window quite calmly, and watched while the group of men and animals in the yard below noiselessly dispersed. There was nothing supernatural in the manner of their disappearance. The figures did not vanish or melt into empty air. One by one I saw the horses led into their separate quarters; one by one the redcoats strolled out of the gates, and the grooms departed, some one way, some another. The scene, but for its noiselessness, was natural enough; and had I been a stranger in the house, I might have fancied that those figures were real□those stables in full occupation.

But I knew that stable-yard and all its range of building to have been disused for more than half a century. Could I believe that, without an hour's warning, the long-deserted quadrangle could be filled—the empty stalls tenanted? Had some hunting-party from the neighbourhood sought shelter here, glad to escape the pitiless rain? That was not impossible, I thought. I was an utter unbeliever in all ghostly things—ready to credit any possibility rather than suppose that I had been looking upon shadows. And yet the noiselessness, the awful sound of that horn—the strange unearthly gleam of that lantern! Little superstitious as I might be, a cold sweat stood out upon my forehead, and I trembled in every limb.

For some minutes I stood by the window, statue-like, staring blankly into the empty quadrangle. Then I roused myself suddenly, and ran softly downstairs by a back staircase leading to the servants' quarters, determined to solve the mystery somehow or other. The way to Mrs Marjorum's room was familiar to me from old experience, and it was thither that I bent my steps, determined to ask the housekeeper the meaning of what I had seen. I had a lurking conviction that it would be well for me not to mention that scene to any member of the family till I had taken counsel with someone who knew the secrets of Chrighton Abbey.

I heard the sound of merry voices and laughter as I passed the kitchen and servants' hall. Men and maids were all busy in the pleasant labour of decorating their rooms for the evening's festival. They were putting the last touches to garlands of holly and laurel, ivy and fir, as I passed the open doors; and in both rooms I saw tables laid for a substantial tea. The housekeeper's room was in a retired nook at the end of a long passage—a charming old room, panelled with dark oak, and full of capacious cupboards, which in my childhood I had looked upon as storehouses of inexhaustible treasures in the way of preserves and other confectionery. It was a shady old room, with a wide old-fashioned fireplace, cool in summer, when the hearth was adorned with a great jar of roses and lavender; and warm in winter, when the logs burnt merrily all day long.

I opened the door softly; and went in. Mrs Marjorum was dozing in a high-backed armchair by the glowing hearth, dressed in her state gown of grey watered silk, and with a cap that was a perfect garden of roses. She opened her eyes as I approached her, and stared at me with a puzzled look for the first moment or so.

'Why, is that you, Miss Sarah?' she exclaimed; 'and looking as pale as a ghost, I can see, even by this firelight! Let me just light a candle, toil then I'll get you some *sal volatile*. Sit down in my armchair, miss; why, I declare you're all of a tremble!'

She put me into her easy-chair before I could resist, and lighted the two candles which stood ready upon her table, while I was trying to speak. My lips were dry, and it seemed at first as if my voice was gone.

'Never mind the *sal volatile*, Marjorum,' I said at last. 'I am not ill; I've been startled, that's all; and I've come to ask you for an explanation of the business that frightened me.'

'What business, Miss Sarah?'

'You must have heard something of it yourself, surely. Didn't you hear a horn just now, a huntsman's horn?'

'A horn! Lord no, Miss Sarah. Whatever could have put such a fancy in to your head?'

I saw that Mrs Marjorum's ruddy cheeks had suddenly lost their colour, that she was now almost as pale as I could have been myself. 'It was no fancy,' I said; 'I heard the sound, and saw the people. A hunting-party has just taken shelter in the north quadrangle. Dogs and horses, and gentlemen and servants.'

'What were they like, Miss Sarah?' the housekeeper asked in a strange voice.

'I can hardly tell you that. I could see that they wore red coats; and I could scarcely see more than that. Yes, I did get a glimpse of one of the gentlemen by the light of the lantern. A tall man, with grey hair and whiskers, and a stoop in his shoulders. I noticed that he wore a short-waisted coat with a very high collar—a coat that looked a hundred years old.'

'The old Squire!' muttered Mrs Marjorum under her breath; and then turning to me, she said with a cheery resolute air, 'You've been dreaming, Miss Sarah, that's just what it is. You've dropped off in your chair before the fire, and had a dream, that's it.'

'No, Marjorum, it was no dream. The horn woke me, and I stood at my window and saw the dogs and huntsmen come in.'

'Do you know, Miss Sarah, that the gates of the north quadrangle have been locked and barred for the last forty years, and that no one ever goes in there except through the house?'

'The gates may have been opened this evening to give shelter to strangers,' I said.

'Not when the only keys that will open them hang yonder in my cupboard, miss,' said the housekeeper, pointing to a corner of the room.

'But I tell you, Marjorum, these people came into the quadrangle; the horses and dogs are in the stables and kennels at this moment. I'll go and ask Mr Chrighton, or my cousin Fanny, or Edward, all about it, since you won't tell me the truth.'

I said this with a purpose, and it answered. Mrs Marjorum caught me eagerly by the wrist.

'No, miss, don't do that; for pity's sake don't do that; don't breathe a word to missus or master.'

'But why not?'

'Because you've seen that which always brings misfortune and sorrow to this house, Miss Sarah. You've seen the dead.'

'What do you mean?' I gasped, awed in spite of myself.

'I daresay you've heard say that there's been something seen at times at the Abbey—many years apart, thank God; for it never came that trouble didn't come after it.'

'Yes,' I answered hurriedly; 'but I could never get anyone to tell me what it was that haunted this place.'

'No, miss. Those that know have kept the secret. But you have seen it all tonight. There's no use in trying to hide it from you any longer. You have seen the old Squire, Meredith Chrighton, whose eldest son was killed by a fall in the hunting-field, brought home dead one December night, an hour after his father and the rest of the party had come safe home to the Abbey.

'The old gentleman had missed his son in the field, but had thought nothing of that, fancying that master John had had enough of the day's sport, and had turned his horse's head homewards. He was found by a labouring-man, poor lad, lying in a ditch with his back broken, and his horse beside him staked. The old Squire never held his head up after that day, and never rode to hounds again, though he was passionately fond of hunting. Dogs and horses were sold, and the north quadrangle has been empty from that day.'

'How long is it since this kind of thing has been seen?'

'A long time, miss. I was a slip of a girl when it last happened. It was in the winter-time—this very night—the night Squire Meredith's son was killed; and the house was full of company, just as it is now. There was a wild young Oxford gentleman sleeping in your room at that time, and he saw the hunting-party come into the quadrangle; and what did he do but throw his window wide open, and give them the view-hallo as loud as ever he could. He had only arrived the day before, and knew nothing about the neighbourhood; so at dinner he began to ask where were his friends the sportsmen, and to hope he should be allowed to have a run with the Abbey hounds next day.

'It was in the time of our master's father; and his lady at the head of the table turned as white as a sheet when she heard this talk. She had good reason, poor soul. Before the week was out her husband was lying dead. He was struck with a fit of apoplexy, and never spoke or knew any one afterwards.'

'An awful coincidence,' I said; 'but it may have been only a coincidence.'

'I've heard other stories, miss—heard them from those that wouldn't deceive—all proving the same thing: that the appearance of the old Squire and his pack is a warning of death to this house.'

'I cannot believe these things,' I exclaimed; 'I cannot believe them. Docs Mr Edward know anything about this?'

'No, miss. His father and mother have been most careful that it should be kept from him.'

'I think he is too strong-minded to be much affected by the fact,' I said.

'And you'll not say anything about what you've seen to my master or my mistress, will you, Miss Sarah?' pleaded the faithful old servant. 'The knowledge of it would be sure to make them nervous and unhappy. And if evil is to come upon this house, it isn't in human power to prevent its coming.'

'God forbid that there is any evil at hand!' I answered. 'I am no believer in visions or omens. After all, I would sooner fancy that I was dreaming—dreaming with my eyes open as I stood at the window—

than that I beheld the shadows of the dead.'

Mrs Marjorum sighed, and said nothing. I could see that she believed firmly in the phantom hunt.

I went back to my room to dress for dinner. However rationally I might try to think of what I had seen, its effect upon my mind and nerves was not the less powerful. I could think of nothing else; and a strange morbid dread of coming misery weighted me down like an actual burden.

There was a very cheerful party in the drawing-room when I went downstairs, and at dinner the talk and laughter were unceasing; but I could see that my cousin Fanny's face was a little graver than usual, and I had no doubt she was thinking of her son's intended visit to Wycherly.

At the thought of this a sudden terror flashed upon me. How if the shadows I had seen that evening were ominous of danger to him—to Edward, the heir and only son of the house? My heart grew cold as I thought of this, and yet in the next moment I despised myself for such weakness.

'It is natural enough for an old servant to believe in such things,' I said to myself; 'but for me—an educated woman of the world—preposterous folly.'

And yet from that moment I began to puzzle myself in the endeavour to devise some means by which Edward's journey might be prevented. Of my own influence I knew that I was powerless to hinder his departure by so much as an hour; but I fancied that Julia Tremaine could persuade him to any sacrifice of his inclination, if she could only humble her pride so far as to entreat it. I determined to appeal to her in the course of the evening.

We were very merry all that evening. The servants and their guests danced in the great hail, while we sat in the gallery above, and in little groups upon the staircase, watching their diversions. I think this arrangement afforded excellent opportunities for flirtation, and that the younger members of our party made good use of their chances—with one exception: Edward Chrighton and his affianced contrived to keep far away from each other all the evening.

While all was going on noisily in the hall below, I managed to get Miss Tremaine apart from the others in the embrasure of a painted window on the stairs, where there was a wide oaken seat.

Seated here side by side, I described to her, under a promise of secrecy, the scene which I had witnessed that afternoon, and my conversation with Mrs Marjorum.

'But, good gracious me, Miss Chrighton!' the young lady exclaimed, lifting her pencilled eyebrows with unconcealed disdain, 'you don't mean to tell me that you believe in such nonsense□ghosts and omens, and old woman's folly like that!'

'I assure you, Miss Tremaine, it is most difficult for me to believe in the supernatural,' I answered earnestly; 'but that which I saw this evening was something more than human. The thought of it has made me very unhappy; and I cannot help connecting it somehow with my cousin Edward's visit to Wycherly. If I had the power to prevent his going, I would do it at any cost; but I have not. You alone have influence enough for that. For heaven's sake use it! do anything to hinder his hunting with the Daleborough hounds.'

'You would have me humiliate myself by asking him to forgo his pleasure, and that after his conduct to me during the last week?'

'I confess that he has done much to offend you. But you love him, Miss Tremaine, though you are too proud to let your love be seen: I am certain that you do love him. For pity's sake speak to him; do not let him hazard his life, when a few words from you may prevent the danger.'

'I don't believe he would give up this visit to please me,' she answered; 'and I shall certainly not put it in his power to humiliate me a refusal. Besides, all this fear of yours is such utter nonsense. As if nobody had ever hunted before. My brothers hunt four times a week every winter, and not one of them has ever been the worse for it.

I did not give up the attempt lightly. I pleaded with this proud obstinate girl for a long time, as long as I could induce her to listen to me; but it was all in vain. She stuck to her text—no one should persuade her to degrade herself by asking a favour of Edward Chrighton. He had chosen to hold himself aloof from her, and she would show him that she could live without him. When she left Chrighton Abbey, they would part as strangers.

So the night closed, and at breakfast next morning I heard that Edward had started for Wycherly soon after daybreak. His absence made, for me at least, a sad blank in our circle. For one other also, I think; for Miss Tremaine's fair proud face was very pale, though she tried to seem gayer than usual, and exerted herself in quite an unaccustomed manner in her endeavour to be agreeable to everyone.

The days passed slowly for me after my cousin's departure. There was a weight upon my mind, a vague anxiety, which I struggled in vain to shake off. The house, full as it was of pleasant people, seemed to me to have become dull and dreary now that Edward was gone. The place where he had sat appeared always vacant to my eyes, though another filled it, and there was no gap on either side of the long dinner-table.

Light-hearted young men still made the billiard-room resonant with their laughter; merry girls flirted as gaily as ever, undisturbed in the smallest degree by the absence of the heir of the house. Yet for me all was changed. A morbid fancy had taken complete possession of me. I found myself continually brooding over the housekeeper's words; those words which had told me that the shadows I had seen boded death and sorrow to the house of Chrighton.

My cousins, Sophy and Agnes, were no more concerned about their brother's welfare than were their guests. They were full of excitement about the New-Year's ball, which was to be a very grand affair. Even one of importance within fifty miles was to be present, every nook and corner of the Abbey would be filled with visitors coming from a great distance, while others were to be billeted upon the better class of tenantry round about. Altogether the organization of this affair was no small business; and Mrs Chrighton's mornings were broken by discussions with the housekeeper, messages from the cook, interviews with the head-gardener on the subject of floral decorations, and other details, which all alike demanded the attention of the chatelaine herself.

With these duties, and with the claims of her numerous guests, my cousin Fanny's time was so fully occupied, that she had little leisure to indulge in anxious feelings about her son, whatever secret uneasiness may have been lurking in her maternal heart. As for the master of the Abbey, he spent so much of his time in the library, where, under the pretext of business with his bailiff, he read Greek, that it was not easy for anyone to discover what he did feel. Once, and once only, I heard him speak of his son, in a tone that betrayed an intense eagerness for his return.

The girls were to have new dresses from a French milliner in Wigmore Street; and as the great event drew near, bulky packages of millinery were continually arriving, and feminine consultations and expositions of finery were being held all day long in bedrooms and dressing-rooms with closed doors. Thus, with a mind always troubled by the same dark shapeless foreboding, I was perpetually being called upon to give an opinion about pink tulle and lilies of the valley, or maize silk and apple-blossoms.

New-Year's morning came at last, after an interval of abnormal length, as it seemed to me. It was a bright clear day, an almost spring-like sunshine lighting up the leafless landscape. The great dining-room was noisy with congratulations and good wishes as we assembled for breakfast on this first morning of a new year, after having seen the old one out cheerily the night before; but Edward had not yet returned, and I missed him sadly. Some touch of sympathy drew me to the side of Julia Tremaine on this particular morning. I had watched her very often during the last few days, and I had seen that her cheek grew paler every day. Today her eyes had the dull heavy look that betokens a sleepless night. Yes, I was sure that she was unhappy—that the proud relentless nature suffered bitterly.

'He must be home today,' I said to her in a low voice, as she sat in stately silence before an untasted breakfast.

'Who must?' she answered, turning towards roe with a cold distant look.

'My cousin Edward. You know he promised to be back in time for the ball.'

'I know nothing of Mr Chrighton's intended movements.' she said in her haughtiest tone; 'but of course it is only natural that he should be here tonight. He would scarcely care to insult half the count by his absence, however little he may value those now staying in his father's house.'

'But you know that there is one here whom he does value better than anyone else in the world, Miss Tremaine,' I answered, anxious to soothe this proud girl.

'I know nothing of the kind. But why do you speak so solemnly about his return? He will come, of course. There is no reason he should not come.'

She spoke in a rapid manner that was strange to her, and looked at me with a sharp enquiring glance, that touched me somehow, it was so unlike herself—it revealed to me so keen an anxiety.

'No, there is no reasonable cause for anything like uneasiness,' I said; 'but you remember what I told you the other night. That has preyed upon my mind, and it will be an unspeakable relief to me when I see my cousin safe at home.'

'I am sorry that you should indulge in such weakness, Miss Chrighton.'

That was all she said; but when I saw her in the drawing-room after breakfast, she had established herself in a window that commanded a view of the long winding drive leading to the front of the Abbey. From this point she could not fail to see anyone approaching the house. She sat there all day; everyone else was more or less busy with arrangements for the evening, or at any rate occupied with an appearance of business; but Julia Tremaine kept her place by the window, pleading a headache as an excuse for sitting still, with a book in her hand, all day, yet obstinately refusing to go to her room and lie down, when her mother entreated her to do so.

'You will be fit for nothing tonight, Julia,' Mrs Tremaine said, almost angrily; 'you have been looking ill for ever so long, and today you are as pale as a ghost.'

I knew that she was watching for him; and I pitied her with all my heart, as the day wore itself out, and he did not come.

We dined earlier than usual, played a game or two of billiards after dinner, made a tour of inspection through the bright rooms, lit with wax-candles only, and odorous with exoties; and then came a long interregnum devoted to the arts and mysteries of the toilet; while maids flitted to and fro laden with frilled muslin petticoats from the laundry, and a faint smell of singed hair pervaded the corridors. At ten o'clock the band were tuning their violins, and pretty girls and elegant-looking men were coming slowly down the broad oak staircase, as the roll of fast-.coming wheels sounded louder without, and stentorian voices announced the best people in the county.

I have no need to dwell long upon the details of that evening's festival. It was very much like other balls—a brilliant success, a night of splendour and enchantment for those whose hearts were light and happy, and who could abandon themselves utterly to the pleasure of the moment; a far-away picture of fair faces and bright-hued dresses, a wearisome kaleidoscopic procession of form and colour for those whose minds were weighed down with the burden of a hidden care.

For me the music had no melody, the dazzling scene no charm. Hour after hour went by; supper was over, and the waltzers were enjoying those latest dances which always seem the most delightful, and yet Edward Chrighton had not appeared amongst us.

There had been innumerable enquiries about him, and Mrs Chrighton had apologized for his absence as best she might. Poor soul, I well knew that his non-return was now a source of poignant anxiety to her, although she greeted all her guests with the same gracious smile, and was able to talk gaily and well upon every subject. Once, when she was sitting alone for a few minutes, watching the dancers, I saw the smile fade from her face, and a look of anguish come over it. I ventured to approach her at this moment, and never shall I forget the look which she turned towards me.

'My son, Sarah!' she said in a low voice—'something has happened to my son!'

I did my best to comfort her; but my own heart was growing heavier and heavier, and my attempt was a very poor one.

Julia Tremaine had danced a little at the beginning of the evening, to keep up appearances, I believe, in order that no one might suppose that she was distressed by her lover's absence; but after the first two or three dances she pronounced herself tired, and withdrew to a seat amongst the matrons. She was looking very lovely in spite of her extreme pallor, dressed in white tulle, a perfect cloud of airy puffings, and with a wreath of ivy-leaves and diamonds crowning her pale golden hair.

The night waned, the dancers were revolving in the last waltz, when I happened to look towards the doorway at the end of the room. I was startled by seeing a man standing there, with his hat in his hand, not in evening costume; a man with a pale anxious-looking face, peering cautiously into the room. My first thought was of evil; but in the next moment the man had disappeared, and I saw no more of him.

I lingered by my cousin Fanny's side till the rooms were empty. Even Sophy and Aggy had gone off to their own apartments, their airy dresses sadly dilapidated by a night's vigorous dancing. There were only Mr and Mrs Chrighton and myself in the long suite of rooms, where the flowers were drooping and the wax-lights dying out one by one in the silver sconces against the walls.

'I think the evening went off very well,' Fanny said, looking rather anxiously at her husband, who was stretching himself and yawning with an air of intense relief.

'Yes, the affair went off well enough. But Edward has committed a terrible breach of manners by not being here. Upon my word, the young men of the present day think of nothing but their own pleasures. I suppose that something especially attractive was going on at Wycherly today, and he couldn't tear himself away.'

'It is so unlike him to break his word,' Mrs Chrighton answered. 'You are not alarmed, Frederick? You don't think that anything has happened—any accident?'

'What should happen? Ned is one of the best riders in the county. I don't think there's any fear of his coming to grief.'

'He might be ill.'

'Not he. He's a young Hercules. And if it were possible for him to be ill—which it is not—we should have had a message from Wycherly.'

The words were scarcely spoken when Truefold the old butler stood by his master's side, with a solemn anxious face.

'There is a—a person who wishes to see you, sir,' he said in a low voice, 'alone.'

Low as the words were, both Fanny and myself heard them. 'Someone from Wycherly?' she exclaimed. 'Let him come here.'

'But, madam, the person most particularly wished to see master alone. Shall I show him into the library, sir? The lights are not out there.'

'Then it is someone from Wycherly,' said my cousin, seizing my wrist with a hand that was icy cold. 'Didn't I tell you so, Sarah? Something has happened to my son. Let the person come here, Truefold, here; I insist upon it.'

The tone of command was quite strange in a wife who was always deferential to her husband, in a mistress who was ever gentle to her servants.

'Let it be so, Truefold,' said Mr Chrighton. 'Whatever ill news has come to us we will hear together.'

He put his arm round his wife's waist. Both were pale as marble, both stood in stony stillness waiting for the blow that was to fall upon them.

The stranger, the man I had seen in the doorway, came in. He was curate of Wycherly church, and chaplain to Sir Francis Wycherly; a grave middle-aged man. He told what he had to tell with all kindness, with all the usual forms of consolation which Christianity and an experience of sorrow could suggest. Vain words, wasted trouble. The blow must fall, and earthly consolation was unable to lighten it by a feather's weight.

There had been a steeplechase at Wycherly—an amateur affair with gentlemen riders—on that bright New-Year's-day, and Edward Chrighton had been persuaded to ride his favourite hunter Pepperbox. There would be plenty of time for him to return to Chrighton after the races. He had consented; and his horse was winning easily, when, at the last fence, a double one, with water beyond, Pepperbox baulked his leap, and went over head-foremost, flinging his rider over a hedge into a field close beside the course, where there was a heavy stone roller.

Upon this stone roller Edward Chrighton had fallen, his head receiving the full force of the concussion. All was told. It was while the curate was relating the fatal catastrophe that I looked round suddenly, and saw Julia Tremaine standing a little way behind the speaker. She had heard all; she uttered no cry, she showed no signs of fainting, but stood calm and motionless, waiting for the end.

I know not how that night ended: there seemed an awful calm upon us all. A carriage was got ready, and Mr and Mrs Chrighton started for Wycherly to look upon their dead son. He had died while they were carrying him from the course to Sir Francis's house. I went with Julia Tremaine to her room, and sat with her while the winter morning dawned slowly upon us—a bitter dawning.

I have little more to tell. Life goes on, though hearts are broken. Upon Chrighton Abbey there came a dreary time of desolation. The master of the house lived in his library, shut from the outer world, buried almost as completely as a hermit in his cell. I have heard that Julia Tremaine was never known to smile after that day. She is still unmarried, and lives entirely at her father's country house; proud and reserved in her conduct to her equals, but a very angel of mercy and compassion amongst the poor of the neighbourhood.

Yes; this haughty girl, who once declared herself unable to endure the hovels of the poor, is now a Sister of Charity in all but the robe. So does a great sorrow change the current of a woman's life.

I have seen my cousin Fanny many times since that awful New-Year's night; for I have always the same welcome at the Abbey. I have seen her calm and cheerful, doing her duty, smiling upon her daughter's children, the honoured mistress of a great household; but I know that the mainspring of life is broken, that for her there hath passed a glory from the earth, and that upon all the pleasures and joys of this world she looks with the solemn calm of one for whom all things are dark with the shadow of a great sorrow.

Reality or Delusion?

Mrs Henry Wood

This is a ghost story. Every word of it is true. And I don't mind confessing that for ages afterwards some of us did not care to pass the spot alone at night. Some people do not care to pass it yet.

It was autumn, and we were at Crabb Cot. Lena had been ailing; and in October Mrs. Todhetley proposed to the squire that they should remove with her there, to see if the change would do her good.

We Worcestershire people call North Crabb a village; but one might count the houses in it, little and great, and not find four-and-twenty. South Crabb, half a mile off, is ever so much larger; but the church and school are at North Crabb.

John Ferrar had been employed by Squire Todhetley as a sort of overlooker on the estate, or working bailiff. He had died the previous winter; leaving nothing behind him except some debts; for he was not provident; and his handsome son Daniel. Daniel Ferrar, who was rather superior as far as education went, disliked work: he would make a show of helping his father, but it came to little. Old Ferrar had not put him to any particular trade or occupation, and Daniel, who was as proud as Lucifer, would not turn to it himself. He liked to be a gentleman. All he did now was to work in his garden, and feed his fowls, ducks, rabbits, and pigeons, of which he kept a great quantity, selling them to the houses around and sending them to market.

But, as everyone said, poultry would not maintain him. Mrs. Lease, in the pretty cottage hard by Ferrar's, grew tired of saying it. This Mrs. Lease and her daughter, Maria, must not be confounded with Lease the pointsman: they were in a better condition of life, and not related to him. Daniel Ferrar used to run in and out of their house at will when a boy, and he was now engaged to be married to Maria. She would have a little money, and the Leases were respected in North Crabb. People began to whisper a query as to how Ferrar got his corn for the poultry: he was not known to buy much: and he would have to go out of his house at Christmas, for its owner, Mr. Coney, had given him notice. Mrs. Lease, anxious about Maria's prospects, asked Daniel what he intended to do then, and he answered, 'Make his fortune: he should begin to do it as soon as he could turn himself round.' But the time was going on, and the turning round seemed to be as far off as ever.

After Midsummer, a niece of the schoolmistress's, Miss Timmens, had come to the school to stay: her name was Harriet Roe. The father, Humphrey Roe, was half-brother to Miss Timmens. He had married a Frenchwoman, and lived more in France than in England until his death. The girl had been christened Henriette; but North Crabb, not understanding much French, converted it into Harriet. She was a showy, free-mannered, good-looking girl, and made speedy acquaintance with Daniel Ferrar; or he with her. They improved upon it so rapidly that Maria Lease grew jealous, and North Crabb began to say he cared for Harriet more than for Maria.

When Tod and I got home the latter end of October, to spend the squire's birthday, things were in this state. James Hill, the bailiff who had been taken on by the squire in John Ferrar's place (but a far inferior man to Ferrar; not much better, in fact, than a common workman, and of whose doings you will hear soon in regard to his little stepson, David Garth) gave us an account of matters in general. Daniel Ferrar had been drinking lately, Hill added, and his head was not strong enough to stand it; and he was also beginning to look as if he had some care upon him.

'A nice lot, he, for them two women to be fighting for,' cried Hill, who was no friend to Ferrar. 'There'll be mischief between 'm if they don't draw in a bit. Maria Lease is next door to mad over it, I know; and t'other, finding herself the best liked, crows over her. It's something like the Bible story of Leah and Rachel, young gents, Dan Ferrar likes the one, and he's bound by promise to the t'other. As to the French jade,' concluded Hill, giving his head a toss, 'she'd make a show of liking any man that followed her, she would; a dozen of 'em on a string.'

It was all very well for surly Hill to call Daniel Ferrar a 'nice lot', but he was the best-looking fellow in the church on Sunday morning well-dressed too. But his colour seemed brighter; and his hands shook as they were raised, often, to push back his hair, that the sun shone upon through the south-window, turning it to gold. He scarcely looked up, not even at Harriet Roe, with her dark eyes roving everywhere, and her streaming pink ribbons. Maria Lease was pale, quiet, and nice, as usual; she had no beauty, but her face was sensible, and her deep grey eyes had a strange and curious earnestness. The new parson preached, a young man just appointed to the parish of Crabb. He went in for great observances of Saints' days, and told his congregation that he should expect to see them at church on the morrow, which would be the Feast of All Saints.

Daniel Ferrar walked home with Mrs. Lease and Maria after service, and was invited to dinner. I ran across to shake hands with the old dame, who had once nursed me through an illness, and promised to look in and see her later. We were going back to school on the morrow. As I turned away, Harriet Roe passed, her pink ribbons and her cheap gay silk dress gleaming in the sunlight. She stared at me, and I stared back again. And now, the explanation of matters being over, the real story begins. But I shall have to tell some of it as it was told by others.

The tea-things waited on Mrs. Lease's table in the afternoon; waited for Daniel Ferrar. He had left them shortly before to go and attend to his poultry. Nothing had been said about his coming back for tea: that he would do so had been looked upon as a matter of course. But he did not make his appearance, and the tea was taken without him. At half-past five the church-bell rang out for evening service, and Maria put her things on. Mrs. Lease did not go out at night.

'You are starting early, Maria. You'll be in church before other people.'

'That won't matter, mother.'

A jealous suspicion lay on Maria—that the secret of Daniel Ferrar's absence was his having fallen in with Harriet Roe: perhaps he had gone of his own accord to seek her. She walked slowly along. The gloom of dusk, and a deep dusk, had stolen over the evening, but the moon would be up later. As Maria passed the schoolhouse, she halted to glance in at the little sitting-room window: the shutters were not closed yet, and the room was lighted by the blazing fire. Harriet was not there. She only saw Miss Timmens, the mistress, who was putting on her bonnet before a hand-glass propped upright on the mantelpiece. Without warning, Miss Timmens turned and threw open the window. It was only for the purpose of pulling-to the shutters, but Maria thought she must have been observed, and spoke.

'Good evening, Miss Timmens.'

'Who is it?' cried out Miss Timmens, in answer, peering into the dusk. 'Oh, it's you, Maria Lease! Have you seen anything of Harriet? She went off somewhere this afternoon, and never came in to tea.'

'I have not seen her.'

'She's gone to the Batleys', I'll be bound. She knows I don't like her to be with the Batley girls: they make her ten times flightier than she would otherwise be.'

Miss Timmens drew in her shutters with a jerk, without which they would not close, and Maria Lease turned away.

'Not at the Batleys', not at the Batleys', but with *him*,' she cried, in bitter rebellion, as she turned away from the church. From the church, not to it. Was Maria to blame for wishing to see whether she was right or not?—for walking about a little in the thought of meeting them? At any rate it is what she did. And had her reward; such as it was.

As she was passing the top of the withy walk, their voices reached her ear. People often walked there, and it was one of the ways to South Crabb. Maria drew back amidst the trees, and they came on: Harriet Roe and Daniel Ferrar, walking arm-in-arm.

'I think I had better take it off,' Harriet was saying. 'No need to invoke a storm upon my head. And that would come in a shower of hail from stiff old Aunt Timmens.'

The answer seemed one of quick accent, but Ferrar spoke low. Maria Lease had hard work to control herself: anger, passion, jealousy, all blazed up. With her arms stretched out to a friendly tree on either side,—with her heart beating,—with her pulses coursing on to fever-heat, she watched them across the bit of common to the road. Harriet went one way then; he another, in the direction of Mrs. Lease's cottage. No doubt to fetch her Maria—to church, with a plausible excuse of having been detained. Until now she had had no proof of his falseness; had never perfectly believed in it.

She took her arms from the trees and went forward, a sharp faint cry of despair breaking forth on the night air. Maria Lease was one of those silent-natured girls who can never speak of a wrong like this. She had to bury it within her; down, down, out of sight and show; and she went into church with her usual quiet step. Harriet Roe with Miss Timmens came next, quite demure, as if she had been singing some of the infant scholars to sleep at their own homes. Daniel Ferrar did not go to church at all: he stayed, as was found afterwards, with Mrs. Lease.

Maria might as well have been at home as at church: better perhaps that she had been. Not a syllable of the service did she hear: her brain was a sea of confusion; the tumult within it rising higher and higher. She did not hear even the text, 'Peace, be still', or the sermon; both so singularly appropriate. The passions in men's minds, the preacher said, raged and foamed just like the angry waves of the sea in a storm, until Jesus came to still them.

I ran after Maria when church was over, and went in to pay the promised visit to old Mother Lease. Daniel Ferrar was sitting in the parlour. He got up and offered Maria a chair at the fire, but she turned her back and stood at the table under the window, taking off her gloves. An open Bible was before Mrs. Lease: I wondered whether she had been reading aloud to Daniel.

'What was the text, child?' asked the old lady.

No answer.

'Do you hear, Maria! What was the text?'

Maria turned at that, as if suddenly awakened. Her face was white; her eyes had in them an uncertain terror.

'The text?' she stammered. 'I—I forget it, mother. It was from Genesis, I think.'

'Was it, Master Johnny?'

'It was from the fourth chapter of St. Mark, 'Peace, be still.''

Mrs. Lease stared at me. 'Why, that is the very chapter I've been reading. Well now, that's curious. But there's never a better in the Bible, and never a better text was taken from it than those three words. I have been telling Daniel here, Master Johnny, that when once that peace, Christ's peace, is got into the heart, storms can't hurt us much. And you are going away again tomorrow, sir?' she added, after a pause. 'It's a short stay?'

I was not going away on the morrow. Tod and I, taking the squire in a genial moment after dinner, had pressed to be let stay until Tuesday, Tod using the argument, and laughing while he did it, that it must be wrong to travel on All Saints' Day, when the parson had specially enjoined us to be at church. The squire told us we were a couple of encroaching rascals, and if he did let us stay it should be upon condition that we did go to church. This I said to them.

'He may send you all the same, sir, when the morning comes,' remarked Daniel Ferrar.

'Knowing Mr. Todhetley as you do Ferrar, you may remember that he never breaks his promises.'

Daniel laughed. 'He grumbles over them, though, Master Johnny.'

'Well, he may grumble tomorrow about our staying, say it is wasting time that ought to be spent in study, but he will not send us back until Tuesday.'

Until Tuesday! If I could have foreseen then what would have happened before Tuesday! If all of us could have foreseen! Seen the few hours between now and then depicted, as in a mirror, event by event! Would it have saved the calamity, the dreadful sin that could never be redeemed? Why, yes; surely it would. Daniel Ferrar turned and looked at Maria.

'Why don't you come to the fire?'

'I am very well here, thank you.'

She had sat down where she was, her bonnet touching the curtain. Mrs. Lease, not noticing that anything was wrong, had begun talking about Lena, whose illness was turning to low fever, when the house door opened and Harriet Roe came in.

'What a lovely night it is!' she said, taking of own accord the chair I had not cared to take, for I kept saying I must go. 'Maria, what went with you after church? I hunted for you everywhere.'

Maria gave no answer. She looked black and angry, and her bosom heaved as if a storm were brewing. Harriet Roe slightly laughed.

'Do you intend to take holiday tomorrow, Mrs. Lease?'

'Me take holiday! what is there in tomorrow to take holiday for?' returned Mrs. Lease.

'I shall,' continued Harriet, not answering the question: 'I have been used to it in France. All Saints' Day is a grand holiday there; we go to church in our best clothes, and pay visits afterwards. Following it, like a dark shadow, comes the gloomy *Jour des Morts*.'

'The what?' cried Mrs. Lease, bending her ear.

'The day of the dead. All Souls' Day. But you English don't go to the cemeteries to pray.'

Mrs. Lease put on her spectacles, which lay upon the open pages of the Bible, and stared at Harriet. Perhaps she thought they might help her to understand. The girl laughed.

'On All Souls' Day, whether it be wet or dry, the French cemeteries are full of kneeling women draped in black; all praying for the repose of their dead relatives, after the manner of the Roman Catholics.'

Daniel Ferrar, who had not spoken a word since she came in, but sat with his face to the fire, turned and looked at her. Upon which she tossed back her head and her pink ribbons, and smiled till all her teeth were seen. Good teeth they were. As to reverence in her tone, there was none.

'I have seen them kneeling when the slosh and wet have been ankle-deep. Did you ever see a ghost?' added she, with energy. 'The French believe that the spirits of the dead come abroad on the night of All Saints' Day. You'd scarcely get a French woman to go out of her house after dark. It is their chief superstition.'

'What *is* the superstition?' questioned Mrs. Lease.

'Why, *that,*' said Harriet. 'They believe that the dead are allowed to revisit the world after dark on the Eve of All Souls; that they hover in the air, waiting to appear to any of their living relatives, who may venture out, lest they should forget to pray on the morrow for the rest of their souls.' (A superstition obtaining amongst some of the lower orders in France.)

'Well, I never!' cried Mrs. Lease, staring excessively. 'Did you ever hear the like of that, sir?' turning to me.

'Yes; I have heard of it.'

Harriet Roe looked up at me; I was standing at the corner of the mantelpiece. She laughed a free laugh.

'I say, wouldn't it be fun to go out tomorrow night, and meet the ghosts? Only, perhaps they don't visit this country, as it is not under Rome.'

'Now just you behave yourself before your betters, Harriet Roe, put in Mrs. Lease, sharply. 'That gentleman is young Mr. Ludlow of Crabb Cot.'

'And very happy I am to make young Mr. Ludlow's acquaintance,' returned easy Harriet, flinging back her mantle from her shoulders. 'How hot your parlour is, Mrs. Lease.'

The hook of the cloak had caught in a thin chain of twisted gold that she wore round her neck, displaying it to view. She hurriedly folded her cloak together, as if wishing to conceal the chain. But Mrs. Lease's spectacles had seen it.

'What's that you've got on, Harriet? A gold chain?'

A moment's pause, and then Harriet Roe flung back her mantle again, defiance upon her face, and touched the chain with her hand.

'That's what it is, Mrs. Lease: a gold chain. And a very pretty one, too.'

'Was it your mother's?'

'It was never anybody's but mine. I had it made a present to me this afternoon; for a keepsake.'

Happening to look at Maria, I was startled at her face, it was so white and dark: white with emotion, dark with an angry despair that

I for one did not comprehend. Harriet Roe, throwing at her a look of saucy triumph, went out with as little ceremony as she had come in, just calling back a general good night; and we heard her footsteps outside getting gradually fainter in the distance. Daniel Ferrar rose.

'I'll take my departure too, I think. You are very unsociable tonight, Maria.'

'Perhaps I am. Perhaps I have cause to be.'

She flung his hand back when he held it out; and in another moment, as if a thought struck her, ran after him into the passage to speak. I, standing near the door in the small room, caught the words.

'I must have an explanation with you, Daniel Ferrar. Now. Tonight. We cannot go on thus for a single hour longer.'

'Not tonight, Maria; I have no time to spare. And I don't know what you mean.'

'You do know. Listen. I will not go to my rest, no, though it were for twenty nights to come, until we have had it out. I vow I will not. There. You are playing with me. Others have long said so, and I know it now.'

He seemed to speak some quieting words to her, for the tone was low and soothing; and then went out, closing the door behind him. Maria came back and stood with her face and its ghastliness turned from us. And still the old mother noticed nothing.

'Why don't you take your things off, Maria?' she asked.

'Presently,' was the answer.

I said goodnight in my turn, and went away. Halfway home I met Tod with the two young Lexoms. The Lexoms made us go in and stay to supper, and it was ten o'clock before we left them.

'We shall catch it,' said Tod, setting off at a run. They never let us stay out late on a Sunday evening, on account of the reading.

But, as it happened, we escaped scot-free this time, for the house was in a commotion about Lena. She had been better in the afternoon, but at nine o'clock the fever returned worse than ever. Her little cheeks and lips were scarlet as she lay on the bed, her wide-open eyes were bright and glistening. The squire had gone up to look at her, and was fuming and fretting in his usual fashion.

'The doctor has never sent the medicine,' said patient Mrs. Todhetley, who must have been worn out with nursing. 'She ought to take it; I am sure she ought.'

'These boys are good to run over to Cole's for that,' cried the squire. 'It won't hurt them; it's a fine night.'

Of course we were good for it. And we got our caps again; being charged to enjoin Mr. Cole to come over the first thing in the morning.

'Do you care much about my going with you, Johnny?' Tod asked as we were turning out at the door. 'I am awfully tired.'

'Not a bit. I'd as soon go alone as not. You'll see me back in half-an-hour.'

I took the nearest way; flying across the fields at a canter, and startling the hares. Mr. Cole lived near South Crabb, and I don't believe more than ten minutes had gone by when I knocked at his door. But to get back as quickly was another thing. The doctor was not at home. He had been called out to a patient at eight o'clock, and had not yet returned.

I went in to wait: the servant said he might be expected to come in from minute to minute. It was of no use to go away without the medicine; and I sat down in the surgery in front of the shelves, and fell asleep counting the white jars and physic bottles. The doctor's entrance awoke me.

'I am sorry you should have had to come over and to wait,' he said. 'When my other patient, with whom I was detained a considerable time, was done with, I went on to Crabb Cot with the child's medicine, which I had in my pocket.'

'They think her very ill tonight, sir.'

'I left her better, and going quietly to sleep. She will soon be well again, I hope.'

'Why! is that the time?' I exclaimed, happening to catch sight of the clock as I was crossing the hall. It was nearly twelve. Mr. Cole laughed, saying time passed quickly when folk were asleep.

I went back slowly. The sleep, or the canter before it, had made me feel as tired as Tod had said he was. It was a night to be abroad in and to enjoy; calm, warm, light. The moon, high in the sky, illumined every blade of grass; sparkled on the water of the little rivulet; brought out the moss on the grey walls of the old church; played on its round-faced clock, then striking twelve.

Twelve o'clock at night at North Crabb answers to about three in the morning in London, for country people are mostly in bed and asleep at ten. Therefore, when loud and angry voices struck up in dispute, just as the last stroke of the hour was dying away on the midnight air, I stood still and doubted my ears.

I was getting near home then. The sounds came from the back of a building standing alone in a solitary place on the left-hand side of the road. It belonged to the squire, and was called the yellow barn, its walls being covered with a yellow wash; but it was in fact used as a storehouse for corn. I was passing in front of it when the voices rose upon the air. Round the building I ran, and saw Maria Lease: and something else that I could not at first comprehend. In the pursuit of her vow, not to go to rest until she had 'had it out' with Daniel Ferrar, Maria had been abroad searching for him. What ill fate brought her looking for him up near our barn?—perhaps because she had fruitlessly searched in every other spot.

At the back of this barn, up some steps, was an unused door. Unused partly because it was not required, the principal entrance being in front; partly because the key of it had been for a long time missing. Stealing out at this door, a bag of corn upon his shoulders, had come Daniel Ferrar in a smock-frock. Maria saw him, and stood back in the shade. She watched him lock the door and put the key in his pocket; she watched him give the heavy bag a jerk as he turned to come down the steps. Then she burst out. Her loud reproaches petrified him, and he stood there as one suddenly turned to stone. It was at that moment that I appeared.

I understood it all soon; it needed not Maria's words to enlighten me. Daniel Ferrar possessed the lost key and could come in and out at will in the midnight hours when the world was sleeping, and help himself to the corn. No wonder his poultry throve; no wonder there had been grumblings at Crabb Cot at the mysterious disappearance of the good grain.

Maria Lease was decidedly mad in those few first moments. Stealing is looked upon in an honest village as an awful thing; a disgrace, a crime; and there was the night's earlier misery besides. Daniel Ferrar was a thief! Daniel Ferrar was false to her! A storm of words and reproaches poured forth from her in confusion, none of it very distinct. 'Living upon theft! Convicted felon! Transportation for life! Squire Todhetley's corn! Fattening poultry on stolen goods! Buying gold chains with the profits for that bold, flaunting French girl, Harriet Roe! Taking his stealthy walks with her!'

My going up to them stopped the charge. There was a pause; and then Maria, in her mad passion, denounced him to me, as representative (so she put it) of the squire—the breaker-in upon our premises! the robber of our stored corn!

Daniel Ferrar came down the steps; he had remained there still as a statue, immovable; and turned his white face to me. Never a word in defence said he: the blow had crushed him; he was a proud man (if anyone can understand that), and to be discovered in this ill-doing was worse than death to him.

'Don't think of me more hardly than you can help, Master Johnny,' he said in a quiet tone. 'I have been almost tired of my life this long while.'

Putting down the bag of corn near the steps, he took the key from his pocket and handed it to me. The man's aspect had so changed; there was something so grievously subdued and sad about him altogether, that I felt as sorry for him as if he had not been guilty. Maria Lease went on in her fiery passion.

'You'll be more tired of it tomorrow when the police are taking you to Worcester gaol. Squire Todhetley will not spare you, though your father was his many-years bailiff. He could not, you know, if he wished; Master Ludlow has seen you in the act.'

'Let me have the key again for a minute, sir,' he said, as quietly as though he had not heard a word. And I gave it to him. I'm not sure but I should have given him my head had he asked for it.

He swung the bag on his shoulders, unlocked the granary door, and put the bag beside the other sacks. The bag was his own, as we found afterwards, but he left it there. Locking the door again, he gave me the key, and went away with a weary step.

'Goodbye, Master Johnny.'

I answered back goodnight civilly, though he had been stealing. When he was out of sight, Maria Lease, her passion full upon her still, dashed off towards her mother's cottage, a strange cry of despair breaking from her lips.

'Where have you been lingering, Johnny?' roared the squire, who was sitting up for me. 'You have been throwing at the owls, sir, that's what you've been at; you have been scudding after the hares.'

I said I had waited for Mr. Cole, and had come back slower than I went; but I said no more, and went up to my room at once. And the squire went to his.

I know I am only a muff; people tell me so, often: but I can't help it; I did not make myself. I lay awake till nearly daylight, first wishing Daniel Ferrar could be screened, and then thinking it might perhaps be done. If he would only take the lesson to heart and go straight for the future, what a capital thing it would be. We had liked old Ferrar; he had done me and Tod many a good turn: and, for the matter of that, we liked Daniel. So I never said a word when morning came of the past night's work.

'Is Daniel at home?' I asked, going to Ferrar's the first thing before breakfast. I meant to tell him that if he would keep right, I would keep counsel.

'He went out at dawn, sir,' answered the old woman who did for him, and sold his poultry at market. 'He'll be in presently: he have had no breakfast yet.'

'Then tell him when he comes, to wait in, and see me: tell him it's all right. Can you remember, Goody? 'It is all right."'

'I'll remember, safe enough, Master Ludlow.'

Tod and I, being on our honour, went to church, and found about ten people in the pews. Harriet Roe was one, with her pink ribbons, the twisted gold chain showing outside a short-cut velvet jacket.

'No, sir; he has not been home yet; I can't think where he can have got to,' was the old Goody's reply when I went again to Ferrar's. And so I wrote a word in pencil, and told her to give it him when he came in, for I could not go dodging there every hour of the day.

After luncheon, strolling by the back of the barn: a certain reminiscence I suppose taking me there, for it was not a frequented spot: I saw Maria Lease coming along.

Well, it was a change! The passionate woman of the previous night had subsided into a poor, wild-looking, sorrow-stricken thing, ready to die of remorse. Excessive passion had wrought its usual consequences; a reaction: a reaction in favour of Daniel Ferrar. She came up to me, clasping her hands in agony—beseeching that I would spare him; that I would not tell of him; that I would give him a chance for the future: and her lips quivered and trembled, and there were dark circles round her hollow eyes.

I said that I had not told and did not intend to tell. Upon which she was going to fall down on her knees, but I rushed off.

'Do you know where he is?' I asked, when she came to her sober senses.

'Oh, I wish I did know! Master Johnny, he is just the man to go and do something desperate. He would never face shame; and I was a mad, hard-hearted, wicked girl to do what I did last night. He might run away to sea; he might go and enlist for a soldier.'

'I dare say he is at home by this time. I have left a word for him there, and promised to go in and see him tonight. If he will undertake not to be up to wrong things again, no one shall ever know of this from me.'

She went away easier, and I sauntered on towards South Crabb. Eager as Tod and I had been for the day's holiday, it did not seem to be turning out much of a boon. In going home again—there was nothing worth staying out for—I had come to the spot by the three-cornered grove where I saw Maria, when a galloping policeman overtook me. My heart stood still; for I thought he must have come after Daniel Ferrar.

'Can you tell me if I am near to Crabb Cot—Squire Todhetley's?' he asked, reining-in his horse.

'You will reach it in a minute or two. I live there. Squire Todhetley is not at home. What do you want with him?'

'It's only to give in an official paper, sir. I have to leave one personally upon all the county magistrates.'

He rode on. When I got in I saw the folded paper upon the hall-table; the man and horse had already gone onwards. It was worse indoors than out; less to be done. Tod had disappeared after church; the squire was abroad; Mrs. Todhetley sat upstairs with Lena: and I strolled out again. It was only three o'clock then.

An hour, or more, was got through somehow; meeting one, talking to another, throwing at the ducks and geese; anything. Mrs. Lease had her head, smothered in a yellow shawl, stretched out over the palings as I passed her cottage.

'Don't catch cold, mother.'

'I am looking for Maria, sir. I can't think what has come to her today, Master Johnny,' she added, dropping her voice to a confidential tone. 'The girl seems demented: she has been going in and out ever since daylight like a dog in a fair.'

'If I meet her I will send her home.'

And in another minute I did meet her. For she was coming out of Daniel Ferrar's yard. I supposed he was at home again.

'No,' she said looking more wild, worn, haggard than before; 'that's what I have been to ask. I am just out of my senses, sir. He has gone for certain. Gone!'

I did not think it. He would not be likely to go away without clothes.

'Well, I know he is, Master Johnny; something tells me. I've been all about everywhere. There's a great dread upon me, sir; I never felt anything like it.'

'Wait until night, Maria; I dare say he will go home then. Your mother is looking out for you; I said if I met you I'd send you in.'

Mechanically she turned towards the cottage, and I went on. Presently, as I was sitting on a gate watching the sunset, Harriet Roe passed towards the withy walk, and gave me a nod in her free but good-natured way.

'Are you going there to look out for the ghosts this evening?' I asked: and I wished not long afterwards I had not said it. 'It will soon be dark.'

'So it will,' she said, turning to the red sky in the west. 'But I have no time to give to the ghosts tonight.'

'Have you seen Ferrar today?' I cried, an idea occurring to me.

'No. And I can't think where he has got to; unless he is off to Worcester. He told me he should have to go there someday this week.'

She evidently knew nothing about him, and went on her way with another free-and-easy nod. I sat on the gate till the sun had gone down, and then thought it was time to be getting homewards.

Close against the yellow barn, the scene of last night's trouble, whom should I come upon but Maria Lease. She was standing still, and turned quickly at the sound of my footsteps. Her face was bright again, but had a puzzled look upon it.

'I have just seen him: he has not gone,' she said in a happy whisper. 'You were right, Master Johnny, and I was wrong.'

'Where did you see him?'

'Here; not a minute ago. I saw him twice. He is angry, very, and will not let me speak to him; both times he got away before I could reach him. He is close by somewhere.'

I looked round, naturally; but Ferrar was nowhere to be seen. There was nothing to conceal him except the barn, and that was locked up. The account she gave was this and her face grew puzzled again as she related it.

Unable to rest indoors, she had wandered up here again, and saw Ferrar standing at the corner of the barn, looking very hard at her. She thought he was waiting for her to come up, but before she got close to him he had disappeared, and she did not see which way. She hastened past the front of the barn, ran round to the back, and there he was. He stood near the steps looking out for her; waiting for her, as it again seemed; and was gazing at her with the same fixed stare. But again she missed him before she could get quite up; and it was at that moment that I arrived on the scene.

I went all round the barn, but could see nothing of Ferrar. It was an extraordinary thing where he could have got to. Inside the barn he could not be: it was securely locked; and there was no appearance of him in the open country. It was, so to say, broad daylight yet, or at least not far short of it; the red light was still in the west. Beyond the field at the back of the barn, was a grove of trees in the form of a triangle; and this grove was flanked by Crabb Ravine, which ran right and left. Crabb Ravine had the reputation of being haunted; for a light was sometimes seen dodging about its deep descending banks at night that no one could account for. A lively spot altogether for those who liked gloom.

'Are you sure it was Ferrar, Maria?'

'Sure!' she returned in surprise. 'You don't think I could mistake him Master Johnny, do you? He wore that ugly seal-skin winter-cap of his tied over his ears, and his thick grey coat. The coat was buttoned closely round him. I have not seen him wear either since last winter.'

That Ferrar must have gone into hiding somewhere seemed quite evident; and yet there was nothing but the ground to receive him. Maria said she lost sight of him the last time in a moment; both times in fact; and it was absolutely impossible that he could have made off to the triangle or elsewhere, as she must have seen him cross the open land. For that matter I must have seen him also.

On the whole, not two minutes had elapsed since I came up, though it seems to have been longer in telling it: when, before we could look further, voices were heard approaching from the direction of Crabb Cot; and Maria, not caring to be seen, went away quickly. I was still puzzling about Ferrar's hiding-place, when they reached me—the squire, Tod, and two or three men. Tod came slowly up, his face dark and grave.

'I say, Johnny, what a shocking thing this is!'

'What is a shocking thing?'

'You have not heard of it?—But I don't see how you could hear it.'

I had heard nothing. I did not know what there was to hear. Tod told me in a whisper.

'Daniel Ferrar's dead, lad.'

'*What?*'

'He has destroyed himself Not more than half-an-hour ago. Hung himself in the grove.'

I turned sick, taking one thing with another, comparing this recollection with that; which I dare say you will think no one but a muff would do.

Ferrar was indeed dead. He had been hiding all day in the three-cornered grove: perhaps waiting for night to get away—perhaps only waiting for night to go home again. Who can tell? About half-past two, Luke Macintosh, a man who sometimes worked for us, sometimes for old Coney happening to go through the grove, saw him there, and talked with him. The same man, passing back a little before sunset, found him hanging from a tree, dead. Macintosh ran with the news to Crabb Cot, and they were now flocking to the scene. When facts came to be examined there appeared only too much reason to think that the unfortunate appearance of the galloping policeman had terrified Ferrar into the act; perhaps—we all hoped it!—had scared his senses quite away. Look at it as we would, it was very dreadful.

But what of the appearance Maria Lease saw? At that time, Ferrar had been dead at least half-an-hour. Was it reality or delusion? That is (as the squire put it), did her eyes see a real, spectral Daniel Ferrar; or were they deceived by some imagination of the brain? Opinions were divided. Nothing can shake her own steadfast belief in its reality; to her it remains an awful certainty, true and sure as heaven.

If I say that I believe in it too, I shall be called a muff and a double muff. But there is no stumbling-block difficult to be got over. Ferrar, when found, was wearing the seal-skin cap tied over the ears and the thick grey coat buttoned up round him, just as Maria Lease had described to me; and he had never worn them since the previous winter, or taken them out of the chest where they were kept. The old woman at his home did not know he had done it then. When told that he had died in these things, she protested that they were in the chest, and ran up to look for them. But the things were gone.

The Open Door

Mrs. J. H. Riddell

Some people do not believe in ghosts. For that matter, some people do not believe in anything. There are persons who even affect incredulity concerning that open door at Ladlow Hall. They say it did not stand wide open—that they could have shut it; that the whole affair was a delusion; that they are sure it must have been a conspiracy; that they are doubtful whether there is such a place as Ladlow on the face of the earth; that the first time they are in Meadowshire they will look it up.

That is the manner in which this story, hitherto unpublished, has been greeted by my acquaintances. How it will be received by strangers is quite another matter. I am going to tell what happened to me exactly as it happened, and readers can credit or scoff at the tale as it pleases them. It is not necessary for me to find faith and comprehension in addition to a ghost story, for the world at large. If such were the case, I should lay down my pen.

Perhaps, before going further, I ought to premise there was a time when I did not believe in ghosts either. If you had asked me one summer's morning years ago when you met me on London Bridge if I held such appearances to be probable or possible, you would have received an emphatic 'No' for answer.

But, at this rate, the story of the Open Door will never be told; so we will, with your permission, plunge into it immediately.

★★★★★★

'Sandy!'

'What do you want?'

'Should you like to earn a sovereign?'

'Of course I should.'

A somewhat curt dialogue, but we were given to curtness in the office of Messrs Frimpton, Frampton and Fryer, auctioneers and estate agents, St Benet's Hill, City.

(My name is not Sandy or anything like it, but the other clerks so styled me because of a real or fancied likeness to some character, an ill-looking Scotchman, they had seen at the theatre. From this it may be inferred I was not handsome. Far from it. The only ugly specimen in my family, I knew I was very plain; and it chanced to be no secret to me either that I felt grievously discontented with my lot. I did not like the occupation of clerk in an auctioneer's office, and I did not like my employers. We are all of us inconsistent, I suppose, for it was a shock to me to find they entertained a most cordial antipathy to me.)

'Because,' went on Parton, a fellow, my senior by many years—a fellow who delighted in chaffing me, 'I can tell you how to lay hands on one.'

'How?' I asked, sulkily enough, for I felt he was having what he called his fun.

'You know that place we let to Carrison, the tea-dealer?'

Carrison was a merchant in the China trade, possessed of fleets of vessels and towns of warehouses; but I did not correct Parton's expression, I simply nodded.

'He took it on a long lease, and he can't live in it; and our governor said this morning he wouldn't mind giving anybody who could find out what the deuce is the matter, a couple of sovereigns and his travelling expenses.'

'Where is the place?' I asked, without turning my head; for the convenience of listening I had put my elbows on the desk and propped up my face with both hands.

'Away down in Meadowshire, in the heart of the grazing country.'

'And what is the matter?' I further enquired.

'A door that won't keep shut.'

'What?'

'A door that will keep open, if you prefer that way of putting it,' said Parton.

'You are jesting.'

'If I am, Carrison is not, or Fryer either. Carrison came here in a nice passion, and Fryer was in a fine rage; I could see he was, though he kept his temper outwardly. They have had an active correspondence it appears, and Carrison went away to talk to his lawyer. Won't make much by that move, I fancy.'

'But tell me,' I entreated, 'why the door won't keep shut?'

'They say the place is haunted.'

'What nonsense!' I exclaimed.

'Then you are just the person to take the ghost in hand. I thought so while old Fryer was speaking.'

'If the door won't keep shut,' I remarked, pursuing my own train of thought, 'why can't they let it stay open?'

'I have not the slightest idea. I only know there are two sovereigns to be made, and that I give you a present of the information.'

And having thus spoken, Parton took down his hat and went out, either upon his own business or that of his employers.

There was one thing I can truly say about our office, we were never serious in it. I fancy that is the case in most offices nowadays; at all events, it was the case in ours. We were always chaffing each other, playing practical jokes, telling stupid stories, scamping our work, looking at the clock, counting the weeks to next St Lubbock's Day, counting the hours to Saturday.

For all that we were all very earnest in our desire to have our salaries raised, and unanimous in the opinion no fellows ever before received such wretched pay. I had twenty pounds a year, which I was aware did not half provide for what I ate at home. My mother and sisters left me in no doubt on the point, and when new clothes were wanted I always hated to mention the fact to my poor worried father.

We had been better off once, I believe, though I never remember the time. My father owned a small property in the country, but owing to the failure of some bank, I never could understand what bank, it had to be mortgaged; then the interest was not paid, and the mortgages foreclosed, and we had nothing left save the half-pay of a major, and about a hundred a year which my mother brought to the common fund.

We might have managed on our income, I think, if we had not been so painfully genteel; but we were always trying to do something quite beyond our means, and consequently debts accumulated, and creditors ruled us with rods of iron.

Before the final smash came, one of my sisters married the younger son of a distinguished family, and even if they had been disposed to live comfortably and sensibly she would have kept her sisters up to the mark. My only brother, too, was an officer, and of course the family thought it necessary he should see we preserved appearances.

It was all a great trial to my father, I think, who had to bear the brunt of the dunning and harass, and eternal shortness of money; and it would have driven me crazy if I had not found a happy refuge when matters were going wrong at home at my aunt's. She was my father's sister, and had married so 'dreadfully below her' that my mother refused to acknowledge the relationship at all.

For these reasons and others, Parton's careless words about the two sovereigns stayed in my memory.

I wanted money badly—I may say I never had sixpence in the world of my own—and I thought if I could earn two sovereigns I might buy some trifles I needed for myself, and present my father with a new umbrella. Fancy is a dangerous little jade to flirt with, as I soon discovered.

She led me on and on. First I thought of the two sovereigns; then I recalled the amount of the rent Mr Carrison agreed to pay for Ladlow Hall; then I decided he would gladly give more than two sovereigns if he could only have the ghost turned out of possession. I fancied I might get ten pounds—twenty pounds. I considered the matter all day, and I dreamed of it all night, and when I dressed myself next morning I was determined to speak to Mr Fryer on the subject.

I did so—I told that gentleman Parton had mentioned the matter to me, and that if Mr Fryer had no objection, I should like to try whether I could not solve the mystery. I told him I had been accustomed to lonely houses, and that I should not feel at all nervous; that I did not believe in ghosts, and as for burglars, I was not afraid of them.

'I don't mind your trying,' he said at last. 'Of course you understand it is no cure, no pay. Stay in the house for a week; if at the end of that time you can keep the door shut, locked, bolted, or nailed up, telegraph for me, and I will go down—if not, come back. If you like to take a companion there is no objection.'

I thanked him, but said I would rather not have a companion.

'There is only one thing, sir, I should like,' I ventured.

'And that—?' he interrupted.

'Is a little more money. If I lay the ghost, or find out the ghost, I think I ought to have more than two sovereigns.'

'How much more do you think you ought to have?' he asked.

His tone quite threw me off my guard, it was so civil and conciliatory, and I answered boldly:

'Well, if Mr Carrison cannot now live in the place perhaps he wouldn't mind giving me a ten-pound note.'

Mr Fryer turned, and opened one of the books lying on his desk. He did not look at or refer to it in any way—I saw that.

'You have been with us how long, Edlyd?' he said.

'Eleven months tomorrow,' I replied.

'And our arrangement was, I think, quarterly payments, and one month's notice on either side?'

'Yes, sir.' I heard my voice tremble, though I could not have said what frightened me.

'Then you will please to take your notice now. Come in before you leave this evening, and I'll pay you three months' salary, and then we shall be quits.'

'I don't think I quite understand,' I was beginning, when he broke in:

'But I understand, and that's enough. I have had enough of you and your airs, and your indifference, and your insolence here. I never had a clerk I disliked as I do you. Coming and dictating terms, forsooth! No, you shan't go to Ladlow. Many a poor chap'—(he said 'devil')—'would have been glad to earn half a guinea, let alone two sovereigns; and perhaps you may be before you are much older.'

'Do you mean that you won't keep me here any longer, sir?' I asked in despair. I had no intention of offending you. I—'

'Now you need not say another word,' he interrupted, 'for I won't bandy words with you.

Since you have been in this place you have never known your position, and you don't seem able to realize it. When I was foolish enough to take you, I did it on the strength of your connections, but your connections have done nothing for me. I have never had a penny out of any one of your friends—if you have any. You'll not do any good in business for yourself or anybody else, and the sooner you go to Australia'—(here he was very emphatic)—'and get off these premises, the better I shall be pleased.'

I did not answer him—I could not. He had worked himself to a white heat by this time, and evidently intended I should leave his premises then and there. He counted five pounds out of his cash-box, and, writing a receipt, pushed it and the money across the table, and bade me sign and be off at once.

My hand trembled so I could scarcely hold the pen, but I had presence of mind enough left to return one pound ten in gold, and three shillings and fourpence I had, quite by the merest good fortune, in my waistcoat pocket.

'I can't take wages for work I haven't done,' I said, as well as sorrow and passion would let me. 'Good-morning,' and I left his office and passed out among the clerks.

I took from my desk the few articles belonging to me, left the papers it contained in order, and then, locking it, asked Parton if he would be so good as to give the key to Mr Fryer.

'What's up?' he asked 'Are you going?'

I said, 'Yes, I am going'.

'Got the sack?'

'That is exactly what has happened.'

'Well, I'm—!' exclaimed Mr Parton.

I did not stop to hear any further commentary on the matter, but bidding my fellow-clerks goodbye, shook the dust of Frimpton's Estate and Agency Office from off my feet.

I did not like to go home and say I was discharged, so I walked about aimlessly, and at length found myself in Regent Street. There I met my father, looking more worried than usual.

'Do you think, Phil,' he said (my name is Theophilus), 'you could get two or three pounds from your employers?'

Maintaining a discreet silence regarding what had passed, I answered:

'No doubt I could.'

'I shall be glad if you will then, my boy,' he went on, 'for we are badly in want of it.'

I did not ask him what was the special trouble. Where would have been the use? There was always something—gas, or water, or poor-rates, or the butcher, or the baker, or the bootmaker. Well, it did not much matter, for we were well accustomed to the life; but, I thought, 'if ever I marry, we will keep within our means'. And then there rose up before me a vision of Patty, my cousin—the blithest, prettiest, most useful, most sensible girl that ever made sunshine in poor man's house.

My father and I had parted by this time, and I was still walking aimlessly on, when all at once an idea occurred to me. Mr Fryer had not treated me well or fairly. I would hoist him on his own petard. I would go to headquarters, and try to make terms with Mr Carrison direct.

No sooner thought than done. I hailed a passing omnibus, and was ere long in the heart of the city. Like other great men, Mr Carrison was difficult of access—indeed, so difficult of access, that the clerk to whom I applied for an audience told me plainly I could not see him at all. I might send in my message if I liked, he was good enough to add, and no doubt it would be attended to. I said I should not send in a message, and was then asked what I would do. My answer was simple. I meant to wait till I did see him. I was told they could not have people waiting about the office in this way.

I said I supposed I might stay in the street. 'Carrison didn't own that,' I suggested.

The clerk advised me not to try that game, or I might get locked up.

I said I would take my chance of it.

After that we went on arguing the question at some length, and we were in the middle of a heated argument, in which several of Carrison's 'young gentlemen', as they called themselves, were good enough to join, when we were all suddenly silenced by a grave-looking individual, who authoritatively enquired:

'What is all this noise about?'

Before anyone could answer I spoke up:

'I want to see Mr Carrison, and they won't let me.'

'What do you want with Mr Carrison?'

'I will tell that to himself only.'

'Very well, say on—I am Mr Carrison.'

For a moment I felt abashed and almost ashamed of my persistency; next instant, however, what Mr Fryer would have called my 'native audacity' came to the rescue, and I said, drawing a step or two nearer to him, and taking off my hat:

'I wanted to speak to you about Ladlow Hall, if you please, sir.'

In an instant the fashion of his face changed, a look of irritation succeeded to that of immobility; an angry contraction of the eyebrows disfigured the expression of his countenance.

'Ladlow Hall!' he repeated; 'and what have you got to say about Ladlow Hall?'

'That is what I wanted to tell you, sir,' I answered, and a dead hush seemed to fall on the office as I spoke.

The silence seemed to attract his attention, for he looked sternly at the clerks, who were not using a pen or moving a finger.

'Come this way, then,' he said abruptly; and next minute I was in his private office.

'Now, what is it?' he asked, flinging himself into a chair, and addressing me, who stood hat in hand beside the great table in the middle of the room.

I began—I will say he was a patient listener—at the very beginning, and told my story straight through. I concealed nothing. I enlarged on nothing. A discharged clerk I stood before him, and in the capacity of a discharged clerk I said what I had to say. He heard me to the end, then he sat silent, thinking.

At last he spoke.

'You have heard a great deal of conversation about Ladlow, I suppose?' he remarked.

'No sir; I have heard nothing except what I have told you.'

'And why do you desire to strive to solve such a mystery?'

'If there is any money to be made, I should like to make it, sir.'

'How old are you?'

'Two-and-twenty last January.'

'And how much salary had you at Frimpton's?'

'Twenty pounds a year.'

'Humph! More than you are worth, I should say.'

'Mr Fryer seemed to imagine so, sir, at any rate,' I agreed, sorrowfully.

'But what do you think?' he asked, smiling in spite of himself.

'I think I did quite as much work as the other clerks,' I answered.

'That is not saying much, perhaps,' he observed. I was of his opinion, but I held my peace.

'You will never make much of a clerk, I am afraid,' Mr Carrison proceeded, fitting his disparaging remarks upon me as he might on a lay figure. 'You don't like desk work?'

'Not much, sir.'

'I should judge the best thing you could do would be to emigrate,' he went on, eyeing me critically.

'Mr Fryer said I had better go to Australia or—' I stopped, remembering the alternative that gentleman had presented.

'Or where?' asked Mr Carrison.

'The ——, sir' I explained, softly and apologetically.

He laughed—he lay back in his chair and laughed—and I laughed myself, though ruefully.

After all, twenty pounds was twenty pounds, though I had not thought much of the salary till I lost it.

We went on talking for a long time after that; he asked me all about my father and my early life, and how we lived, and where we lived, and the people we knew; and, in fact, put more questions than I can well remember.

'It seems a crazy thing to do,' he said at last; 'and yet I feel disposed to trust you. The house is standing perfectly empty. I can't live in it, and I can't get rid of it; all my own furniture I have removed, and there is nothing in the place except a few old-fashioned articles belonging to Lord Ladlow. The place is a loss to me. It is of no use trying to let it, and thus, in fact, matters are at a deadlock. You won't be able to find out anything, I know, because, of course, others have tried to solve the mystery ere now; still, if you like to try you may. I will make this bargain with you. If you like to go down, I will pay your reasonable expenses for a fortnight; and if you do any good for me, I will give you a ten-pound note for yourself. Of course I must be satisfied that what you have told me is true and that you are what you represent. Do you know anybody in the city who would speak for you?'

I could think of no one but my uncle. I hinted to Mr Carrison he was not grand enough or rich enough, perhaps, but I knew nobody else to whom I could refer him.

'What!' he said, 'Robert Dorland, of Cullum Street. He does business with us. If he will go bail for your good behaviour I shan't want any further guarantee. Come along.' And to my intense amazement, he rose, put on his hat, walked me across the outer office and along the pavements till we came to Cullum Street.

'Do you know this youth, Mr Dorland?' he said, standing in front of my uncle's desk, and laying a hand on my shoulder.

'Of course I do, Mr Carrison,' answered my uncle, a little apprehensively; for, as he told me afterwards, he could not imagine what mischief I had been up to. 'He is my nephew.'

'And what is your opinion of him—do you think he is a young fellow I may safely trust?'

My uncle smiled, and answered, 'That depends on what you wish to trust him with.'

'A long column of addition, for instance.'

'It would be safer to give that task to somebody else.'

'Oh, uncle!' I remonstrated; for I had really striven to conquer my natural antipathy to figures—worked hard, and every bit of it against the collar.

My uncle got off his stool, and said, standing with his back to the empty fire-grate. 'Tell me what you wish the boy to do, Mr Carrison, and I will tell you whether he will suit your purpose or not. I know him, I believe, better than he knows himself.'

In an easy, affable way, for so rich a man, Mr Carrison took possession of the vacant stool, and nursing his right leg over his left knee, answered:

'He wants to go and shut the open door at Ladlow for me. Do you think he can do that?'

My uncle looked steadily back at the speaker, and said, 'I thought, Mr Carrison, it was quite settled no one could shut it?'

Mr Carrison shifted a little uneasily on his seat, and replied: 'I did not set your nephew the task he fancies he would like to undertake.'

'Have nothing to do with it, Phil,' advised my uncle, shortly.

'You don't believe in ghosts, do you, Mr Dorland?' asked Mr Carrison, with a slight sneer.

'Don't you, Mr Carrison?' retorted my uncle.

There was a pause—an uncomfortable pause—during the course of which I felt the ten pounds, which, in imagination, I had really spent, trembling in the scale. I was not afraid. For ten pounds, or half the money, I would have faced all the inhabitants of spirit land. I longed to tell them so; but something in the way those two men looked at each other stayed my tongue.

'If you ask me the question here in the heart of the city, Mr Dorland,' said Mr Carrison, at length, slowly and carefully, 'I answer "No"; but it you were to put it to me on a dark night at Ladlow, I should beg time to consider. I do not believe in supernatural phenomena myself, and yet—the door at Ladlow is as much beyond my comprehension as the ebbing and flowing of the sea.'

And you can't live at Ladlow?' remarked my uncle.

'I can't live at Ladlow, and what is more, I can't get anyone else to live at Ladlow.'

'And you want to get rid of your lease?'

'I want so much to get rid of my lease that I told Fryer I would give him a handsome sum if he could induce anyone to solve the mystery. Is there any other information you desire, Mr Dorland? Because if here is, you have only to ask and have. I feel I am not here in a prosaic office in the city of London, but in the Palace of Truth.'

My uncle took no notice of the implied compliment. When wine is good it needs no bush. If a man is habitually honest in his speech and in his thoughts, he desires no recognition of the fact.

'I don't think so,' he answered; 'it is for the boy to say what he will do. If he be advised by me he will stick to his ordinary work in his employers' office, and leave ghost-hunting and spirit-laying alone.'

Mr Carrison shot a rapid glance in my direction, a glance which, implying a secret understanding, might have influenced my uncle could I have stooped to deceive my uncle.

'I can't stick to my work there any longer,' I said. 'I got my marching orders today.'

'What *had* you been doing, Phil?' asked my uncle.

'I wanted ten pounds to go and lay the ghost!' I answered, so dejectedly, that both Mr Carrison and my uncle broke out laughing.

'Ten pounds!' cried my uncle, almost between laughing and crying. 'Why, Phil boy, I had rather, poor man though I am, have given thee ten pounds than that thou should'st go ghost-hunting or ghostlaying.'

When he was very much in earnest my uncle went back to thee and thou of his native dialect. I liked the vulgarism, as my mother called it, and I knew my aunt loved to hear him use the caressing words to her. He had risen, not quite from the ranks it is true, but if ever a gentleman came ready born into the world it was Robert Dorland, upon whom at our home everyone seemed to look down.

'What will you do, Edlyd?' asked Mr Carrison; 'you hear what your uncle says, "Give up the enterprise", and what I say; I do not want either to bribe or force your inclinations.'

'I will go, sir,' I answered quite steadily. I am not afraid, and I should like to show you—' I stopped. I had been going to say, 'I should like to show you I am not such a fool as you all take me for,' but I felt such an address would be too familiar, and refrained.

Mr Carrison looked at me curiously. I think he supplied the end of the sentence for himself, but he only answered:

'I should like you to show me that door fast shut; at any rate, if you can stay in the place alone for a fortnight, you shall have your money.'

'I don't like it, Phil,' said my uncle: 'I don't like this freak at all.'

'I am sorry for that, uncle,' I answered, 'for I mean to go.

'When?' asked Mr Carrison.

'Tomorrow morning,' I replied.

'Give him five pounds, Dorland, please, and I will send you my cheque. You will account to me for that sum, you understand,' added Mr Carrison, turning to where I stood.

'A sovereign will be quite enough,' I said.

'You will take five pounds, and account to me for it,' repeated Mr Carrison, firmly; 'also, you will write to me every day, to my private address, and if at any moment you feel the thing too much for you, throw it up. Good afternoon,' and without more formal leave-taking he departed.

'It is of no use talking to you, Phil, I suppose?' said my uncle.

'I don't think it is,' I replied; 'you won't say anything to them at home, will you?'

'I am not very likely to meet any of them, am I?' he answered, without a shade of bitterness—merely stating a fact.

'I suppose I shall not see you again before I start,' I said, 'so I will bid you goodbye now.'

'Goodbye, my lad; I wish I could see you a bit wiser and steadier.'

I did not answer him; my heart was very full, and my eyes too. I had tried, but office-work was not in me, and I felt it was just as vain to ask me to sit on a stool and pore over writing and figures as to think a person born destitute of musical ability could compose an opera.

Of course I went straight to Patty; though we were not then married, though sometimes it seemed to me as if we never should be married, she was my better half then as she is my better half now.

She did not throw cold water on the project; she did not discourage me. What she said, with her dear face aglow with excitement, was, 'I only wish, Phil, I was going with you.' Heaven knows, so did I.

Next morning I was up before the milkman. I had told my people overnight I should be going out of town on business. Patty and I settled the whole plan in detail. I was to breakfast and dress there, for I meant to go down to Ladlow in my volunteer garments. That was a subject upon which my poor father and I never could agree; he called volunteering child's play, and other things equally hard to bear; whilst my brother, a very carpet warrior to my mind, was never weary of ridiculing the force, and chaffing me for imagining I was 'a soldier'.

Patty and I had talked matters over, and settled, as I have said, that I should dress at her father's.

A young fellow I knew had won a revolver at a raffle, and willingly lent it to me. With that and my rifle I felt I could conquer an army.

It was a lovely afternoon when I found myself walking through leafy lanes in the heart of Meadowshire. With every vein of my heart I loved the country, and the country was looking its best just then: grass ripe for the mower, grain forming in the ear, rippling streams, dreamy rivers, old orchards, quaint cottages.

'Oh that I had never to go back to London,' I thought, for I am one of the few people left on earth who love the country and hate cities. I walked on, I walked a long way, and being uncertain as to my road, asked a gentleman who was slowly riding a powerful roan horse under arching trees—a gentleman accompanied by a young lady mounted on a stiff white pony—my way to Ladlow Hall.

'That is Ladlow Hall,' he answered, pointing with his whip over the fence to my left hand. I thanked him and was going on, when he said:

'No one is living there now.'

'I am aware of that,' I answered.

He did not say anything more, only courteously bade me good-day, and rode off. The young lady inclined her head in acknowledgement of my uplifted cap, and smiled kindly. Altogether I felt pleased, little things always did please me. It was a good beginning—halfway to a good ending!

When I got to the Lodge I showed Mr Carrison's letter to the woman, and received the key.

'You are not going to stop up at the Hall alone, are you, sir?' she asked.

'Yes, I am,' I answered, uncompromisingly, so uncompromisingly that she said no more.

The avenue led straight to the house; it was uphill all the way, and bordered by rows of the most magnificent limes I ever beheld. A light iron fence divided the avenue from the park, and between the trunks of the trees I could see the deer browsing and cattle grazing. Ever and *anon* there came likewise to my ear the sound of a sheep-bell.

It was a long avenue, but at length I stood in front of the Hall—a square, solid-looking, old-fashioned house, three storeys high, with no basement; a flight of steps up to the principal entrance; four windows to the right of the door, four windows to the left; the whole building flanked and backed with trees; all the blinds pulled down, a dead silence brooding over the place: the sun westering behind the great trees studding the park. I took all this in as I approached, and afterwards as I stood for a moment under the ample porch; then, remembering the business which had brought me so far, I fitted the great key in the lock, turned the handle, and entered Ladlow Hall.

For a minute—stepping out of the bright sunlight—the place looked to me so dark that I could scarcely distinguish the objects by which I was surrounded; but my eyes soon grew accustomed to the comparative darkness, and I found I was in an immense hall, lighted from the roof, a magnificent old oak staircase conducted to the upper rooms.

The floor was of black and white marble. There were two fireplaces, fitted with dogs for burning wood; around the walls hung pictures, antlers, and horns, and in odd niches and corners stood groups of statues, and the figures of men in complete suits of armour.

To look at the place outside, no one would have expected to find such a hall. I stood lost in amazement and admiration, and then I began to glance more particularly around.

Mr Carrison had not given me any instructions by which to identify the ghostly chamber—which I concluded would most probably be found on the first floor.

I knew nothing of the story connected with it—if there were a story. On that point I had left London as badly provided with mental as with actual luggage—worse provided, indeed, for a hamper, packed by Patty, and a small bag were coming over from the station; but regarding the mystery I was perfectly unencumbered. I had not the faintest idea in which apartment it resided.

Well, I should discover that, no doubt, for myself ere long.

I looked around me—doors—doors—doors I had never before seen so many doors together all at once. Two of them stood open—one wide, the other slightly ajar.

'I'll just shut them as a beginning,' I thought, 'before I go upstairs.'

The doors were of oak, heavy, well-fitting, furnished with good locks and sound handles. After I had closed I tried them. Yes, they were quite secure. I ascended the great staircase feeling curiously like an intruder, paced the corridors, entered the many bedchambers—some quite bare of furniture, others containing articles of an ancient fashion, and no doubt of considerable value—chairs, antique dressing-tables, curious wardrobes, and such like. For the most part the doors were closed, and I shut those that stood open before making my way into the attics.

I was greatly delighted with the attics. The windows lighting them did not, as a rule, overlook the front of the Hall, but commanded wide views over wood, and valley, and meadow. Leaning out of one, I could see, that to the right of the Hall the ground, thickly planted, shelved down to a stream, which came out into the daylight a little distance beyond the plantation, and meandered through the deer park. At the back of the Hall the windows looked out on nothing save a dense wood and a portion of the stable-yard, whilst on the side nearest the point from whence I had come there were spreading gardens surrounded by thick yew hedges, and kitchen-gardens protected by high walls; and further on a farmyard, where I could perceive cows and oxen, and, further still, luxuriant meadows, and fields glad with waving corn.

'What a beautiful place!' I said. 'Carrison must have been a duffer to leave it.' And then I thought what a great ramshackle house it was for anyone to be in all alone.

Getting heated with my long walk, I suppose, made me feel chilly, for I shivered as I drew my head in from the last dormer window, and prepared to go downstairs again.

In the attics, as in the other parts of the house I had as yet explored, I closed the doors, when there were keys locking them; when there were not, trying them, and in all cases, leaving them securely fastened.

When I reached the ground floor the evening was drawing on apace, and I felt that if I wanted to explore the whole house before dusk I must hurry my proceedings.

'I'll take the kitchens next,' I decided, and so made my way to a wilderness of domestic offices lying to the rear of the great hall. Stone passages, great kitchens, an immense servants'-hall, larders, pantries, coal-cellars, beer-cellars, laundries, brewhouses, housekeeper's room—it was not of any use lingering over these details. The mystery that troubled Mr Carrison could scarcely lodge amongst cinders and empty bottles, and there did not seem much else left in this part of the building.

I would go through the living-rooms, and then decide as to the apartments I should occupy myself.

The evening shadows were drawing on apace, so I hurried back into the hall, feeling it was a weird position to be there all alone with those ghostly hollow figures of men in armour, and the statues on which the moon's beams must fall so coldly. I would just look through the lower apartments and then kindle a fire. I had seen quantities of wood in a cupboard close at hand, and felt that beside a blazing hearth, and after a good cup of tea, I should not feel the solitary sensation which was oppressing me.

The sun had sunk below the horizon by this time, for to reach Ladlow I had been obliged to travel by cross lines of railway, and wait besides for such trains as condescended to carry third-class passengers; but there was still light enough in the hall to see all objects distinctly. With my own eyes I saw that one of the doors I had shut with my own hands was standing wide!

I turned to the door on the other side of the hall. It was as I had left it—closed. This, then, was the room—this with the open door For a second I stood appalled; I think I was fairly frightened.

That did not last long, however. There lay the work I had desired to undertake, the foe I had offered to fight; so without more ado I shut the door and tried it.

'Now I will walk to the end of the hall and see what happens,' I considered. I did so. I walked to the foot of the grand staircase and back again, and looked.

The door stood wide open.

I went into the room, after just a spasm of irresolution—went in and pulled up the blinds: a good-sized room, twenty by twenty (I knew, because I paced it afterwards), lighted by two long windows.

The floor, of polished oak, was partially covered with a Turkey carpet. There were two recesses beside the fireplace, one fitted up as a bookcase, the other with an old and elaborately caned cabinet. I was astonished also to find a bedstead in an apartment so little retired from the traffic of the house; and there were also some chairs of an obsolete make, covered, so far as I could make out, with faded tapestry. Beside the bedstead, which stood against the wall opposite to the door, I perceived another door. It was fast locked, the only locked door I had as yet met with in the interior of the house. It was a dreary, gloomy room: the dark panelled walls; the black, shining floor; the windows high from the ground; the antique furniture; the dull four-poster bedstead, with dingy velvet curtains; the gaping chimney; the silk counterpane that looked like a pall.

'Any crime might have been committed in such a room,' I thought pettishly; and then I looked at the door critically.

Someone had been at the trouble of fitting bolts upon it, for when I passed out I not merely shut the door securely, but bolted it as well.

'I will go and get some wood, and then look at it again,' I soliloquized. When I came back it stood wide open once more.

'Stay open, then!' I cried in a fury. 'I won't trouble myself any more with you tonight!'

Almost as I spoke the words, there came a ring at the front door. Echoing through the desolate house, the peal in the then state of my nerves startled me beyond expression.

It was only the man who had agreed to bring over my traps. I bade him lay them down in the hall, and, while looking out some small silver, asked where the nearest post-office was to be found. Not far from the park gates, he said; if I wanted any letter sent, he would drop it in the box for me; the mail-cart picked up the bag at ten o'clock.

I had nothing ready to post then, and told him so. Perhaps the money I gave was more than he expected, or perhaps the dreariness of my position impressed him as it had impressed me, for he paused with his hand on the lock, and asked:

'Are you going to stop here all alone, master?'

'All alone,' I answered, with such cheerfulness as was possible under the circumstances.

'That's the room, you know,' he said, nodding in the direction of the open door, and dropping his voice to a whisper.

'Yes, I know,' I replied.

'What you've been trying to shut it already, have you? Well, you are a game one!' And with this complementary if not very respectful comment he hastened out of the house. Evidently he had no intention of proffering his services towards the solution of the mystery.

I cast one glance at the door—it stood wide open. Through the windows I had left bare to the night, moonlight was beginning to stream cold and silvery. Before I did aught else I felt I must write to Mr Carrison and Patty, so straightway I hurried to one of the great tables in the hall, and lighting a candle my thoughtful link girl had provided, with many other things, sat down and dashed off the two epistles.

Then down the long avenue, with its mysterious lights and shades, with the moonbeams glinting here and there, playing at hide-and-seek round the boles of the trees and through the tracery of quivering leaf and stem, I walked as fast as if I were doing a match against time.

It was delicious, the scent of the summer odours, the smell of the earth; if it had not been for the door I should have felt too happy. As it was—

'Look here, Phil,' I said, all of a sudden; 'life's not child's play, as uncle truly remarks. That door is just the trouble you have now to face, and you must face it! But for that door you would never have been here. I hope you are not going to turn coward the very first night. Courage!—that is your enemy—conquer it.'

'I will try,' my other self answered back. 'I can but try. I can but fail.'

The post-office was at Ladlow Hollow, a little hamlet through which the stream I had remarked dawdling on its way across the park flowed swiftly, spanned by an ancient bridge.

As I stood by the door of the little shop, asking some questions of the postmistress, the same gentleman I had met in the afternoon mounted on his roan horse, passed on foot. He wished me goodnight as he went by, and nodded familiarly to my companion, who curtseyed her acknowledgements.

'His lordship ages fast,' she remarked, following the retreating figure with her eyes.

'His lordship,' I repeated. 'Of whom are you speaking?'

'Of Lord Ladlow,' she said.

'Oh! I have never seen him,' I answered, puzzled.

'Why, *that* was Lord Ladlow!' she exclaimed.

You may be sure I had something to think about as I walked back to the Hall—something beside the moonlight and the sweet night-scents, and the rustle of beast and bird and leaf, that make silence seem more eloquent than noise away down in the heart of the country.

Lord Ladlow! my word, I thought he was hundreds, thousands of miles away; and here I find him—he walking in the opposite direction from his own home—I an inmate of his desolate abode. Hi!—what was that? I heard a noise in a shrubbery close at hand, and in an instant I was in the thick of the underwood. Something shot out and darted into the cover of the further plantation. I followed, but I could catch never a glimpse of it. I did not know the lie of the ground sufficiently to course with success, and I had at length to give up the hunt—heated, baffled, and annoyed.

When I got into the house the moon's beams were streaming down upon the hall; I could see every statue, every square of marble, every piece of armour. For all the world it seemed to me like something in a dream; but I was tired and sleepy, and decided I would not trouble about fire or food, or the open door, till the next morning: I would go to sleep.

With this intention I picked up some of my traps and carried them to a room on the first floor I had selected as small and habitable. I went down for the rest, and this time chanced to lay my hand on my rifle.

It was wet. I touched the floor—it was wet likewise.

I never felt anything like the thrill of delight which shot through me. I had to deal with flesh and blood, and I would deal with it, heaven helping me.

The next morning broke clear and bright. I was up with the lark—had washed, dressed, breakfasted, explored the house before the postman came with my letters.

One from Mr Carrison, one from Patty, and one from my uncle: I gave the man half a crown, I was so delighted, and said I was afraid my being at the Hall would cause him some additional trouble.

'No, sir,' he answered, profuse in his expressions of gratitude; 'I pass here every morning on my way to her ladyship's.'

'Who is her ladyship?' I asked.

'The Dowager Lady Ladlow,' he answered—'the old lord's widow.'

'And where is her place?' I persisted.

'If you keep on through the shrubbery and across the waterfall, you come to the house about a quarter of a mile further up the stream.'

He departed, after telling me there was only one post a day; and I hurried back to the room in which I had breakfasted, carrying my letters with me.

I opened Mr Carrison's first. The gist of it was, 'Spare no expense; if you run short of money telegraph for it.'

I opened my uncle's next. He implored me to return; he had always thought me hair-brained, but he felt a deep interest in and affection for me, and thought he could get me a good berth if I would only try to settle down and promise to stick to my work. The last was from Patty. O Patty, God bless you! Such women, I fancy, the men who fight best in battle, who stick last to a sinking ship, who are firm in life's struggles, who are brave to resist temptation, must have known and loved. I can't tell you more about the letter, except that it gave me strength to go on to the end.

I spent the forenoon considering that door. I looked at it from within and from without. I eyed it critically. I tried whether there was any reason why it should fly open, and I found that so long as I remained on the threshold it remained closed; if I walked even so far away as the opposite side of the hall, it swung wide.

Do what I would, it burst from latch and bolt. I could not lock it because there was no key.

Well, before two o'clock I confess I was baffled.

At two there came a visitor—none other than Lord Ladlow himself. Sorely I wanted to take his horse round to the stables, but he would not hear of it.

'Walk beside me across the park, if you will be so kind,' he said; 'I want to speak to you.'

We went together across the park, and before we parted I felt I could have gone through fire and water for this simple-spoken nobleman.

'You must not stay here ignorant of the rumours which are afloat,' he said. 'Of course, when I let the place to Mr Carrison I knew nothing of the open door.'

'Did you not, sir?—my lord, I mean,' I stammered.

He smiled. 'Do not trouble yourself about my title, which, indeed, carries a very empty state with it, but talk to me as you might to a friend. I had no idea there was any ghost story connected with the Hall, or I should have kept the place empty.'

I did not exactly know what to answer, so I remained silent.

'How did you chance to be sent here?' he asked, after a pause.

I told him. When the first shock was over, a lord did not seem very different from anybody else. If an emperor had taken a morning canter across the park, I might, supposing him equally affable, have spoken as familiarly to him as to Lord Ladlow. My mother always said I entirely lacked the bump of veneration!

Beginning at the beginning, I repeated the whole story, from Parton's remark about the sovereign to Mr Carrison's conversation with my uncle. When I had left London behind in the narrative, however, and arrived at the Hall, I became somewhat more reticent. After all, it was *his* Hall people could not live in—*his* door that would not keep shut; and it seemed to me these were facts he might dislike being forced upon his attention.

But he would have it. What had *I* seen? What did *I* think of the matter? Very honestly I told him I did not know what to say. The door certainly would not remain shut, and there seemed no human agency to account for its persistent opening; but then, on the other hand, ghosts generally did not tamper with firearms, and my rifle, though not loaded, had been tampered with—I was sure of that.

My companion listened attentively. 'You are not frightened, are you?' he enquired at length.

'Not now,' I answered. 'The door did give me a start last evening, but I am not afraid of that since I find someone else is afraid of a bullet.'

He did not answer for a minute; then he said:

'The theory people have set up about the open door is this: As in that room my uncle was murdered, they say the door will never remain shut till the murderer is discovered.'

'Murdered!' I did not like the word at all; it made me feel chill and uncomfortable.

'Yes—he was murdered sitting in his chair, and the assassin has never been discovered. At first many persons inclined to the belief that I killed him; indeed, many are of that opinion still.'

'But you did not, sir—there is not a word of truth in that story, is there?'

He laid his hand on my shoulder as he said:

'No, my lad; not a word. I loved the old man tenderly. Even when he disinherited me for the sake of his young wife, I was sorry, but not angry; and when he sent for me and assured me he had resolved to repair that wrong, I tried to induce him to leave the lady a handsome sum in addition to her jointure. "If you do not, people may think she has not been the source of happiness you expected," I added.

'"Thank you, Hal," he said. "You are a good fellow; we will talk further about this tomorrow."

'And then he bade me goodnight.

'Before morning broke—it was in the summer two years ago—the household was aroused by a fearful scream. It was his death-cry. He had been stabbed from behind in the neck. He was seated in his chair writing—writing a letter to me. But for that I might have found it harder to clear myself than was in the case; for his solicitors came forward and said he had signed a will leaving all his personalty to me—he was very rich—unconditionally, only three days previously. That, of course, supplied the motive, as my lady's lawyer put it. She was very vindictive, spared no expense in trying to prove my guilt, and said openly she would never rest till she saw justice done, if it cost her the whole of her fortune.

'The letter lying before the dead man, over which blood had spurted, she declared must have been placed on his table by me; but the coroner saw there was an animus in this, for the few opening lines stated my uncle's desire to confide in me his reasons for changing his will—reasons, he said, that involved his honour, as they had destroyed his peace. "In the statement you will find sealed up with my will in—" At that point he was dealt his death-blow. The papers were never found, and the will was never proved. My lady put in the former will, leaving her everything. Ill as I could afford to go to law, I was obliged to dispute the matter, and the lawyers are at it still, and very likely will continue at it for years.

'When I lost my good name, I lost my good health, and had to go abroad; and while I was away Mr Carrison took the Hall. Till I returned, I never heard a word about the open door. My solicitor said Mr Carrison was behaving badly; but I think now I must see them or him, and consider what can be done in the affair. As for yourself, it is of vital importance to me that this mystery should be cleared up, and if you are really not timid, stay on. I am too poor to make rash promises, but you won't find me ungrateful.'

'Oh, my lord!' I cried—the address slipped quite easily and naturally off my tongue—'I don't want any more money or anything, if I can only show Patty's father I am good for something—'

'Who is Patty?' he asked.

He read the answer in my face, for he said no more.

'Should you like to have a good dog for company?' he enquired after a pause.

I hesitated; then I said:

'No, thank you. I would rather watch and hunt for myself.'

And as I spoke, the remembrance of that 'something' in the shrubbery recurred to me, and I told him I thought there had been someone about the place the previous evening.

'Poachers,' he suggested; but I shook my head.

'A girl or a woman I imagine. However, I think a dog might hamper me.'

He went away, and I returned to the house. I never left it all day. I did not go into the garden, or the stable-yard, or the shrubbery, or anywhere; I devoted myself solely and exclusively to that door.

If I shut it once, I shut it a hundred times, and always with the same result. Do what I would, it swung wide. Never, however, when I was looking at it. So long as I could endure to remain, it stayed shut—the instant I turned my back, it stood open.

About four o'clock I had another visitor; no other than Lord Ladlow's daughter—the Honourable Beatrice, riding her funny little white pony.

She was a beautiful girl of fifteen or thereabouts, and she had the sweetest smile you ever saw.

'Papa sent me with this,' she said; 'he would not trust any other messenger,' and she put a piece of paper in my hand.

> Keep your food under lock and key; buy what you require yourself. Get your water from the pump in the stable-yard. I am going from home; but if you want anything, go or send to my daughter.

'Any answer?' she asked, patting her pony's neck.

'Tell his lordship, if you please, I will "keep my powder dry"!' I replied.

'You have made papa look so happy,' she said, still patting that fortunate pony.

'If it is in my power, I will make him look happier still, Miss —' and I hesitated, not knowing how to address her.

'Call me Beatrice,' she said, with an enchanting grace; then added, slily, 'Papa promises me I shall be introduced to Patty ere long,' and before I could recover from my astonishment, she had tightened the bit and was turning across the park.

'One moment, please,' I cried. 'You can do something for me.'

'What is it?' and she came back, trotting over the great sweep in front of the house.

'Lend me your pony for a minute.'

She was off before I could even offer to help her alight—off, and gathering up her habit dexterously with one hand, led the docile old sheep forward with the other.

I took the bridle—when I was with horses I felt amongst my own kind—stroked the pony, pulled his ears, and let him thrust his nose into my hand.

Miss Beatrice is a countess now, and a happy wife and mother; but I sometimes see her, and the other night she took me carefully into a conservatory and asked:

'Do you remember Toddy, Mr Edlyd?'

'Remember him!' I exclaimed; 'I can never forget him!'

'He is dead!' she told me, and there were tears in her beautiful eyes as she spoke the words.

'Mr Edlyd, I *loved* Toddy!'

Well, I took Toddy up to the house, and under the third window to the right hand. He was a docile creature, and let me stand on the saddle while I looked into the only room in Ladlow Hall I had been unable to enter.

It was perfectly bare of furniture, there was not a thing in it—not a chair or table, not a picture on the walls, or ornament on the chimney-piece.

'That is where my grand-uncle's valet slept,' said Miss Beatrice. 'It was he who first ran in to help him the night he was murdered.'

'Where is the valet?' I asked.

'Dead,' she answered. 'The shock killed him. He loved his master more than he loved himself.'

I had seen all I wished, so I jumped off the saddle, which I had carefully dusted with a branch plucked from a lilac tree; between jest and earnest pressed the hem of Miss Beatrice's habit to my lips as I arranged its folds; saw her wave her hand as she went at a hand-gallop across the park; and then turned back once again into the lonely house, with the determination to solve the mystery attached to it or die in the attempt.

Why, I cannot explain, but before I went to bed that night I drove a gimlet I found in the stables hard into the floor, and said to the door:

'Now *I* am keeping you open.'

When I went down in the morning the door was close shut, and the handle of the gimlet, broken off short, lying in the hall.

I put my hand to wipe my forehead; it was dripping with perspiration. I did not know what to make of the place at all! I went out into the open air for a few minutes; when I returned the door again stood wide.

If I were to pursue in detail the days and nights that followed, I should weary my readers. I can only say they changed my life. The solitude, the solemnity, the mystery, produced an effect I do not profess to understand, but that I cannot regret.

I have hesitated about writing of the end, but it must come, so let me hasten to it.

Though feeling convinced that no human agency did or could keep the door open, I was certain that some living person had means of access to the house which I could not discover, This was made apparent in trifles which might well have escaped unnoticed had several, or even two people occupied the mansion, but that in my solitary position it was impossible to overlook. A chair would be misplaced, for instance; a path would be visible over a dusty floor; my papers I found were moved; my clothes touched—letters I carried about with me, and kept under my pillow at night; still, the fact remained that when I went to the post-office, and while I was asleep, someone did wander over the house.

On Lord Ladlow's return I meant to ask him for some further particulars of his uncle's death, and I was about to write to Mr Carrison and beg permission to have the door where the valet had slept broken open, when one morning, very early indeed, I spied a hairpin lying close beside it.

What an idiot I had been! If I wanted to solve the mystery of the open door, of course I must keep watch in the room itself. The door would not stay wide unless there was a reason for it, and most certainly a hairpin could not have got into the house without assistance.

I made up my mind what I should do—that I would go to the post early, and take up my position about the hour I had hitherto started for Ladlow Hollow. I felt on the eve of a discovery, and longed for the day to pass, that the night might come.

It was a lovely morning; the weather had been exquisite during the whole week, and I flung the hall-door wide to let in the sunshine and the breeze. As I did so, I saw there was a basket on the top step—a basket filled with rare and beautiful fruit and flowers.

Mr Carrison had let off the gardens attached to Ladlow Hall for the season—he thought he might as well save something out of the fire, he said, so my fare had not been varied with delicacies of that kind. I was very fond of fruit in those days, and seeing a card addressed to me, I instantly selected a tempting peach, and ate it a little greedily perhaps.

I might say I had barely swallowed the last morsel, when Lord Ladlow's caution recurred to me. The fruit had a curious flavour—there was a strange taste hanging about my palate. For a moment, sky, trees and park swam before my eyes; then I made up my mind what to do.

I smelt the fruit—it had all the same faint odour; then I put some in my pocket—took the basket and locked it away—walked round to the farmyard—asked for the loan of a horse that was generally driven in a light cart, and in less than half an hour was asking in Ladlow to be directed to a doctor.

Rather cross at being disturbed so early, he was at first inclined to pooh-pooh my idea; but I made him cut open a pear and satisfy himself the fruit had been tampered with.

'It is fortunate you stopped at the first peach,' he remarked, after giving me a draught, and some medicine to take back, and advising me to keep in the open air as much as possible. 'I should like to retain this fruit and see you again tomorrow.'

We did not think then on how many morrows we should see each other!

Riding across to Ladlow, the postman had given me three letters, but I did not read them till I was seated under a great tree in the park, with a basin of milk and a piece of bread beside me.

Hitherto, there had been nothing exciting in my correspondence. Patty's epistles were always delightful, but they could not be regarded as sensational; and about Mr Carrison's there was a monotony I had begun to find tedious. On this occasion, however, no fault could be found on that score. The contents of his letter greatly surprised me. He said Lord Ladlow had released him from his bargain—that I could, therefore, leave the Hall at once. He enclosed me ten pounds, and said he would consider how he could best advance my interests; and that I had better call upon him at his private house when I returned to London.

'I do not think I shall leave Ladlow yet awhile,' I considered, as I replaced his letter in its envelope. 'Before I go I should like to make it hot for whoever sent me that fruit; so unless Lord Ladlow turns me out I'll stay a little longer.'

Lord Ladlow did not wish me to leave. The third letter was from him. He wrote:

> I shall return home tomorrow night, and see you on Wednesday. I have arranged satisfactorily with Mr Carrison, and as the Hall is my own again, I mean to try to solve the mystery it contains myself. If you choose to stop and help me to do so, you would confer a favour, and I will try to make it worth your while.

'I will keep watch tonight, and see if I cannot give you some news tomorrow,' I thought. And then I opened Patty's letter—the best, dearest, sweetest letter any postman in all the world could have brought me.

If it had not been for what Lord Ladlow said about his sharing my undertaking, I should not have chosen that night for my vigil. I felt ill and languid—fancy, no doubt, to a great degree inducing these sensations. I had lost energy in a most unaccountable manner. The long, lonely days had told upon my spirits—the fidgety feeling which took me a hundred times in the twelve hours to look upon the open door, to close it, and to count how many steps I could take before it opened again, had tried my mental strength as a perpetual blister might have worn away my physical. In no sense was I fit for the task I had set myself, and yet I determined to go through with it. Why had I never before decided to watch in that mysterious chamber? Had I been at the bottom of my heart afraid? In the bravest of us there are depths of cowardice that lurk unsuspected till they engulf our courage.

The day wore on—the long, dreary day; evening approached—the night shadows closed over the Hall. The moon would not rise for a couple of hours more. Everything was still as death. The house had never before seemed to me so silent and so deserted.

I took a light, and went up to my accustomed room, moving about for a time as though preparing for bed; then I extinguished the candle, softly opened the door, turned the key, and put it in my pocket, slipped softly downstairs, across the hall, through the open door. Then I knew I had been afraid, for I felt a thrill of terror as in the dark I stepped over the threshold. I paused and listened—there was not a sound—the night was still and sultry, as though a storm were brewing.

Not a leaf seemed moving—the very mice remained in their holes! Noiselessly I made my way to the other side of the room. There was an old-fashioned easy-chair between the bookshelves and the bed; I sat down in it, shrouded by the heavy curtain.

The hours passed—were ever hours so long? The moon rose, came and looked in at the windows, and then sailed away to the west; but not a sound, no, not even the cry of a bird. I seemed to myself a mere collection of nerves. Every part of my body appeared twitching. It was agony to remain still; the desire to move became a form of torture. Ah! a streak in the sky; morning at last, Heaven be praised! Had ever anyone before so welcomed the dawn? A thrush began to sing—was there ever heard such delightful music? It was the morning twilight, soon the sun would rise; soon that awful vigil would be over, and yet I was no nearer the mystery than before. Hush! what was that? *It had come.* After the hours of watching and waiting; after the long night and the long suspense, it came in a moment.

The locked door opened—so suddenly, so silently, that I had barely time to draw back behind the curtain, before I saw a woman in the room. She went straight across to the other door and closed it, securing it as I saw with bolt and lock. Then just glancing around, she made her way to the cabinet, and with a key she produced shot back the wards. I did not stir, I scarcely breathed, and yet she seemed uneasy. Whatever she wanted to do she evidently was in haste to finish, for she took out the drawers one by one, and placed them on the floor; then, as the light grew better, I saw her first kneel on the floor, and peer into every aperture, and subsequently repeat the same process, standing on a chair she drew forward for the purpose. A slight, lithe woman, not a lady, clad all in black—not a bit of white about her. What on earth could she want? In a moment it flashed upon me—*The will and the letter! She is searching for them.*

I sprang from my concealment—I had her in my grasp; but she tore herself out of my hands, fighting like a wild-cat: she hit, scratched, kicked, shifting her body as though she had not a bone in it, and at last slipped herself free, and ran wildly towards the door by which she had entered.

If she reached it, she would escape me. I rushed across the room and just caught her dress as she was on the threshold. My blood was up, and I dragged her back: she had the strength of twenty devils, I think, and struggled as surely no woman ever did before.

'I do not want to kill you,' I managed to say in gasps, 'but I will if you do not keep quiet.'

'Bah!' she cried; and before I knew what she was doing she had the revolver out of my pocket and fired.

She missed: the ball just glanced off my sleeve. I fell upon her—I can use no other expression, for it had become a fight for life, and no man can tell the ferocity there is in him till he is placed as I was then—fell upon her, and seized the weapon. She would not let it go, but I held her so tight she could not use it. She bit my face; with her disengaged hand she tore my hair. She turned and twisted and slipped about like a snake, but I did not feel pain or anything except a deadly horror lest my strength should give out.

Could I hold out much longer? She made one desperate plunge, I felt the grasp with which I held her slackening; she felt it too, and seizing her advantage tore herself free, and at the same instant fired again blindly, and again missed.

Suddenly there came a look of horror into her eyes—a frozen expression of fear.

'See!' she cried; and flinging the revolver at me, fled.

I saw, as in a momentary flash, that the door I had beheld locked stood wide—that there stood beside the table an awful figure, with uplifted hand—and then I saw no more. I was struck at last; as she threw the revolver at me she must have pulled the trigger, for I felt something like red-hot iron enter my shoulder, and I could but rush from the room before I fell senseless on the marble pavement of the ball.

When the postman came that morning, finding no one stirring, be looked through one of the long windows that flanked the door; then he ran to the farmyard and called for help.

'There is something wrong inside,' he cried. 'That young gentleman is lying on the floor in a pool of blood.'

As they rushed round to the front of the house they saw Lord Ladlow riding up the avenue, and breathlessly told him what had happened.

'Smash in one of the windows,' he said; 'and go instantly for a doctor.'

They laid me on the bed in that terrible room, and telegraphed for my father. For long I hovered between life and death, but at length I recovered sufficiently to be removed to the house Lord Ladlow owned on the other side of the Hollow.

Before that time I had told him all I knew, and begged him to make instant search for the will.

'Break up the cabinet if necessary,' I entreated, 'I am sure the papers are there.'

And they were. His lordship got his own, and as to the scandal and the crime, one was hushed up and the other remained unpunished. The dowager and her maid went abroad the very morning I lay on the marble pavement at Ladlow Hall—they never returned.

My lord made that one condition of his silence.

Not in Meadowshire, but in a fairer county still, I have a farm which I manage, and make both ends meet comfortably.

Patty is the best wife any man ever possessed—and I—well, I am just as happy if a trifle more serious than of old; but there are times when a great horror of darkness seems to fall upon me, and at such periods I cannot endure to be left alone.

An Account of Some Strange Disturbances in Aungier Street

J. Sheridan Le Fanu

It is not worth telling, this story of mine—at least, not worth writing. Told, indeed, as I have sometimes been called upon to tell it, to a circle of intelligent and eager faces, lighted up by a good after-dinner fire on a winter's evening, with a cold wind rising and wailing outside, and all snug and cosy within, it has gone off—though I say it, who should not—indifferent well. But it is a venture to do as you would have me. Pen, ink, and paper are cold vehicles for the marvellous, and a "reader" decidedly a more critical animal than a "listener." If, however, you can induce your friends to read it after nightfall, and when the fireside talk has run for a while on thrilling tales of shapeless terror; in short, if you will secure me the *mollia tempora fandi*, I will go to my work, and say my say, with better heart. Well, then, these conditions presupposed, I shall waste no more words, but tell you simply how it all happened.

My cousin (Tom Ludlow) and I studied medicine together. I think he would have succeeded, had he stuck to the profession; but he preferred the Church, poor fellow, and died early, a sacrifice to contagion, contracted in the noble discharge of his duties. For my present purpose, I say enough of his character when I mention that he was of a sedate but frank and cheerful nature; very exact in his observance of truth, and not by any means like myself—of an excitable or nervous temperament.

My Uncle Ludlow—Tom's father—while we were attending lectures, purchased three or four old houses in Aungier Street, one of which was unoccupied. *He* resided in the country, and Tom proposed that we should take up our abode in the untenanted house, so long as it should continue unlet; a move which would accomplish the double end of settling us nearer alike to our lecture-rooms and to our amusements, and of relieving us from the weekly charge of rent for our lodgings.

Our furniture was very scant—our whole equipage remarkably modest and primitive; and, in short, our arrangements pretty nearly as simple as those of a bivouac. Our new plan was, therefore, executed almost as soon as conceived. The front drawing-room was our sitting-room. I had the bedroom over it, and Tom the back bedroom on the same floor, which nothing could have induced me to occupy.

The house, to begin with, was a very old one. It had been, I believe, newly fronted about fifty years before; but with this exception, it had nothing modern about it. The agent who bought it and looked into the titles for my uncle, told me that it was sold, along with much other forfeited property, at Chichester House, I think, in 1702; and had belonged to Sir Thomas Hacket, who was Lord Mayor of Dublin in James II.'s time. How old it was *then*, I can't say; but, at all events, it had seen years and changes enough to have contracted all that mysterious and saddened air, at once exciting and depressing, which belongs to most old mansions.

There had been very little done in the way of modernising details; and, perhaps, it was better so; for there was something queer and by-gone in the very walls and ceilings—in the shape of doors and windows—in the odd diagonal site of the chimney-pieces—in the beams and ponderous cornices—not to mention the singular solidity of all the woodwork, from the banisters to the windowframes, which hopelessly defied disguise, and would have emphatically proclaimed their antiquity through any conceivable amount of modern finery and varnish.

An effort had, indeed, been made, to the extent of papering the drawing-rooms; but somehow, the paper looked raw and out of keeping; and the old woman, who kept a little dirt-pie of a shop in the lane, and whose daughter—a girl of two and fifty—was our solitary handmaid, coming in at sunrise, and chastely receding again as soon as she had made all ready for tea in our state apartment;—this woman, I say, remembered it, when old Judge Horrocks (who, having earned the reputation of a particularly "hanging judge," ended by hanging himself, as the coroner's jury found, under an impulse of "temporary insanity," with a child's skipping-rope, over the massive old banisters) resided there, entertaining good company, with fine venison and rare old port. In those halcyon days, the drawing-rooms were hung with gilded leather, and, I dare say, cut a good figure, for they were really spacious rooms.

The bedrooms were wainscoted, but the front one was not gloomy; and in it the cosiness of antiquity quite overcame its sombre associations. But the back bedroom, with its two queerly-placed melancholy windows, staring vacantly at the foot of the bed, and with the shadowy recess to be found in most old houses in Dublin, like a large ghostly closet, which, from congeniality of temperament, had amalgamated with the bedchamber, and dissolved the partition. At night-time, this "alcove"—as our "maid" was wont to call it—had, in my eyes, a specially sinister and suggestive character. Tom's distant and solitary candle glimmered vainly into its darkness. *There* it was always overlooking him—always itself impenetrable. But this was only part of the effect.

The whole room was, I can't tell how, repulsive to me. There was, I suppose, in its proportions and features, a latent discord—a certain mysterious and indescribable relation, which jarred indistinctly upon some secret sense of the fitting and the safe, and raised indefinable suspicions and apprehensions of the imagination. On the whole, as I began by saying, nothing could have induced me to pass a night alone in it.

I had never pretended to conceal from poor Tom my superstitious weakness; and he, on the other hand, most unaffectedly ridiculed my tremors. The sceptic was, however, destined to receive a lesson, as you shall hear.

We had not been very long in occupation of our respective dormitories, when I began to complain of uneasy nights and disturbed sleep. I was, I suppose, the more impatient under this annoyance, as I was usually a sound sleeper, and by no means prone to nightmares. It was now, however, my destiny, instead of enjoying my customary repose, every night to "sup full of horrors." After a preliminary course of disagreeable and frightful dreams, my troubles took a definite form, and the same vision, without an appreciable variation in a single detail, visited me at least (on an average) every second night in the week.

Now, this dream, nightmare, or infernal illusion—which you please—of which I was the miserable sport, was on this wise:—

I saw, or thought I saw, with the most abominable distinctness, although at the time in profound darkness, every article of furniture and accidental arrangement of the chamber in which I lay. This, as you know, is incidental to ordinary nightmare. Well, while in this clairvoyant condition, which seemed but the lighting up of the theatre in which was to be exhibited the monotonous tableau of horror, which made my nights insupportable, my attention invariably became, I know not why, fixed upon the windows opposite the foot of my bed; and, uniformly with the same effect, a sense of dreadful anticipation always took slow but sure possession of me.

I became somehow conscious of a sort of horrid but undefined preparation going forward in some unknown quarter, and by some unknown agency, for my torment; and, after an interval, which always seemed to me of the same length, a picture suddenly flew up to the window, where it remained fixed, as if by an electrical attraction, and my discipline of horror then commenced, to last perhaps for hours. The picture thus mysteriously glued to the window-panes, was the portrait of an old man, in a crimson flowered silk dressing-gown, the folds of which I could now describe, with a countenance embodying a strange mixture of intellect, sensuality, and power, but withal sinister and full of malignant omen.

His nose was hooked, like the beak of a vulture; his eyes large, grey, and prominent, and lighted up with a more than mortal cruelty and coldness. These features were surmounted by a crimson velvet cap, the hair that peeped from under which was white with age, while the eyebrows retained their original blackness. Well I remember every line, hue, and shadow of that stony countenance, and well I may! The gaze of this hellish visage was fixed upon me, and mine returned it with the inexplicable fascination of nightmare, for what appeared to me to be hours of agony. At last——

The cock he crew, away then flew

the fiend who had enslaved me through the awful watches of the night; and, harassed and nervous, I rose to the duties of the day.

I had—I can't say exactly why, but it may have been from the exquisite anguish and profound impressions of unearthly horror, with which this strange phantasmagoria was associated—an insurmountable antipathy to describing the exact nature of my nightly troubles to my friend and comrade. Generally, however, I told him that I was haunted by abominable dreams; and, true to the imputed materialism of medicine, we put our heads together to dispel my horrors, not by exorcism, but by a tonic.

I will do this tonic justice, and frankly admit that the accursed portrait began to intermit its visits under its influence. What of that? Was this singular apparition—as full of character as of terror—therefore the creature of my fancy, or the invention of my poor stomach? Was it, in short, *subjective* (to borrow the technical slang of the day) and not the palpable aggression and intrusion of an external agent? That, good friend, as we will both admit, by no means follows. The evil spirit, who enthralled my senses in the shape of that portrait, may have been just as near me, just as energetic, just as malignant, though I saw him not.

What means the whole moral code of revealed religion regarding the due keeping of our own bodies, soberness, temperance, etc.? here is an obvious connexion between the material and the invisible; the healthy tone of the system, and its unimpaired energy, may, for aught we can tell, guard us against influences which would otherwise render life itself terrific. The mesmerist and the electro-biologist will fail upon an average with nine patients out of ten—so may the evil spirit. Special conditions of the corporeal system are indispensable to the production of certain spiritual phenomena. The operation succeeds sometimes—sometimes fails—that is all.

I found afterwards that my would-be sceptical companion had his troubles too. But of these I knew nothing yet. One night, for a wonder, I was sleeping soundly, when I was roused by a step on the lobby outside my room, followed by the loud clang of what turned out to be a large brass candlestick, flung with all his force by poor Tom Ludlow over the banisters, and rattling with a rebound down the second flight of stairs; and almost concurrently with this, Tom burst open my door, and bounced into my room backwards, in a state of extraordinary agitation.

I had jumped out of bed and clutched him by the arm before I had any distinct idea of my own whereabouts. There we were—in our shirts—standing before the open door—staring through the great old banister opposite, at the lobby window, through which the sickly light of a clouded moon was gleaming.

"What's the matter, Tom? What's the matter with you? What the devil's the matter with you, Tom?" I demanded shaking him with nervous impatience.

He took a long breath before he answered me, and then it was not very coherently.

"It's nothing, nothing at all—did I speak?—what did I say?—where's the candle, Richard? It's dark; I—I had a candle!"

"Yes, dark enough," I said; "but what's the matter?—what *is* it?—why don't you speak, Tom?—have you lost your wits?—what is the matter?"

"The matter?—oh, it is all over. It must have been a dream—nothing at all but a dream—don't you think so? It could not be anything more than a dream."

"Of *course*" said I, feeling uncommonly nervous, "it *was* a dream."

"I thought," he said, "there was a man in my room, and—and I jumped out of bed; and—and—where's the candle?"

"In your room, most likely," I said, "shall I go and bring it?"

"No; stay here—don't go; it's no matter—don't, I tell you; it was all a dream. Bolt the door, Dick; I'll stay here with you—I feel nervous. So, Dick, like a good fellow, light your candle and open the window—I am in a *shocking state*."

I did as he asked me, and robing himself like Granuaile in one of my blankets, he seated himself close beside my bed.

Everybody knows how contagious is fear of all sorts, but more especially that particular kind of fear under which poor Tom was at that moment labouring. I would not have heard, nor I believe would he have recapitulated, just at that moment, for half the world, the details of the hideous vision which had so unmanned him.

"Don't mind telling me anything about your nonsensical dream, Tom," said I, affecting contempt, really in a panic; "let us talk about something else; but it is quite plain that this dirty old house disagrees with us both, and hang me if I stay here any longer, to be pestered with indigestion and—and—bad nights, so we may as well look out for lodgings—don't you think so?—at once."

Tom agreed, and, after an interval, said—

"I have been thinking, Richard, that it is a long time since I saw my father, and I have made up my mind to go down tomorrow and return in a day or two, and you can take rooms for us in the meantime."

I fancied that this resolution, obviously the result of the vision which had so profoundly scared him, would probably vanish next morning with the damps and shadows of night. But I was mistaken. Off went Tom at peep of day to the country, having agreed that so soon as I had secured suitable lodgings, I was to recall him by letter from his visit to my Uncle Ludlow.

Now, anxious as I was to change my quarters, it so happened, owing to a series of petty procrastinations and accidents, that nearly a week elapsed before my bargain was made and my letter of recall on the wing to Tom; and, in the meantime, a trifling adventure or two had occurred to your humble servant, which, absurd as they now appear, diminished by distance, did certainly at the time serve to whet my appetite for change considerably.

A night or two after the departure of my comrade, I was sitting by my bedroom fire, the door locked, and the ingredients of a tumbler of hot whisky-punch upon the crazy spider-table; for, as the best mode of keeping the

Black spirits and white,
Blue spirits and grey,

with which I was environed, at bay, I had adopted the practice recommended by the wisdom of my ancestors, and "kept my spirits up by pouring spirits down." I had thrown aside my volume of Anatomy, and was treating myself by way of a tonic, preparatory to my punch and bed, to half-a-dozen pages of the *Spectator*, when I heard a step on the flight of stairs descending from the attics. It was two o'clock, and the streets were as silent as a churchyard—the sounds were, therefore, perfectly distinct. There was a slow, heavy tread, characterised by the emphasis and deliberation of age, descending by the narrow staircase from above; and, what made the sound more singular, it was plain that the feet which produced it were perfectly bare, measuring the descent with something between a pound and a flop, very ugly to hear.

I knew quite well that my attendant had gone away many hours before, and that nobody but myself had any business in the house. It was quite plain also that the person who was coming down stairs had no intention whatever of concealing his movements; but, on the contrary, appeared disposed to make even more noise, and proceed more deliberately, than was at all necessary. When the step reached the foot of the stairs outside my room, it seemed to stop; and I expected every moment to see my door open spontaneously, and give admission to the original of my detested portrait. I was, however, relieved in a few seconds by hearing the descent renewed, just in the same manner, upon the staircase leading down to the drawing-rooms, and thence, after another pause, down the next flight, and so on to the hall, whence I heard no more.

Now, by the time the sound had ceased, I was wound up, as they say, to a very unpleasant pitch of excitement. I listened, but there was not a stir. I screwed up my courage to a decisive experiment—opened my door, and in a stentorian voice bawled over the banisters, "Who's there?" There was no answer but the ringing of my own voice through the empty old house,—no renewal of the movement; nothing, in short, to give my unpleasant sensations a definite direction. There is,

I think, something most disagreeably disenchanting in the sound of one's own voice under such circumstances, exerted in solitude, and in vain. It redoubled my sense of isolation, and my misgivings increased on perceiving that the door, which I certainly thought I had left open, was closed behind me; in a vague alarm, lest my retreat should be cut off, I got again into my room as quickly as I could, where I remained in a state of imaginary blockade, and very uncomfortable indeed, till morning.

Next night brought no return of my barefooted fellow-lodger; but the night following, being in my bed, and in the dark—somewhere, I suppose, about the same hour as before, I distinctly heard the old fellow again descending from the garrets.

This time I had had my punch, and the *morale* of the garrison was consequently excellent. I jumped out of bed, clutched the poker as I passed the expiring fire, and in a moment was upon the lobby. The sound had ceased by this time—the dark and chill were discouraging; and, guess my horror, when I saw, or thought I saw, a black monster, whether in the shape of a man or a bear I could not say, standing, with its back to the wall, on the lobby, facing me, with a pair of great greenish eyes shining dimly out. Now, I must be frank, and confess that the cupboard which displayed our plates and cups stood just there, though at the moment I did not recollect it.

At the same time I must honestly say, that making every allowance for an excited imagination, I never could satisfy myself that I was made the dupe of my own fancy in this matter; for this apparition, after one or two shiftings of shape, as if in the act of incipient transformation, began, as it seemed on second thoughts, to advance upon me in its original form. From an instinct of terror rather than of courage, I hurled the poker, with all my force, at its head; and to the music of a horrid crash made my way into my room, and double-locked the door. Then, in a minute more, I heard the horrid bare feet walk down the stairs, till the sound ceased in the hall, as on the former occasion.

If the apparition of the night before was an ocular delusion of my fancy sporting with the dark outlines of our cupboard, and if its horrid eyes were nothing but a pair of inverted teacups, I had, at all events, the satisfaction of having launched the poker with admirable effect, and in true "fancy" phrase, "knocked its two daylights into one," as the commingled fragments of my tea-service testified. I did my best to gather comfort and courage from these evidences; but it would not do. And then what could I say of those horrid bare feet, and the regular tramp, tramp, tramp, which measured the distance of the entire staircase through the solitude of my haunted dwelling, and at an hour when no good influence was stirring? Confound it!—the whole affair was abominable. I was out of spirits, and dreaded the approach of night.

It came, ushered ominously in with a thunder-storm and dull torrents of depressing rain. Earlier than usual the streets grew silent; and by twelve o'clock nothing but the comfortless pattering of the rain was to be heard.

I made myself as snug as I could. I lighted *two* candles instead of one. I forswore bed, and held myself in readiness for a sally, candle in hand; for, *coute qui coute*, I was resolved to *see* the being, if visible at all, who troubled the nightly stillness of my mansion. I was fidgety and nervous and tried in vain to interest myself with my books. I walked up and down my room, whistling in turn martial and hilarious music, and listening ever and anon for the dreaded noise. I sate down and stared at the square label on the solemn and reserved-looking black bottle, until "FLANAGAN & CO'S BEST OLD MALT WHISKY" grew into a sort of subdued accompaniment to all the fantastic and horrible speculations which chased one another through my brain.

Silence, meanwhile, grew more silent, and darkness darker. I listened in vain for the rumble of a vehicle, or the dull clamour of a distant row. There was nothing but the sound of a rising wind, which had succeeded the thunder-storm that had travelled over the Dublin mountains quite out of hearing. In the middle of this great city I began to feel myself alone with nature, and Heaven knows what beside. My courage was ebbing. Punch, however, which makes beasts of so many, made a man of me again—just in time to hear with tolerable nerve and firmness the lumpy, flabby, naked feet deliberately descending the stairs again.

I took a candle, not without a tremor. As I crossed the floor I tried to extemporise a prayer, but stopped short to listen, and never finished it. The steps continued. I confess I hesitated for some seconds at the door before I took heart of grace and opened it. When I peeped out the lobby was perfectly empty—there was no monster standing on the staircase; and as the detested sound ceased, I was reassured enough to venture forward nearly to the banisters. Horror of horrors! within a stair or two beneath the spot where I stood the unearthly tread smote the floor. My eye caught something in motion; it was about the size of Goliah's foot—it was grey, heavy, and flapped with a dead weight from one step to another. As I am alive, it was the most monstrous grey rat I ever beheld or imagined.

Shakespeare says—"*Some men there are cannot abide a gaping pig, and some that are mad if they behold a cat.*" I went well-nigh out of my wits when I beheld this *rat*; for, laugh at me as you may, it fixed upon me, I thought, a perfectly human expression of malice; and, as it shuffled about and looked up into my face almost from between my feet, I saw, I could swear it—I felt it then, and know it now, the infernal gaze and the accursed countenance of my old friend in the portrait, transfused into the visage of the bloated vermin before me.

I bounced into my room again with a feeling of loathing and horror I cannot describe, and locked and bolted my door as if a lion had been at the other side. D—n him or *it*; curse the portrait and its original! I felt in my soul that the rat—yes, the *rat*, the RAT I had just seen, was that evil being in masquerade, and rambling through the house upon some infernal night lark.

Next morning I was early trudging through the miry streets; and, among other transactions, posted a peremptory note recalling Tom. On my return, however, I found a note from my absent "chum," announcing his intended return next day. I was doubly rejoiced at this, because I had succeeded in getting rooms; and because the change of scene and return of my comrade were rendered specially pleasant by the last night's half ridiculous half horrible adventure.

I slept extemporaneously in my new quarters in Digges' Street that night, and next morning returned for breakfast to the haunted mansion, where I was certain Tom would call immediately on his arrival.

I was quite right—he came; and almost his first question referred to the primary object of our change of residence.

"Thank God," he said with genuine fervour, on hearing that all was arranged. "On *your* account I am delighted. As to myself, I assure you that no earthly consideration could have induced me ever again to pass a night in this disastrous old house."

"Confound the house!" I ejaculated, with a genuine mixture of fear and detestation, "we have not had a pleasant hour since we came to live here"; and so I went on, and related incidentally my adventure with the plethoric old rat.

"Well, if that were *all*," said my cousin, affecting to make light of the matter, "I don't think I should have minded it very much."

"Ay, but its eye—its countenance, my dear Tom," urged I; "if you had seen *that*, you would have felt it might be *anything* but what it seemed."

"I inclined to think the best conjurer in such a case would be an able-bodied cat," he said, with a provoking chuckle.

"But let us hear your own adventure," I said tartly.

At this challenge he looked uneasily round him. I had poked up a very unpleasant recollection.

"You shall hear it, Dick; I'll tell it to you," he said. "Begad, sir, I should feel quite queer, though, telling it *here*, though we are too strong a body for ghosts to meddle with just now."

Though he spoke this like a joke, I think it was serious calculation. Our Hebe was in a corner of the room, packing our cracked delft tea and dinner-services in a basket. She soon suspended operations, and with mouth and eyes wide open became an absorbed listener. Tom's experiences were told nearly in these words:—

"I saw it three times, Dick—three distinct times; and I am perfectly certain it meant me some infernal harm. I was, I say, in danger—in *extreme* danger; for, if nothing else had happened, my reason would most certainly have failed me, unless I had escaped so soon. Thank God. I *did* escape.

"The first night of this hateful disturbance, I was lying in the attitude of sleep, in that lumbering old bed. I hate to think of it. I was really wide awake, though I had put out my candle, and was lying as quietly as if I had been asleep; and although accidentally restless, my thoughts were running in a cheerful and agreeable channel.

"I think it must have been two o'clock at least when I thought I heard a sound in that—that odious dark recess at the far end of the bedroom. It was as if someone was drawing a piece of cord slowly along the floor, lifting it up, and dropping it softly down again in coils. I sate up once or twice in my bed, but could see nothing, so I concluded it must be mice in the wainscot. I felt no emotion graver than curiosity, and after a few minutes ceased to observe it.

"While lying in this state, strange to say; without at first a suspicion of anything supernatural, on a sudden I saw an old man, rather stout and square, in a sort of roan-red dressing-gown, and with a black cap on his head, moving stiffly and slowly in a diagonal direction, from the recess, across the floor of the bedroom, passing my bed at the foot, and entering the lumber-closet at the left. He had something under his arm; his head hung a little at one side; and, merciful God! when I saw his face."

Tom stopped for a while, and then said—

"That awful countenance, which living or dying I never can forget, disclosed what he was. Without turning to the right or left, he passed beside me, and entered the closet by the bed's head.

"While this fearful and indescribable type of death and guilt was passing, I felt that I had no more power to speak or stir than if I had been myself a corpse. For hours after it had disappeared, I was too terrified and weak to move. As soon as daylight came, I took courage, and examined the room, and especially the course which the frightful intruder had seemed to take, but there was not a vestige to indicate anybody's having passed there; no sign of any disturbing agency visible among the lumber that strewed the floor of the closet.

"I now began to recover a little. I was fagged and exhausted, and at last, overpowered by a feverish sleep. I came down late; and finding you out of spirits, on account of your dreams about the portrait, whose *original* I am now certain disclosed himself to me, I did not care to talk about the infernal vision. In fact, I was trying to persuade myself that the whole thing was an illusion, and I did not like to revive in their intensity the hated impressions of the past night—or to risk the constancy of my scepticism, by recounting the tale of my sufferings.

"It required some nerve, I can tell you, to go to my haunted chamber next night, and lie down quietly in the same bed," continued Tom. "I did so with a degree of trepidation, which, I am not ashamed to say, a very little matter would have sufficed to stimulate to downright panic. This night, however, passed off quietly enough, as also the next; and so too did two or three more. I grew more confident, and began to fancy that I believed in the theories of spectral illusions, with which I had at first vainly tried to impose upon my convictions.

"The apparition had been, indeed, altogether anomalous. It had crossed the room without any recognition of my presence: I had not disturbed *it*, and *it* had no mission to *me*. What, then, was the imaginable use of its crossing the room in a visible shape at all? Of course it might have *been* in the closet instead of *going* there, as easily as it introduced itself into the recess without entering the chamber in a shape discernible by the senses. Besides, how the deuce *had* I seen it? It was a dark night; I had no candle; there was no fire; and yet I saw it as distinctly, in colouring and outline, as ever I beheld human form! A cataleptic dream would explain it all; and I was determined that a dream it should be.

"One of the most remarkable phenomena connected with the practice of mendacity is the vast number of deliberate lies we tell ourselves, whom, of all persons, we can least expect to deceive. In all this, I need hardly tell you, Dick, I was simply lying to myself, and did not believe one word of the wretched humbug. Yet I went on, as men will do, like persevering charlatans and impostors, who tire people into credulity by the mere force of reiteration; so I hoped to win myself over at last to a comfortable scepticism about the ghost.

"He had not appeared a second time—that certainly was a comfort; and what, after all, did I care for him, and his queer old toggery and strange looks? Not a fig! I was nothing the worse for having seen him, and a good story the better. So I tumbled into bed, put out my candle, and, cheered by a loud drunken quarrel in the back lane, went fast asleep.

"From this deep slumber I awoke with a start. I knew I had had a horrible dream; but what it was I could not remember. My heart was thumping furiously; I felt bewildered and feverish; I sate up in the bed and looked about the room. A broad flood of moonlight came in through the curtainless window; everything was as I had last seen it; and though the domestic squabble in the back lane was, unhappily for me, allayed, I yet could hear a pleasant fellow singing, on his way home, the then popular comic ditty called, 'Murphy Delany.' Taking advantage of this diversion I lay down again, with my face towards the fireplace, and closing my eyes, did my best to think of nothing else but the song, which was every moment growing fainter in the distance:—

"' *Twas Murphy Delany, so funny and frisky,*
Stept into a shebeen shop to get his skin full;
He reeled out again pretty well lined with whiskey,
As fresh as a shamrock, as blind as a bull.

"The singer, whose condition I dare say resembled that of his hero, was soon too far off to regale my ears anymore; and as his music died away, I myself sank into a doze, neither sound nor refreshing. Somehow the song had got into my head, and I went meandering on through the adventures of my respectable fellow-countryman, who, on emerging from the 'shebeen shop,' fell into a river, from which he was fished up to be 'sat upon' by a coroner's jury, who having learned from a 'horse-doctor' that he was 'dead as a door-nail, so there was an end,' returned their verdict accordingly, just as he returned to his senses, when an angry altercation and a pitched battle between the body and the coroner winds up the lay with due spirit and pleasantry.

"Through this ballad I continued with a weary monotony to plod, down to the very last line, and then *da capo*, and so on, in my uncomfortable half-sleep, for how long, I can't conjecture. I found myself at last, however, muttering, '*dead* as a door-nail, so there was an end'; and something like another voice within me, seemed to say, very faintly, but sharply, 'dead! dead! *dead*! and may the Lord have mercy on your soul!' and instantaneously I was wide awake, and staring right before me from the pillow.

"Now—will you believe it, Dick?—I saw the same accursed figure standing full front, and gazing at me with its stony and fiendish countenance, not two yards from the bedside."

Tom stopped here, and wiped the perspiration from his face. I felt very queer. The girl was as pale as Tom; and, assembled as we were in the very scene of these adventures, we were all, I dare say, equally grateful for the clear daylight and the resuming bustle out of doors.

"For about three seconds only I saw it plainly; then it grew indistinct; but, for a long time, there was something like a column of dark vapour where it had been standing, between me and the wall; and I felt sure that he was still there. After a good while, this appearance went too. I took my clothes downstairs to the hall, and dressed there, with the door half open; then went out into the street, and walked about the town till morning, when I came back, in a miserable state of nervousness and exhaustion. I was such a fool, Dick, as to be ashamed to tell you how I came to be so upset. I thought you would laugh at me; especially as I had always talked philosophy, and treated *your* ghosts with contempt. I concluded you would give me no quarter; and so kept my tale of horror to myself.

"Now, Dick, you will hardly believe me, when I assure you, that for many nights after this last experience, I did not go to my room at all. I used to sit up for a while in the drawing-room after you had gone up to your bed; and then steal down softly to the hall-door, let myself out, and sit in the 'Robin Hood' tavern until the last guest went off; and then I got through the night like a sentry, pacing the streets till morning.

"For more than a week I never slept in bed. I sometimes had a snooze on a form in the 'Robin Hood,' and sometimes a nap in a chair during the day; but regular sleep I had absolutely none.

"I was quite resolved that we should get into another house; but I could not bring myself to tell you the reason, and I somehow put it off from day to day, although my life was, during every hour of this procrastination, rendered as miserable as that of a felon with the constables on his track. I was growing absolutely ill from this wretched mode of life.

"One afternoon I determined to enjoy an hour's sleep upon your bed. I hated mine; so that I had never, except in a stealthy visit every day to unmake it, lest Martha should discover the secret of my nightly absence, entered the ill-omened chamber.

"As ill-luck would have it, you had locked your bedroom, and taken away the key. I went into my own to unsettle the bedclothes, as usual, and give the bed the appearance of having been slept in. Now, a variety of circumstances concurred to bring about the dreadful scene through which I was that night to pass. In the first place, I was literally overpowered with fatigue, and longing for sleep; in the next place, the effect of this extreme exhaustion upon my nerves resembled that of a narcotic, and rendered me less susceptible than, perhaps, I should in any other condition have been, of the exciting fears which had become habitual to me. Then again, a little bit of the window was open, a pleasant freshness pervaded the room, and, to crown all, the cheerful sun of day was making the room quite pleasant. What was to prevent my enjoying an hour's nap *here*? The whole air was resonant with the cheerful hum of life, and the broad matter-of-fact light of day filled every corner of the room.

"I yielded—stifling my qualms—to the almost overpowering temptation; and merely throwing off my coat, and loosening my cravat, I lay down, limiting myself to *half*-an-hour's doze in the unwonted enjoyment of a feather bed, a coverlet, and a bolster.

"It was horribly insidious; and the demon, no doubt, marked my infatuated preparations. Dolt that I was, I fancied, with mind and body worn out for want of sleep, and an arrear of a full week's rest to my credit, that such measure as *half*-an-hour's sleep, in such a situation, was possible. My sleep was death-like, long, and dreamless.

"Without a start or fearful sensation of any kind, I waked gently, but completely. It was, as you have good reason to remember, long past midnight—I believe, about two o'clock. When sleep has been deep and long enough to satisfy nature thoroughly, one often wakens in this way, suddenly, tranquilly, and completely.

"There was a figure seated in that lumbering, old sofa-chair, near the fireplace. Its back was rather towards me, but I could not be mistaken; it turned slowly round, and, merciful heavens! there was the stony face, with its infernal lineaments of malignity and despair, gloating on me. There was now no doubt as to its consciousness of my presence, and the hellish malice with which it was animated, for it arose, and drew close to the bedside. There was a rope about its neck, and the other end, coiled up, it held stiffly in its hand.

"My good angel nerved me for this horrible crisis. I remained for some seconds transfixed by the gaze of this tremendous phantom. He came close to the bed, and appeared on the point of mounting upon it. The next instant I was upon the floor at the far side, and in a moment more was, I don't know how, upon the lobby.

"But the spell was not yet broken; the valley of the shadow of death was not yet traversed. The abhorred phantom was before me there; it was standing near the banisters, stooping a little, and with one end of the rope round its own neck, was poising a noose at the other, as if to throw over mine; and while engaged in this baleful pantomime, it wore a smile so sensual, so unspeakably dreadful, that my senses were nearly overpowered. I saw and remember nothing more, until I found myself in your room.

"I had a wonderful escape, Dick—there is no disputing *that*—an escape for which, while I live, I shall bless the mercy of heaven. No one can conceive or imagine what it is for flesh and blood to stand in the presence of such a thing, but one who has had the terrific experience. Dick, Dick, a shadow has passed over me—a chill has crossed my blood and marrow, and I will never be the same again—never, Dick—never!"

Our handmaid, a mature girl of two-and-fifty, as I have said, stayed her hand, as Tom's story proceeded, and by little and little drew near to us, with open mouth, and her brows contracted over her little, beady black eyes, till stealing a glance over her shoulder now and then, she established herself close behind us. During the relation, she had made various earnest comments, in an undertone; but these and her ejaculations, for the sake of brevity and simplicity, I have omitted in my narration.

"It's often I heard tell of it," she now said, "but I never believed it rightly till now—though, indeed, why should not I? Does not my mother, down there in the lane, know quare stories, God bless us, beyant telling about it? But you ought not to have slept in the back bedroom. She was loath to let me be going in and out of that room even in the day time, let alone for any Christian to spend the night in it; for sure she says it was his own bedroom."

"*Whose* own bedroom?" we asked, in a breath.

"Why, *his*—the ould Judge's—Judge Horrock's, to be sure, God rest his sowl"; and she looked fearfully round.

"Amen!" I muttered. "But did he die there?"

"Die there! No, not quite *there*," she said. "Shure, was not it over the banisters he hung himself, the ould sinner, God be merciful to us all? and was not it in the alcove they found the handles of the skipping-rope cut off, and the knife where he was settling the cord, God bless us, to hang himself with? It was his housekeeper's daughter owned the rope, my mother often told me, and the child never throve after, and used to be starting up out of her sleep, and screeching in the night time, wid dhrames and frights that cum an her; and they said how it was the speerit of the ould Judge that was tormentin' her; and she used to be roaring and yelling out to hould back the big ould fellow with the crooked neck; and then she'd screech 'Oh, the master! the master! he's stampin' at me, and beckoning to me! Mother, darling, don't let me go!' And so the poor crathure died at last, and the docthers said it was wather on the brain, for it was all they could say."

"How long ago was all this?" I asked.

"Oh, then, how would I know?" she answered. "But it must be a wondherful long time ago, for the housekeeper was an ould woman, with a pipe in her mouth, and not a tooth left, and better nor eighty years ould when my mother was first married; and they said she was a rale buxom, fine-dressed woman when the ould Judge come to his end; an', indeed, my mother's not far from eighty years ould herself this day; and what made it worse for the unnatural ould villain, God rest his soul, to frighten the little girl out of the world the way he did, was what was mostly thought and believed by everyone. My mother says how the poor little crathure was his own child; for he was by all accounts an ould villain every way, an' the hangin'est judge that ever was known in Ireland's ground."

"From what you said about the danger of sleeping in that bedroom," said I, "I suppose there were stories about the ghost having appeared there to others."

"Well, there was things said—quare things, surely," she answered, as it seemed, with some reluctance. "And why would not there? Sure was it not up in that same room he slept for more than twenty years? and was it not in the *alcove* he got the rope ready that done his own business at last, the way he done many a betther man's in his lifetime?—and was not the body lying in the same bed after death, and put in the coffin there, too, and carried out to his grave from it in Pether's churchyard, after the coroner was done? But there was quare stories—my mother has them all—about how one Nicholas Spaight got into trouble on the head of it."

"And what did they say of this Nicholas Spaight?" I asked.

"Oh, for that matther, it's soon told," she answered.

And she certainly did relate a very strange story, which so piqued my curiosity, that I took occasion to visit the ancient lady, her mother, from whom I learned many very curious particulars. Indeed, I am tempted to tell the tale, but my fingers are weary, and I must defer it. But if you wish to hear it another time, I shall do my best.

When we had heard the strange tale I have *not* told you, we put one or two further questions to her about the alleged spectral visitations, to which the house had, ever since the death of the wicked old Judge, been subjected.

"No one ever had luck in it," she told us. "There was always cross accidents, sudden deaths, and short times in it. The first that tuck, it was a family—I forget their name—but at any rate there was two young ladies and their papa. He was about sixty, and a stout healthy gentleman as you'd wish to see at that age. Well, he slept in that unlucky back bedroom; and, God between us an' harm! sure enough he was found dead one morning, half out of the bed, with his head as black as a sloe, and swelled like a puddin', hanging down near the floor. It was a fit, they said. He was as dead as a mackerel, and so *he* could not say what it was; but the ould people was all sure that it was nothing at all but the ould Judge, God bless us! that frightened him out of his senses and his life together.

"Sometime after there was a rich old maiden lady took the house. I don't know which room *she* slept in, but she lived alone; and at any rate, one morning, the servants going down early to their work, found her sitting on the passage-stairs, shivering and talkin' to herself, quite mad; and never a word more could any of *them* or her friends get from her ever afterwards but, 'Don't ask me to go, for I promised to wait for him.' They never made out from her who it was she meant by *him*, but of course those that knew all about the ould house were at no loss for the meaning of all that happened to her.

"Then afterwards, when the house was let out in lodgings, there was Micky Byrne that took the same room, with his wife and three little children; and sure I heard Mrs. Byrne myself telling how the children used to be lifted up in the bed at night, she could not see by what mains; and how they were starting and screeching every hour, just all as one as the housekeeper's little girl that died, till at last one night poor Micky had a dhrop in him, the way he used now and again;

and what do you think in the middle of the night he thought he heard a noise on the stairs, and being in liquor, nothing less id do him but out he must go himself to see what was wrong. Well, after that, all she ever heard of him was himself sayin', 'Oh, God!' and a tumble that shook the very house; and there, sure enough, he was lying on the lower stairs, under the lobby, with his neck smashed double undher him, where he was flung over the banisters."

Then the handmaiden added—

"I'll go down to the lane, and send up Joe Gavvey to pack up the rest of the taythings, and bring all the things across to your new lodgings."

And so we all sallied out together, each of us breathing more freely, I have no doubt, as we crossed that ill-omened threshold for the last time.

Now, I may add thus much, in compliance with the immemorial usage of the realm of fiction, which sees the hero not only through his adventures, but fairly out of the world. You must have perceived that what the flesh, blood, and bone hero of romance proper is to the regular compounder of fiction, this old house of brick, wood, and mortar is to the humble recorder of this true tale. I, therefore, relate, as in duty bound, the catastrophe which ultimately befell it, which was simply this—that about two years subsequently to my story it was taken by a quack doctor, who called himself Baron Duhlstoerf, and filled the parlour windows with bottles of indescribable horrors preserved in brandy, and the newspapers with the usual grandiloquent and mendacious advertisements. This gentleman among his virtues did not reckon sobriety, and one night, being overcome with much wine, he set fire to his bed curtains, partially burned himself, and totally consumed the house. It was afterwards rebuilt, and for a time an undertaker established himself in the premises.

I have now told you my own and Tom's adventures, together with some valuable collateral particulars; and having acquitted myself of my engagement, I wish you a very goodnight, and pleasant dreams.

The Botathen Ghost

R S Hawker

There was something very painful and peculiar in the position of the clergy in the west of England throughout the seventeenth century. The Church of those days was in a transitory state, and her ministers, like her formularies, embodied a strange mixture of the old belief with the new interpretation. Their wide severance also from the great metropolis of life and manners, the city of London (which in those times was civilized England, much as the Paris of our own day is France), divested the Cornish clergy in particular of all personal access to the master-minds of their age and body. Then, too, the barrier interposed by the rude rough roads of their country, and by their abode in wilds that were almost inaccessible, rendered the existence of a bishop rather a doctrine suggested to their belief than a fact revealed to the actual vision of each in his generation.

Hence it came to pass that the Cornish clergyman, insulated within his own limited sphere, often without even the presence of a country squire (and unchecked by the influence of the Fourth Estate—for until the beginning of this nineteenth century, *Flindell's Weekly Miscellany*, distributed from house to house from the pannier of a mule, was the only light of the West), became developed about middle life into an original mind and man, sole and absolute within his parish boundary, eccentric when compared with his brethren in civilized regions, and yet, in German phrase, 'a whole and seldom man' in his dominion of souls.

He was 'the parson', in canonical phrase—that is to say, The Person, the somebody of consequence among his own people. These men were not, however, smoothed down into a monotonous aspect of life and manners by this remote and secluded existence. They imbibed, each in his own peculiar circle, the hue of surrounding objects, and were tinged into a distinctive colouring and character by many a contrast of scenery and people.

There was the 'light of other days', the curate by the sea-shore, who professed to check the turbulence of the 'smugglers' landing by his presence on the sands, and who 'held the lantern' for the guidance of his flock when the nights were dark, as the only proper ecclesiastical part he could take in the proceedings. He was soothed and silenced by the gift of a keg of hollands or a chest of tea. There was the merry minister of the mines, whose cure was honeycombed by the underground men. He must needs have been artist and poet in his way, for he had to enliven his people three or four times a-year, by mastering the arrangements of a 'guary.', or religious mystery, which was duly performed in the topmost hollow of a green barrow or hill, of which many survive, scooped out into vast amphitheatres and surrounded by benches of turf which held two thousand spectators.

Such were the historic plays, *The Creation* and *Noe's Flood*, which still exist in the original Celtic as well as the English text, and suggest what critics and antiquaries these Cornish curates, masters of such revels, must have been—for the native language of Cornwall did not lapse into silence until the end of the seventeenth century. Then, moreover, here and there would be one parson more learned than his kind in the mysteries of a deep and thrilling lore of peculiar fascination. He was a man so highly honoured at college for natural gifts and knowledge of learned books which nobody else could read, that when he 'took his second orders' the bishop gave him a mantle of scarlet silk to wear upon his shoulders in church, and his lordship had put such power into it that, when the parson had it rightly on, he could 'govern any ghost or evil spirit', and even 'stop an earthquake'.

Such a powerful minister, in combat with supernatural visitations, was one Parson Rudall, of Launceston, whose existence and exploits we gather from the local tradition of his time, from surviving letters and other memoranda, and indeed from his own 'diurnal' which fell by chance into the hands of the present writer. Indeed, the legend of Parson Rudall and the Botathen Ghost will be recognized by many Cornish people as a local remembrance of their boyhood.

It appears, then, from the diary of this learned master of the grammar school—for such was his office as well as perpetual curate of the parish—'that a pestilential disease did break forth in our town in the beginning of the year *A.D* 1665; yea, and it likewise invaded my school, insomuch that therewithal certain of the chief scholars sickened and died.

'Among others who yielded to the malign influence was Master John Eliot, the eldest son and the worshipful heir of Edward Eliot, Esquire, of Trebursey, a stripling of sixteen years of age, but of uncommon parts and hopeful ingenuity. At his own especial motion and earnest desire, I did consent to preach his funeral sermon.' It should he remembered here that, howsoever strange and singular it may sound to us that a mere lad should formally solicit such a performance at the hands of his master, it was in consonance with the habitual usage of those times. The old services for dead had been abolished by law, and in the stead of sacrament and ceremony, month's mind and year's mind, the sole substitute which survived was the general desire 'to partake', as they called it, of a posthumous discourse, replete with lofty eulogy and flattering remembrance of the living and the dead. The diary proceeds:

'I fulfilled my undertaking, and preached over the coffin in the presence of a full assemblage of mourners and lachrymose friends. An ancient gentleman, who was then and there in the church, a Mr Bligh, of Botathen, was much affected with my discourse, and he was heard to repeat to himself certain parentheses therefrom, especially a phrase from Maro Virgilius, which I had applied to the deceased youth, "*Et puer ipse fuit cantari dignus*."

'The cause wherefore this old gentleman was moved by my applications was this: He had a first-born and only son—a child who, but a very few months before, had been not unworthy the character I drew of young Master Eliot, but who, by some strange accident, had of late quite fallen away from his parent's hopes, and become moody, and sullen, and distraught. When the funeral obsequies were over, I had no sooner come out of church than I was accosted by this aged parent, and he besought me incontinently, with a singular energy, that I would resort with him forthwith to his abode at Botathen that very night; nor could I have delivered myself from his importunity, had not Mr Eliot urged his claim to enjoy my company at his own house. Hereupon I got loose, but not until I had pledged a fast assurance that I would pay him, faithfully, an early visit the next day.'

'The Place', as it was called, of Botathen, where old Mr Bligh resided, was a low-roofed gabled manor-house of the fifteenth century, walled and mullioned, and with clustered chimneys of dark-grey stone from the neighbouring quarries of Ventorgan. The mansion was flanked by a pleasance or enclosure in one space, of garden and lawn, and it was surrounded by a solemn grove of stag-horned trees. It had the sombre aspect of age and of solitude, and looked the very scene of strange and supernatural events. A legend might well belong to every gloomy glade around, and there must surely be a haunted room somewhere within its walls. Hither, according to his appointment, on the morrow, Parson Rudall betook himself. Another clergyman, as it appeared, had been invited to meet him, who, very soon after his arrival, proposed a walk together in the pleasance, on the pretext of showing him, as a stranger, the walks and trees, until the dinner-hell should strike. There, with much prolixity, and with many a solemn pause, his brother minister proceeded to 'unfold the mystery'.

A singular infelicity, he declared, had befallen young Master Bligh, once the hopeful heir of his parents and of the lands of Botathen. Whereas he had been from childhood a blithe and merry boy, 'the gladness', like Isaac of old, of his father's age, he had suddenly, and of late, become morose and silent—nay, even austere and stern—dwelling apart, always solemn, often in tears. The lad had at first repulsed all questions as to the origin of this great change, but of late he had yielded to the importune researches of his parents, and had disclosed the secret cause. It appeared that he resorted every day, by a pathway across the fields, to this very clergyman's house, who had charge of his education, and grounded him in the studies suitable to his age.

In the course of his daily walk he had to pass a certain heath or down where the road wound along through tall blocks of granite with open spaces of grassy sward between. There in a certain spot, and always in one and the same place, the lad declared that he encountered, every day, a woman with a pale and troubled face, clothed in a long loose garment of frieze, with one hand always stretched forth, and the other pressed against her side. Her name, he said, was Dorothy Dinglet, for he had known her well from his childhood, and she often used to come to his parents' house; but that which troubled him was, that she had now been dead three years, and he himself had been with the neighbours at her burial; so that, as the youth alleged, with great simplicity, since he had seen her body laid in the grave, this that he saw every day must needs he her soul or ghost.

'Questioned again and again,' said the clergyman, 'he never contradicts himself; but he relates the same and the simple tale as a thing that cannot be gain-said. Indeed, the lad's observance is keen and calm for a boy of his age. The hair of the appearance, sayeth he, is not like anything alive, but it is so soft and light that it seemeth to melt away while you look; but her eyes are set, and never blink—no, not when the sun shineth lull upon her face. She maketh no steps, but seemeth to swim along the top of the grass; and her hand, which is stretched out alway, seemeth to point at something far away, out of sight. It is her continual coming; for she never faileth to meet him, and to pass on, that hath quenched his spirits; and although he never seeth her by night, yet cannot he get his natural rest.

'Thus far the clergyman; whereupon the dinner-clock did sound, and we went into the house. After dinner, when young Master Bligh had withdrawn with his tutor, under excuse of their books, the parents did forthwith beset me as to my thoughts about their son. Said I, warily, "The case is strange but by no means impossible. It is one that I will study, and fear not to handle, if the lad will be free with me, and fulfil all that I desire." The mother was overjoyed, but I perceived that old Mr thigh turned pale, and was downcast with some thought which, however, he did not express. Then they bade that Master Bligh should be called to meet me in the pleasance forthwith. The boy came, and he rehearsed to me his talc with an open countenance, and, withal, a pretty modesty of speech. Verily he seemed *ingenui vultus puer ingenuique pudoris.* Then I signified to him my purpose. "Tomorrow," said I, "we will go together to the place; and if, as I doubt not, the woman shall appear, it will be for me to proceed according to knowledge, and by rules laid down in my hooks."'

The unaltered scenery of the legend still survives, and, like the field of the forty footsteps in another history, the place is still visited by those who take interest in the supernatural tales of old. The pathway leads along a moorland waste, where large masses of rock stand up here and there from the grassy turf, and clumps of heath and gorse weave their tapestry of golden and purple garniture on every side. Amidst all these, and winding along between the rocks, is a natural footway worn by the scant, rare tread of the village traveller. Just midway, a somewhat larger stretch than usual of green sod expands, which is skirted by the path, and which is still identified as the legendary haunt of the phantom, by the name of Parson Rudall's Ghost.

But we must draw the record of the first interview between the minister and Dorothy from his own words.

'We met', thus he writes, 'in the pleasance very early, and before any others in the house were awake; and together the lad and myself proceeded towards the field. The youth was quite composed, and carried his Bible under his arm, from whence he read to me verses, which he said he had lately picked out, to have always in his mind. These were Job vii. 14, "*Thou scarest me with dreams, and terrifiest me through visions*", and Deuteronomy xxviii. 67, "*In the morning thou shalt say, Would to God it were evening, and in the evening thou shalt say, Would to God it were morning; for the tear of thine heart wherewith thou shalt fear, and for the sight of thine eyes which thou shalt see.*"

'I was much pleased with the lad's ingenuity in these pious applications, but for mine own part I was somewhat anxious and out of cheer. For aught I knew this might be a *daemonium meridianum*, the most stubborn spirit to govern and guide that any man can meet, and the most perilous withal. We had hardly reached the accustomed spot, when we both saw her at once gliding towards us; punctually as the ancient writers describe the motion of their "lemures, which swoon along the ground, neither marking the sand nor bending the herbage". The aspect of the woman was exactly that which had been related by the lad. There was the pale and stony face, the strange and misty hair, the eyes firm and fixed, that gazed, yet not on us, but on something that they saw far, far away; one hand and arm stretched out, and the other grasping the girdle of her waist. She floated along the field like a sail upon a stream, and glided past the spot where we stood, pausingly. But so deep was the awe that overcame me, as I stood there in the light of day, face to face with a human soul separate from her bones and flesh, that my heart and purpose both failed me.

'I had resolved to speak to the spectre in the appointed form of words, but I did not. I stood like one amazed and speechless, until she had passed clean out of sight. One thing remarkable came to pass. A spaniel dog, the favourite of young Master Bligh, had followed us, and lo! when the woman drew nigh, the poor creature began to yell and hark piteously, and ran backward and away, like a thing dismayed and appalled. We returned to the house, and after I had said all that I could to pacify the lad, and to soothe the aged people, I took my leave for that time, with a promise that when I had fulfilled certain business elsewhere, which I then alleged, I would return and take orders to assuage these disturbances and their cause.

January 7, 1665. At my own house, I find, by my hooks, what is expedient to be done; and then *Apage, Sathanas!*

'*January 9*, 1665. This day I took leave of my wife and family, under pretext of engagements elsewhere, and made my secret journey to our diocesan city, wherein the good and venerable bishop then abode.

'*January 10. Deo gratias*, in safe arrival in Exeter; craved and obtained immediate audience of his lordship; pleading it was for counsel and admonition on a weighty and pressing cause; called to the presence; made obeisance; then and by command stated my case—the Botathen perplexity—which I moved with strong and earnest instances and solemn asseverations of that which I had myself seen and heard. Demanded by his lordship, what was the succour that I had come to entreat at his hands. Replied, licence for my exorcism, that so I might, ministerially, allay this spiritual visitant, and thus render to the living and the dead release from this surprise. "But," said our bishop, "on what authority do you allege that I am entrusted with faculty so to do? Our Church, as is well known, hath abjured certain branches of her ancient power, on grounds of perversion and abuse."

'"Nay, my lord," I humbly answered, "under favour, the seventy-second of the canons ratified and enjoined on us, the clergy, anno Domini 1604, doth expressly provide, that 'no minister, unless he hath the licence of his diocesan bishop, shall essay to exorcise a spirit, evil or good.' Therefore it was," I did here mildly allege, "that I did not presume to enter on such a work without lawful privilege under your lordship's hand and seal."

'Hereupon did our wise and learned bishop, sitting in his chair, condescend upon the theme at some length with many gracious interpretations from ancient writers and from Holy Scriptures, and I did humbly rejoin and reply, till the upshot was that he did call in his secretary and command him to draw the aforesaid faculty, forthwith and without further delay, assigning him a form, insomuch that the matter was incontinently done; and after I had disbursed into the secretary's hands certain moneys for signitary purposes, as the manner of such officers hath always been, the bishop did himself affix his signature under the *sigillum* of his see, and deliver the document into my hands. When I knelt down to receive his benediction, he softly said, "Let it be secret, Mr R. Weak brethren! weak brethren!"'

This interview with the bishop, and the success with which he vanquished his lordship's scruples, would seem to have confirmed Parson Rudall very strongly in his own esteem, and to have invested him with that courage which he evidently lacked at his first encounter with the ghost.

The entries proceed:

'*January 11,* 1665. Therewithal did I hasten home and prepare my instruments, and cast my figures for the onset of the next day. Took out my ring of brass, and put it on the index-finger of my right hand, with the *scutum Davidis* traced thereon.

'*January 12*, 1665. Rode into the gateway at Botathen, armed at all points, but not with Saul's armour, and ready. There is danger from the demons, but so there is in the surrounding air every day. At early morning then, and alone—for so the usage ordains—I betook me towards the field. It was void, and I had thereby due time to prepare. First, I paced and measured out my circle on the grass. Then I did mark my pentacle in the very midst, and at the intersection of the five angles I did set up and fix my crutch of raun (rowan). Lastly, I took my station south, at the true line of the meridian, and stood facing due north. I waited and watched for a long time.

'At last there was a kind of trouble in the air, a soft and rippling sound, and all at once the shape appeared, and came on towards me gradually. I opened my parchment-scroll, and read aloud the command. She paused, and seemed to waver and doubt; stood still; then I rehearsed the sentence again, sounding out every syllable like a chant. She drew near my ring, but halted at first outside, on the brink. I sounded again, and now at the third time I gave the signal in Syriac—the speech which is used, they say, where such ones dwell and converse in thoughts that glide.

'She was at last obedient, and swam into the midst of the circle, and there stood still, suddenly. I saw, moreover, that she drew back her pointing hand. All this while I do confess that my knees shook under me, and the drops of sweat ran down my flesh like rain. But now, although face to face with the spirit, my heart grew calm, and my mind was composed. I knew that the pentacle would govern her, and the ring must hind, until I gave the word. Then I called to mind the rule laid down of old, that no angel or fiend, no spirit, good or evil, will ever speak until they have been first spoken to.

'N.B. This is the great law of prayer. God Himself will not yield reply until man hath made vocal entreaty, once and again. So, I went on to demand, as the books advise; and the phantom made answer, willingly.

'Questioned wherefore not at rest. Unquiet, because of a certain sin. Asked what, and by whom. Revealed it; but it is *sub sigillo*, and therefore *nefas dictu*; more *anon*. Enquired, what sign she could give that she was a true spirit and not a false fiend. Stated, before next

Yule-tide a fearful pestilence would lay waste the land and myriads of souls would be loosened from their flesh, until, as she piteously said, "our valleys will be full". Asked again, why she so terrified the lad. Replied: "It is the law: we must seek a youth or a maiden of clean life, and under age, to receive messages and admonitions." We conversed with many more words, but it is not lawful for me to set them down. Pen and ink would degrade and defile the thoughts she uttered, and which my mind received that day. I broke the ring and she passed, but to return once more next day. At even-song, a long discourse with that ancient transgressor, Mr B. Great horror and remorse; entire atonement and penance; whatsoever I enjoin; full acknowledgement before pardon.

'*January 13*, 1665.—At sunrise I was again in the field. She came in at once, and, as it seemed, with freedom. Enquired if she knew my thoughts, and what I was going to relate? Answered, "Nay, we only know what we perceive and hear; we cannot see the heart." Then I rehearsed the penitent words of the man she had come up to denounce, and the satisfaction he would perform. Then said she, "Peace in our midst." I went through the proper forms of dismissal, and fulfilled all as it was set down and written in my memoranda; and then, with certain fixed rites, I did dismiss that troubled ghost, until she peacefully withdrew, gliding towards the west. Neither did she ever afterward appear, but was allayed until she shall come in her second flesh to the valley of Armageddon on the last day.'

These quaint and curious details from the 'diurnal' of a simple-hearted clergyman of the seventeenth century appear to betoken his personal persuasion of the truth of what he saw and said, although the statements are strongly tinged with what some may term the superstition, and others the excessive belief, of those times. It is a singular fact, however, that the canon which authorizes exorcism under episcopal licence is still a part of the ecclesiastical law of the Anglican Church, although it might have a singular effect on the nerves of certain of our bishops if their clergy were to resort to them for the faculty which Parson Rudall obtained.

The general facts stated in his diary are to this day matters of belief in that neighbourhood; and it has been always accounted a strong proof of the veracity of the Parson and the Ghost, that the plague, fatal to so many thousands, did break nut in London at the close of that very year. We may well excuse a triumphant entry, on a subsequent page of the 'diurnal', with the date of July to, 1665:

'How sorely must the *infidels* and heretics of this generation be dismayed when they know that this Black Death, which is now swallowing its thousands in the streets of the great city, was foretold six months agone, under the exorcisms of a county minister, by a visible and suppliant ghost! And what pleasures and improvements do such deny themselves who scorn and avoid all opportunity of intercourse with souls separate, and the spirits, glad and sorrowful, which inhabit the unseen world!'

The Doll's Ghost

F. Marion Crawford

It was a terrible accident, and for one moment the splendid machinery of Cranston House got out of gear and stood still. The butler emerged from the retirement in which he spent his elegant leisure, two grooms of the chambers appeared simultaneously from opposite directions, there were actually housemaids on the grand staircase, and those who remember the facts most exactly assert that Mrs. Pringle herself positively stood upon the landing. Mrs. Pringle was the housekeeper. As for the head nurse, the under nurse, and the nursery maid, their feelings cannot be described. The head-nurse laid one hand upon the polished marble balustrade and stared stupidly before her, the under-nurse stood rigid and pale, leaning against the polished marble wall, and the nursery-maid collapsed and sat down upon the polished marble step, just beyond the limits of the velvet carpet, and frankly burst into tears.

The Lady Gwendolen Lancaster-Douglas-Scroop, youngest daughter of the ninth Duke of Cranston, and aged six years and three months, picked herself up quite alone, and sat down on the third step from the foot of the grand staircase in Cranston House.

"Oh!" ejaculated the butler, and he disappeared again.

"Ah!" responded the grooms of the chambers, as they also went away.

"It's only that doll," Mrs. Pringle was distinctly heard to say, in a tone of contempt.

The under nurse heard her say it. Then the three nurses gathered round Lady Gwendolen and patted her, and gave her unhealthy things out of their pockets, and hurried her out of Cranston House as fast as they could, lest it should be found out upstairs that they had allowed the Lady Gwendolen Lancaster-Douglas-Scroop to tumble down the grand staircase with her doll in her arms. And as the doll was badly broken, the nursery-maid carried it, with the pieces, wrapped up in Lady Gwendolen's little cloak. It was not far to Hyde Park, and when they had reached a quiet place they took means to find out that Lady Gwendolen had no bruises. For the carpet was very thick and soft, and there was thick stuff under it to make it softer.

Lady Gwendolen Douglas-Scroop sometimes yelled, but she never cried. It was because she had yelled that the nurse had allowed her to go downstairs alone with Nina, the doll, under one arm, while she steadied herself with her other hand on the balustrade, and trod upon the polished marble steps beyond the edge of the carpet. So she had fallen, and Nina had come to grief.

When the nurses were quite sure that she was not hurt, they unwrapped the doll and looked at her in her turn. She had been a very beautiful doll, very large, and fair, and healthy, with real yellow hair, and eyelids that would open and shut over very grown-up dark eyes. Moreover, when you moved her right arm up and down she said "Pa-pa," and when you moved the left she said "Ma-ma," very distinctly.

"I heard her say 'Pa', when she fell," said the under-nurse, who heard everything. "But she ought to have said 'Pa-pa'."

"That's because her arm went up when she hit the step," said the head nurse. "She'll say the other 'Pa' when I put it down again."

"Pa," said Nina, as her right arm was pushed down, and speaking through her broken face. It was cracked right across, from the upper corner of the forehead, with a hideous gash, through the nose and down to the little frilled collar of the pale green silk Mother Hubbard frock, and two little three-cornered pieces of porcelain had fallen out.

"I m sure it's a wonder she can speak at all, being all smashed," said the under-nurse.

"You'll have to take her to Mr. Puckler," said her superior. "it's not far, and you'd better go at once."

Lady Gwendolen was occupied in digging a hole in the ground with a little spade, and paid no attention to the nurses.

"What are you doing?" enquired the nursery maid, looking on.

"Nina's dead, and I'm diggin' her a grave," replied her ladyship thoughtfully.

"Oh, she'll come to life again all right," said the nursery-maid.

The under-nurse wrapped Nina up again and departed. Fortunately a kind soldier, with very long legs and a very small cap, happened to be there; and as he had nothing to do, he offered to see the under nurse safely to Mr. Puckler's and back.

Mr. Bernard Puckler and his little daughter lived in a little house in a little alley, which led out off a quiet little street not very far from Belgrave Square. He was the great doll doctor, and his extensive practice lay in the most aristocratic quarter. He mended dolls of all sizes and ages, boy dolls and girl dolls, baby dolls in long clothes, and grown-up dolls in fashionable gowns, talking dolls and dumb dolls, those that shut their eyes when they lay down, and those whose eyes had to be shut for them by means of a mysterious wire. His daughter Else was only just over twelve years old, but she was already very clever at mending dolls clothes, and at doing their hair, which is harder than you might think, though the dolls sit quite still while it is being done.

Mr. Puckler had originally been a German, but he had dissolved his nationality in the ocean of London many years ago, like a great many foreigners. He still had one or two German friends, however, who came on Saturday evenings, and smoked with him and played picquet or "*skat*" with him for farthing points, and called him "*Herr Doctor*," which seemed to please Mr. Puckler very much.

He looked older than he was, for his beard was rather long and ragged, his hair was grizzled and thin, and he wore horn-rimmed spectacles. As for Else, she was a thin, pale child, very quiet and neat, with dark eyes and brown hair that was plaited down her back and tied with a bit of black ribbon. She mended the dolls' clothes and took the dolls back to their homes when they were quite strong again.

The house was a little one, but too big for the two people who lived in it. There was a small sitting-room on the street, and the work shop was at the back, and there were three rooms upstairs. But the father and daughter lived most of their time in the workshop, because they were generally at work, even in the evenings.

Mr. Puckler laid Nina on the table and looked at her a long time, till the tears began to fill his eyes behind the horn-rimmed spectacles. He was a very susceptible man, and he often fell in love with the dolls he mended, and found it hard to part with them when they had smiled at him for a few days. They were real little people to him, with characters and thoughts and feelings of their own, and he was very tender with them all. But some attracted him especially from the first, and when they were brought to him maimed and injured, their state seemed so pitiful to him that the tears came easily. You must remember that he had lived among dolls during a great part of his life, and understood them.

"How do you know that they feel nothing?" he went on to say to

Else. "You must be gentle with them. It costs nothing to be kind to the little beings, and perhaps it makes a difference to them."

And Else understood him, because she was a child, and she knew that she was more to him than all the dolls.

He fell in love with Nina at first sight, perhaps because her beautiful brown glass eyes were something like Else's own, and he loved Else first and best, with all his heart. And, besides, it was a very sorrowful case. Nina had evidently not been long in the world, for her complexion was perfect, her hair was smooth where it should be smooth, and curly where it should be curly, and her silk clothes were perfectly new. But across her face was that frightful gash, like a sabre-cut, deep and shadowy within, but clean and sharp at the edges. When he tenderly pressed her head to close the gaping wound, the edges made a fine grating sound, that was painful to hear, and the lids of the dark eyes quivered and trembled as though Nina were suffering dreadfully.

"Poor Nina!" he exclaimed sorrowfully. "But I shall not hurt you much, though you will take a long time to get strong."

He always asked the names of the broken dolls when they were brought to him, and sometimes the people knew what the children called them, and told him. He liked "Nina" for a name. Altogether and in every way she pleased him more than any doll he had seen for many years, and he felt drawn to her, and made up his mind to make her perfectly strong and sound, no matter how much labour it might cost him.

Mr. Puckler worked patiently a little at a time, and Else watched him. She could do nothing for poor Nina, whose clothes needed no mending. The longer the doll doctor worked, the more fond he became of the yellow hair and the beautiful brown glass eyes. He sometimes forgot all the other dolls that were waiting to be mended, lying side by side on a shelf, and sat for an hour gazing at Nina's face, while he racked his ingenuity for some new invention by which to hide even the smallest trace of the terrible accident.

She was wonderfully mended. Even he was obliged to admit that; but the scar was still visible to his keen eyes, a very fine line right across the face, downwards from right to left. Yet all the conditions had been most favourable for a cure, since the cement had set quite hard at the first attempt and the weather had been fine and dry, which makes a great difference in a dolls hospital.

At last he knew that he could do no more, and the under-nurse had already come twice to see whether the job was finished, as she coarsely expressed it.

"Nina is not quite strong yet," Mr. Puckler had answered each time, for he could not make up his mind to face the parting.

And now he sat before the square deal table at which he worked, and Nina lay before him for the last time with a big brown paper box beside her. It stood there like her coffin, waiting for her, he thought. He must put her into it, and lay tissue paper over her dear face, and then put on the lid, and at the thought of tying the string his sight was dim with tears again. He was never to look into the glassy depths of the beautiful brown eyes any more, nor to hear the little wooden voice say "Pa-pa" and "Ma-ma." It was a very painful moment.

In the vain hope of gaining time before the separation, he took up the little sticky bottles of cement and glue and gum and colour, looking at each one in turn, and then at Nina's face. And all his small tools lay there, neatly arranged in a row, but he knew that he could not use them again for Nina. She was quite strong at last, and in a country where there should be no cruel children to hurt her she might live a hundred years, with only that almost imperceptible line across her face to tell of the fearful thing that had befallen her on the marble steps of Cranston House.

Suddenly Mr. Puckler's heart was quite full, and he rose abruptly from his seat and turned away.

"Else," he said unsteadily, "you must do it for me. I cannot bear to see her go into the box."

So he went and stood at the window with his back turned, while Else did what he had not the heart to do.

"Is it done?" he asked, not turning round. "Then take her away, my dear. Put on your hat, and take her to Cranston House quickly, and when you are gone I will turn round."

Else was used to her father's queer ways with the dolls, and though she had never seen him so much moved by a parting, she was not much surprised.

"Come back quickly," he said, when he heard her hand on the latch. "It is growing late, and I should not send you at this hour. But I cannot bear to look forward to it anymore."

When Else was gone, he left the window and sat down in his place before the table again, to wait for the child to come back. He touched the place where Nina had lain, very gently, and he recalled the softly tinted pink face, and the glass eyes, and the ringlets of yellow hair, till he could almost see them.

The evenings were long, for it was late in the spring. But it began to grow dark soon, and Mr. Puckler wondered why Else did not come back. She had been gone an hour and a half, and that was much longer than he had expected, for it was barely half a mile from Belgrave Square to Cranston House. He reflected that the child might have been kept waiting, but as the twilight deepened he grew anxious, and walked up and down in the dim workshop, no longer thinking of Nina, but of Else, his own living child, whom he loved.

An undefinable, disquieting sensation came upon him by fine degrees, a chilliness and a faint stirring of his thin hair, joined with a wish to be in any company rather than to be alone much longer. It was the beginning of fear.

He told himself in strong German-English that he was a foolish old man, and he began to feel about for the matches in the dusk. He knew just where they should be, for he always kept them in the same place, close to the little tin box that held bits of sealing-wax of various colours, for some kinds of mending. But somehow he could not find the matches in the gloom.

Something had happened to Else, he was sure, and as his fear increased, he felt as though it might be allayed if he could get a light and see what time it was. Then he called himself a foolish old man again, and the sound of his own voice startled him in the dark. He could not find the matches.

The window was grey still; he might see what time it was if he went close to it, and he could go and get matches out of the cupboard afterwards.

He stood back from the table, to get out of the way of the chair, and began to cross the board floor.

Something was following him in the dark. There was a small pattering, as of tiny feet upon the boards. He stopped and listened, and the roots of his hair tingled. It was nothing, and he was a foolish old man. He made two steps more, and he was sure that he heard the little pattering again. He turned his back to the window, leaning against the sash so that the panes began to crack, and he faced the dark. Everything was quite still, and it smelt of paste and cement and wood-filings as usual.

"Is that you, Else?" he asked, and he was surprised by the fear in his voice.

There was no answer in the room, and he held up his watch and tried to make out what time it was by the grey dusk that was just not darkness. So far as he could see, it was within two or three minutes of ten o'clock. He had been a long time alone. He was shocked, and frightened for Else, out in London, so late, and he almost ran across the room to the door. As he fumbled for the latch, he distinctly heard the running of the little feet after him.

"Mice!" he exclaimed feebly, just as he got the door open.

He shut it quickly behind him, and felt as though some cold thing had settled on his back and were writhing upon him. The passage was quite dark, but he found his hat and was out in the alley in a moment, breathing more freely, and surprised to find how much light there still was in the open air. He could see the pavement clearly under his feet, and far off in the street to which the alley led he could hear the laughter and calls of children, playing some game out of doors. He wondered how he could have been so nervous, and for an instant he thought of going back into the house to wait quietly for Else. But instantly he felt that nervous fright of something stealing over him again. In any case it was better to walk up to Cranston House and ask the servants about the child. One of the women had perhaps taken a fancy to her, and was even now giving her tea and cake.

He walked quickly to Belgrave Square, and then up the broad streets, listening as he went, whenever there was no other sound, for the tiny footsteps. But he heard nothing, and was laughing at himself when he rang the servants' bell at the big house. Of course, the child must be there.

The person who opened the door was quite an inferior person, for it was a back door, but affected the manners of the front, and stared at Mr. Puckler superciliously under the strong light.

No little girl had been seen, and he knew "nothing about no dolls."

"She is my little girl, said Mr. Puckler tremulously, for all his anxiety was returning tenfold, "and I am afraid something has happened."

The inferior person said rudely that "nothing could have happened to her in that house, because she had not been there, which was a jolly good reason why;" and Mr. Puckler was obliged to admit that the man ought to know, as it was his business to keep the door and let people in. He wished to be allowed to speak to the under-nurse, who knew him; but the man was ruder than ever, and finally shut the door in his face.

When the doll doctor was alone in the street, he steadied himself by the railing, for he felt as though he were breaking in two, just as some dolls break, in the middle of the backbone.

Presently he knew that he must be doing something to find Else, and that gave him strength. He began to walk as quickly as he could through the streets, following every highway and byway which his little girl might have taken on her errand. He also asked several policemen in vain if they had seen her, and most of them answered him kindly, for they saw that he was a sober man and in his right senses, and some of them had little girls of their own.

It was one o'clock in the morning when he went up to his own door again, worn out and hopeless and broken-hearted. As he turned the key in the lock, his heart stood still, for he knew that he was awake and not dreaming, and that he really heard those tiny footsteps pattering to meet him inside the house along the passage.

But he was too unhappy to be much frightened any more, and his heart went on again with a dull regular pain, that found its way all through him with every pulse. So he went in, and hung up his hat in the dark, and found the matches in the cupboard and the candlestick in its place in the corner.

Mr. Puckler was so much overcome and so completely worn out that he sat down in his chair before the work-table and almost fainted, as his face dropped forward upon his folded hands. Beside him the solitary candle burned steadily with a low flame in the still warm air.

"Else! Else!" he moaned against his yellow knuckles. And that was all he could say, and it was no relief to him. On the contrary, the very sound of the name was a new and sharp pain that pierced his ears and his head and his very soul. For every time he repeated the name it meant that little Else was dead, somewhere out in the streets of London in the dark.

He was so terribly hurt that he did not even feel something pulling gently at the skirt of his old coat, so gently that it was like the nibbling of a tiny mouse. He might have thought that it was really a mouse if he had noticed it.

"Else! Else!" he groaned right against his hands.

Then a cool breath stirred his thin hair, and the low flame of the one candle dropped down almost to a mere spark, not flickering as though a draught were going to blow it out, but just dropping down as if it were tired out. Mr. Puckler felt his hands stiffening with fright under his face; and there was a faint rustling sound, like some small silk thing blown in a gentle breeze. He sat up straight, stark and scared, and a small wooden voice spoke in the stillness.

"Pa-pa," it said, with a break between the syllables.

Mr. Puckler stood up in a single jump, and his chair fell over backwards with a smashing noise upon the wooden floor. The candle had almost gone out.

It was Nina's doll voice that had spoken, and he should have known it among the voices of a hundred other dolls. And yet there was something more in it, a little human ring, with a pitiful cry and a call for help, and the wail of a hurt child. Mr. Puckler stood up, stark and stiff, and tried to look round, but at first he could not, for he seemed to be frozen from head to foot.

Then he made a great effort, and he raised one hand to each of his temples, and pressed his own head round as he would have turned a doll's. The candle was burning so low that it might as well have been out altogether, for any light it gave, and the room seemed quite dark at first. Then he saw something. He would not have believed that he could be more frightened than he had been just before that. But he was, and his knees shook, for he saw the doll standing in the middle of the floor, shining with a faint and ghostly radiance, her beautiful glassy brown eyes fixed on his. And across her face the very thin line of the break he had mended shone as though it were drawn in light with a fine point of white flame.

Yet there was something more in the eyes, too; there was something human, like Else's own, but as if only the doll saw him through them, and not Else. And there was enough of Else to bring back all his pain and to make him forget his fear.

"Else! my little Else!" he cried aloud.

The small ghost moved, and its doll-arm slowly rose and fell with a stiff, mechanical motion.

"Pa-pa," it said.

It seemed this time that there was even more of Else's tone echoing somewhere between the wooden notes that reached his ears so distinctly, and yet so far away. Else was calling him, he was sure.

His face was perfectly white in the gloom, but his knees did not shake any more, and he felt that he was less frightened.

"Yes, child! But where? Where?" he asked. "Where are you, Else?"

"Pa-pa!"

The syllables died away in the quiet room. There was a low rustling of silk, the glassy brown eyes turned slowly away, and Mr. Puckler heard the pitter-patter of the small feet in the bronze kid slippers as the figure ran straight to the door. Then the candle burned high again, the room was full of light, and he was alone.

Mr. Puckler passed his hand over his eyes and looked about him. He could see everything quite clearly, and he felt that he must have been dreaming, though he was standing instead of sitting down, as he should have been if he had just waked up. The candle burned brightly now. There were the dolls to be mended, lying in a row with their toes up. The third one had lost her right shoe, and Else was making one. He knew that, and he was certainly not dreaming now. He had not been dreaming when he had come in from his fruitless search and had heard the doll's footsteps running to the door. He had not fallen asleep in his chair. How could he possibly have fallen asleep when his heart was breaking? He had been awake all the time.

He steadied himself, set the fallen chair upon its legs, and said to himself again very emphatically that he was a foolish old man. He ought to be out in the streets looking for his child, asking questions, and enquiring at the police stations, where all accidents were reported as soon as they were known, or at the hospitals.

"Pa-pa!"

The longing, wailing, pitiful little wooden cry rang from the passage, outside the door, and Mr. Puckler stood for an instant with white face, transfixed and rooted to the spot. A moment later his hand was on the latch. Then he was in the passage, with the light streaming from the open door behind him.

Quite at the other end he saw the little phantom shining clearly in the shadow, and the right hand seemed to beckon to him as the arm rose and fell once more. He knew all at once that it had not come to frighten him but to lead him, and when it disappeared, and he walked boldly towards the door, he knew that it was in the street outside, waiting for him. He forgot that he was tired and had eaten no supper, and had walked many miles, for a sudden hope ran through and through him, like a golden stream of life.

And sure enough, at the corner of the alley, and at the corner of the street, and out in Belgrave Square, he saw the small ghost flitting before him. Sometimes it was only a shadow, where there was other light, but then the glare of the lamps made a pale green sheen on its little Mother Hubbard frock of silk; and sometimes, where the streets were dark and silent, the whole figure shone out brightly, with its yellow curls and rosy neck.

It seemed to trot along like a tiny child, and Mr. Puckler could almost hear the pattering of the bronze kid slippers on the pavement as it ran. But it went very fast, and he could only just keep up with it, tearing along with his hat on the back of his head and his thin hair blown by the night breeze, and his horn-rimmed spectacles firmly set upon his broad nose.

On and on he went, and he had no idea where he was. He did not even care, for he knew certainly that he was going the right way.

Then at last, in a wide, quiet street, he was standing before a big, sober-looking door that had two lamps on each side of it, and a polished brass bell-handle, which he pulled.

And just inside, when the door was opened, in the bright light, there was the little shadow, and the pale green sheen of the little silk dress, and once more the small cry came to his ears, less pitiful, more longing.

"Pa-pa!"

The shadow turned suddenly bright, and out of the brightness the beautiful brown glass eyes were turned up happily to his, while the rosy mouth smiled so divinely that the phantom doll looked almost like a little angel just then.

"A little girl was brought in soon after ten o clock," said the quiet voice of the hospital door keeper. "I think they thought she was only stunned. She was holding a big brown-paper box against her, and they could not get it out of her arms. She had a long plait of brown hair that hung down as they carried her."

"She is my little girl," said Mr. Puckler, but he hardly heard his own voice.

He leaned over Else's face in the gentle light of the children's ward, and when he had stood there a minute the beautiful brown eyes opened and looked up to his.

"Pa-pa!" cried Else, softly, "I knew you would come!"

Then Mr. Puckler did not know what he did or said for a moment, and what he felt was worth all the fear and terror and despair that had almost killed him that night. But by and by Else was telling her story, and the nurse let her speak, for there were only two other children in the room, who were getting well and were sound asleep.

"They were big boys with bad faces," said Else, "and they tried to get Nina away from me, but I held on and fought as well as I could till one of them hit me with something, and I don't remember any more, for I tumbled down, and I suppose the boys ran away, and somebody found me there. But I'm afraid Nina is all smashed."

"Here is the box," said the nurse. "We could not take it out of her arms till she came to herself. Should you like to see if the doll is broken?"

And she undid the string cleverly, but Nina was all smashed to pieces. Only the gentle light of the children's ward made a pale green sheen in the folds of the little Mother Hubbard frock.

The Ghost at the Rath

Rosa Mulholland

Many may disbelieve this story, yet there are some still living who can remember hearing, when children, of the events which it details, and of the strange sensation which their publicity excited. The tale, in its present form, is copied, by permission, from a memoir written by the chief actor in the romance, and preserved as a sort of heirloom in the family whom it concerns.

In the year —— I, John Thunder, Captain in the —— Regiment, having passed many years abroad following my profession, received notice that I had become owner of certain properties which I had never thought to inherit. I set off for my native land, arrived in Dublin, found that my good fortune was real, and at once began to look about me for old friends. The first I met with, quite by accident, was curly-headed Frank O'Brien, who had been at school with me, though I was ten years his senior. He was curly-headed still, and handsome, as he had promised to be, but careworn and poor. During an evening spent at his chambers I drew all his history from him. He was a briefless barrister.

As a man he was not more talented than he had been as a boy. Hard work and anxiety had not brought him success, only broken his health and soured his mind. He was in love, and he could not marry. I soon knew all about Mary Leonard, his *fiancée*, whom he had met at a house in the country somewhere, in which she was governess. They had now been engaged for two years—she active and hopeful, he sick and despondent. From the letters of hers which he showed me, I thought she was worth all the devotion he felt for her. I considered a good deal about what could be done for Frank, but I could not easily hit upon a plan to assist him. For ten chances you have of helping a sharp man, you have not two for a dull one.

In the meantime, my friend must regain his health, and a change of air and scene was necessary. I urged him to make a voyage of discovery to the Rath, an old house and park which had come into my possession as portion of my recently acquired estates. I had never been to the place myself; but it had once been the residence of Sir Luke Thunder, of generous memory, and I knew that it was furnished, and provided with a caretaker. I pressed him to leave Dublin at once, and promised to follow him as soon as I found it possible to do so.

So, Frank went down to the Rath. The place was two hundred miles away; he was a stranger there, and far from well. When the first week came to an end, and I had heard nothing from him, I did not like the silence; when a fortnight had passed, and still not a word to say he was alive, I felt decidedly uncomfortable; and when the third week of his absence arrived at Saturday without bringing me news, I found myself whizzing through a part of the country I had never travelled before, in the same train in which I had seen Frank seated at our parting.

I reached D——, and, shouldering my knapsack, walked right into the heart of a lovely woody country. Following the directions, I had received, I made my way to a lonely road, on which I met not a soul, and which seemed cut out of the heart of a forest, so closely were the trees ranked on either side, and so dense was the twilight made by the meeting and intertwining of the thick branches overhead. In these shades I came upon a gate, like a gate run to seed, with tall, thin, brick pillars, brandishing long grasses from their heads, and spotted with a melancholy crust of creeping moss. I jangled a cracked bell, and an old man appeared from the thickets within, stared at me, then admitted me with a rusty key. I breathed freely on hearing that my friend was well and to be seen. I presented a letter to the old man, having a fancy not to avow myself.

I found my friend walking up and down the alleys of a neglected orchard, with the lichened branches tangled above his head, and ripe apples rotting about his feet. His hands were locked behind his back, and his head was set on one side, listening to the singing of a bird. I never had seen him look so well; yet there was a vacancy about his whole air which I did not like. He did not seem at all surprised to see me, asked had he really not written to me; thought he had; was so comfortable that he had forgotten everything else. He fancied he had only been there about three days; could not imagine how the time had passed. He seemed to talk wildly, and this, coupled with the unusual happy placidity of his manner, confounded me. The place knew him, he told me confidentially; the place belonged to him, or should; the birds sang him this, the very trees bent before him as he passed, the air whispered him that he had been long expected, and should be poor no more. Wrestling with my judgment ere it might pronounce him mad, I followed him indoors.

The Rath was no ordinary old country-house. The acres around it were so wildly overgrown that it was hard to decide which had been pleasure-ground and where the thickets had begun. The plan of the house was fine, with mullioned windows, and here and there a fleck of stained glass flinging back the challenge of an angry sunset. The vast rooms were full of a dusky glare from the sky as I strolled through them in the twilight. The antique furniture had many a blood-red stain on the abrupt notches of its dark carvings; the dusty mirrors flared back at the windows, while the faded curtains produced streaks of uncertain colour from the depths of their sullen foldings.

Dinner was laid for us in the library, a long wainscoted room, with an enormous fire roaring up the chimney, sending a dancing light over the dingy titles of long unopened books. The old man who had unlocked the gate for me served us at table, and, after drawing the dusty curtains, and furnishing us with a plentiful supply of fuel and wine, left us. His clanking hobnailed shoes went echoing away in the distance over the unmatted tiles of the vacant hall till a door closed with a resounding clang very far away, letting us know that we were shut up together for the night in this vast, mouldy, oppressive old house.

I felt as if I could scarcely breathe in it. I could not eat with my usual appetite. The air of the place seemed heavy and tainted. I grew sick and restless. The very wine tasted badly, as if it had been drugged. I had a strange feeling that I had been in the house before, and that something evil had happened to me in it. Yet such could not be the case. What puzzled me most was, that I should feel dissatisfied at seeing Frank looking so well, and eating so heartily. A little time before I should have been glad to suffer something to see him as he looked now; and yet not quite as he looked now. There was a drowsy contentment about him which I could not understand. He did not talk of his work, or of any wish to return to it. He seemed to have no thought of anything but the delight of hanging about that old house, which had certainly cast a spell over him.

About midnight he seized a light, and proposed retiring to our rooms. "I have such delightful dreams in this place," he said. He volunteered, as we issued into the hall, to take me upstairs and show me the upper regions of his paradise.

I said, "Not tonight."

I felt a strange creeping sensation as I looked up the vast black staircase, wide enough for a coach to drive down, and at the heavy darkness bending over it like a curse, while our lamps made drips of light down the first two or three gloomy steps. Our bedrooms were on the ground floor, and stood opposite one another off a passage which led to a garden. Into mine Frank conducted me, and left me for his own.

The uneasy feeling which I have described did not go from me with him, and I felt a restlessness amounting to pain when left alone in my chamber. Efforts had evidently been made to render the room habitable, but there was a something antagonistic to sleep in every angle of its many crooked corners. I kicked chairs out of their prim order along the wall, and banged things about here and there; finally, thinking that a good night's rest was u the best cure for an inexplicably disturbed frame of mind, I undressed as quickly as possible, and laid my head on my pillow under a canopy, like the wings of a gigantic bird of prey wheeling above me ready to pounce.

But I could not sleep. The wind grumbled in the chimney, and the boughs swished in the garden outside; and between these noises I thought I heard sounds coming from the interior of the old house, where all should have been still as the dead down in their vaults. I could not make out what these sounds were.

Sometimes I thought I heard feet running about, sometimes I could have sworn there were double knocks, tremendous *tantararaaras* at the great hall door. Sometimes I heard the clashing of dishes, the echo of voices calling, and the dragging about of furniture. Whilst I sat up in bed trying to account for these noises, my door suddenly flew open, a bright light streamed in from the passage without, and a powdered servant in an elaborate livery of antique pattern stood holding the handle of the door in his hand, and bowing low to me in the bed.

"Her ladyship, my mistress, desires your presence in the drawing-room, sir."

This was announced in the measured tone of a well-trained domestic. Then with another bow he retired, the door closed, and I was left in the dark to determine whether I had not suddenly awakened from a tantalising dream. In spite of my very wakeful sensations, I believe I should have endeavoured to convince myself that I had been sleeping, but that I perceived light shining under my door, and through the keyhole, from the passage. I got up, lit my lamp, and dressed myself as hastily as I was able.

I opened my door, and the passage down which a short time before I had almost groped my way, with my lamp blinking in the dense foggy darkness, was now illuminated with a light as bright as gas. I walked along it quickly, looking right and left to see whence the glare proceeded. Arriving at the hall, I found it also blazing with light, and filled with perfume. Groups of choice plants, heavy with blossoms, made it look like a garden. The mosaic floor was strewn with costly mats. Soft colours and gilding shone from the walls, and canvases that had been black gave forth faces of men and women looking brightly from their burnished frames.

Servants were running about, the dining-room and drawing-room doors were opening and shutting, and as I looked through each I saw *vistas* of light and colour, the moving of brilliant crowds, the waving of feathers, and glancing of brilliant dresses and uniforms. A festive hum reached me with a drowsy subdued sound, as if I were listening with stuffed ears. Standing aside by an orange tree, I gave up speculating on what this might be, and concentrated all my powers on observation.

Wheels were heard suddenly, and a resounding knock banged at the door till it seemed that the very rooks in the chimneys must be startled out of their nests. The door flew open, a flaming of lanterns was seen outside, and a dazzling lady came up the steps and swept into the hall. When she held up her cloth of silver train, I could see the diamonds that twinkled on her feet. Her bosom was covered with roses, and there was a red light in her eyes like the reflection from a hundred glowing fires.

Her black hair went coiling about her head, and couched among the braids lay a jewel not unlike the head of a snake. She was flashing and glowing with gems and flowers. Her beauty and brilliance made me dizzy. Then came a faintness in the air, as if her breath had poisoned it. A whirl of storm came in with her, and rushed up the staircase like a moan. The plants shuddered and shed their blossoms, and all the lights grew dim a moment, then flared up again.

Now the drawing-room door opened, and a gentleman came out with a young girl leaning on his arm. He was a fine-looking, middle-aged gentleman, with a mild countenance.

The girl was a slender creature, with golden hair and a pale face. She was dressed in pure white, with a large ruby like a drop of blood at her throat. They advanced together to receive the lady who had arrived. The gentleman offered his arm to the stranger, and the girl who was displaced for her fell back, and walked behind them with a downcast air. I felt irresistibly impelled to follow them, and passed with them into the drawing-room. Never had I mixed in a finer, gayer crowd. The costumes were rich and of an old-fashioned pattern. Dancing was going forward with spirit—minuets and country dances. The stately gentleman was evidently the host, and moved among the company, introducing the magnificent lady right and left. He led her to the head of the room presently, and they mixed in the dance. The arrogance of her manner and the fascination of her beauty were wonderful.

I cannot attempt to describe the strange manner in which I was in this company, and yet not of it. I seemed to view all I beheld through some fine and subtle medium. I saw clearly, yet I felt that it was not with my ordinary naked eyesight. I can compare it to nothing but looking at a scene through a piece of smoked or coloured glass. And just in the same way (as I have said before) all sounds seemed to reach me as if I were listening with ears imperfectly stuffed. No one present took any notice of me. I spoke to several, and they made no reply—did not even turn their eyes upon me, nor show in any way that they heard me. I planted myself straight in the way of a fine fellow in a general's uniform, but he, swerving neither to right nor left by an inch, kept on his way, as though I were a streak of mist, and left me behind him.

Everyone I touched eluded me somehow. Substantial as they all looked, I could not contrive to lay my hand on anything that felt like solid flesh. Two or three times I felt a momentary relief from the oppressive sensations which distracted me, when I firmly believed I saw Frank's head at some distance among the crowd, now in one room and now in another, and again in the conservatory, which was hung with lamps, and filled with people walking about among the flowers. But, whenever I approached, he had vanished. At last I came upon him, sitting by himself on a couch behind a curtain watching the dancers. I laid my hand upon his shoulder. Here was something substantial at last. He did not look up; he seemed aware neither of my touch nor my speech. I looked in his staring eyes, and found that he was sound asleep. I could not wake him.

Curiosity would not let me remain by his side. I again mixed with the crowd, and found the stately host still leading about the magnificent lady. No one seemed to notice that the golden-haired girl was sitting weeping in a corner; no one but the beauty in the silver train, who sometimes glanced at her contemptuously. Whilst I watched her distress a group came between me and her, and I wandered into another room, where, as though I had turned from one picture of her to look at another, I beheld her dancing gaily, in the full glee of Sir Roger de Coverley, with a fine-looking youth, who was more plainly dressed than any other person in the room. Never was a better-matched pair to look at. Down the middle they danced, hand in hand, his face full of tenderness, hers beaming with joy, right and left bowing and curtseying, parted and meeting again, smiling and whispering; but over the heads of smaller women there were the fierce eyes of the magnificent beauty scowling at them. Then again, the crowd shifted around me, and this scene was lost.

For some time, I could see no trace of the golden-haired girl in any of the rooms. I looked for her in vain, till at last I caught a glimpse of her standing smiling in a doorway with her finger lifted, beckoning. At whom? Could it be at me? Her eyes were fixed on mine. I hastened into the hall, and caught sight of her white dress passing up the wide black staircase from which I had shrunk some hours earlier. I followed her, she keeping some steps in advance. It was intensely dark, but by the gleaming of her gown I was able to trace her flying figure.

Where we went I knew not, up how many stairs, down how many passages, till we arrived at a low-roofed large room with sloping roof and queer windows where there was a dim light, like the sanctuary light in a deserted church. Here, when I entered, the golden head was glimmering over something which I presently discerned to be a cradle wrapped round with white curtains, and with a few fresh flowers fastened up on the hood of it, as if to catch a baby's eye.

The fair sweet face looked up at me with a glow of pride on it, smiling with happy dimples. The white hands unfolded the curtains, and stripped back the coverlet. Then, suddenly there went a rushing moan all round the weird room, that seemed like a gust of wind forcing in through the crannies, and shaking the jingling old windows in their sockets. The cradle was an empty one. The girl fell back with a look of horror on her pale face that I shall never forget, then, flinging her arms above her head, she dashed from the room.

I followed her as fast as I was able, but the wild white figure was too swift for me. I had lost her before I reached the bottom of the staircase. I searched for her, first in one room, then in another, neither could I see her foe (as I already believed to be), the lady of the silver train. At length I found myself in a small ante-room, where a lamp was expiring on the table. A window was open, close by it the golden-haired girl was lying sobbing in a chair, while the magnificent lady was bending over her as if soothingly, and offering her something to drink in a goblet. The moon was rising behind the two figures.

The shuddering light of the lamp was flickering over the girl's bright head, the rich embossing of the golden cup, the lady's silver robes, and, I thought, the jewelled eyes of the serpent looked out from her bending head. As I watched, the girl raised her face and drank, then suddenly dashed the goblet away; while a cry such as I never heard but once, and shiver to remember, rose to the very roof of the old house, and the clear sharp word "*Poisoned!*" rang and reverberated from hall and chamber in a thousand echoes, like the clash of a peal of bells. The girl dashed herself from the open window, leaving the cry clamouring behind her. I heard the violent opening of doors and running of feet, but I waited for nothing more. Maddened by what I had witnessed, I would have felled the murderess, but she glided unhurt from under my vain blow.

I sprang from the window after the wretched white figure. I saw it flying on before me with a speed I could not overtake. I ran till I was dizzy. I called like a madman, and heard the owls croaking back to me. The moon grew huge and bright, the trees grew out before it like the bushy heads of giants, the river lay keen and shining like a long unsheathed sword, couching for deadly work among the rushes. The white figure shimmered and vanished, glittered brightly on before me, shimmered and vanished again, shimmered, staggered, fell, and disappeared in the river. Of what she was, phantom or reality, I thought not at the moment; she had the semblance of a human being going to destruction, and I had the frenzied impulse to save her. I rushed forward with one last effort, struck my foot against the root of a tree, and was dashed to the ground. I remember a crash, momentary pain and confusion; then nothing more.

When my senses returned, the red clouds of the dawn were shining in the river beside me. I arose to my feet, and found that, though much bruised, I was otherwise unhurt. I busied my mind in recalling the strange circumstances which had brought me to that place in the dead of the night. The recollection of all I had witnessed was vividly present to my mind. I took my way slowly to the house, almost expecting to see the marks of wheels and other indications of last night's revel, but the rank grass that covered the gravel was uncrushed, not a blade disturbed, not a stone displaced. I shook one of the drawing-room windows till I shook off the old rusty hasp inside, flung up the creaking sash, and entered. Where were the brilliant draperies and carpets, the soft gilding, the vases teeming with flowers, the thousand sweet odours of the night before? Not a trace of them; no, nor even a ragged cobweb swept away, nor a stiff chair moved an inch from its melancholy place, nor the face of a mirror relieved from one speck of its obscuring dust!

Coming back into the open air, I met the old man from the gate walking up one of the weedy paths. He eyed me meaningly from head to foot, but I gave him good-morrow cheerfully.

"You see I am poking about early," I said.

"I' faith, sir," said he, "an' ye look like a man that had been pokin' about *all night*."

"How so?" said I.

"Why, ye see, sir," said he, "I'm used to 't, an' I can read it in yer face like prent. Some sees one thing an' some another, an' some only feels an' hears. The poor jintleman inside, *he* says nothin', but he has beautyful dhrames. An' for the Lord's sake, sir, take him out o' this, for I've seen him wandherin' about like a ghost himself in the heart of the night, an' him that sound sleepin' that I couldn't wake him!"

At breakfast I said nothing to Frank of my strange adventures. He had rested well, he said, and boasted of his enchanting dreams. I asked him to describe them, when he grew perplexed and annoyed. He remembered nothing, but that his spirit had been delightfully entertained whilst his body reposed. I now felt a curiosity to go through the old house, and was not surprised, on pushing open a door at the end of a remote mouldy passage, to enter the identical chamber into which I had followed the pale-faced girl when she beckoned me out of the drawing-room.

There were the low brooding roof and slanting walls, the short wide latticed windows to which the noonday sun was trying to pierce through a forest of leaves. The hangings rotting with age shook like dreary banners at the opening of the door, and there in the middle of the room was the cradle; only the curtains that had been white were blackened with dirt, and laced and overlaced with cobwebs. I parted the curtains, bringing down a shower of dust upon the floor, and saw lying upon the pillow, within, a child's tiny shoe, and a toy. I need not describe the rest of the house. It was vast and rambling, and, as far as furniture and decorations were concerned, the wreck of grandeur.

Having strange subject for meditation, I walked alone in the orchard that evening. This orchard sloped towards the river I have mentioned before. The trees were old and stunted, and the branches tangled overhead. The ripe apples were rolling in the long, bleached grass. A row of taller trees, sycamores and chestnuts, straggled along by the river's edge, ferns and tall weeds grew round and amongst them, and between their trunks, and behind the rifts in the foliage, the water was seen to flow. Walking up and down one of the paths I alternately faced these trees and turned my back upon them.

Once when coming towards them I chanced to lift my glance, started, drew my hands across my eyes, looked again, and finally stood still gazing in much astonishment. I saw distinctly the figure of a lady standing by one of the trees, bending low towards the grass. Her face was a little turned away, her dress a bluish-white, her mantle a dun-brown colour. She held a spade in her hand, and her foot was upon it, as if she were in the act of digging. I gazed at her for some time, vainly trying to guess at whom she might be, then I advanced towards her.

As I approached, the outlines of her figure broke up and disappeared, and I found that she was only an illusion presented to me by the curious accidental grouping of the lines of two trees which had shaped the space between them into the semblance of the form I have described. A patch of the flowing water had been her robe, a piece of russet moorland her cloak. The spade was an awkward young shoot slanting up from the root of one of the trees. I stepped back and tried to piece her out again bit by bit, but could not succeed.

That night I did not feel at all inclined to return to my dismal chamber, and lie awaiting such another summons as I had once received. When Frank bade me goodnight, I heaped fresh coals on the fire, took down from the shelves a book, from which I lifted the dust in layers with my penknife, and, dragging an armchair close to the hearth, tried to make myself as comfortable as might be. I am a strong, robust man, very unimaginative, and little troubled with affections of the nerves, but I confess that my feelings were not enviable, sitting thus alone in that queer old house, with last night's strange pantomime still vividly present to my memory. In spite of my efforts at coolness, I was excited by the prospect of what yet might be in store for me before morning. But these feelings passed away as the night wore on, and I nodded asleep over my book.

I was startled by the sound of a brisk light step walking overhead.

Wide awake at once, I sat up and listened. The ceiling was low, but I could not call to mind what room it was that lay above the library in which I sat. Presently I heard the same step upon the stairs, and the loud sharp rustling of a silk dress sweeping against the banisters. The step paused at the library door, and then there was silence. I got up, and with all the courage I could summon seized a light, and opened the door; but there was nothing in the hall but the usual heavy darkness and damp mouldy air. I confess I felt more uncomfortable at that moment than I had done at any time during the preceding night. All the visions that had then appeared to me had produced nothing like the horror of thus feeling a supernatural presence which my eyes were not permitted to behold.

I returned to the library, and passed the night there. Next day I sought for the room above it in which I had heard the footsteps, but could discover no entrance to any such room. Its windows, indeed, I counted from the outside, though they were so overgrown with ivy I could hardly discern them, but in the interior of the house I could find no door to the chamber. I asked Frank about it, but he knew and cared nothing on the subject; I asked the old man at the lodge, and he shook his head.

"Och!" he said, "don't ask about that room. The door's built up, and flesh and blood have no consarn wid it. It was *her own* room."

"Whose own?" I asked.

"Ould Lady Thunder's. An' whist, sir! *that's her grave!*"

"What do you mean?" I said. "Are you out of your mind?"

He laughed queerly, drew nearer, and lowered his voice. "Nobody has asked about the room these years but yourself," he said. "Nobody misses it goin' over the house. My grandfather was an old retainer o' the Thunder family, my father was in the service too, an' I was born myself before the ould lady died. Yon was her room, an' she left her eternal curse on her family if so be they didn't lave her coffin there. *She* wasn't goin' undher the ground to the worms. So, there it was left, an' they built up the door. God love ye, sir, an' don't go near it. I wouldn't have told you, only I know ye've seen plenty about already, an' ye have the look o' one that'd be ferretin' things out, savin' yer presence."

He looked at me knowingly, but I gave him no information, only thanked him for putting me on my guard. I could scarcely credit what he told me about the room; but my curiosity was excited regarding it. I made up my mind that day to try and induce Frank to quit the place on the morrow. I felt more and more convinced that the atmosphere was not healthful for his mind, whatever it might be for his body. The sooner we left the spot the better for us both; but the remaining night which I had to pass there I resolved on devoting to the exploring of the walled-up chamber. What impelled me to this resolve I do not know.

The undertaking was not a pleasant one, and I should hardly have ventured on it had I been forced to remain much longer at the Rath. But I knew there was little chance of sleep for me in that house, and I thought I might as well go and seek for my adventures as sit waiting for them to come for me, as I had done the night before. I felt a relish for my enterprise, and expected the night with satisfaction. I did not say anything of my intention either to Frank or the old man at the lodge. I did not want to make a fuss, and have my doings talked of all over the country. I may as well mention here that again, on this evening, when walking in the orchard, I saw the figure of the lady digging between the trees. And again, I saw that this figure was an illusive appearance; that the water was her gown, and the moorland her cloak, and a willow in the distance her tresses.

As soon as the night was pretty far advanced, I placed a ladder against the window which was least covered over with the ivy, and mounted it, having provided myself with a dark lantern. The moon rose full behind some trees that stood like a black bank against the horizon, and glimmered on the panes as I ripped away branches and leaves with a knife, and shook the old crazy casement open. The sashes were rotten, and the fastenings easily gave way. I placed my lantern on a bench within, and was soon standing beside it in the chamber. The air was insufferably close and mouldy, and I flung the window open to the widest, and beat the bowering ivy still further back from about it, so as to let the fresh air of heaven blow into the place. I then took my lantern in hand, and began to look about me.

The room was vast and double; a velvet curtain hung between me and an inner chamber. The darkness was thick and irksome, and the scanty light of my lantern only tantalised me. My eyes fell on some tall spectral-looking candelabra furnished with wax candles, which, though black with age, still bore the marks of having been guttered by a draught that had blown on them fifty years ago. I lighted these; they burned up with a ghastly flickering, and the apartment, with its fittings, was revealed to me. These latter had been splendid in the days of their freshness: the appointments of the rest of the house were mean in comparison. The ceiling was painted with fine allegorical figures, also spaces of the walls between the dim mirrors and the sumptuous hangings of crimson velvet, with their tarnished golden tassels and fringes. The carpet still felt luxurious to the tread, and the dust could not altogether obliterate the elaborate fancy of its flowery design.

There were gorgeous cabinets laden with curiosities, wonderfully carved chairs, rare vases, and antique glasses of every description, under some of which lay little heaps of dust which had once no doubt been blooming flowers. There was a table laden with books of poetry and science, drawings and drawing materials, which showed that the occupant of the room had been a person of mind. There was also a writing-table scattered over with yellow papers, and a work-table at a window, on which lay reels, a thimble, and a piece of what had once been white muslin, but was now saffron colour, sewn with gold thread, a rusty needle sticking in it. This and the pen lying on the ink-stand, the paper-knife between the leaves of a book, the loose sketches shaken out by the side of a portfolio, and the ashes of a fire on the wide mildewed hearth-place, all suggested that the owner of this retreat had been snatched from it without warning, and that whoever had thought proper to build up the doors, had also thought proper to touch nothing that had belonged to her.

Having surveyed all these things, I entered the inner room, which was a bedroom. The furniture of this was in keeping with that of the other chamber. I saw dimly a bed enveloped in lace, and a dressing-table fancifully garnished and draped. Here I espied more candelabra, and going forward to set the lights burning, I stumbled against something. I turned the blaze of my lantern on this something, and started with a sudden thrill of horror. It was a large stone coffin.

I own that I felt very strangely for the next few minutes. When I had recovered the shock, I set the wax-candles burning, and took a better survey of this odd burial-place. A wardrobe stood open, and I saw dresses hanging within. A gown lay upon a chair, as if just thrown off, and a pair of dainty slippers were beside it. The toilet-table looked as if only used yesterday, judging by the litter that covered it; hair-brushes lying this way and that way, essence-bottles with the stoppers out, paint pots uncovered, a ring here, a wreath of artificial flowers there, and in front of all that coffin, the tarnished Cupids that bore the mirror between their hands smirking down at it with a grim complacency.

On the corner of this table was a small golden salver, holding a plate of some black mouldered food, an antique decanter filled with wine, a glass, and a phial with some thick black liquid, uncorked. I felt weak and sick with the atmosphere of the place, and I seized the decanter, wiped the dust from it with my handkerchief, tasted, found that the wine was good, and drank a moderate draught. Immediately it was swallowed I felt a horrid giddiness, and sank upon the coffin. A raging pain was in my head and a sense of suffocation in my chest. After a few intolerable moments I felt better, but the heavy air pressed on me stiflingly, and I rushed from this inner room into the larger and outer chamber. Here a blast of cool air revived me, and I saw that the place was changed.

A dozen other candelabra besides those I had lighted were flaming round the walls, the hearth was all ruddy with a blazing fire, everything that had been dim was bright, the lustre had returned to the gilding, the flowers bloomed in the vases. A lady was sitting before the hearth in a low arm-chair. Her light loose gown swept about her on the carpet, her black hair fell round her to her knees, and into it her hands were thrust as she leaned her forehead upon them, and stared between them into the fire.

I had scarcely time to observe her attitude when she turned her head quickly towards me, and I recognised the handsome face of the magnificent lady who had played such a sinister part in the strange scenes that had been enacted before me two nights ago. I saw something dark looming behind her chair, but I thought it was only her shadow thrown backward by the firelight.

She arose and came to meet me, and I recoiled from her. There was something horridly fixed and hollow in her gaze, and filmy in the stirring of her garments. The shadow, as she moved, grew more firm and distinct in outline, and followed her like a servant where she went.

She crossed half of the room, then beckoned me, and sat down at the writing-table. The shadow waited beside her, adjusted her paper, placed the ink-bottle near her and the pen between her fingers. I felt impelled to approach her, and to take my place at her left shoulder, so as to be able to see what she might write. The shadow stood motionless at her other hand. As I became accustomed to the shadow's presence he grew more visibly loathsome and hideous. He was quite distinct from the lady, and moved independently of her with long ugly limbs. She hesitated about beginning to write, and he made a wild gesture with his arm, which brought her hand quickly to the paper, and her pen began to move at once. I needed not to bend and scrutinise in order to read. Every word as it was formed flashed before me like a meteor.

> I am the spirit of Madeline, Lady Thunder, who lived and died in this house, and whose coffin stands in yonder room among the vanities in which I delighted. I am constrained to make my confession to you, John Thunder, who are the present owner of the estates of your family.

Here the hand trembled and stopped writing. But the shadow made a threatening gesture, and the hand fluttered on.

> I was beautiful, poor, and ambitious, and when I entered this house first on the night of a ball given by Sir Luke Thunder, I determined to become its mistress. His daughter, Mary Thunder, was the only obstacle in my way. She divined my intention, and stood between me and her father. She was a gentle, delicate girl, and no match for me. I pushed her aside, and became Lady Thunder. After that I hated her, and made her dread me. I had gained the object of my ambition, but I was jealous of the influence possessed by her over her father, and I revenged myself by crushing the joy out of her young life. In this I defeated my own purpose. She eloped with a young man who was devoted to her, though poor, and beneath her in station. Her father was indignant at first, and my malice was satisfied; but as time passed on I had no children, and she had a son, soon after whose birth her husband died. Then her father took her back to his heart, and the boy was his idol and heir.

Again, the hand stopped writing, the ghostly head drooped, and the whole figure was convulsed. But the shadow gesticulated fiercely, and, cowering under its menace, the wretched spirit went on:

> I caused the child to be stolen away. I thought I had done it cunningly, but she tracked the crime home to me. She came and accused me of it, and in the desperation of my terror at discovery, I gave her poison to drink. She rushed from me and from the house in frenzy, and in her mortal anguish fell in the river. People thought she had gone mad from grief for her child, and committed suicide. I only knew the horrible truth.
>
> Sorrow brought an illness upon her father, of which he died. Up to the day of his death he had search made for the child. Believing that it was alive, and must be found, he willed all his

> property to it, his rightful heir, and to its heirs for ever. I buried the deeds under a tree in the orchard, and forged a will, in which all was bequeathed to me during my lifetime.
>
> I enjoyed my state and grandeur till the day of my death, which came upon me miserably, and, after that, my husband's possessions went to a distant relation of his family. Nothing more was heard of the fate of the child who was stolen; but he lived and married, and his daughter now toils for her bread—his daughter, who is the rightful owner of all that is said to belong to you, John Thunder. I tell you this that you may devote yourself to the task of discovering this wronged girl, and giving up to her that which you are unlawfully possessed of.
>
> Under the thirteenth tree standing on the brink of the river at the foot of the orchard you will find buried the genuine will of Sir Luke Thunder. When you have found and read it, do justice, as you value your soul. In order that you may know the grandchild of Mary Thunder when you find her, you shall behold her in a vision—

The last words grew dim before me; the lights faded away, and all the place was in darkness, except one spot on the opposite wall. On this spot the light glimmered softly, and against the brightness the outlines of a figure appeared, faintly at first, but, growing firm and distinct, became filled in and rounded at last to the perfect semblance of life. The figure was that of a young girl in a plain black dress, with a bright, happy face, and pale gold hair softly banded on her fair forehead. She might have been the twin-sister of the pale-faced girl whom I had seen bending over the cradle two nights ago; but her healthier, gladder, and prettier sister.

When I had gazed on her some moments, the vision faded away as it had come; the last vestige of the brightness died out upon the wall, and I found myself once more in total darkness. Stunned for a time by the sudden changes, I stood watching for the return of the lights and figures; but in vain. By-and-by my eyes grew accustomed to the obscurity, and I saw the sky glimmering behind the little window which I had left open. I could soon discern the writing-table beside me, and possessed myself of the slips of loose paper which lay upon it. I then made my way to the window. The first streaks of dawn were in the sky as I descended my ladder, and I thanked God that I breathed the fresh morning air once more, and heard the cheering sound of the cocks crowing.

All thought of acting immediately upon last night's strange revelations, almost all memory of them, was for the time banished from my mind by the unexpected trouble of the next few days. That morning I found an alarming change in Frank. Feeling sure that he was going to be ill, I engaged a lodging in a cottage in the neighbourhood, whither we removed before nightfall, leaving the accursed Rath behind us. Before midnight he was in the delirium of a raging fever.

I thought it right to let his poor little *fiancée* know his state, and wrote to her, trying to alarm her no more than was necessary. On the evening of the third day after my letter went I was sitting by Frank's bedside, when an unusual bustle outside aroused my curiosity, and going into the cottage kitchen I saw a figure standing in the firelight which seemed a third appearance of that vision of the pale-faced golden-haired girl which was now thoroughly imprinted on my memory,—a third, with all the woe of the first and all the beauty of the second. But this was a living, breathing apparition. She was throwing off her bonnet and shawl, and stood there at home in a moment in her plain black dress. I drew my hand across my eyes to make sure that they did not deceive me. I had beheld so many supernatural visions lately that it seemed as though I could scarcely believe in the reality of anything till I had touched it.

"Oh, sir," said the visitor, " I am Mary Leonard, and are you poor Frank's friend ? Oh, sir, we are all the world to one another, and I could not let him die without coming to see him!"

And here the poor little traveller burst into tears.

I cheered her as well as I could, telling her that Frank would soon, I trusted, be out of all danger. She told me that she had thrown up her situation in order to come and nurse him. I said we had got a more experienced nurse than she could be, and then I gave her to the care of our landlady, a motherly country-woman. After that I went back to Frank's bedside, nor left it for long till he was convalescent. The fever had swept away all that strangeness in his manner which had afflicted me, and he was quite himself again.

There was a joyful meeting of the lovers. The more I saw of Mary Leonard's bright face the more thoroughly was I convinced that she was the living counterpart of the vision I had seen in the burial chamber. I made inquiries as to her birth, and her father's history, and found that she was indeed the grandchild of that Mary Thunder whose history had been so strangely related to me, and the rightful heiress of all those properties which for a few months only had been mine. Under the tree in the orchard, the thirteenth, and that by which I had seen the lady digging, were found the buried deeds which had been described to me. I made an immediate transfer of property, whereupon some others who thought they had a chance of being my heirs disputed the matter with me, and went to law. Thus, the affair has gained publicity, and become a nine days' wonder.

Many things have been in my favour, however: the proving of Mary's birth and of Sir Luke's will, the identification of Lady Thunder's handwriting on the slips of paper which I had brought from the burial chamber; also, other matters which a search in that chamber brought to light. I triumphed, and I now go abroad, leaving Frank and his Mary made happy by the possession of what could only have been a burden to me.

So, the MS. ends. Major Thunder fell in battle a few years after the adventure it relates. Frank O'Brien's grandchildren hear of him with gratitude and awe. The Rath has been long since totally dismantled and left to go to ruin.

The Miniature

J.Y. Akerman

Calling one day on a friend, who had amassed a large collection of autographs, and other manuscript curiosities, he showed me a small quarto volume, which had been bequeathed to him by a relative, a physician, who for many years had been in extensive practice in London.

'He attended the patients at a private asylum for insane persons of the better classes,' said my friend, 'and I have often heard him speak of the writer of that beautiful MS, a gentleman of good family, who had been an inmate of —— House upwards of thirty years, at the time he was first called to attend him.'

On looking over the volume, I found it filled with scraps of poetry, extracts from classic authors, and even from the Talmudic writers; but what interested me most was a narrative of several pages, which appeared so circumstantially related as to leave little doubt of its being partly, if not wholly, founded on fact. I begged permission to make a transcript, which was readily granted, and the result is before the reader:

'We laugh at what we call the folk of our ancestors, and their notions of destiny, and the malignant influences of the stars. For what will our children deride us? Perhaps for dreaming that friendship was a reality, and that constant love dwelt upon earth. I once believed that friendship was not a vain name, and thought, with the antique sage, that one mind sometimes dwelt in two bodies. I dreamt, and woke to find that I had been dreaming!

'George S—— was my chum at school, and my inseparable companion at college. We quitted it at the same time, he to proceed to London, where he was in expectation of obtaining a lucrative appointment in one of the English colonies, and I to return for a short period to the family mansion, When I reached —— Hall, I found several visitors, among whom was my cousin, Maria D——. She had grown a woman since I had last met her, and I now thought I had never seen a more perfect figure, or a more bewitching countenance. Then she sang like a siren, and was an elegant horsewoman. Will those who read this wonder that I fell in love with her, that I spent nearly the whole of the day in her company, and that I could think of nothing in the world besides.

'Something occurred to delay my friend George's departure from England, and, as he was idling about town, I invited him to —— Hall. Great as was my regard for him, I now, however, discovered that I could live less in his company. No marvel! I preferred the society of my lovely cousin, upon whose heart, I had the happiness to learn, my constant attentions had already made a sensible impression. I hesitated to make her an offer, though I had even reason to believe our attachment was mutual, partly, perhaps, from that excessive delicacy which constantly attends on true love, and partly because I wished to do so when my friend should have left us less exposed to intrusion. Would that the deep sea had swallowed him up, or that he had rotted under a tropical sun, ere he had come to —— Hall!

'One morning I arose earlier than usual, and was looking from my chamber window on the beautiful prospect which the house commanded. Wrapped in a delightful reverie, of which my lovely cousin was the principal subject, I paid but little attention to the sound of voices below.

'Suddenly, however, I awoke to consciousness: for the sweet tones of a woman in earnest conversation struck on my ear. Yes, it was hers—it was Maria's. What could have called her forth at so early an hour? As I looked earnestly towards the walk which ran through the plantation, I saw emerge from it my cousin and my friend! My heart rose to my lips, and choked my utterance, or I should have cried out at the sight. I withdrew from the window, and threw myself on the sofa, tormented with surmises a thousand times more painful even than realities.

'At the breakfast table, I was moody and thoughtful, which my friend perceiving, attempted a joke; but I was in no humour to receive it, when Maria, in a compassionating tone, remarked that I looked unwell, and that I should take a walk or ride before breakfast, adding, that she and George S—— had walked for an hour and more in the plantation near the house. Though this announcement was certainly but ill calculated to afford perfect case to my mind, it was yet made with such an artless air, that my more gloomy surmises vanished, and I rallied; but I wished my friend would take his departure. Right truly says the Italian proverb, "*Love's guerdon is jealousy*."

'After breakfast, George S—— proposed a stroll on foot to the ruins of the Cistercian Abbey, about a mile distant from the Hall, to which I at once assented. As we walked along the beautiful and shady lane which led to the ruin, George was as loquacious as ever, talked of everybody and everything, and of his confident expectation of realizing a fortune abroad. I was, however, in no humour for talking, and made few remarks in reply; but he appeared not to heed my taciturnity, and, when he arrived at the spot, broke forth into raptures at the sight of the noble ruin.

'And truly it was a scene the contemplation of which might have lulled the minds of most men!

'A thousand birds were carolling around us; the grass near the ruin was not long and rank, but short, close, studded with trefoil, and soft as a rich carpet. Luxuriant ivy climbed the shattered walls, bleached by the winds of centuries; and the lizards, basking in the sun, darted beneath the fallen fragments at the sound of our footsteps as we approached the spot.

'We both sat down on a large stone, and surveyed the noble oriel. I was passionately fond of Gothic architecture, and had often admired this window, but I thought I had never seen it look so beautiful before. My moody thoughts fled, and I was wrapped in the contemplation of the exquisite tracery, when I was suddenly roused by my friend, who, patting me familiarly on the back, exclaimed, 'It is a beautiful ruin, Dick! How I wish thy sweet cousin, Maria, had accompanied us!"

'I was struck dumb by this declaration; but my look was sufficiently eloquent to be understood by him, and he did not fail to interpret it aright. He appeared confused, and I, regaining my self-possession, arose from my seat with the laconic remark, "Indeed!"

'George S—— attempted a laugh, but it failed; he was evidently as much disconcerted and disquieted as myself How lynx-eyed is love! We mutually read each other's hearts at the same moment.

'"I am sorry for you, Dick," said he, after a short pause, affecting very awkwardly an air of indifference; "'pon my soul, I am; but I'm over head and ears in love with the girl, and should die at the bare thought of her encouraging another."

'I wished for the strength of Milo, that I might have dashed out his brains against the huge stone on which we had been sitting. I felt my very blood seethe and simmer at the declaration, and with my clenched fist I struck him a violent and stunning blow, which, though it did not beat him to the ground, sent him staggering several paces backward.

'"Liar!" screamed I frantically, "take that! You dare not proceed with your folly."

'Recovering his feet, George S—— laid his hand on his sword, which he half unsheathed; but, as if conscious of there being no witness present, or wishing, perhaps, still further to convince me of the advantage he possessed, he did not draw.

'"Nay," said I, "out with your weapon; nothing less will do. I would rather lose my birth-right than yield to thee one, without whom life would be valueless."

'He smiled bitterly, wiped his bruised and bloody face, and slowly drew from his bosom a small miniature, encircled with diamonds, which he held before my eyes. One glance was sufficient, it was a portrait of Maria! It was that face which, sleeping or waking, has haunted me these thirty years past.

'"Villain!" I cried, clutching at the portrait with my left hand, while I snatched with my right hand my sword from its sheath, "you have stolen it."

'With assumed coolness, which it was impossible he could feel, he smiled again, put back the miniature in his bosom, and drew his sword. The next moment our weapons crossed with an angry clash, and were flashing in the morning's sun.

'My adversary was a perfect master of his weapon, and he pressed upon me with a vigour which any attempt to retaliate would have rendered dangerous in one so much inferior to him in skill. Maddened as I was, I yet restrained myself, and stood on my guard, my eyes fixed on his, and watching every glance: my wish to destroy him was intense. The fiend nerved my arm, and, while he warmed with the conflict, I became more cool and vigilant. At length, he appeared to grow weary, and then I pressed upon him with the fixed determination of taking his life; but he rallied instantly, and, in returning a thrust, which I intended for his heart, and which he parried scarcely in time, his foot slipped, and he fell on one knee, the point of my sword entering the left breast by accident.

'It was not a deep wound, and perhaps he felt it not; for he attempted to master my sword with his left hand, while he shortened his own weapon, and thrust fiercely at my throat, making at the same time a spring to regain his feet. But his fate was sealed: as he rose, I dashed aside the thrust intended for me, and sheathed my weapon in his left breast. I believe I must have pierced his heart; for he sank on his knees with a gasp, and the next moment fell heavily on his face, with his sword still clutched tightly in his hand.'

'Wearied, and panting from the effects of the violent struggle, I threw myself on the large stone which had so recently served us for a seat, and looked on the body of my adversary. He was dead!—that fatal thrust had destroyed all rivalry, but at the price of murder, the murder of one who had been my friend from boyhood upwards! A thousand conflicting emotions racked me as I beheld the piteous sight. Hatred was extinguished, and remorse succeeded; yet I still thought of the audacity of him who had provoked such deadly resentment. Fear, too, fear of the consequences of this fatal encounter in a solitary spot, without witnesses, added to the intensity of my misery, and I groaned in anguish. What was to be done? Should I go and deliver myself up to justice, and declare the whole truth? Should I fly, and leave the body of my friend to tell the dismal tale?—or should I bury him secretly, and leave it to be supposed that he had been robbed and murdered? As each suggestion was canvassed and rejected, in my despair, I even thought of dying by my own hand.

'"Ah! miserable wretch!" I exclaimed, "what hast thou done?—to what dire necessity has a fair and false face driven thee? Yet I will look once more on those bewitching features which have brought me to this wretched pass!"

'I stooped, and turned the dead man on his back. His pallid face was writhen and distorted, his lips were bloody, and his eyes, which were wide open, seemed still to glare with hatred and defiance, as when he stood before me in the desperate struggle for life and death. I tore open his vest, and discovered the wound which had killed him. It had collapsed, and looked no bigger than the puncture of a bodkin: but one little round crimson spot was visible, the haemorrhage was internal. There lay the miniature which, a few minutes before, had been held up exultingly to my frantic gaze. I seized, and pressed it to my lips, forgetting in my transports how dearly I had purchased it.

'This delirium, however, soon subsided, and my next thoughts were of the dead body. I looked about me for some nook where I might deposit it. There was a chasm in the ground among the ruins a few yards off, where the vaulted roof of the crypt had fallen in. It was scarcely large enough to admit the corpse; but I raised it in my arms, bore it thither, and with some difficulty thrust it through the aperture. I heard it fall, as if to some distance, with a dull, heavy sound; and, casting in after it my adversary's hat and sword, I hurried from the spot like another Cain.

'At dinner, one glance from Maria, as I replied, in answer to her enquiry after George S——, that he was gone to make a call a few miles oft—one glance, I say, thrilled through my very soul, and almost caused me to betray myself. All noticed my perturbed look, and, complaining of violent headache, I withdrew from the table ere the meal was ended, and betook myself to my chamber.

'How shall I paint the horror of that evening, of the night that succeeded it, and the mental darkness which fell upon my wretched self ere the morning dawned! Night came; I rang for lights, and attempted to read, but in vain; and, after pacing my chamber for some hours, overpowered by fatigue, I threw myself on the bed and slept, how long I know not. A succession of hideous dreams haunted my slumbers, still I was not awakened by them; the scenes shifted when arrived at their climax, and a new ordeal of horrors succeeded, yet, like him who suffers from nightmare, with a vague consciousness that all was not real, I wished to awake.

'Last of all, I dreamt that I was arraigned for the murder of my friend. The judge summed up the evidence, which, though purely circumstantial, was sufficient to condemn me; and, amidst the silence of the crowded court, broken only by the sobs of anxious and sympathizing friends and relatives, I received sentence of death, and was hurried back to my cell. Here, abandoned by all hope, I lay grovelling on my straw bed, and cursed the hour of my birth. A figure entered, and in gentle accents, which I thought I recognized, bade me arise, quit my prison-house, and follow. The figure was that of a woman closely veiled. She led the way, and passed the gaolers, who seemed buried in profound sleep. We left the town crossed the common, and entered a wood, when I threw myself at the feet of my deliverer, and passionately besought her to unveil. She shook her head mournfully, bade me wait a while till she should return with a change of apparel, and departed.

'I cast myself down at the foot of an aged oak, drew from my bosom the portrait of Maria, and, rapt in the contemplation of those lovely features, I did not perceive the approach of a man, the ranger of the forest, who, recognizing my prison-dress, darted upon me, exclaiming, "Villain! you have escaped from gaol, and stolen that miniature from the Hall!"

'I sprang to my tact, thrust the fatal portrait into my bosom, and would have fled; but he seized, and closed with me. In the struggle which followed we both fell, I undermost. At that moment, I awoke; I was in reality struggling with someone, but whom I could not tell; for my candles had burnt out, and the chamber was in total darkness! A powerful, bony hand grasped me tightly by the throat, while another was thrust into my bosom, as if in search of the miniature, which I had placed there previous to lying down.

'With a desperate effort, I disengaged myself and leaped from the bed; but I was again seized, and again my assailant attempted to reach my fatal prize. We struggled violently; at one time, I seemed to be overpowering him, and for several moments there was a pause, during which I heard my own breathing, and felt my own heart throbbing violently; but he with whom I contended seemed to breathe not, nor to feel like a warm and living man. An indescribable tremor shook my frame; I attempted to cry out, but my throat was rigid, and incapable of articulation. I made another effort to disengage myself from the grasp of my assailant, and in doing so drew him, as I found by the curtains, near to the window. Again, the hand was thrust into my bosom, and again I repelled it.

'Panting with the violence of the struggle, while a cold sweat burst out at every pore, I disengaged my right hand, and, determined to see whom I was contending with, I dashed aside the curtain. The dim light of the waning moon shone into the chamber; it fell upon the face of my antagonist, and one glance froze the blood in my veins. It was he!—it was George S——;—he whom I had murdered, glaring upon me with eyes which no mortal could look upon a second time! My brain whirled, a sound like the discharge of artillery shook the place, and I fell to the ground, blasted at the sight!

Here follows a few incoherent sentences, which I have not deemed it necessary to transcribe. The reader will probably supply the sequel to this sad story.

The Recrudescence of Imray

(A.k.a. *The Return of Imray*)
Rudyard Kipling

The doors were wide, the story saith,
Out of the night came the patient wraith,
He might not speak, and he could not stir
A hair of the Baron's minniver—
Speechless and strengthless, a shadow thin,
He roved the castle to seek his kin.
And oh, 'twas a piteous thing to see
The dumb ghost follow his enemy!

The Baron

Imray achieved the impossible. Without warning, for no conceivable motive, in his youth, at the threshold of his career he chose to disappear from the world—which is to say, the little Indian station where he lived.

Upon a day he was alive, well, happy, and in great evidence among the billiard-tables at his club. Upon a morning, he was not, and no manner of search could make sure where he might be. He had stepped out of his place; he had not appeared at his office at the proper time, and his dogcart was not upon the public roads. For these reasons, and because he was hampering, in a microscopical degree, the administration of the Indian Empire, that empire paused for one microscopical moment to make inquiry into the fate of Imray. Ponds were dragged, wells were plumbed, telegrams were despatched down the lines of railways and to the nearest seaport town—twelve hundred miles away; but Imray was not at the end of the drag-ropes nor the telegraph wires. He was gone, and his place knew him no more. Then the work of the great Indian Empire swept forward, because it could not be delayed, and Imray from being a man became a mystery—such a thing as men talk over at their tables in the club for a month, and then forget utterly. His guns, horses, and carts were sold to the highest bidder. His superior officer wrote an altogether absurd letter to his mother, saying that Imray had unaccountably disappeared, and his bungalow stood empty.

After three or four months of the scorching hot weather had gone by, my friend Strickland, of the police, saw fit to rent the bungalow from the native landlord. This was before he was engaged to Miss Youghal—an affair which has been described in another place—and while he was pursuing his investigations into native life. His own life was sufficiently peculiar, and men complained of his manners and customs. There was always food in his house, but there were no regular times for meals. He ate, standing up and walking about, whatever he might find at the sideboard, and this is not good for human beings. His domestic equipment was limited to six rifles, three shot-guns, five saddles, and a collection of stiff-jointed *mahseer*-rods, bigger and stronger than the largest salmon-rods.

These occupied one-half of his bungalow, and the other half was given up to Strickland and his dog Tietjens—an enormous Rampur slut who devoured daily the rations of two men. She spoke to Strickland in a language of her own; and whenever, walking abroad, she saw things calculated to destroy the peace of Her Majesty the Queen Empress, she returned to her master and laid information. Strickland would take steps at once, and the end of his labours was trouble and fine and imprisonment for other people. The natives believed that Tietjens was a familiar spirit, and treated her with the great reverence that is born of hate and fear.

One room in the bungalow was set apart for her special use. She owned a bedstead, a blanket, and a drinking-trough, and if any one came into Strickland's room at night her custom was to knock down the invader and give tongue till someone came with a light. Strickland owed his life to her, when he was on the Frontier, in search of a local murderer, who came in the gray dawn to send Strickland much farther than the Andaman Islands. Tietjens caught the man as he was crawling into Strickland's tent with a dagger between his teeth; and after his record of iniquity was established in the eyes of the law he was hanged. From that date Tietjens wore a collar of rough silver, and employed a monogram on her night-blanket; and the blanket was of double woven Kashmir cloth, for she was a delicate dog.

Under no circumstances would she be separated from Strickland; and once, when he was ill with fever, made great trouble for the doctors, because she did not know how to help her master and would not allow another creature to attempt aid. Macarnaght, of the Indian Medical Service, beat her over her head with a gun-butt before she could understand that she must give room for those who could give quinine.

A short time after Strickland had taken Imray's bungalow, my business took me through that station, and naturally, the club quarters being full, I quartered myself upon Strickland. It was a desirable bungalow, eight-roomed and heavily thatched against any chance of leakage from rain. Under the pitch of the roof ran a ceiling-cloth which looked just as neat as a white-washed ceiling. The landlord had repainted it when Strickland took the bungalow. Unless you knew how Indian bungalows were built you would never have suspected that above the cloth lay the dark three-cornered cavern of the roof, where the beams and the underside of the thatch harboured all manner of rats, bats, ants, and foul things.

Tietjens met me in the verandah with a bay like the boom of the bell of St. Paul's, putting her paws on my shoulder to show she was glad to see me. Strickland had contrived to claw together a sort of meal which he called lunch, and immediately after it was finished went out about his business. I was left alone with Tietjens and my own affairs. The heat of the summer had broken up and turned to the warm damp of the rains. There was no motion in the heated air, but the rain fell like ramrods on the earth, and flung up a blue mist when it splashed back. The bamboos, and the custard-apples, the poinsettias, and the mango-trees in the garden stood still while the warm water lashed through them, and the frogs began to sing among the aloe hedges. A little before the light failed, and when the rain was at its worst, I sat in the back verandah and heard the water roar from the eaves, and scratched myself because I was covered with the thing, called prickly-heat. Tietjens came out with me and put her head in my lap and was very sorrowful; so I gave her biscuits when tea was ready, and I took tea in the back verandah on account of the little coolness found there. The rooms of the house were dark behind me. I could smell Strickland's saddlery and the oil on his guns, and I had no desire to sit among these things.

My own servant came to me in the twilight, the muslin of his clothes clinging tightly to his drenched body, and told me that a gentleman had called and wished to see someone. Very much against my will, but only because of the darkness of the rooms, I went into the naked drawing-room, telling my man to bring the lights. There might or might not have been a caller waiting—it seemed to me that I saw a figure by one of the windows but when the lights came there was nothing save the spikes of the rain without, and the smell of the drinking earth in my nostrils. I explained to my servant that he was no wiser than he ought to be, and went back to the verandah to talk to Tietjens. She had gone out into the wet, and I could hardly coax her back to me; even with biscuits with sugar tops. Strickland came home, dripping wet, just before dinner, and the first thing he said was,

'Has anyone called?'

I explained, with apologies, that my servant had summoned me into the drawing-room on a false alarm; or that some loafer had tried to call on Strickland, and thinking better of it had fled after giving his name. Strickland ordered dinner, without comment, and since it was a real dinner with a white tablecloth attached, we sat down.

At nine o'clock Strickland wanted to go to bed, and I was tired too. Tietjens, who had been lying underneath the table, rose up, and swung into the least exposed verandah as soon as her master moved to his own room, which was next to the stately chamber set apart for Tietjens. If a mere wife had wished to sleep out of doors in that pelting rain it would not have mattered; but Tietjens was a dog, and therefore the better animal. I looked at Strickland, expecting to see him flay her with a whip. He smiled queerly, as a man would smile after telling some unpleasant domestic tragedy. 'She has done this ever since I moved in here,' said he. 'Let her go.'

The dog was Strickland's dog, so I said nothing, but I felt all that Strickland felt in being thus made light of. Tietjens encamped outside my bedroom window, and storm after storm came up, thundered on the thatch, and died away. The lightning spattered the sky as a thrown egg spatters a barn-door, but the light was pale blue, not yellow; and, looking through my split bamboo blinds, I could see the great dog standing, not sleeping, in the verandah, the hackles alift on her back and her feet anchored as tensely as the drawn wire-rope of a suspension bridge. In the very short pauses of the thunder I tried to sleep, but it seemed that someone wanted me very urgently. He, whoever he was, was trying to call me by name, but his voice was no more than a husky whisper. The thunder ceased, and Tietjens went into the garden and howled at the low moon. Somebody tried to open my door, walked about and about through the house and stood breathing heavily in the verandahs, and just when I was falling asleep I fancied that I heard a wild hammering and clamouring above my head or on the door.

I ran into Strickland's room and asked him whether he was ill, and had been calling for me. He was lying on his bed half dressed, a pipe in his mouth. 'I thought you'd come,' he said. 'Have I been walking round the house recently?'

I explained that he had been tramping in the dining-room and the smoking-room and two or three other places; and he laughed and told me to go back to bed. I went back to bed and slept till the morning, but through all my mixed dreams I was sure I was doing some one an injustice in not attending to his wants. What those wants were I could not tell; but a fluttering, whispering, bolt-fumbling, lurking, loitering Someone was reproaching me for my slackness, and, half awake, I heard the howling of Tietjens in the garden and the threshing of the rain.

I lived in that house for two days. Strickland went to his office daily, leaving me alone for eight or ten hours with Tietjens for my only companion. As long as the full light lasted I was comfortable, and so was Tietjens; but in the twilight she and I moved into the back verandah and cuddled each other for company. We were alone in the house, but none the less it was much too fully occupied by a tenant with whom I did not wish to interfere. I never saw him, but I could see the curtains between the rooms quivering where he had just passed through; I could hear the chairs creaking as the bamboos sprung under a weight that had just quitted them; and I could feel when I went to get a book from the dining-room that somebody was waiting in the shadows of the front verandah till I should have gone away. Tietjens made the twilight more interesting by glaring into the darkened rooms with every hair erect, and following the motions of something that I could not see. She never entered the rooms, but her eyes moved interestedly: that was quite sufficient. Only when my servant came to trim the lamps and make all light and habitable she would come in with me and spend her time sitting on her haunches, watching an invisible extra man as he moved about behind my shoulder. Dogs are cheerful companions.

I explained to Strickland, gently as might be, that I would go over to the club and find for myself quarters there. I admired his hospitality, was pleased with his guns and rods, but I did not much care for his house and its atmosphere. He heard me out to the end, and then smiled very wearily, but without contempt, for he is a man who understands things. 'Stay on,' he said, 'and see what this thing means. All you have talked about I have known since I took the bungalow. Stay on and wait. Tietjens has left me. Are you going too?'

I had seen, him through one little affair, connected with a heathen idol, that had brought me to the doors of a lunatic asylum, and I had no desire to help him through further experiences. He was a man to whom unpleasantnesses arrived as do dinners to ordinary people.

Therefore I explained more clearly than ever that I liked him immensely, and would be happy to see him in the daytime; but that I did not care to sleep under his roof. This was after dinner, when Tietjens had gone out to lie in the verandah.

''Pon my soul, I don't wonder,' said Strickland, with his eyes on the ceiling-cloth. 'Look at that!'

The tails of two brown snakes were hanging between the cloth and the cornice of the wall. They threw long shadows in the lamplight.

'If you are afraid of snakes of course—' said Strickland.

I hate and fear snakes, because if you look into the eyes of any snake you will see that it knows all and more of the mystery of man's fall, and that it feels all the contempt that the Devil felt when Adam was evicted from Eden. Besides which its bite is generally fatal, and it twists up trouser legs.

'You ought to get your thatch overhauled,' I said. 'Give me a *mahseer*-rod, and we'll poke 'em down.'

' They'll hide among the roof-beams,' said Strickland. 'I can't stand snakes overhead. I'm going up into the roof. If I shake 'em down, stand by with a cleaning-rod and break their backs.'

I was not anxious to assist Strickland in his work, but I took the cleaning-rod and waited in the dining-room, while Strickland brought a gardener's ladder from the verandah, and set it against the side of the room. The snake-tails drew themselves up and disappeared. We could hear the dry rushing scuttle of long bodies running over the baggy ceiling-cloth. Strickland took a lump with him, while I tried to make clear to him the danger of hunting roof-snakes between a ceiling-cloth and a thatch, apart from the deterioration of property caused by ripping out ceiling-cloths.

'Nonsense!' said Strickland. 'They're sure to hide near the walls by the cloth. The bricks are too cold for 'em, and the heat of the room is just what they like.' He put his hand to the corner of the stuff and ripped it from the cornice. It gave with a great sound of tearing, and Strickland put his head through the opening into the dark of the angle of the roof-beams. I set my teeth and lifted the rod, for I had not the least knowledge of what might descend.

'H'm!' said Strickland, and his voice rolled and rumbled in the roof. 'There's room for another set of rooms up here, and, by Jove, someone is occupying 'em!'

'Snakes?' I said from below.

'No. It's a buffalo. Hand me up the two last joints of a *mahseer*-rod, and I'll prod it. It's lying on the main roof-beam.'

I handed up the rod.

'What a nest for owls and serpents! No wonder the snakes live here,' said Strickland, climbing farther into the roof. I could see his elbow thrusting with the rod. 'Come out of that, whoever you are! Heads below there! It's falling.'

I saw the ceiling cloth nearly in the centre of the room bag with a shape that was pressing it downwards and downwards towards the lighted lamp on the table. I snatched the lamp out of danger and stood back. Then the cloth ripped out from the walls, tore, split, swayed, and shot down upon the table something that I dared not look at, till Strickland had slid down the ladder and was standing by my side.

He did not say much, being a man of few words; but he picked up the loose end of the tablecloth and threw it over the remnants on the table.

'It strikes me,' said he, putting down the lamp, 'our friend Imray has come back. Oh! you would, would you?'

There was a movement under the cloth, and a little snake wriggled out, to be back-broken by the butt of the *mahseer*-rod. I was sufficiently sick to make no remarks worth recording.

Strickland meditated, and helped himself to drinks. The arrangement under the cloth made no more signs of life.

'Is it Imray?' I said.

Strickland turned back the cloth for a moment, and looked.

'It is Imray,' he said; 'and his throat is cut from ear to ear.'

Then we spoke, both together and to ourselves: 'That's why he whispered about the house.'

Tietjens, in the garden, began to bay furiously. A little later her great nose heaved open the dining-room door.

She snuffed and was still. The tattered ceiling-cloth hung down almost to the level of the table, and there was hardly room to move away from the discovery.

Tietjens came in and sat down; her teeth bared under her lip and her forepaws planted. She looked at Strickland.

'It's a bad business, old lady,' said he. 'Men don't climb up into the roofs of their bungalows to die, and they don't fasten up the ceiling cloth behind 'em. Let's think it out.'

'Let's think it out somewhere else,' I said.

'Excellent idea! Turn the lamps out. We'll get into my room.'

I did not turn the lamps out. I went into Strickland's room first, and allowed him to make the darkness. Then he followed me, and we lit tobacco and thought. Strickland thought. I smoked furiously, because I was afraid.

'Imray is back,' said Strickland. 'The question is—who killed Imray? Don't talk, I've a notion of my own. When I took this bungalow I took over most of Imray's servants. Imray was guileless and inoffensive, wasn't he?'

I agreed; though the heap under the cloth had looked neither one thing nor the other.

'If I call in all the servants they will stand fast in a crowd and lie like Aryans. What do you suggest?'

'Call 'em in one by one,' I said.

'They'll run away and give the news to all their fellows,' said Strickland. 'We must segregate 'em. Do you suppose your servant knows anything about it?'

'He may, for aught I know; but I don't think it's likely. He has only been here two or three days,' I answered. 'What's your notion?'

'I can't quite tell. How the dickens did the man get the wrong side of the ceiling-cloth?'

There was a heavy coughing outside Strickland's bedroom door. This showed that Bahadur Khan, his body-servant, had waked from sleep and wished to put Strickland to bed.

'Come in,' said Strickland. 'It's a very warm night, isn't it?'

Bahadur Khan, a great, green-turbaned, six-foot Mahomedan, said that it was a very warm night; but that there was more rain pending, which, by His Honour's favour, would bring relief to the country.

'It will be so, if God pleases,' said Strickland, tugging off his boots. 'It is in my mind, Bahadur Khan, that I have worked thee remorselessly for many days—ever since that time when thou first earnest into my service. What time was that?'

'Has the Heaven-born forgotten? It was when Imray Sahib went secretly to Europe without warning given; and I—even I—came into the honoured service of the protector of the poor.'

'And Imray Sahib went to Europe?'

'It is so said among those who were his servants.

'And thou wilt take service with him when he returns?'

'Assuredly, *sahib*. He was a good master, and cherished his dependants.'

'That is true. I am very tired, but I go buck-shooting tomorrow. Give me the little sharp rifle that I use for black-buck; it is in the case yonder.'

The man stooped over the case; handed barrels, stock, and fore-end to Strickland, who fitted all together, yawning dolefully. Then he reached down to the gun-case, took a solid-drawn cartridge, and slipped it into the breech of the .360 Express.

'And Imray Sahib has gone to Europe secretly! That is very strange, Bahadur Khan, is it not?'

'What do I know of the ways of the white man, Heaven-born?'

'Very little, truly. But thou shalt know more *anon*. It has reached me that Imray Sahib has returned from his so long journeyings, and that even now he lies in the next room, waiting his servant.'

'*Sahib*!'

The lamplight slid along the barrels of the rifle as they levelled themselves at Bahadur Khan's broad breast.

'Go and look!' said Strickland. 'Take a lamp. Thy master is tired, and he waits thee. Go!'

The man picked up a lamp, and went into the dining-room, Strickland following, and almost pushing him with the muzzle of the rifle. He looked for a moment at the black depths behind the ceiling-cloth; at the writhing snake under foot; and last, a gray glaze settling on his face, at the thing under the tablecloth.

'Hast thou seen?' said Strickland after a pause.

'I have seen. I am clay in the white man's hands. What does the Presence do?'

'Hang thee within the month. What else?'

'For killing him? Nay, *sahib*, consider. Walking among us, his servants, he cast his eyes upon my child, who was four years old. Him he bewitched, and in ten days he died of the fever—my child!'

'What said Imray Sahib?'

'He said he was a handsome child, and patted him on the head; wherefore my child died. Wherefore I killed Imray Sahib in the twilight, when he had come back from office, and was sleeping. Wherefore I dragged him up into the roof-beams and made all fast behind him. The Heaven-born knows all things. I am the servant of the Heaven-born.'

Strickland looked at me above the rifle, and said, in the vernacular, 'Thou art witness to this saying? He has killed.'

Bahadur Khan stood ashen gray in the light of the one lamp. The need for justification came upon him very swiftly. 'I am trapped,' he said, 'but the offence was that man's. He cast an evil eye upon my child, and I killed and hid him. Only such as are served by devils,' he glared at Tietjens, couched stolidly before him, 'only such could know what I did.'

'It was clever. But thou shouldst have lashed him to the beam with a rope. Now, thou thyself wilt hang by a rope. Orderly!'

A drowsy policeman answered Strickland's call. He was followed by another, and Tietjens sat wondrous still.

'Take him to the police-station,' said Strickland. 'There is a case toward.'

'Do I hang, then?' said Bahadur Khan, making no attempt to escape, and keeping his eyes on the ground.

'If the sun shines or the water runs—yes!' said Strickland.

Bahadur Khan stepped back one long pace, quivered, and stood still. The two policemen waited further orders.

'Go!' said Strickland.

'Nay; but I go very swiftly,' said Bahadur Khan. 'Look! I am even now a dead man.'

He lifted his foot, and to the little toe there clung the head of the half-killed snake, firm fixed in the agony of death.

'I come of land-holding stock,' said Bahadur Khan, rocking where he stood. 'It were a disgrace to me to go to the public scaffold: therefore I take this way. Be it remembered that the *sahib's* shirts are correctly enumerated, and that there is an extra piece of soap in his wash-basin. My child was bewitched, and I slew the wizard. Why should you seek to slay me with the rope? My honour is saved, and—and—I die.'

At the end of an hour he died, as they die who are bitten by the little brown *karait*, and the policemen bore him and the thing under the tablecloth to their appointed places. All were needed to make clear the disappearance of Imray.

'This,' said Strickland, very calmly, as he climbed into bed, 'is called the nineteenth century. Did you hear what that man said?'

'I heard,' I answered. 'Imray made a mistake.'

'Simply and solely through not knowing the nature of the Oriental, and the coincidence of a little seasonal fever. Bahadur Khan had been with him for four years.'

I shuddered. My own servant had been with me for exactly that length of time. When I went over to my own room I found my man waiting, impassive as the copper head on a penny, to pull off my boots.

'What has befallen Bahadur Khan?' said I.

'He was bitten by a snake and died. The rest the *sahib* knows,' was the answer.

'And how much of this matter hast thou known?'

'As much as might be gathered from One coming in in the twilight to seek satisfaction. Gently, *sahib*. Let me pull off those boots.'

I had just settled to the sleep of exhaustion when I heard Strickland shouting from his side of the house—

'Tietjens has come back to her place!'

And so she had. The great deerhound was couched stately on her own bedstead on her own blanket, while, in the next room, the idle, empty, ceiling-cloth waggled as it trailed on the table.

The Shadow of a Shade

Tom Hood

My sister Lettie has lived with me ever since I had a home of my own. She was my little housekeeper before I married. Now she is my wife's constant companion, and the 'darling auntie' of my children, who go to her for comfort, advice, and aid in all their little troubles and perplexities.

But, though she has a comfortable home, and loving hearts around her, she wears a grave, melancholy look on her face, which puzzles acquaintances and grieves friends.

A disappointment! Yes, the old story of a lost lover is the reason for Lettie's looks. She has had good offers often; but since she lost the first love of her heart she has never indulged in the happy dream of loving and being loved.

George Mason was a cousin of my wife's—a sailor by profession. He and Lettie met one another at our wedding, and fell in love at first sight. George's father had seen service before him on the great mysterious sea, and had been especially known as a good Arctic sailor, having shared in more than one expedition in search of the North Pole and the North-West Passage.

It was not a matter of surprise to me, therefore, when George volunteered to go out in the *Pioneer*, which was being fitted out for a cruise in search of Franklin and his missing expedition.

There was a fascination about such an undertaking that I felt I could not have resisted had I been in his place. Of course, Lettie did not like the idea at all, but he silenced her by telling her that men who volunteered for Arctic search were never lost sight of, and that he should not make as much advance in his profession in a dozen years as he would in the year or so of this expedition.

I cannot say that Lettie, even after this, was quite satisfied with the notion of his going, but, at all events, she did not argue against it any longer. But the grave look, which is now habitual with her, but was a rare thing in her young and happy days, passed over her face sometimes when she thought no one was looking.

My younger brother, Harry, was at this time an academy student. He was only a beginner then.

Now he is pretty well known in the art world, and his pictures command fair prices. Like all beginners in art, he was full of fancies and theories. He would have been a pre-Raphaelite, only pre-Raphaelism had not been invented then. His peculiar craze was for what he styled the Venetian School. Now, it chanced that George had a fine Italian-looking head, and Harry persuaded him to sit to him for his portrait. It was a fair likeness, but a very moderate work of art. The background was so very dark, and George's naval costume so very deep in colour, that the face came out too white and staring. It was a three-quarter picture; but only one hand showed in it, leaning on the hilt of a sword. As George said, he looked much more like the commander of a Venetian galley than a modern mate.

However, the picture pleased Lettie, who did not care much about art provided the resemblance was good. So, the picture was duly framed—in a tremendously heavy frame, of Harry's ordering—and hung up in the dining-room.

And now the time for George's departure was growing nearer. The *Pioneer* was nearly ready to sail, and her crew only waited orders. The officers grew acquainted with each other before sailing, which was an advantage. George took up very warmly with the surgeon, Vincent Grieve, and, with my permission, brought him to dinner once or twice.

'Poor chap, he has no friends nearer than the Highlands, and it's precious lonely work.'

'Bring him by all means, George! You know that any friends of yours will be welcome here.'

So, Vincent Grieve came. I am bound to say I was not favourably impressed by him, and almost wished I had not consented to his coming. He was a tall, pale, fair young man, with a hard Scotch face and a cold, grey eye. There was something in his expression, too, that was unpleasant—something cruel or crafty, or both.

I considered that it was very bad taste for him to pay such marked attention to Lettie, coming, as he did, as the friend of her *fiancé*. He kept by her constantly and anticipated George in all the little attentions which a lover delights to pay. I think George was a little put out about it, though he said nothing, attributing his friend's offence to lack of breeding.

Lettie did not like it at all. She knew that she was not to have George with her much longer, and she was anxious to have him to herself as much as possible. But as Grieve was her lover's friend she bore the infliction with the best possible patience.

The surgeon did not seem to perceive in the least that he was interfering where he had no business. He was quite self-possessed and happy, with one exception. The portrait of George seemed to annoy him. He had uttered a little impatient exclamation when he first saw it which drew my attention to him; and I noticed that he tried to avoid looking at it. At last, when dinner came, he was told to sit exactly facing the picture. He hesitated for an instant and then sat down, but almost immediately rose again.

'It's very childish and that sort of thing,' he stammered, 'but I cannot sit opposite that picture.'

'It is not high art,' I said, 'and may irritate a critical eye.'

'I know nothing about art,' he answered, 'but it is one of those unpleasant pictures whose eyes follow you about the room. I have an inherited horror of such pictures. My mother married against her father's will, and when I was born she was so ill she was hardly expected to live.

When she was sufficiently recovered to speak without delirious rambling she implored them to remove a picture of my grandfather that hung in the room, and which she vowed made threatening faces at her. It's superstitious, but constitutional—I have a horror of such paintings!'

I believe George thought this was a ruse of his friends to get a seat next to Lettie; but I felt sure it was not, for I had seen the alarmed expression of his face.

At night, when George and his friend were leaving, I took an opportunity to ask the former, half in a joke, if he should bring the surgeon to see us again. George made a very hearty assertion to the contrary, adding that he was pleasant enough company among men at an inn, or onboard ship, but not where ladies were concerned.

But the mischief was done. Vincent Grieve took advantage of the introduction and did not wait to be invited again. He called the next day, and nearly ever' day after. He was a more frequent visitor than George now, for George was obliged to attend to his duties, and they kept him on board the Pioneer pretty constantly, whereas the surgeon, having seen to the supply of drugs, etc., was pretty well at liberty. Lettie avoided him as much as possible, but he generally brought, or professed to bring, some little message from George to her, so that he had an excuse for asking to see her.

On the occasion of his last visit—the day before the *Pioneer* sailed—Lettie came to me in great distress. The young cub had actually the audacity to tell her he loved her. He knew, he said, about her engagement to George, but that did not prevent another man from loving her too. A man could no more help falling in love than he could help taking a fever. Lettie stood upon her dignity and rebuked him severely; but he told her he could see no harm in telling her of his passion, though he knew it was a hopeless one.

'A thousand things may happen,' he said at last, 'to bring your engagement with George Mason to an end. Then perhaps you will not forget that another loves you!'

I was very angry, and was forthwith going to give him my opinion on his conduct, when Lettie told me he was gone, that she had bade him go and had forbidden him the house. She only told me in order to protect herself, for she did not intend to say anything to George, for fear it should lead to a duel or some other violence.

That was the last we saw ofVincent Grieve before the *Pioneer* sailed.

George came the same evening, and was with us till daybreak, when he had to tear himself away and join his ship.

After shaking hands with him at the door, in the cold, grey, drizzly dawn, I turned back into the dining-room, where poor Lettie was sobbing on the sofa.

I could not help starting when I looked at George's portrait, which hung above her. The strange light of daybreak could hardly account for the extraordinary pallor of the face. I went close to it and looked hard at it. I saw that it was covered with moisture, and imagined that I hat possibly made it look so pale. As for the moisture, I supposed poor Lettie had been kissing the beloved's portrait, and that the moisture was caused by her tears.

It was not till a long time after, when I was jestingly telling Harry how his picture had been caressed, that I learnt the error of my conjecture. Lettie assured me most solemnly that I was mistaken in supposing she had kissed it.

'It was the varnish blooming, I expect,' said Harry. And thus, the subject was dismissed, for I said no more, though I knew well enough, in spite of my not being an artist, that the bloom of varnish was quite another sort of thing.

The *Pioneer* sailed. We received—or, rather, Lettie received—two letters from George, which he had taken the opportunity of sending by homeward-bound whalers. In the second he said it was hardly likely he should have an opportunity of sending another, as they were sailing into high latitudes—into the solitary sea, to which none but expedition ships ever penetrated. They were all in high spirits, he said, for they had encountered very little ice and hoped to find clear water further north than usual. Moreover, he added, Grieve had held a sinecure so far, for there had not been a single case of illness on board.

Then came a long silence, and a year crept away very slowly for poor Lettie. Once we heard of the expedition from the papers. They were reported as pushing on and progressing favourably by a wandering tribe of Esquimaux with whom the captain of a Russian vessel fell in. They had laid the ship up for the winter, and were taking the boats on sledges, and believed they had met with traces of the lost crews that seemed to show they were on the right track.

The winter passed again, and spring came. It was a balmy, bright spring such as we get occasionally, even in this changeable and uncertain climate of ours.

One evening we were sitting in the dining-room with the window open, for, although we had long given up fires, the room was so oppressively warm that we were glad of the breath of the cool evening breeze.

Lettie was working. Poor child, though she never murmured, she was evidently pining at George's long absence. Harry was leaning out of the window, studying the evening effect on the fruit blossom, which was wonderfully early and plentiful, the season was so mild. I was sitting at the table, near the lamp, reading the paper.

Suddenly there swept into the room a chill. It was not a gust of cold wind, for the curtain by the open window did not swerve in the least. But the deathly cold pervaded the room—came, and was gone in an instant. Lettie shuddered, as I did, with the intense icy feeling.

She looked up. 'How curiously cold it has got all in a minute,' she said.

'We are having a taste of poor George's Polar weather,' I said with a smile.

At the same moment, I instinctively glanced towards his portrait. What I saw struck me dumb, A rush of blood, at fever heat, dispelled the numbing influence of the chill breath that had seemed to freeze me.

I have said the lamp was lighted; but it was only that I might read with comfort, for the violet twilight was still so full of sunset that the room was not dark. But as I looked at the picture I saw it had undergone a strange change. I saw it as plainly as possible. It was no delusion, coined for the eye by the brain.

I saw, in the place of George's head, a ginning skull! I stared at it hard; but it was no trick of fancy. I could see the hollow orbits, the gleaming teeth, the fleshless cheekbones—it was the head of death!

Without saying a word, I rose from my chair and walked straight up to the painting. As I drew nearer a sort of mist seemed to pass before it; and as I stood close to it, I saw only the face of George. The spectral skull had vanished.

'Poor George!' I said unconsciously.

Lettie looked up. The tone of my voice had alarmed her, the expression of my face did not reassure her.

'What do you mean? Have you heard anything? Oh, Robert, in mercy tell me!'

She got up and came over to me and, laying her hands on my arm, looked up into my face imploringly.

'No, my dear; how should I hear? Only I could not help thinking of the privation and discomfort he must have gone through. I was reminded of it by the cold—'

'Cold!' said Harry, who had left the window by this time. 'Cold! what on earth are you talking about? Cold, such an evening as this! You must have had a touch of ague, I should think.'

'Both Lettie and I felt it bitterly cold a minute or two ago. Did not you feel it?'

'Not a bit; and as I was three parts out of the window I ought to have felt it if anyone did.'

It was curious, but that strange chill had been felt only in the room. It was not the night wind, but some supernatural breath connected with the dread apparition I had seen. It was, indeed, the chill of polar winter—the icy shadow of the frozen North.

'What is the day of the month, Harry?' I asked.

'Today—the 23rd, I think,' he answered; then added, taking up the newspaper I had been reading: 'Yes, here you are. Tuesday, February the 23rd, if the *Daily News* tells truth, which I suppose it does. Newspapers can afford to tell the truth about dates, whatever they may do about art.' Harry had been rather roughly handled by the critic of a morning paper for one of his pictures a few days before, and he was a little angry with journalism generally.

Presently Lettie left the mom, and I told Harry what I had felt and seen, and told him to take note of the date, for I feared that some mischance had befallen George.

I'll put it down in my pocket-book, Bob. But you and Lettie must have had a touch of the cold shivers, and your stomach or fancy misled you—they're the same thing, you know. Besides, as regards the picture, there's nothing in that! There is a skull there, of course. As Tennyson says:

Any face, however full,
Padded round with flesh and fat,
Is but modelled on a skull.

The skull's there—just as in even good figure-subject the nude is there under the costumes. You fancy that is a mere coat of paint. Nothing of the kind! Art lives, sir! That is just as much a real head as yours is with all the muscles and bones, just the same. That's what makes the difference between art and rubbish.'

This was a favourite theory of Harry's, who had not yet developed from the dreamer into the worker. As I did not care to argue with him, I allowed the subject to drop after we had written down the date in our pocket-books. Lettie sent down word presently that she did not feel well and had gone to bed. My wife came down presently and asked what had happened. She had been up with the children and had gone in to see what was the matter with Lettie.

'I think it was very imprudent to sit with the window open, dear. I know the evenings are warm, but the night air strikes cold at times—at any rate, Lettie seems to have caught a violent cold, for she is shivering very much. I am afraid she has got a chill from the open windows.'

I did not say anything to her then, except that both Lettie and I had felt a sudden coldness; for I did not care to enter into an explanation again, for I could see Harry was inclined to laugh at me for being so superstitious.

At night, however, in our own room, I told my wife what had occurred, and what my apprehensions were. She was so upset and alarmed that I almost repented having done so.

The next morning Lettie was better again, and as we did not either of us refer to the events of the preceding night the circumstance appeared to be forgotten by us all.

But from that day I was ever inwardly dreading the arrival of bad news. And at last it came, as I expected.

One morning, just as I was coming downstairs to breakfast, there came a knock at the door, and Harry made his appearance. It was a very early visit from him, for he generally used to spend his mornings at the studio, and drop in on his way home at night.

He was looking pale and agitated.

'Lettie's not down, is she, yet?' he asked; and then, before I could answer, added another question:

'What newspaper do you take?'

'The *Daily News*,' I answered. 'Why?'

'She's not down?'

'No.'

'Thank God! Look here!'

He took a paper from his pocket and gave it to me, pointing out a short paragraph at the bottom of one of the columns.

I knew what was coming the moment he spoke about Lettie.

The paragraph was headed, 'Fatal Accident to one of the Officers of the *Pioneer* Expedition Ship'. It stated that news had been received at the Admiralty stating that the expedition had failed to find the missing crews, but had come upon some traces of them. Want of stores and necessaries had compelled them to turn back without following those traces up; but the commander was anxious, as soon as the ship could be refitted, to go out and take up the trail where he left it. An unfortunate accident had deprived him of one of his most promising officers, Lieutenant Mason, who was precipitated from an iceberg and killed while out shooting with the surgeon. He was beloved by all, and his death had flung a gloom over the gallant little troop of explorers.

'It's not in the *News* today, thank goodness, Bob,' said Harry, who had been searching that paper while I was reading the one he brought—'but you must keep a sharp look-out for some days and not let Lettie see it when it appears, as it is certain to do sooner or later.'

Then we both of us looked at each other with tears in our eyes. 'Poor George!—poor Lettie!' we sighed softly.

'But she must be told at some time or other?' I said despairingly.

'I suppose so,' said Harry; 'but it would kill her to come on it suddenly like this. Where's your wife?'

She was with the children, but I sent up for her and told her the ill-tidings.

She had a hard struggle to conceal her emotion, for Lettie's sake. But the tears would flow in spite of her efforts.

'How shall I ever find courage to tell her?' she asked.

'Hush!' said Harry, suddenly grasping her arm and looking towards the door.

I turned. There stood Lettie, with her face pale as death, with her lips apart, and with a blind look about her eyes. She had come in without our hearing her. We never learnt how much of the story she had overheard; but it was enough to tell her the worst. We all sprang towards her; but she only waved us away, turned round, and went upstairs again without saying a word. My wife hastened up after her and found her on her knees by the bed, insensible.

'The doctor was sent for, and restoratives were promptly administered. She came to herself again, but lay dangerously ill for some weeks from the shock.

It was about a month after she was well enough to come downstairs again that I saw in the paper an announcement of the arrival of the *Pioneer*. The news had no interest for any of us now, so I said nothing about it. The mere mention of the vessel's name would have caused the poor girl pain.

One afternoon shortly after this, as I was writing a letter, there came a loud knock at the front door. I looked up from my writing and listened; for the voice which enquired if I was in sounded strange, but yet not altogether unfamiliar. As I looked up, puzzling whose it could he, my eye rested accidentally upon poor George's portrait. Was I dreaming or awake?

I have told you that the one hand was resting on a sword. I could see now distinctly that the forefinger was raised, as if in warning. I looked at it hard, to assure myself it was no fancy, and then I perceived, standing out bright and distinct on the pale face, two large drops, as if of blood.

I walked up to it, expecting the appearance to vanish, as the skull had done. It did not vanish; but the uplifted finger resolved itself into a little white moth which had settled on the canvas. The red drops were fluid, and certainly not blood, though I was at a loss for the time to account for them.

The moth seemed to be in a torpid state, so I took it off the picture and placed it under an inverted wine-glass on the mantelpiece. All this took less time to do than to describe. As I turned from the mantelpiece the servant brought in a card, saying the gentleman was waiting in the hall to know if I would see him.

On the card was the name of 'Vincent Grieve, of the exploring vessel *Pioneer*'.

'Thank Heaven, Lettie is out,' thought I; and then added aloud to the servant, 'Show him in here; and Jane, if your mistress and Miss Lettie come in before the gentleman goes, tell them I have someone with me on business and do not wish to be disturbed.'

I went to the door to meet Grieve. As he crossed the threshold, and before he could have seen the portrait, he stopped, shuddered and turned white, even to his thin lips.

'Cover that picture before I come in,' he said hurriedly, in a low voice. 'You remember the effect it had upon me. Now, with the memory of poor Mason, it would be worse than ever.'

I could understand his feelings better now than at first; for I had come to look on the picture with some awe myself. So, I took the cloth off a little round table that stood under the window and hung it over the portrait.

When I had done so Grieve came in. He was greatly altered. He was thinner and paler than ever; hollow-eyed and hollow-checked. He had acquired a strange stoop, too, and his eyes had lost the crafty look for a look of terror, like that of a hunted beast. I noticed that he kept glancing sideways every instant, as if unconsciously. It looked as if he heard someone behind him.

I had never liked the man; but now I felt an insurmountable repugnance to him—so great a repugnance that, when I came to think of it, I felt pleased that the incident of covering the picture at his request had led to my not shaking hands with him.

I felt that I could not speak otherwise than coldly to him; indeed, I had to speak with painful plainness.

I told him that, of course, I was glad to see him back, but that I could not ask him to continue to visit us. I should be glad to hear the particulars of poor George's death, but that I could not let him see my sister, and hinted, as delicately as I could, at the impropriety of which he had been guilty when he last visited.

He took it all very quietly, only giving a long, wean sigh when I told him I must beg him not to repeat his visit. He looked so weak and ill that I was obliged to ask him to take a glass of wine—an offer which he seemed to accept with great pleasure.

I got out the sherry and biscuits and placed them on the table between us, and he took a glass and drank it off greedily.

It was not without some difficulty that I could get him to tell me of George's death. He related, with evident reluctance, how they had gone out to shoot a white bear which they had seen on an iceberg stranded along the shore. The top of the berg was ridged like the roof of a house, sloping down on one side to the edge of a tremendous overhanging precipice. They had scrambled along the ridge in order to get nearer the game, when George incautiously ventured on the sloping side.

'I called out to him', said Grieve, 'and begged him to come back, but too late. The surface was as smooth and slippery as glass. He tried to turn back, but slipped and fell. And then began a horrible scene. Slowly, slowly, but with ever-increasing motion, he began to slide down towards the edge. There was nothing to grasp at—no irregularity or projection on the smooth face of the ice. I tore off my coat, and hastily attaching it to the stock of my gun, pushed the latter towards him; but it did not reach far enough. Before I could lengthen it, by tying my cravat to it, he had slid yet further away, and more quickly. I shouted in agony; but there was no one within hearing. He, too, saw his fate was sealed; and he could only tell me to bring his last farewell to you, and—and to her!'—Here Grieve's voice broke—'and it was all over! He clung to the edge of the precipice instinctively for one second, and was gone!'

Just as Grieve uttered the last word, his jaw fell; his eyeballs seemed ready to start from his head; he sprang to his feet, pointed at something behind me, and then flinging up his arms, fell, with a scream, as if he had been shot. He was seized with an epileptic fit.

I instinctively looked behind me as I hurried to raise him from the floor. The cloth had fallen from the picture, where the face of George, made paler than ever by the gouts of red, looked sternly down.

I rang the bell. Luckily, Harry had come in; and, when the servant told him what was the matter, he came in and assisted me in restoring Grieve to consciousness. Of course, I covered the painting up again.

When he was quite himself again, Grieve told me he was subject to fits occasionally.

He seemed very anxious to learn if he had said or done anything extraordinary while he was in the fit, and appeared reassured when I said he had not. He apologised for the trouble he had given, and said as soon as he was strong enough he would take his leave. He was leaning on the mantelpiece as he said this. The little white moth caught his eye.

'So, you have had someone else from the *Pioneer* here before me?' he said, nervously.

I answered in the negative, asking what made him think so.

'Why, this little white moth is never found in such southern latitudes. It is one of the last signs of life northward. Where did you get it?'

'I caught it here, in this room,' I answered.

'That is very strange. I never heard of such a thing before. We shall hear of showers of blood soon, I should not wonder.'

'What do you mean?' I asked.

'Oh, these little fellows emit little drops of a red-looking fluid at certain seasons, and sometimes so plentifully that the superstitious think it is a shower of blood. I have seen the snow quite stained in places. Take care of it, it is a rarity in the south.'

I noticed, after he left, which he did almost immediately, that there was a drop of red fluid on the marble under the wine-glass. The blood-stain on the picture was accounted for; but how came the moth here?

And there was another strange thing about the man, which I had scarcely been able to assure myself of in the room, where there were cross-lights, but about which there was no possible mistake, when I saw him walking away up the street.

'Harry, here—quick!' I called to my brother, who at once came to the window. 'You're an artist, tell me, is there anything strange about that man?'

'No; nothing that I can see,' said Harry, but then suddenly, in an altered tone, added, 'Yes, there is. By Jove, he has a double shadow!'

That was the explanation of his sidelong glances, of the habitual stoop. There was a something always at his side, which none could see, but which east a shadow.

He turned, presently, and saw us at the window. Instantly, he crossed the road to the shady side of the street. I told Harry all that had passed, and we agreed that it would be as well not to say a word to Lettie.

Two days later, when I returned from a visit to Harry's studio, I found the whole house in confusion.

I learnt from Lettie that while my wife was upstairs, Grieve had called, had not waited for the servant to announce him, but had walked straight into the dining-room, where Lettie was sitting.

She noticed that he avoided looking at the picture, and, to make sure of not seeing it, had seated himself on the sofa just beneath it. He had then, in spite of Lettie's angry remonstrances, renewed his offer of love, strengthening it finally by assuring her that poor George with his dying breath had implored him to seek her, and watch over her, and marry her.

'I was so indignant I hardly knew how to answer him,' said Lettie. 'When, suddenly, just as he uttered the last words, there came a twang like the breaking of a guitar—and—I hardly know how to describe it—but the portrait had fallen, and the corner of the heavy frame had struck him on the head, cutting it open, and rendering him insensible.'

They had carried him upstairs, by the direction of the doctor, for whom my wife at once sent on hearing what had occurred. He was laid on the couch in my dressing-room, where I went to see him. I intended to reproach him for coming to the house, despite my prohibition, but I found him delirious. The doctor said it was a queer case; for, though the blow was a severe one, it was hardly enough to account for the symptoms of brain-fever. When he learnt that Grieve had but just returned in the *Pioneer* from the North, he said it was possible that the privation and hardship had told on his constitution and sown the seeds of the malady.

We sent for a nurse, who was to sit up with him, by the doctor's directions.

The rest of my story is soon told. In the middle of the night I was roused by a loud scream. I slipped on my clothes, and rushed out to find the nurse, with Lettie in her arms, in a faint. We carried her into her room, and then the nurse explained the mystery to us.

It appears that about midnight Grieve sat up in bed, and began to talk. And he said such terrible things that the nurse became alarmed. Nor was she much reassured when she became aware that the light of her single candle flung what seemed to be two shadows of the sick man on the wall.

Terrified beyond measure, she had crept into Lettie's room, and confided her fears to her; and Lettie, who was a courageous and kindly girl, dressed herself, and said she would sit with her.

She, too, saw the double shadow—but what she heard was far more terrible.

Grieve was sitting up in bed, gazing at the unseen figure to which the shadow belonged. In a voice that trembled with emotion, he begged the haunting spirit to leave him, and prayed its forgiveness.

'You know the crime was not premeditated. It was a sudden temptation of the devil that made me strike the blow, and fling you over the precipice. It was the devil tempting me with the recollection of her exquisite face—of the tender love that might have been mine, but for you. But she will not listen to me. See, she turns away from me, as if she knew I was your murderer, George Mason!'

It was Lettie who repeated in a horrified whisper this awful confession.

I could see it all now! As I was about to tell Lettie of the many strange things I had concealed from her, the nurse, who had gone to see her patient, came running back in alarm.

Vincent Grieve had disappeared. He had risen in his delirious terror, had opened the window, and leaped out. Two days later his body was found in the river.

A curtain hangs now before poor George's portrait, though it is no longer connected with any supernatural marvels; and never, since the night of Vincent Grieve's death, have we seen aught of that most mysterious haunting presence—the Shadow of a Shade.

The Story of Mary Ancel

William Makepeace Thackeray,

"Go, my nephew," said old Father Jacob to me, "and complete thy studies at Strasburg: Heaven surely hath ordained thee for the ministry in these times of trouble, and my excellent friend Schneider will work out the divine intention."

Schneider was an old college friend of Uncle Jacob's, was a Benedictine monk, and a man famous for his learning; as for me, I was at that time my uncle's chorister, clerk, and sacristan; I swept the church, chanted the prayers with my shrill treble, and swung the great copper incense-pot on Sundays and feasts; and I toiled over the Fathers for the other days of the week.

The old gentleman said that my progress was prodigious, and, without vanity, I believe he was right, for I then verily considered that praying was my vocation, and not fighting, as I have found since.

You would hardly conceive (said the Captain, swearing a great oath) how devout and how learned I was in those days; I talked Latin faster than my own beautiful patois of Alsacian French; I could utterly overthrow in argument every Protestant (heretics we called them) parson in the neighborhood, and there was a confounded sprinkling of these unbelievers in our part of the country. I prayed half a dozen times a day; I fasted thrice in a week; and, as for penance, I used to scourge my little sides, till they had no more feeling than a peg-top: such was the godly life I led at my Uncle Jacob's in the village of Steinbach.

Our family had long dwelt in this place, and a large farm and a pleasant house were then in the possession of another uncle—uncle Edward. He was the youngest of the three sons of my grandfather; but Jacob, the elder, had shown a decided vocation for the church, from, I believe, the age of three, and now was by no means tired of it at sixty. My father, who was to have inherited the paternal property, was, as I hear, a terrible scamp and scapegrace, quarrelled with his family, and disappeared altogether, living and dying at Paris; so far we knew through my mother, who came, poor woman, with me, a child of six months, on her bosom, was refused all shelter by my grandfather, but was housed and kindly cared for by my good Uncle Jacob.

Here she lived for about seven years, and the old gentleman, when she died, wept over her grave a great deal more than I did, who was then too young to mind anything but toys or sweetmeats.

During this time my grandfather was likewise carried off: he left, as I said, the property to his son Edward, with a small proviso in his will that something should be done for me, his grandson.

Edward was himself a widower, with one daughter, Mary, about three years older than I, and certainly she was the dearest little treasure with which Providence ever blessed a miserly father; by the time she was fifteen, five farmers, three lawyers, twelve Protestant parsons, and a lieutenant of dragoons had made her offers: it must not be denied that she was an heiress as well as a beauty, which, perhaps, had something to do with the love of these gentlemen. However, Mary declared that she intended to live single, turned away her lovers one after another, and devoted herself to the care of her father.

Uncle Jacob was as fond of her as he was of any saint or martyr. As for me, at the mature age of twelve I had made a kind of divinity of her, and when we sang "*Ave Maria*" on Sundays I could not refrain from turning to her, where she knelt, blushing and praying and looking like an angel, as she was. Besides her beauty, Mary had a thousand good qualities; she could play better on the harpsichord, she could dance more lightly, she could make better pickles and puddings, than any girl in Alsace; there was not a want or a fancy of the old hunks her father, or a wish of mine or my uncle's, that she would not gratify if she could; as for herself, the sweet soul had neither wants nor wishes except to see us happy.

I could talk to you for a year of all the pretty kindnesses that she would do for me; how, when she found me of early mornings among my books, her presence "would cast a light upon the day;" how she used to smooth and fold my little surplice, and embroider me caps and gowns for high feast-days; how she used to bring flowers for the altar, and who could deck it so well as she? But sentiment does not come glibly from under a grizzled moustache, so I will drop it, if you please.

Amongst other favors she showed me, Mary used to be particularly fond of kissing me: it was a thing I did not so much value in those days, but I found that the more I grew alive to the extent of the benefit, the less she would condescend to confer it on me; till at last, when I was about fourteen, she discontinued it altogether, of her own wish at least; only sometimes I used to be rude, and take what she had now become so mighty unwilling to give.

I was engaged in a contest of this sort one day with Mary, when, just as I was about to carry off a kiss from her cheek, I was saluted with a staggering slap on my own, which was bestowed by uncle Edward, and sent me reeling some yards down the garden.

The old gentleman, whose tongue was generally as close as his purse, now poured forth a flood of eloquence which quite astonished me. I did not think that so much was to be said on any subject as he managed to utter on one, and that was abuse of me; he stamped, he swore, he screamed; and then, from complimenting me, he turned to Mary, and saluted her in a manner equally forcible and significant; she, who was very much frightened at the commencement of the scene, grew very angry at the coarse words he used, and the wicked motives he imputed to her.

"The child is but fourteen," she said; "he is your own nephew, and a candidate for holy orders:—father, it is a shame that you should thus speak of me, your daughter, or of one of his holy profession."

I did not particularly admire this speech myself, but it had an effect on my uncle, and was the cause of the words with which this history commences. The old gentleman persuaded his brother that I must be sent to Strasburg, and there kept until my studies for the church were concluded. I was furnished with a letter to my uncle's old college chum, Professor Schneider, who was to instruct me in theology and Greek.

I was not sorry to see Strasburg, of the wonders of which I had heard so much; but felt very loth as the time drew near when I must quit my pretty cousin, and my good old uncle. Mary and I managed, however, a parting walk, in which a number of tender things were said on both sides. I am told that you Englishmen consider it cowardly to cry; as for me, I wept and roared incessantly: when Mary squeezed me, for the last time, the tears came out of me as if I had been neither more nor less than a great wet sponge. My cousin's eyes were stoically dry; her ladyship had a part to play, and it would have been wrong for her to be in love with a young chit of fourteen—so she carried herself with perfect coolness, as if there was nothing the matter. I should not have known that she cared for me, had it not been for a letter which she wrote me a month afterwards—*then*, nobody was by, and the consequence was that the letter was half washed away with her weeping; if she had used a watering-pot the thing could not have been better done.

Well, I arrived at Strasburg—a dismal, old-fashioned, rickety town in those days—and straightway presented myself and letter at Schneider's door; over it was written—

COMITÉ DE SALUT PUBLIC.

Would you believe it? I was so ignorant a young fellow, that I had no idea of the meaning of the words; however, I entered the citizen's room without fear, and sat down in his ante-chamber until I could be admitted to see him.

Here I found very few indications of his reverence's profession; the walls were hung round with portraits of Robespierre, Marat, and the like; a great bust of Mirabeau, mutilated, with the word *Traître* underneath; lists and republican proclamations, tobacco-pipes and firearms. At a deal-table, stained with grease and wine, sat a gentleman, with a huge pigtail dangling down to that part of his person which immediately succeeds his back, and a red nightcap, containing a Tricolor cockade as large as a pancake. He was smoking a short pipe, reading a little book, and sobbing as if his heart would break. Every now and then he would make brief remarks upon the personages or the incidents of his book, by which I could judge that he was a man of the very keenest sensibilities—"Ah, brigand!" "*O malheureuse!*" "O Charlotte, Charlotte!" The work which this gentleman was perusing is called *The Sorrows of Werter*; it was all the rage, in those days, and my friend was only following the fashion. I asked him if I could see Father Schneider? he turned towards me a hideous, pimpled face, which I dream of now at forty years' distance.

"Father who?" said he. "Do you imagine that citizen Schneider has not thrown off the absurd mummery of priesthood? If you were a little older you would go to prison for calling him Father Schneider—many a man has died for less;" and he pointed to a picture of a guillotine, which was hanging in the room.

I was in amazement.

"What is he? Is he not a teacher of Greek, an *abbé*, a monk, until monasteries were abolished, the learned editor of the songs of 'Anacreon?'"

"He *was* all this," replied my grim friend; "he is now a Member of the Committee of Public Safety, and would think no more of ordering your head off than of drinking this tumbler of beer."

He swallowed, himself, the frothy liquid, and then proceeded to give me the history of the man to whom my uncle had sent me for instruction.

Schneider was born in 1756: was a student at Wurzburg, and afterwards entered a convent, where he remained nine years. He here became distinguished for his learning and his talents as a preacher, and became chaplain to Duke Charles of Württemberg. The doctrines of the Illuminati began about this time to spread in Germany, and Schneider speedily joined the sect. He had been a professor of Greek at Cologne; and being compelled, on account of his irregularity, to give up his chair, he came to Strasburg at the commencement of the French Revolution, and acted for some time a principal part as a revolutionary agent at Strasburg.

("Heaven knows what would have happened to me had I continued long under his tuition!" said the Captain. "I owe the preservation of my morals entirely to my entering the army. A man, sir, who is a soldier, has very little time to be wicked; except in the case of a siege and the sack of a town, when a little license can offend nobody.")

By the time that my friend had concluded Schneider's biography, we had grown tolerably intimate, and I imparted to him (with that experience so remarkable in youth) my whole history—my course of studies, my pleasant country life, the names and qualities of my dear relations, and my occupations in the vestry before religion was abolished by order of the Republic. In the course of my speech I recurred so often to the name of my cousin Mary, that the gentleman could not fail to perceive what a tender place she had in my heart.

Then we reverted to *The Sorrows of Werter*, and discussed the merits of that sublime performance. Although I had before felt some misgivings about my new acquaintance, my heart now quite yearned towards him. He talked about love and sentiment in a manner which made me recollect that I was in love myself; and you know that when a man is in that condition, his taste is not very refined, any maudlin trash of prose or verse appearing sublime to him, provided it correspond, in some degree, with his own situation.

"Candid youth!" cried my unknown, "I love to hear thy innocent story and look on thy guileless face. There is, alas! so much of the contrary in this world, so much terror and crime and blood, that we who mingle with it are only too glad to forget it. Would that we could shake off our cares as men, and be boys, as thou art, again!"

Here my friend began to weep once more, and fondly shook my hand. I blessed my stars that I had, at the very outset of my career, met with one who was so likely to aid me. What a slanderous world it is, thought I; the people in our village call these Republicans wicked and bloody-minded; a lamb could not be more tender than this sentimental bottle-nosed gentleman! The worthy man then gave me to understand that he held a place under Government. I was busy in endeavoring to discover what his situation might be, when the door of the next apartment opened, and Schneider made his appearance.

At first he did not notice me, but he advanced to my new acquaintance, and gave him, to my astonishment, something very like a blow.

"You drunken, talking fool," he said, "you are always after your time. Fourteen people are cooling their heels yonder, waiting until you have finished your beer and your sentiment!"

My friend slunk muttering out of the room.

"That fellow," said Schneider, turning to me, "is our public executioner: a capital hand too if he would but keep decent time; but the brute is always drunk, and blubbering over *The Sorrows of Werter!*"

I know not whether it was his old friendship for my uncle, or my proper merits, which won the heart of this the sternest ruffian of Robespierre's crew; but certain it is, that he became strangely attached to me, and kept me constantly about his person. As for the priesthood and the Greek, they were of course very soon out of the question. The Austrians were on our frontier; every day brought us accounts of battles won; and the youth of Strasburg, and of all France, indeed, were bursting with military ardor. As for me, I shared the general mania, and speedily mounted a cockade as large as that of my friend, the executioner.

The occupations of this worthy were unremitting. Saint Just, who had come down from Paris to preside over our town, executed the laws and the aristocrats with terrible punctuality; and Schneider used to make country excursions in search of offenders with this fellow, as a provost-marshal, at his back. In the meantime, having entered my sixteenth year, and being a proper lad of my age, I had joined a regiment of cavalry, and was scampering now after the Austrians who menaced us, and now threatening the *émigrés*, who were banded at Coblentz. My love for my dear cousin increased as my whiskers grew; and when I was scarcely seventeen, I thought myself man enough to marry her, and to cut the throat of any one who should venture to say me nay.

I need not tell you that during my absence at Strasburg, great changes had occurred in our little village, and somewhat of the revolutionary rage had penetrated even to that quiet and distant place. The hideous "*Fête* of the Supreme Being" had been celebrated at Paris; the practice of our ancient religion was forbidden; its professors were most of them in concealment, or in exile, or had expiated on the scaffold their crime of Christianity. In our poor village my uncle's church was closed, and he, himself, an inmate in my brother's house, only owing his safety to his great popularity among his former flock, and the influence of Edward Ancel.

The latter had taken in the Revolution a somewhat prominent part; that is, he had engaged in many contracts for the army, attended the clubs regularly, corresponded with the authorities of his department, and was loud in his denunciations of the aristocrats in the neighborhood. But owing, perhaps, to the German origin of the peasantry, and their quiet and rustic lives, the revolutionary fury which prevailed in the cities had hardly reached the country people. The occasional visit of a commissary from Paris or Strasburg served to keep the flame alive, and to remind the rural swains of the existence of a Republic in France.

Now and then, when I could gain a week's leave of absence, I returned to the village, and was received with tolerable politeness by my uncle, and with a warmer feeling by his daughter.

I won't describe to you the progress of our love, or the wrath of my uncle Edward, when he discovered that it still continued. He swore and he stormed; he locked Mary into her chamber, and vowed that he would withdraw the allowance he made me, if ever I ventured near her. His daughter, he said, should never marry a hopeless, penniless subaltern; and Mary declared she would not marry without his consent. What had I to do? — to despair and to leave her. As for my poor Uncle Jacob, he had no counsel to give me, and, indeed, no spirit left: his little church was turned into a stable, his surplice torn off his shoulders, and he was only too lucky in keeping *his head* on them. A bright thought struck him: suppose you were to ask the advice of my old friend Schneider regarding this marriage? he has ever been your friend, and may help you now as before.

(Here the Captain paused a little.) You may fancy (continued he) that it was droll advice of a reverend gentleman like uncle Jacob to counsel me in this manner, and to bid me make friends with such a murderous cut-throat as Schneider; but we thought nothing of it in those days; guillotining was as common as dancing, and a man was only thought the better patriot the more severe he might be. I departed forthwith to Strasburg, and requested the vote and interest of the Citizen President of the Committee of Public Safety.

He heard me with a great deal of attention. I described to him most minutely the circumstance, expatiated upon the charms of my dear Mary, and painted her to him from head to foot. Her golden hair and her bright blushing cheeks, her slim waist and her tripping tiny feet; and furthermore, I added that she possessed a fortune which ought, by rights, to be mine, but for the miserly old father. "Curse him for an aristocrat!" concluded I, in my wrath.

As I had been discoursing about Mary's charms Schneider listened with much complacency and attention: when I spoke about her fortune, his interest redoubled; and when I called her father an aristocrat, the worthy ex-Jesuit gave a grin of satisfaction, which was really quite terrible. O fool that I was to trust him so far!

The very same evening an officer waited upon me with the following note from Saint Just:—

> Strasburg,
>
> Fifth year of the Republic, one and indivisible, 11 *Ventose*.
>
> The citizen Pierre Ancel is to leave Strasburg within two hours, and to carry the enclosed despatches to the President of the Committee of Public Safety at Paris. The necessary leave of absence from his military duties has been provided. Instant punishment will follow the slightest delay on the road.
>
> *Salut et Fraternité*

There was no choice but obedience, and off I sped on my weary way to the capital.

As I was riding out of the Paris gate I met an equipage which I knew to be that of Schneider. The ruffian smiled at me as I passed, and wished me a bon voyage. Behind his chariot came a curious machine, or cart; a great basket, three stout poles, and several planks, all painted red, were lying in this vehicle, on the top of which was seated my friend with the big cockade. It was the *portable guillotine* which Schneider always carried with him on his travels. The *bourreau* was reading *The Sorrows of Werter*, and looked as sentimental as usual.

I will not speak of my voyage in order to relate to you Schneider's. My story had awakened the wretch's curiosity and avarice, and he was determined that such a prize as I had shown my cousin to be should fall into no hands but his own. No sooner, in fact, had I quitted his room than he procured the order for my absence, and was on the way to Steinbach as I met him.

The journey is not a very long one; and on the next day my uncle Jacob was surprised by receiving a message that the citizen Schneider was in the village, and was coming to greet his old friend. Old Jacob was in an ecstasy, for he longed to see his college acquaintance, and he hoped also that Schneider had come into that part of the country upon the marriage-business of your humble servant. Of course Mary was summoned to give her best dinner, and wear her best frock; and her father made ready to receive the new State dignitary.

Schneider's carriage speedily rolled into the courtyard, and Schneider's Cart followed, as a matter of course. The ex-priest only entered the house; his companion remaining with the horses to dine in private. Here was a most touching meeting between him and Jacob. They talked over their old college pranks and successes; they capped Greek verses, and quoted ancient epigrams upon their tutors, who had been dead since the Seven Years' War. Mary declared it was quite touching to listen to the merry friendly talk of these two old gentlemen.

After the conversation had continued for a time in this strain, Schneider drew up all of a sudden, and said quietly, that he had come on particular and unpleasant business—hinting about troublesome times, spies, evil reports, and so forth. Then he called Uncle Edward aside, and had with him a long and earnest conversation: so Jacob went out and talked with Schneider's *friend*; they speedily became very intimate, for the ruffian detailed all the circumstances of his interview with me. When he returned into the house, some time after this pleasing colloquy, he found the tone of the society strangely altered. Edward Ancel, pale as a sheet, trembling, and crying for mercy; poor Mary weeping; and Schneider pacing energetically about the apartment, raging about the rights of man, the punishment of traitors, and the one and indivisible republic.

"Jacob," he said, as my uncle entered the room, "I was willing, for the sake of our old friendship, to forget the crimes of your brother. He is a known and dangerous aristocrat; he holds communications with the enemy on the frontier; he is a possessor of great and ill-gotten wealth, of which he has plundered the Republic. Do you know," said he, turning to Edward Ancel, "where the least of these crimes, or the mere suspicion of them, would lead you?"

Poor Edward sat trembling in his chair, and answered not a word.

He knew full well how quickly, in this dreadful time, punishment followed suspicion; and, though guiltless of all treason with the enemy, perhaps he was aware that, in certain contracts with the Government, he had taken to himself a more than patriotic share of profit.

"Do you know," resumed Schneider, in a voice of thunder, "for what purpose I came hither, and by whom I am accompanied? I am the administrator of the justice of the Republic. The life of yourself and your family is in my hands: yonder man, who follows me, is the executor of the law; he has rid the nation of hundreds of wretches like yourself. A single word from me, and your doom is sealed without hope, and your last hour is come. Ho! Grégoire!" shouted he; "is all ready?"

Grégoire replied from the court, "I can put up the machine in half an hour. Shall I go down to the village and call the troops and the law people?"

"Do you hear him?" said Schneider. "The guillotine is in the courtyard; your name is on my list, and I have witnesses to prove your crime. Have you a word in your defence?"

Not a word came; the old gentleman was dumb; but his daughter, who did not give way to his terror, spoke for him.

"You cannot, sir," said she, "although you say it, *feel* that my father is guilty; you would not have entered our house thus alone if you had thought it. You threaten him in this manner because you have something to ask and to gain from us: what is it, citizen? — tell us how much you value our lives, and what sum we are to pay for our ransom?"

"Sum!" said uncle Jacob; "he does not want money of us: my old friend, my college chum, does not come hither to drive bargains with anybody belonging to Jacob Ancel?"

"Oh, no, sir, no, you can't want money of us," shrieked Edward; "we are the poorest people of the village: ruined, Monsieur Schneider, ruined in the cause of the Republic."

"Silence, father," said my brave Mary; "this man wants a *price*: he comes, with his worthy friend yonder, to frighten us, not to kill us. If we die, he cannot touch a *sou* of our money; it is confiscated to the State. Tell us, sir, what is the price of our safety?"

Schneider smiled, and bowed with perfect politeness.

"Mademoiselle Marie," he said, "is perfectly correct in her surmise. I do not want the life of this poor drivelling old man: my intentions are much more peaceable, be assured. It rests entirely with this accomplished young lady (whose spirit I like, and whose ready wit I admire), whether the business between us shall be a matter of love or death. I humbly offer myself, citizen Ancel, as a candidate for the hand of your charming daughter. Her goodness, her beauty, and the large fortune which I know you intend to give her, would render her a desirable match for the proudest man in the republic, and, I am sure, would make me the happiest."

"This must be a jest, Monsieur Schneider," said Mary, trembling, and turning deadly pale: "you cannot mean this; you do not know me: you never heard of me until today."

"Pardon me, *belle dame,*" replied he; "your cousin Pierre has often talked to me of your virtues; indeed, it was by his special suggestion that I made the visit."

"It is false!—it is a base and cowardly lie!" exclaimed she (for the young lady's courage was up),—"Pierre never could have forgotten himself and me so as to offer me to one like you. You come here with a lie on your lips—a lie against my father, to swear his life away, against my dear cousin's honor and love. It is useless now to deny it: father, I love Pierre Ancel; I will marry no other but him—no, though our last penny were paid to this man as the price of our freedom."

Schneider's only reply to this was a call to his friend Grégoire.

"Send down to the village for the maire and some *gendarmes*; and tell your people to make ready."

"Shall I put *the machine* up?" shouted he of the sentimental turn.

"You hear him," said Schneider; "Marie Ancel, you may decide the fate of your father. I shall return in a few hours," concluded he, "and will then beg to know your decision."

The advocate of the rights of man then left the apartment, and left the family, as you may imagine, in no very pleasant mood.

Old Uncle Jacob, during the few minutes which had elapsed in the enactment of this strange scene, sat staring wildly at Schneider, and holding Mary on his knees: the poor little thing had fled to him for protection, and not to her father, who was kneeling almost senseless at the window, gazing at the executioner and his hideous preparations. The instinct of the poor girl had not failed her; she knew that Jacob was her only protector, if not of her life— heaven bless him!—of her honor. "Indeed," the old man said, in a stout voice, "this must never be, my dearest child—you must not marry this man. If it be the will of Providence that we fall, we shall have at least the thought to console us that we die innocent. Any man in France at a time like this, would be a coward and traitor if he feared to meet the fate of the thousand brave and good who have preceded us."

"Who speaks of dying?" said Edward. "You, Brother Jacob? —you would not lay that poor girl's head on the scaffold, or mine, your dear brother's. You will not let us die, Mary; you will not, for a small sacrifice, bring your poor old father into danger?"

Mary made no answer. "Perhaps," she said, "there is time for escape: he is to be here but in two hours; in two hours we may be safe, in concealment, or on the frontier." And she rushed to the door of the chamber, as if she would have instantly made the attempt: two gendarmes were at the door. "We have orders, *Mademoiselle*," they said, "to allow no one to leave this apartment until the return of the citizen Schneider."

Alas! all hope of escape was impossible. Mary became quite silent for a while; she would not speak to uncle Jacob; and, in reply to her father's eager questions, she only replied, coldly, that she would answer Schneider when he arrived.

The two dreadful hours passed away only too quickly; and, punctual to his appointment, the ex-monk appeared. Directly he entered, Mary advanced to him, and said, calmly,—

"Sir, I could not deceive you if I said that I freely accepted the offer which you have made me. I will be your wife; but I tell you that I love another; and that it is only to save the lives of those two old men that I yield my person up to you."

Schneider bowed, and said,—

"It is bravely spoken. I like your candor—your beauty. As for the love, excuse me for saying that is a matter of total indifference. I have no doubt, however, that it will come as soon as your feelings in favor of the young gentleman, your cousin, have lost their present fervor. That engaging young man has, at present, another mistress—Glory. He occupies, I believe, the distinguished post of corporal in a regiment which is about to march to—Perpignan, I believe."

It was, in fact, Monsieur Schneider's polite intention to banish me as far as possible from the place of my birth; and he had, accordingly, selected the Spanish frontier as the spot where I was to display my future military talents.

Mary gave no answer to this sneer: she seemed perfectly resigned and calm: she only said,—

"I must make, however, some conditions regarding our proposed marriage, which a gentleman of Monsieur Schneider's gallantry cannot refuse."

"Pray command me," replied the husband elect. "Fair lady, you know I am your slave."

"You occupy a distinguished political rank, citizen representative," said she; "and we in our village are likewise known and beloved. I should be ashamed, I confess, to wed you here; for our people would wonder at the sudden marriage, and imply that it was only by compulsion that I gave you my hand. Let us, then, perform this ceremony at Strasburg, before the public authorities of the city, with the state and solemnity which befits the marriage of one of the chief men of the Republic."

"Be it so, madam," he answered, and gallantly proceeded to embrace his bride.

Mary did not shrink from this ruffian's kiss; nor did she reply when poor old Jacob, who sat sobbing in a corner, burst out, and said,—

"O Mary, Mary, I did not think this of thee!"

"Silence, brother!" hastily said Edward; "my good son-in-law will pardon your ill-humor."

I believe uncle Edward in his heart was pleased at the notion of the marriage; he only cared for money and rank, and was little scrupulous as to the means of obtaining them.

The matter then was finally arranged; and presently, after Schneider had transacted the affairs which brought him into that part of the country, the happy bridal party set forward for Strasburg. Uncles Jacob and Edward occupied the back seat of the old family carriage, and the young bride and bridegroom (he was nearly Jacob's age) were seated majestically in front. Mary has often since talked to me of this dreadful journey. She said she wondered at the scrupulous politeness of Schneider during the route; nay, that at another period she could have listened to and admired the singular talent of this man, his great learning, his fancy, and wit; but her mind was bent upon other things, and the poor girl firmly thought that her last day was come.

In the meantime, by a blessed chance, I had not ridden three leagues from Strasburg, when the officer of a passing troop of a cavalry regiment, looking at the beast on which I was mounted, was pleased to take a fancy to it, and ordered me, in an authoritative tone, to descend, and to give up my steed for the benefit of the Republic. I represented to him, in vain, that I was a soldier, like himself, and the bearer of despatches to Paris. "Fool!" he said; "do you think they would send despatches by a man who can ride at best but ten leagues a day?" And the honest soldier was so wroth at my supposed duplicity, that he not only confiscated my horse, but my saddle, and the little portmanteau which contained the chief part of my worldly goods and treasure. I had nothing for it but to dismount, and take my way on foot back again to Strasburg. I arrived there in the evening, determining the next morning to make my case known to the citizen St. Just; and though I made my entry without a *sou*, I don't know what secret exultation I felt at again being able to return.

The ante-chamber of such a great man as St. Just was, in those days, too crowded for an unprotected boy to obtain an early audience; two days passed before I could obtain a sight of the friend of Robespierre. On the third day, as I was still waiting for the interview, I heard a great bustle in the courtyard of the house, and looked out with many others at the spectacle.

A number of men and women, singing epithalamiums, and dressed in some absurd imitation of Roman costume, a troop of soldiers and gendarmerie, and an immense crowd of the badauds of Strasburg, were surrounding a carriage which then entered the court of the mayoralty. In this carriage, great God! I saw my dear Mary, and Schneider by her side. The truth instantly came upon me: the reason for Schneider's keen inquiries and my abrupt dismissal; but I could not believe that Mary was false to me. I had only to look in her face, white and rigid as marble, to see that this proposed marriage was not with her consent.

I fell back in the crowd as the procession entered the great room in which I was, and hid my face in my hands: I could not look upon her as the wife of another,—upon her so long loved and truly—the saint of my childhood—the pride and hope of my youth—torn from me for ever, and delivered over to the unholy arms of the murderer who stood before me.

The door of St. Just's private apartment opened, and he took his seat at the table of mayoralty just as Schneider and his cort?ge arrived before it.

Schneider then said that he came in before the authorities of the Republic to espouse the *citoyenne* Marie Ancel.

"Is she a minor?" asked St. Just.

"She is a minor, but her father is here to give her away."

"I am here," said uncle Edward, coming eagerly forward and bowing. "Edward Ancel, so please you, citizen representative. The worthy citizen Schneider has done me the honor of marrying into my family."

"But my father has not told you the terms of the marriage," said

Mary, interrupting him, in a loud, clear voice.

Here Schneider seized her hand, and endeavored to prevent her from speaking. Her father turned pale, and cried, "Stop, Mary, stop! For heaven's sake, remember your poor old father's danger!"

"Sir, may I speak?"

"Let the young woman speak," said St. Just, "if she have a desire to talk." He did not suspect what would be the purport of her story.

"Sir," she said, "two days since the citizen Schneider entered for the first time our house; and you will fancy that it must be a love of very sudden growth which has brought either him or me before you today. He had heard from a person who is now unhappily not present, of my name and of the wealth which my family was said to possess; and hence arose this mad design concerning me. He came into our village with supreme power, an executioner at his heels, and the soldiery and authorities of the district entirely under his orders. He threatened my father with death if he refused to give up his daughter; and I, who knew that there was no chance of escape, except here before you, consented to become his wife. My father I know to be innocent, for all his transactions with the State have passed through my hands. Citizen representative, I demand to be freed from this marriage; and I charge Schneider as a traitor to the Republic, as a man who would have murdered an innocent citizen for the sake of private gain."

During the delivery of this little speech, uncle Jacob had been sobbing and panting like a broken-winded horse; and when Mary had done, he rushed up to her and kissed her, and held her tight in his arms. "Bless thee, my child!" he cried, "for having had the courage to speak the truth, and shame thy old father and me, who dared not say a word."

"The girl amazes me," said Schneider, with a look of astonishment. "I never saw her, it is true, till yesterday; but I used no force: her father gave her to me with his free consent, and she yielded as gladly. Speak, Edward Ancel, was it not so?"

"It was, indeed, by my free consent," said Edward, trembling.

"For shame, brother!" cried old Jacob. "Sir, it was by Edward's free consent and my niece's; but the guillotine was in the courtyard! Question Schneider's famulus, the man Grégoire, him who reads 'The Sorrows of Werter.'"

Grégoire stepped forward, and looked hesitatingly at Schneider, as he said, "I know not what took place within doors; but I was ordered to put up the scaffold without; and I was told to get soldiers, and let no one leave the house."

"Citizen St. Just," cried Schneider, "you will not allow the testimony of a ruffian like this, of a foolish girl, and a mad ex- priest, to weigh against the word of one who has done such service to the Republic: it is a base conspiracy to betray me; the whole family is known to favor the interest of the *émigrés*."

"And therefore you would marry a member of the family, and allow the others to escape; you must make a better defence, citizen Schneider," said St. Just, sternly.

Here I came forward, and said that, three days since, I had received an order to quit Strasburg for Paris immediately after a conversation with Schneider, in which I had asked him his aid in promoting my marriage with my cousin, Mary Ancel; that he had heard from me full accounts regarding her father's wealth; and that he had abruptly caused my dismissal, in order to carry on his scheme against her.

"You are in the uniform of a regiment of this town; who sent you from it?" said St. Just.

I produced the order, signed by himself, and the despatches which Schneider had sent me.

"The signature is mine, but the despatches did not come from my office. Can you prove in any way your conversation with Schneider?"

"Why," said my sentimental friend Grégoire, "for the matter of that, I can answer that the lad was always talking about this young woman: he told me the whole story himself, and many a good laugh I had with citizen Schneider as we talked about it."

"The charge against Edward Ancel must be examined into," said St. Just. "The marriage cannot take place. But if I had ratified it, Mary Ancel, what then would have been your course?"

Mary felt for a moment in her bosom, and said—"*He would have died tonight—I would have stabbed him with this dagger*." (This reply, and, indeed, the whole of the story, is historical. An account, by Charles Nodier, in the *Revue de Paris*, suggested it to the writer.)

The rain was beating down the streets, and yet they were thronged; all the world was hastening to the market-place, where the worthy Grégoire was about to perform some of the pleasant duties of his office. On this occasion, it was not death that he was to inflict; he was only to expose a criminal who was to be sent on afterwards to Paris. St. Just had ordered that Schneider should stand for six hours in the public place of Strasburg, and then be sent on to the capital to be dealt with as the authorities might think fit.

The people followed with execrations the villain to his place of punishment; and Grégoire grinned as he fixed up to the post the man whose orders he had obeyed so often—who had delivered over to disgrace and punishment so many who merited it not.

Schneider was left for several hours exposed to the mockery and insults of the mob; he was then, according to his sentence, marched on to Paris, where it is probable that he would have escaped death, but for his own fault. He was left for some time in prison, quite unnoticed, perhaps forgotten: day by day fresh victims were carried to the scaffold, and yet the Alsacian tribune remained alive; at last, by the mediation of one of his friends, a long petition was presented to Robespierre, stating his services and his innocence, and demanding his freedom. The reply to this was an order for his instant execution: the wretch died in the last days of Robespierre's reign. His comrade, St. Just, followed him, as you know; but Edward Ancel had been released before this, for the action of my brave Mary had created a strong feeling in his favour.

"And Mary?" said I.

Here a stout and smiling old lady entered the Captain's little room: she was leaning on the arm of a military-looking man of some forty years, and followed by a number of noisy, rosy children.

"This is Mary Ancel," said the Captain, "and I am Captain Pierre, and yonder is the Colonel, my son; and you see us here assembled in force, for it is the *fête* of little Jacob yonder, whose brothers and sisters have all come from their schools to dance at his birthday."

The Tapestried Chamber; or, The Lady in the Square

Sir Walter Scott

About the end of the American war, when the officers of Lord Cornwallis's army which surrendered at Yorktown, and others, who had been made prisoners during the impolitic and ill-fated controversy, were returning to their own country, to relate their adventures and repose themselves after their fatigues, there was amongst them a general officer, to whom Miss S. gave the name of Browne, but merely, as I understood, to save the inconvenience of introducing a nameless agent in the narrative. He was an officer of merit, as well as a gentleman of high consideration for family and attainments.

Some business had carried General Browne upon a tour through the western counties, when, in the conclusion of a morning stage, he found himself in the vicinity of a small country town, which presented a scene of uncommon beauty and of a character peculiarly English.

The little town, with its stately old church whose tower bore testimony to the devotion of ages long past, lay amidst pasture and cornfields of small extent, but bounded and divided with hedgerow timber of great age and size. There were few marks of modern improvement. The environs of the place intimated neither the solitude of decay, nor the bustle of novelty; the houses were old, but in good repair; and the beautiful little river murmured freely on its way to the left of the town, neither restrained by a dam, nor bordered by a towing-path.

Upon a gentle eminence, nearly a mile to the southward of the town, were seen amongst many venerable oaks and tangled thickets the turrets of a castle, as old as the wars of York and Lancaster, but which seemed to have received important alterations during the age of Elizabeth and her successors. It had not been a place of great size;

but whatever accommodation it formerly afforded, was, it must be supposed, still to be obtained within its walls; at least, such was the inference which General Browne drew from observing the smoke arise merrily from several of the ancient wreathed and carved chimney-stalks.

The wall of the park ran alongside of the highway for two or three hundred yards, and, through the different points by which the eye found glimpses into the woodland scenery, it seemed to be well stocked. Other points of view opened in succession; now a full one, of the front of the old castle, and now a side glimpse at its particular towers; the former rich in all the bizarrerie of the Elizabethan school, while the simple and solid strength of other parts of the building seemed to show that they had been raised more for defence than ostentation.

Delighted with the partial glimpses which he obtained of the castle through the woods and glades by which this ancient feudal fortress was surrounded, our military traveller was determined to inquire whether it might not deserve a nearer view, and whether it contained family pictures or other objects of curiosity worthy of a stranger's visit, when, leaving the vicinity of the park, he rolled through a clean and well-paved street, and stopped at the door of a well-frequented inn.

Before ordering horses to proceed on his journey, General Browne made inquiries concerning the proprietor of the *château* which had so attracted his admiration, and was equally surprised and pleased at hearing in reply a nobleman named whom we shall call Lord Woodville. How fortunate! Much of Browne's early recollections, both at school and at college, had been connected with young Woodville, whom, by a few questions, he now ascertained to be the same with the owner of this fair domain. He had been raised to the peerage by the decease of his father a few months before, and, as the general learned from the landlord, the term of mourning being ended, was now taking possession of his paternal estate in the jovial season of merry autumn, accompanied by a select party of friends to enjoy the sports of a country famous for game.

This was delightful news to our traveller. Frank Woodville had been Richard Browne's fag at Eton, and his chosen intimate at Christ Church; their pleasures and their tasks had been the same; and the honest soldier's heart warmed to find his early friend in possession of so delightful a residence, and of an estate, as the landlord assured him with a nod and a wink, fully adequate to maintain and add to his dignity. Nothing was more natural than that the traveller should suspend a journey, which there was nothing to render hurried, to pay a visit to an old friend under such agreeable circumstances.

The fresh horses, therefore, had only the brief task of conveying the General's travelling-carriage to Woodville Castle. A porter admitted them at a modern Gothic lodge, built in that style to correspond with the castle itself, and at the same time rang a bell to give warning of the approach of visitors. Apparently the sound of the bell had suspended the separation of the company, bent on the various amusements of the morning; for, on entering the court of the château, several young men were lounging about in their sporting-dresses, looking at, and criticizing, the dogs which the keepers held in readiness to attend their pastime.

As General Browne alighted, the young lord came to the gate of the hall, and for an instant gazed, as at a stranger, upon the countenance of his friend, on which war, with its fatigues and its wounds, had made a great alteration. But the uncertainty lasted no longer than till the visitor had spoken, and the hearty greeting which followed was such as can only be exchanged betwixt those who have passed together merry days of careless boyhood or early youth.

"If I could have formed a wish, my dear Browne," said Lord Woodville, "it would have been to have you here, of all men, upon this occasion, which my friends are good enough to hold as a sort of holiday. Do not think you have been unwatched during the years you have been absent from us. I have traced you through your dangers, your triumphs, your misfortunes, and was delighted to see that, whether in victory or defeat, the name of my old friend was always distinguished with applause."

The General made a suitable reply, and congratulated his friend on his new dignities, and the possession of a place and domain so beautiful.

"Nay, you have seen nothing of it as yet," said Lord Woodville, "and I trust you do not mean to leave us till you are better acquainted with it. It is true, I confess, that my present party is pretty large, and the old house, like other places of the kind, does not possess so much accommodation as the extent of the outward walls appears to promise. But we can give you a comfortable old-fashioned room, and I venture to suppose that your campaigns have taught you to be glad of worse quarters."

The General shrugged his shoulders, and laughed. "I presume," he said, "the worst apartment in your château is considerably superior to the old tobacco-cask, in which I was fain to take up my night's lodging when I was in the Bush, as the Virginians call it, with the light corps. There I lay, like Diogenes himself, so delighted with my covering from the elements, that I made a vain attempt to have it rolled on to my next quarters; but my commander for the time would give way to no such luxurious provision, and I took farewell of my beloved cask with tears in my eyes."

"Well, then, since you do not fear your quarters," said Lord Woodville "you will stay with me a week at least. Of guns, dogs, fishing-rods, flies, and means of sport by sea and land, we have enough and to spare: you cannot pitch on an amusement, but we will pitch on the means of pursuing it. But if you prefer the gun and pointers, I will go with you myself, and see whether you have mended your shooting since you have been amongst the Indians of the back settlements."

The General gladly accepted his friendly host's proposal in all its points. After a morning of manly exercise, the company met at dinner, where it was the delight of Lord Woodville to conduce to the display of the high properties of his recovered friend, so as to recommend him to his guests, most of whom were persons of distinction. He led General Browne to speak of the scenes he had witnessed; and as every word marked alike the brave officer and the sensible man, who retained possession of his cool judgement under the most imminent dangers, the company looked upon the soldier with general respect, as on one who had proved himself possessed of an uncommon portion of personal courage—that attribute, of all others, of which everybody desires to be thought possessed.

The day at Woodville Castle ended as usual in such mansions. The hospitality stopped within the limits of good order; music, in which the young lord was a proficient, succeeded to the circulation of the bottle; cards and billiards, for those who preferred such amusements, were in readiness; but the exercise of the morning required early hours, and not long after eleven o'clock the guests began to retire to their several apartments.

The young lord himself conducted his friend, General Browne, to the chamber destined for him, which answered the description he had given of it, being comfortable, but old-fashioned. The bed was of the massive form used in the end of the seventeenth century, and the curtains of faded silk, heavily trimmed with tarnished gold. But then the sheets, pillows, and blankets looked delightful to the campaigner, when he thought of his "mansion, the cask."

There was an air of gloom in the tapestry hangings which, with their worn-out graces, curtained the walls of the little chamber, and gently undulated as the autumnal breeze found its way through the ancient lattice-window, which pattered and whistled as the air gained entrance. The toilet too, with its mirror, turbaned, after the manner of the beginning of the century, with a coiffure of murrey-coloured silk, and its hundred strange-shaped boxes, providing for arrangements which had been obsolete for more than fifty years, had an antique, and in so far a melancholy, aspect. But nothing could blaze more brightly and cheerfully than the two large wax candles; or if aught could rival them, it was the flaming bickering fagots in the chimney, that sent at once their gleam and their warmth through the snug apartment; which, notwithstanding the general antiquity of its appearance, was not wanting in the least convenience that modern habits rendered either necessary or desirable.

"This is an old-fashioned sleeping apartment, General," said the young lord; "but I hope you will find nothing that makes you envy your old tobacco-cask."

"I am not particular respecting my lodgings," replied the General; "yet were I to make any choice, I would prefer this chamber by many degrees, to the gayer and more modern rooms of your family mansion. Believe me that when I unite its modern air of comfort with its venerable antiquity, and recollect that it is your lordship's property, I shall feel in better quarters here, than if I were in the best hotel London could afford."

"I trust—I have no doubt—that you will find yourself as comfortable as I wish you, my dear General," said the young nobleman; and once more bidding his guest good night, he shook him by the hand and withdrew.

The General once more looked round him, and internally congratulating himself on his return to peaceful life, the comforts of which were endeared by the recollection of the hardships and dangers he had lately sustained, undressed himself, and prepared himself for a luxurious night's rest.

Here, contrary to the custom of this species of tale, we leave the General in possession of his apartment until the next morning.

The company assembled for breakfast at an early hour, but without the appearance of General Browne, who seemed the guest that Lord Woodville was desirous of honouring above all whom his hospitality had assembled around him. He more than once expressed surprise at the General's absence, and at length sent a servant to make inquiry after him. The man brought back information that General Browne had been walking abroad since an early hour of the morning, in defiance of the weather, which was misty and ungenial.

"The custom of a soldier," said the young nobleman to his friends: "many of them acquire habitual vigilance, and cannot sleep after the early hour at which their duty usually commands them to be alert."

Yet the explanation which Lord Woodville thus offered to the company seemed hardly satisfactory to his own mind, and it was in a fit of silence and abstraction that he awaited the return of the General. It took place near an hour after the breakfast-bell had rung. He looked fatigued and feverish. His hair, the powdering and arrangement of which was at this time one of the most important occupations of a man's whole day, and marked his fashion as much as, in the present time, the tying of a cravat or the want of one, was dishevelled, uncurled, void of powder, and dank with dew. His clothes were huddled on with a careless negligence, remarkable in a military man, whose real or supposed duties are usually held to include some attention to the toilet; and his looks were haggard and ghastly in a peculiar degree.

"So you have stolen a march upon us this morning, my dear General," said Lord Woodville; "or you have not found your bed so much to your mind as I had hoped and you seemed to expect. How did you rest last night?"

"Oh, excellently well—remarkably well—never better in my life!" said General Browne rapidly, and yet with an air of embarrassment which was obvious to his friend. He then hastily swallowed a cup of tea, and, neglecting or refusing whatever else was offered, seemed to fall into a fit of abstraction.

"You will take the gun to-day, General?" said his friend and host, but had to repeat the question twice ere he received the abrupt answer, "No, my Lord; I am sorry I cannot have the honour of spending another day with your lordship; my post horses are ordered, and will be here directly."

All who were present showed surprise, and Lord Woodville immediately replied, "Post horses, my good friend! What can you possibly want with them, when you promised to stay with me quietly for at least a week?"

"I believe," said the General, obviously much embarrassed, "that I might, in the pleasure of my first meeting with your lordship, have said something about stopping here a few days; but I have since found it altogether impossible."

"That is very extraordinary," answered the young nobleman. "You seemed quite disengaged yesterday, and you cannot have had a summons today; for our post has not come up from the town, and therefore you cannot have received any letters."

General Browne, without giving any further explanation, muttered something of indispensable business, and insisted on the absolute necessity of his departure in a manner which silenced all opposition on the part of his host, who saw that his resolution was taken, and forbore further importunity.

"At least, however," he said, "permit me, my dear Browne, since go you will or must, to show you the view from the terrace, which the mist that is now rising, will soon display."

He threw open a sash-window, and stepped down upon the terrace as he spoke. The General followed him mechanically, but seemed little to attend to what his host was saying, as, looking across an extended and rich prospect, he pointed out the different objects worthy of observation. Thus they moved on till Lord Woodville had attained his purpose of drawing his guest entirely apart from the rest of the company, when, turning round upon him with an air of great solemnity, he addressed him thus:

"Richard Browne, my old and very dear friend, we are now alone. Let me conjure you to answer me upon the word of a friend, and the honour of a soldier. How did you in reality rest during last night?"

"Most wretchedly indeed, my lord," answered the General, in the same tone of solemnity; "so miserably, that I would not run the risk of such a second night, not only for all the lands belonging to this castle, but for all the country which I see from this elevated point of view."

"This is most extraordinary," said the young lord, as if speaking to himself; "then there must be something in the reports concerning that apartment." Again turning to the General, he said, "For God's sake, my dear friend, be candid with me, and let me know the disagreeable particulars which have befallen you under a roof where, with consent of the owner, you should have met nothing save comfort."

The General seemed distressed by this appeal, and paused a moment before he replied. "My dear lord," he at length said, "what happened to me last night is of nature so peculiar and so unpleasant, that I could hardly bring myself to detail it even to your lordship, were it not that, independent of my wish to gratify any request of yours, I think that sincerity on my part may lead to some explanation about a circumstance equally painful and mysterious. To others, the communications I am about to make, might place me in the light of a weak-minded, superstitious fool who suffered his own imagination to delude and bewilder him; but you have known me in childhood and youth, and will not suspect me of having adopted in manhood the feelings and frailties from which my early years were free." Here he paused, and his friend replied:

"Do not doubt my perfect confidence in the truth of your communication, however strange it may be," replied Lord Woodville. "I know your firmness of disposition too well, to suspect you could be made the object of imposition, and am aware that your honour and your friendship will equally deter you from exaggerating whatever you may have witnessed."

"Well then," said the General, "I will proceed with my story as well as I can, relying upon your candour; and yet distinctly feeling that I would rather face a battery than recall to my mind the odious recollections of last night."

He paused a second time, and then perceiving that Lord Woodville remained silent and in an attitude of attention, he commenced, though not without obvious reluctance, the history of his night's adventures in the Tapestried Chamber.

"I undressed and went to bed, so soon as your lordship left me yesterday evening; but the wood in the chimney, which nearly fronted my bed, blazed brightly and cheerfully, and, aided by a hundred exciting recollections of my childhood and youth, which had been recalled by the unexpected pleasure of meeting your lordship, prevented me from falling immediately asleep. I ought, however, to say that these reflections were all of a pleasant and agreeable kind, grounded on a sense of having for a time exchanged the labour, fatigues, and dangers of my profession, for the enjoyments of a peaceful life, and the reunion of those friendly and affectionate ties which I had torn asunder at the rude summons of war.

"While such pleasing reflections were stealing over my mind, and gradually lulling me to slumber, I was suddenly aroused by a sound like that of the rustling of a silken gown, and the tapping of a pair of high-heeled shoes, as if a woman were walking in the apartment. Ere I could draw the curtain to see what the matter was, the figure of a little woman passed between the bed and the fire. The back of this form was turned to me, and I could observe, from the shoulders and neck, it was that of an old woman, whose dress was an old-fashioned gown, which, I think, ladies call a sacque—that is, a sort of robe, completely loose in the body, but gathered into broad plaits upon the neck and shoulders, which fall down to the ground, and terminate in a species of train.

"I thought the intrusion singular enough, but never harboured for a moment the idea that what I saw was anything more than the mortal form of some old woman about the establishment, who had a fancy to dress like her grandmother, and who, having perhaps (as your lordship mentioned that you were rather straitened for room) been dislodged from her chamber for my accommodation, had forgotten the circumstance, and returned by twelve to her old haunt. Under this persuasion I moved myself in bed and coughed a little, to make the intruder sensible of my being in possession of the premises. She turned slowly round, but gracious Heaven! My lord, what a countenance did she display to me!

"There was no longer any question what she was, or any thought of her being a living being. Upon a face which wore the fixed features of a corpse, were imprinted the traces of the vilest and most hideous passions which had animated her while she lived. The body of some atrocious criminal seemed to have been given up from the grave, and the soul restored from the penal fire, in order to form, for a space, a union with the ancient accomplice of its guilt. I started up in bed, and sat upright, supporting myself on my palms, as I gazed on this horrible spectre. The hag made, as it seemed, a single and swift stride to the bed where I lay, and squatted herself down upon it, in precisely the same attitude which I had assumed in the extremity of horror, advancing her diabolical countenance within half a yard of mine, with a grin which seemed to intimate the malice and the derision of an incarnate fiend."

Here General Browne stopped, and wiped from his brow the cold perspiration with which the recollection of his horrible vision had covered it.

"My lord," he said, "I am no coward. I have been in all the mortal dangers incidental to my profession, and I may truly boast that no man ever knew Richard Browne dishonour the sword he wears; but in these horrible circumstances, under the eyes, and as it seemed, almost in the grasp of an incarnation of an evil spirit, all firmness forsook me, all manhood melted from me like wax in the furnace, and I felt my hair individually bristle. The current of my life-blood ceased to flow, and I sank back in a swoon, as very a victim to panic terror as ever was a village girl or a child of ten years old. How long I lay in this condition I cannot pretend to guess.

"But I was roused by the castle clock striking one, so loud that it seemed as if it were in the very room. It was some time before I dared open my eyes, lest they should again encounter the horrible spectacle. When, however, I summoned courage to look up, she was no longer visible. My first idea was to pull my bell, wake the servants, and remove to a garret or a hay-loft, to be ensured against a second visitation. Nay, I will confess the truth, that my resolution was altered, not by the shame of exposing myself, but by the very fear that, as the bell-cord hung by the chimney, I might, in making my way to it, be again crossed by the fiendish hag, who, I figured to myself, might be still lurking about some corner of the apartment.

"I will not pretend to describe what hot and cold fever-fits tormented me for the rest of the night, through broken sleep, weary vigils, and that dubious state which forms the neutral ground between them. An hundred terrible objects appeared to haunt me; but there was the great difference betwixt the vision which I have described, and those which followed, that I knew the last to be deceptions of my own fancy and overexcited nerves.

"Day at last appeared, and I rose from my bed ill in health, and humiliated in mind. I was ashamed of myself as a man and a soldier, and still more so, at feeling my own extreme desire to escape from the haunted apartment, which, however, conquered all other considerations; so that, huddling on my clothes with the most careless haste, I made my escape from your lordship's mansion, to seek in the open air some relief to my nervous system, shaken as it was by this horrible rencountre with a visitant, for such I must believe her, from the other world. Your lordship has now heard the cause of my discomposure, and of my sudden desire to leave your hospitable castle. In other places I trust we may often meet; but God protect me from ever spending a second night under that roof!"

Strange as the General's tale was, he spoke with such a deep air of conviction, that it cut short all the usual commentaries which are made on such stories. Lord Woodville never once asked him if he was sure he did not dream of the apparition, or suggested any of the possibilities by which it is fashionable to explain supernatural appearances, as wild vagaries of the fancy or deceptions of the optic nerves. On the contrary, he seemed deeply impressed with the truth and reality of what he had heard; and, after a considerable pause, regretted, with much appearance of sincerity, that his early friend should in his house have suffered so severely.

"I am the more sorry for your pain, my dear Browne," he continued, "that it is the unhappy, though most unexpected, result of an experiment of my own. You must know that, for my father and grandfather's time, at least, the apartment which was assigned to you last night had been shut on account of reports that it was disturbed by supernatural sights and noises. When I came, a few weeks since, into possession of the estate, I thought the accommodation which the castle afforded for my friends was not extensive enough to permit the inhabitants of the invisible world to retain possession of a comfortable sleeping-apartment. I therefore caused the Tapestried Chamber, as we call it, to be opened; and without destroying its air of antiquity, I had such new articles of furniture placed in it as became the modern times.

"Yet, as the opinion that the room was haunted very strongly prevailed among the domestics, and was also known in the neighbourhood and to many of my friends, I feared some prejudice might be entertained by the first occupant of the Tapestried Chamber, which might tend to revive the evil report which it had laboured under, and so disappoint my purpose of rendering it a useful part of the house. I must confess, my dear Browne, that your arrival yesterday, agreeable to me for a thousand reasons besides, seemed the most favourable opportunity of removing the unpleasant rumours which attached to the room, since your courage was indubitable, and your mind free of any preoccupation on the subject. I could not, therefore, have chosen a more fitting subject for my experiment."

"Upon my life," said General Browne, somewhat hastily, "I am infinitely obliged to your lordship—very particularly indebted indeed. I am likely to remember for some time the consequences of the experiment, as your lordship is pleased to call it."

"Nay, now you are unjust, my dear friend," said Lord Woodville. "You have only to reflect for a single moment, in order to be convinced that I could not augur the possibility of the pain to which you have been so unhappily exposed. I was yesterday morning a complete sceptic on the subject of supernatural appearances. Nay, I am sure that, had I told you what was said about that room, those very reports would have induced you, by your own choice, to select it for your accommodation. It was my misfortune, perhaps my error, but really cannot be termed my fault, that you have been afflicted so strangely."

"Strangely indeed!" said the General, resuming his good temper; "and I acknowledge that I have no right to be offended with your lordship for treating me like what I used to think myself, a man of some firmness and courage. But I see my post-horses are arrived, and I must not detain your lordship from your amusement."

"Nay, my old friend," said Lord Woodville, "since you cannot stay with us another day, which, indeed, I can no longer urge, give me at least half an hour more. You used to love pictures, and I have a gallery of portraits, some of them by Vandyke, representing ancestry to whom this property and castle formerly belonged. I think that several of them will strike you as possessing merit."

General Browne accepted the invitation, though somewhat unwillingly. It was evident he was not to breathe freely or at ease until he left Woodville Castle far behind him. He could not refuse his friend's invitation, however; and the less so, that he was a little ashamed of the peevishness which he had displayed towards his well-meaning entertainer.

The general, therefore, followed Lord Woodville through several rooms, into a long gallery hung with pictures, which the latter pointed out to his guest, telling the names, and giving some account, of the personages whose portraits presented themselves in progression. General Browne was but little interested in the details which these accounts conveyed to him. They were, indeed, of the kind which are usually found in an old family gallery. Here was a cavalier who had ruined the estate in the royal cause; there, a fine lady who had reinstated it by contracting a match with a wealthy Roundhead. There hung a gallant who had been in danger for corresponding with the exiled court at St. Germain's; here, one who had taken arms for William at the Revolution; and there, a third that had thrown his weight alternately into the scale of Whig and Tory.

While Lord Woodville was cramming these words into his guest's ear, "against the stomach of his sense," they gained the middle of the gallery, when he beheld General Browne suddenly start, and assume an attitude of the utmost surprise, not unmixed with fear, as his eyes were caught and suddenly riveted by a portrait of an old lady in a sacque, the fashionable dress of the end of the 17th century.

"There she is!" he exclaimed—"there she is, in form and features, though inferior in demoniac expression to the accursed hag who visited me last night!"

"If that be the case," said the young nobleman, "there can remain no longer any doubt of the horrible reality of your apparition. That is the picture of a wretched ancestress of mine, of whose crimes a black and fearful catalogue is recorded in a family history in my charter-chest. The recital of them would be too horrible; it is enough to say, that in yon fatal apartment incest and unnatural murder were committed. I will restore it to the solitude to which the better judgement of those who preceded me had consigned it; and never shall any one, so long as I can prevent it, be exposed to a repetition of the supernatural horrors which could shake such courage as yours."

Thus the friends, who had met with such glee, parted in a very different mood—Lord Woodville to command the Tapestried Chamber to be unmantled and the door built up; and General Browne to seek in some less beautiful country, and with some less dignified friend, forgetfulness of the painful night which he had passed in Woodville Castle.

The Tell-Tale Heart

Edgar Allan Poe

True!—nervous—very, very dreadfully nervous I had been and am; but why will you say that I am mad? The disease had sharpened my senses—not destroyed—not dulled them. Above all was the sense of hearing acute. I heard all things in the heaven and in the earth. I heard many things in hell. How, then, am I mad? Hearken! and observe how healthily—how calmly I can tell you the whole story.

It is impossible to say how first the idea entered my brain; but once conceived, it haunted me day and night. Object there was none. Passion there was none. I loved the old man. He had never wronged me. He had never given me insult. For his gold, I had no desire. I think it was his eye! yes, it was this! He had the eye of a vulture—a pale blue eye, with a film over it. Whenever it fell upon me, my blood ran cold; and so, by degrees—very gradually—I made up my mind to take the life of the old man, and thus rid myself of the eye forever.

Now this is the point. You fancy me mad. Madmen know nothing. But you should have seen me. You should have seen how wisely I proceeded—with what caution—with what foresight—with what dissimulation I went to work! I was never kinder to the old man than during the whole week before I killed him. And every night, about midnight, I turned the latch of his door and opened it—oh so gently! And then, when I had made an opening sufficient for my head, I put in a dark lantern, all closed, closed, that no light shone out, and then I thrust in my head. Oh, you would have laughed to see how cunningly I thrust it in! I moved it slowly—very, very slowly, so that I might not disturb the old man's sleep. It took me an hour to place my whole head within the opening so far that I could see him as he lay upon his bed. Ha! would a madman have been so wise as this.

And then, when my head was well in the room, I undid the lantern cautiously-oh, so cautiously—cautiously (for the hinges creaked)—I undid it just so much that a single thin ray fell upon the vulture eye. And this I did for seven long nights—every night just at midnight—but I found the eye always closed; and so, it was impossible to do the work; for it was not the old man who vexed me, but his Evil Eye. And every morning, when the day broke, I went boldly into the chamber, and spoke courageously to him, calling him by name in a hearty tone, and inquiring how he has passed the night. So, you see he would have been a very profound old man, indeed, to suspect that every night, just at twelve, I looked in upon him while he slept.

Upon the eighth night, I was more than usually cautious in opening the door. A watch's minute hand moves more quickly than did mine. Never before that night had I felt the extent of my own powers—of my sagacity. I could scarcely contain my feelings of triumph. To think that there I was, opening the door, little by little, and he not even to dream of my secret deeds or thoughts. I fairly chuckled at the idea; and perhaps he heard me; for he moved on the bed suddenly, as if startled. Now you may think that I drew back—but no. His room was as black as pitch with the thick darkness, (for the shutters were close fastened, through fear of robbers,) and so I knew that he could not see the opening of the door, and I kept pushing it on steadily, steadily.

I had my head in, and was about to open the lantern, when my thumb slipped upon the tin fastening, and the old man sprang up in bed, crying out—"Who's there?"

I kept quite still and said nothing. For a whole hour, I did not move a muscle, and in the meantime, I did not hear him lie down. He was still sitting up in the bed listening;—just as I have done, night after night, hearkening to the death watches in the wall.

Presently I heard a slight groan, and I knew it was the groan of mortal terror. It was not a groan of pain or of grief—oh, no!—it was the low stifled sound that arises from the bottom of the soul when overcharged with awe. I knew the sound well. Many a night, just at midnight, when all the world slept, it has welled up from my own bosom, deepening, with its dreadful echo, the terrors that distracted me. I say I knew it well. I knew what the old man felt, and pitied him, although I chuckled at heart. I knew that he had been lying awake ever since the first slight noise, when he had turned in the bed. His fears had been ever since growing upon him. He had been trying to fancy them causeless, but could not. He had been saying to himself—"It is nothing but the wind in the chimney—it is only a mouse crossing the floor," or "It is merely a cricket which has made a single chirp." Yes, he had been trying to comfort himself with these suppositions: but he had found all in vain. All in vain; because Death, in approaching him had stalked with his black shadow before him, and enveloped the victim. And it was the mournful influence of the unperceived shadow that caused him to feel—although he neither saw nor heard—to feel the presence of my head within the room.

When I had waited a long time, very patiently, without hearing him lie down, I resolved to open a little—a very, very little crevice in the lantern. So, I opened it—you cannot imagine how stealthily, stealthily—until, at length a simple dim ray, like the thread of the spider, shot from out the crevice and fell full upon the vulture eye.

It was open—wide, wide open—and I grew furious as I gazed upon it. I saw it with perfect distinctness—all a dull blue, with a hideous veil over it that chilled the very marrow in my bones; but I could see nothing else of the old man's face or person: for I had directed the ray as if by instinct, precisely upon the damned spot.

And have I not told you that what you mistake for madness is but over-acuteness of the sense?—now, I say, there came to my ears a low, dull, quick sound, such as a watch makes when enveloped in cotton. I knew that sound well, too. It was the beating of the old man's heart. It increased my fury, as the beating of a drum stimulates the soldier into courage.

But even yet I refrained and kept still. I scarcely breathed. I held the lantern motionless. I tried how steadily I could maintain the ray upon the eve. Meantime the hellish tattoo of the heart increased. It grew quicker and quicker, and louder and louder every instant. The old man's terror must have been extreme! It grew louder, I say, louder every moment!—do you mark me well I have told you that I am nervous: so I am. And now at the dead hour of the night, amid the dreadful silence of that old house, so strange a noise as this excited me to uncontrollable terror. Yet, for some minutes longer I refrained and stood still. But the beating grew louder, louder! I thought the heart must burst. And now a new anxiety seized me—the sound would be heard by a neighbour! The old man's hour had come! With a loud yell, I threw open the lantern and leaped into the room. He shrieked once—once only.

In an instant, I dragged him to the floor, and pulled the heavy bed over him. I then smiled gaily, to find the deed so far done. But, for many minutes, the heart beat on with a muffled sound. This, however, did not vex me; it would not be heard through the wall. At length, it ceased. The old man was dead. I removed the bed and examined the corpse. Yes, he was stone, stone dead. I placed my hand upon the heart and held it there many minutes. There was no pulsation. He was stone dead. His eve would trouble me no more.

If still you think me mad, you will think so no longer when I describe the wise precautions I took for the concealment of the body. The night waned, and I worked hastily, but in silence. First of all I dismembered the corpse. I cut off the head and the arms and the legs.

I then took up three planks from the flooring of the chamber, and deposited all between the scantlings. I then replaced the boards so cleverly, so cunningly, that no human eye—not even his—could have detected any thing wrong. There was nothing to wash out—no stain of any kind—no blood-spot whatever. I had been too wary for that. A tub had caught all—ha! ha!

When I had made an end of these labors, it was four o'clock—still dark as midnight. As the bell sounded the hour, there came a knocking at the street door. I went down to open it with a light heart,—for what had I now to fear? There entered three men, who introduced themselves, with perfect suavity, as officers of the police. A shriek had been heard by a neighbour during the night; suspicion of foul play had been aroused; information had been lodged at the police office, and they (the officers) had been deputed to search the premises.

I smiled,—for what had I to fear? I bade the gentlemen welcome. The shriek, I said, was my own in a dream. The old man, I mentioned, was absent in the country. I took my visitors all over the house. I bade them search—search well. I led them, at length, to his chamber. I showed them his treasures, secure, undisturbed. In the enthusiasm of my confidence, I brought chairs into the room, and desired them here to rest from their fatigues, while I myself, in the wild audacity of my perfect triumph, placed my own seat upon the very spot beneath which reposed the corpse of the victim.

The officers were satisfied. My manner had convinced them. I was singularly at ease. They sat, and while I answered cheerily, they chatted of familiar things. But, ere long, I felt myself getting pale and wished them gone. My head ached, and I fancied a ringing in my ears: but still they sat and still chatted. The ringing became more distinct:—It continued and became more distinct: I talked more freely to get rid of the feeling: but it continued and gained definiteness—until, at length, I found that the noise was not within my ears.

No doubt I now grew very pale;—but I talked more fluently, and with a heightened voice. Yet the sound increased—and what could I do? It was a low, dull, quick sound—much such a sound as a watch makes when enveloped in cotton. I gasped for breath—and yet the officers heard it not. I talked more quickly—more vehemently; but the noise steadily increased. I arose and argued about trifles, in a high key and with violent gesticulations; but the noise steadily increased. Why would they not be gone? I paced the floor to and fro with heavy strides, as if excited to fury by the observations of the men—but the noise steadily increased.

Oh God! what could I do? I foamed—I raved—I swore! I swung the chair upon which I had been sitting, and grated it upon the boards, but the noise arose over all and continually increased. It grew louder—louder—louder! And still the men chatted pleasantly, and smiled. Was it possible they heard not? Almighty God!—no, no! They heard!—they suspected!—they knew!—they were making a mockery of my horror!-this I thought, and this I think. But anything was better than this agony! Anything was more tolerable than this derision! I could bear those hypocritical smiles no longer! I felt that I must scream or die! and now—again!—hark! louder! louder! louder! louder!

"Villains!" I shrieked, "dissemble no more! I admit the deed!—tear up the planks! here, here!—It is the beating of his hideous heart!"

The Terrible Old Man

H. P. Lovecraft

It was the design of Angelo Ricci and Joe Czanek and Manuel Silva to call on the Terrible Old Man. This old man dwells all alone in a very ancient house on Water Street near the sea, and is reputed to be both exceedingly rich and exceedingly feeble; which forms a situation very attractive to men of the profession of Messrs. Ricci, Czanek, and Silva, for that profession was nothing less dignified than robbery.

The inhabitants of Kingsport say and think many things about the Terrible Old Man which generally keep him safe from the attention of gentlemen like Mr. Ricci and his colleagues, despite the almost certain fact that he hides a fortune of indefinite magnitude somewhere about his musty and venerable abode. He is, in truth, a very strange person, believed to have been a captain of East India clipper ships in his day; so old that no one can remember when he was young, and so taciturn that few know his real name. Among the gnarled trees in the front yard of his aged and neglected place he maintains a strange collection of large stones, oddly grouped and painted so that they resemble the idols in some obscure Eastern temple. This collection frightens away most of the small boys who love to taunt the Terrible Old Man about his long white hair and beard, or to break the small-paned windows of his dwelling with wicked missiles; but there are other things which frighten the older and more curious folk who sometimes steal up to the house to peer in through the dusty panes.

These folk say that on a table in a bare room on the ground floor are many peculiar bottles, in each a small piece of lead suspended pendulum-wise from a string. And they say that the Terrible Old Man talks to these bottles, addressing them by such names as Jack, Scar-Face, Long Tom, Spanish Joe, Peters, and Mate Ellis, and that whenever he speaks to a bottle the little lead pendulum within makes certain definite vibrations as if in answer. Those who have watched the tall, lean, Terrible Old Man in these peculiar conversations, do not watch him again.

But Angelo Ricci and Joe Czanek and Manuel Silva were not of Kingsport blood; they were of that new and heterogeneous alien stock which lies outside the charmed circle of New England life and traditions, and they saw in the Terrible Old Man merely a tottering, almost helpless greybeard, who could not walk without the aid of his knotted cane, and whose thin, weak hands shook pitifully. They were really quite sorry in their way for the lonely, unpopular old fellow, whom everybody shunned, and at whom all the dogs barked singularly. But business is business, and to a robber whose soul is in his profession, there is a lure and a challenge about a very old and very feeble man who has no account at the bank, and who pays for his few necessities at the village store with Spanish gold and silver minted two centuries ago.

Messrs. Ricci, Czanek, and Silva selected the night of April 11th for their call. Mr. Ricci and Mr. Silva were to interview the poor old gentleman, whilst Mr. Czanek waited for them and their presumable metallic burden with a covered motor-car in Ship Street, by the gate in the tall rear wall of their host's grounds. Desire to avoid needless explanations in case of unexpected police intrusions prompted these plans for a quiet and unostentatious departure.

As prearranged, the three adventurers started out separately in order to prevent any evil-minded suspicions afterward. Messrs. Ricci and Silva met in Water Street by the old man's front gate, and although they did not like the way the moon shone down upon the painted stones through the budding branches of the gnarled trees, they had more important things to think about than mere idle superstition. They feared it might be unpleasant work making the Terrible Old Man loquacious concerning his hoarded gold and silver, for aged sea-captains are notably stubborn and perverse.

Still, he was very old and very feeble, and there were two visitors. Messrs. Ricci and Silva were experienced in the art of making unwilling persons voluble, and the screams of a weak and exceptionally venerable man can be easily muffled. So, they moved up to the one lighted window and heard the Terrible Old Man talking childishly to his bottles with pendulums. Then they donned masks and knocked politely at the weather-stained oaken door.

Waiting seemed very long to Mr. Czanek as he fidgeted restlessly in the covered motorcar by the Terrible Old Man's back gate in Ship Street. He was more than ordinarily tender-hearted, and he did not like the hideous screams he had heard in the ancient house just after the hour appointed for the deed. Had he not told his colleagues to be as gentle as possible with the pathetic old sea-captain? Very nervously he watched that narrow oaken gate in the high and ivy-clad stone wall. Frequently he consulted his watch, and wondered at the delay. Had the old man died before revealing where his treasure was hidden, and had a thorough search become necessary?

Mr. Czanek did not like to wait so long in the dark in such a place. Then he sensed a soft tread or tapping on the walk inside the gate, heard a gentle fumbling at the rusty latch, and saw the narrow, heavy door swing inward. And in the pallid glow of the single dim street-lamp he strained his eyes to see what his colleagues had brought out of that sinister house which loomed so close behind. But when he looked, he did not see what he had expected; for his colleagues were not there at all, but only the Terrible Old Man leaning quietly on his knotted cane and smiling hideously. Mr. Czanek had never before noticed the colour of that man's eyes; now he saw that they were yellow.

Little things make considerable excitement in little towns, which is the reason that Kingsport people talked all that spring and summer about the three unidentifiable bodies, horribly slashed as with many cutlasses, and horribly mangled as by the tread of many cruel boot-heels, which the tide washed in. And some people even spoke of things as trivial as the deserted motor-car found in Ship Street, or certain especially inhuman cries, probably of a stray animal or migratory bird, heard in the night by wakeful citizens. But in this idle village gossip the Terrible Old Man took no interest at all. He was by nature reserved, and when one is aged and feeble one's reserve is doubly strong. Besides, so ancient a sea-captain must have witnessed scores of things much more stirring in the far-off days of his unremembered youth.

Uncle Cornelius His Story

George MacDonald,

It was a dull evening in November. A drizzling mist had been falling all day about the old farm. Harry Heywood and his two sisters sat in the house-place, expecting a visit from their uncle, Cornelius Heywood. This uncle lived alone, occupying the first floor above a chemist's shop in the town, and had just enough of money over to buy books that nobody seemed ever to have heard of but himself; for he was a student in all those regions of speculation in which anything to be called knowledge is impossible.

"What a dreary night!" said Kate. "I wish uncle would come and tell us a story."

"A cheerful wish," said Harry. "Uncle Cornie is a lively companion—isn't he? He can't even blunder through a Joe Miller without tacking a moral to it, and then trying to persuade you that the joke of it depends on the moral."

"Here he comes!" said Kate, as three distinct blows with the knob of his walking-stick announced the arrival of Uncle Cornelius. She ran to the door to open it.

The air had been very still all day, but as he entered he seemed to have brought the wind with him, for the first moan of it pressed against rather than shook the casement of the low-ceiled room.

Uncle Cornelius was very tall, and very thin, and very pale, with large grey eyes that looked greatly larger because he wore spectacles of the most delicate hair-steel, with the largest pebble-eyes that ever were seen. He gave them a kindly greeting, but too much in earnest even in shaking hands to smile over it. He sat down in the armchair by the chimney corner.

I have been particular in my description of him, in order that my reader may give due weight to his words. I am such a believer in words, that I believe everything depends on who says them. Uncle Cornelius Heywood's story told word for word by Uncle Timothy Warren, would not have been the same story at all. Not one of the listeners would have believed a syllable of it from the lips of round-bodied, red-faced, small-eyed, little Uncle Tim; whereas from Uncle Cornie—disbelieve one of his stories if you could!

One word more concerning him. His interest in everything conjectured or believed relative to the awful borderland of this world and the next, was only equalled by his disgust at the vulgar, unimaginative forms which curiosity about such subjects has assumed in the present day. With a yearning after the unseen like that of a child for the lifting of the curtain of a theatre, he declared that, rather than accept such a spirit-world as the would-be seers of the nineteenth century thought or pretended to reveal,—the prophets of a pauperised, workhouse immortality, invented by a poverty-stricken soul, and a sense so greedy that it would gorge on carrion,—he would rejoice to believe that a man had just as much of a soul as the cabbage of Iamblichus, namely, an aerial double of his body.

"I'm so glad you're come, uncle!" said Kate. "Why wouldn't you come to dinner? We have been so gloomy!"

"Well, Katey, you know I don't admire eating. I never could bear to see a cow tearing up the grass with her long tongue." As he spoke he looked very much like a cow. He had a way of opening his jaws while he kept his lips closely pressed together, that made his cheeks fall in, and his face look awfully long and dismal. "I consider eating," he went on, "such an animal exercise that it ought always to be performed in private. You never saw me dine, Kate."

"Never, uncle; but I have seen you drink;—nothing but water, I must confess."

"Yes, that is another affair. According to one eyewitness that is no more than the disembodied can do. I must confess, however, that, although well attested, the story is to me scarcely credible. Fancy a glass of Bavarian beer lifted into the air without a visible hand, turned upside down, and set empty on the table!—and no splash on the floor or anywhere else!"

A solitary gleam of humour shone through the great eyes of the spectacles as he spoke.

"Oh, uncle! how can you believe such nonsense!" said Janet.

"I did not say I believed it—did I? But why not? The story has at least a touch of imagination in it."

"That is a strange reason for believing a thing, uncle," said Harry.

"You might have a worse, Harry. I grant it is not sufficient; but it is better than that commonplace aspect which is the ground of most faith. I believe I did say that the story puzzled me."

"But how can you give it any quarter at all, uncle?"

"It does me no harm. There it is—between the boards of an old German book. There let it remain."

"Well, you will never persuade me to believe such things," said Janet.

"Wait till I ask you, Janet," returned her uncle, gravely. "I have not the slightest desire to convince you. How did we get into this unprofitable current of talk? We will change it at once. How are consols, Harry?"

"Oh, uncle!" said Kate, "we were longing for a story, and just as I thought you were coming to one, off you go to consols!"

"I thought a ghost story at least was coming," said Janet.

"You did your best to stop it, Janet," said Harry.

Janet began an angry retort, but Cornelius interrupted her. "You never heard me tell a ghost story, Janet."

"You have just told one about a drinking ghost, uncle," said Janet—in such a tone that Cornelius replied—

"Well, take that for your story, and let us talk of something else."

Janet apparently saw that she had been rude, and said as sweetly as she might—"Ah! but you didn't make that one, uncle. You got it out of a German book."

"Make it!—Make a ghost story!" repeated Cornelius. "No; that I never did."

"Such things are not to be trifled with, are they?" said Janet.

"I at least have no inclination to trifle with them."

"But, really and truly, uncle," persisted Janet, "you don't believe in such things?"

"Why should I either believe or disbelieve in them? They are not essential to salvation, I presume."

"You must do the one or the other, I suppose."

"I beg your pardon. You suppose wrong. It would take twice the proof I have ever had to make me believe in them; and exactly your prejudice, and allow me to say ignorance, to make me disbelieve in them. Neither is within my reach. I postpone judgment. But you, young people, of course, are wiser, and know all about the question."

"Oh, uncle! I'm so sorry!" said Kate. "I'm sure I did not mean to vex you."

"Not at all, not at all, my dear.—It wasn't you."

"Do you know," Kate went on, anxious to prevent anything unpleasant, for there was something very black perched on Janet's forehead, "I have taken to reading about that kind of thing."

"I beg you will give it up at once. You will bewilder your brains till you are ready to believe anything, if only it be absurd enough. Nay, you may come to find the element of vulgarity essential to belief. I should be sorry to the heart to believe concerning a horse or dog what they tell you nowadays about Shakespeare and Burns. What have you been reading, my girl?"

"Don't be alarmed, uncle. Only some Highland legends, which are too absurd either for my belief or for your theories."

"I don't know that, Kate."

"Why, what could you do with such shapeless creatures as haunt their fords and pools for instance? They are as featureless as the faces of the mountains."

"And so much the more terrible."

"But that does not make it easier to believe in them," said Harry.

"I only said," returned his uncle, "that their shapelessness adds to their horror."

"But you allowed—almost, at least, uncle," said Kate, "that you could find a place in your theories even for those shapeless creatures."

Cornelius sat silent for a moment; then, having first doubled the length of his face, and restored it to its natural condition, said thoughtfully, "I suspect, Katey, if you were to come upon an ichthyosaurus or a pterodactyl asleep in the shrubbery, you would hardly expect your report of it to be believed all at once either by Harry or Janet."

"I suppose not, uncle. But I can't see what—"

"Of course, such a thing could not happen here and now. But there was a time when and a place where such a thing may have happened. Indeed, in my time, a traveller or two have got pretty soundly disbelieved for reporting what they saw,—the last of an expiring race, which had strayed over the natural verge of its history, coming to life in some neglected swamp, itself a remnant of the slime of Chaos."

"I never heard you talk like that before, uncle," said Harry. "If you go on like that, you'll land me in a swamp, I'm afraid."

"I wasn't talking to you at all, Harry. Kate challenged me to find a place for kelpies, and such like, in the theories she does me the honour of supposing I cultivate."

"Then you think, uncle, that all these stories are only legends which, if you could follow them up, would lead you back to some one of the awful monsters that have since quite disappeared from the earth."

"It is possible those stories may be such legends; but that was not what I intended to lead you to. I gave you that only as something like what I am going to say now. What if,—mind, I only suggest it,—what if the direful creatures, whose report lingers in these tales, should have an origin far older still? What if they were the remnants of a vanishing period of the earth's history long antecedent to the birth of mastodon and iguanodon; a stage, namely, when the world, as we call it, had not yet become quite visible, was not yet so far finished as to part from the invisible world that was its mother, and which, on its part, had not then become quite invisible—was only almost such; and when, as a credible consequence, strange shapes of those now invisible regions, Gorgons and Chimaeras dire, might be expected to gloom out occasionally from the awful Fauna of an ever-generating world upon that one which was being born of it. Hence, the life-periods of a world being long and slow, some of these huge, unformed bulks of half-created matter might, somehow, like the megatherium of later times,—a baby creation to them,—roll at age-long intervals, clothed in a mighty terror of shapelessness into the half-recognition of human beings, whose consternation at the uncertain vision were barrier enough to prevent all further knowledge of its substance."

"I begin to have some notion of your meaning, uncle," said Kate.

"But then," said Janet, "all that must be over by this time. That world has been invisible now for many years."

"Ever since you were born, I suppose, Janet. The changes of a world are not to be measured by the changes of its generations."

"Oh, but, uncle, there can't be any such things. You know that as well as I do."

"Yes, just as well, and no better."

"There can't be any ghosts now. Nobody believes such things."

"Oh, as to ghosts, that is quite another thing. I did not know you were talking with reference to them. It is no wonder if one can get nothing sensible out of you, Janet, when your discrimination is no greater than to lump everything marvellous, kelpies, ghosts, vampires, doubles, witches, fairies, nightmares, and I don't know what all, under the one head of ghosts; and we haven't been saying a word about them. If one were to disprove to you the existence of the afreets of

Eastern tales, you would consider the whole argument concerning the reappearance of the departed upset. I congratulate you on your powers of analysis and induction, Miss Janet. But it matters very little whether we believe in ghosts, as you say, or not, provided we believe that we are ghosts—that within this body, which so many people are ready to consider their own very selves, their lies a ghostly embryo, at least, which has an inner side to it God only can see, which says I concerning itself, and which will soon have to know whether or not it can appear to those whom it has left behind, and thus solve the question of ghosts for itself, at least."

"Then you do believe in ghosts, uncle?" said Janet, in a tone that certainly was not respectful.

"Surely, I said nothing of the sort, Janet. The man most convinced that he had himself had such an interview as you hint at, would find—ought to find it impossible to convince anyone else of it."

"You are quite out of my depth, uncle," said Harry. "Surely any honest man ought to be believed?"

"Honesty is not all, by any means, that is necessary to being believed. It is impossible to convey a conviction of anything. All you can do is to convey a conviction that you are convinced. Of course, what satisfied you might satisfy another; but, till you can present him with the sources of your conviction, you cannot present him with the conviction—and perhaps not even then."

"You can tell him all about, it, can't you?"

"Is telling a man about a ghost, affording him the source of your conviction? Is it the same as a ghost appearing to him? Really, Harry!—You cannot even convey the impression a dream has made upon you."

"But isn't that just because it is only a dream?"

"Not at all. The impression may be deeper and clearer on your mind than any fact of the next morning will make. You will forget the next day altogether, but the impression of the dream will remain through all the following whirl and storm of what you call facts. Now a conviction may be likened to a deep impression on the judgment or the reason, or both. No one can feel it but the person who is convinced. It cannot be conveyed."

"I fancy that is just what those who believe in spirit-rapping would say."

"There are the true and false of convictions, as of everything else. I mean that a man may take that for a conviction in his own mind which is not a conviction, but only resembles one. But those to whom you refer profess to appeal to facts. It is on the ground of those facts, and with the more earnestness the more reason they can give for receiving them as facts, that I refuse all their deductions with abhorrence. I mean that, if what they say is true, the thinker must reject with contempt the claim to anything like revelation therein."

"Then you do not believe in ghosts, after all?" said Kate, in a tone of surprise.

"I did not say so, my dear. Will you be reasonable, or will you not?"

"Dear uncle, do tell us what you really think."

"I have been telling you what I think ever since I came, Katey; and you won't take in a word I say."

"I have been taking in every word, uncle, and trying hard to understand it as well.—Did you ever see a ghost, uncle?"

Cornelius Heywood was silent. He shut his lips and opened his jaws till his cheeks almost met in the vacuum. A strange expression crossed the strange countenance, and the great eyes of his spectacles looked as if, at the very moment, they were seeing something no other spectacles could see. Then his jaws closed with a snap, his countenance brightened, a flash of humour came through the goggle eyes of pebble, and, at length, he actually smiled as he said—"Really, Katey, you must take me for a simpleton!"

"How, uncle?"

"To think, if I had ever seen a ghost, I would confess the fact before a set of creatures like you—all spinning your webs like so many spiders to catch and devour old Daddy Longlegs."

By this time Harry had grown quite grave. "Indeed, I am very sorry, uncle," he said, "if I have deserved such a rebuke."

"No, no, my boy," said Cornelius; "I did not mean it more than half. If I had meant it, I would not have said it. If you really would like—" Here he paused.

"Indeed, we should, uncle," said Kate, earnestly. "You should have heard what we were saying just before you came in."

"All you were saying, Katey?"

"Yes," answered Kate, thoughtfully. "The worst we said was that you could not tell a story without—well, we did say tacking a moral to it."

"Well, well! I mustn't push it. A man has no right to know what people say about him. It unfits him for occupying his real position amongst them. He, least of all, has anything to do with it. If his friends won't defend him, he can't defend himself. Besides, what people say is so often untrue!—I don't mean to others, but to themselves. Their hearts are more honest than their mouths. But Janet doesn't want a strange story, I am sure."

Janet certainly was not one to have chosen for a listener to such a tale. Her eyes were so small that no satisfaction could possibly come of it. "Oh! I don't mind, uncle," she said, with half-affected indifference, as she searched in her box for silk to mend her gloves.

"You are not very encouraging, I must say," returned her uncle, making another cow-face."

"I will go away, if you like," said Janet, pretending to rise.

"No, never mind," said her uncle hastily. "If you don't want me to tell it, I want you to hear it; and, before I have done, that may have come to the same thing perhaps."

"Then you really are going to tell us a ghost story!" said Kate, drawing her chair nearer to her uncle's; and then, finding this did not satisfy her sense of propinquity to the source of the expected pleasure, drawing a stool from the corner, and seating herself almost on the hearth-rug at his knee.

"I did not say so," returned Cornelius, once more. "I said I would tell you a strange story. You may call it a ghost story if you like; I do not pretend to determine what it is. I confess it will look like one, though."

After so many delays, Uncle Cornelius now plunged almost hurriedly into his narration.

"In the year 1820," he said, "in the month of August, I fell in love." Here the girls glanced at each other. The idea of Uncle Cornie in love, and in the very same century in which they were now listening to the confession, was too astonishing to pass without ocular remark; but, if he observed it, he took no notice of it; he did not even pause. "In the month of September, I was refused. Consequently, in the month of October, I was ready to fall in love again. Take particular care of yourself, Harry, for a whole month, at least, after your first disappointment; for you will never be more likely to do a foolish thing. Please yourself after the second. If you are silly then, you may take what you get, for you will deserve it—except it be good fortune."

"Did you do a foolish thing then, uncle?" asked Harry, demurely.

"I did, as you will see; for I fell in love again."

"I don't see anything so very foolish in that."

"I have repented it since, though. Don't interrupt me again, please.

In the middle of October, then, in the year 1820, in the evening, I was walking across Russell Square, on my way home from the British Museum, where I had been reading all day. You see I have a full intention of being precise, Janet."

"I'm sure I don't know why you make the remark to me, uncle," said Janet, with an involuntary toss of her head. Her uncle only went on with his narrative.

"I begin at the very beginning of my story," he said; "for I want to be particular as to everything that can appear to have had anything to do with what came afterwards. I had been reading, I say, all the morning in the British Museum; and, as I walked, I took off my spectacles to ease my eyes. I need not tell you that I am short-sighted now, for that you know well enough. But I must tell you that I was short-sighted then, and helpless enough without my spectacles, although I was not quite so much so as I am now;—for I find it all nonsense about short-sighted eyes improving with age. Well, I was walking along the south side of Russell Square, with my spectacles in my hand, and feeling a little bewildered in consequence—for it was quite the dusk of the evening, and short-sighted people require more light than others. I was feeling, in fact, almost blind.

"I had got more than half-way to the other side, when, from the crossing that cuts off the corner in the direction of Montagu Place, just as I was about to turn towards it, an old lady stepped upon the kerbstone of the pavement, looked at me for a moment, and passed—an occurrence not very remarkable, certainly. But the lady was remarkable, and so was her dress. I am not good at observing, and I am still worse at describing dress, therefore I can only say that hers reminded me of an old picture—that is, I had never seen anything like it, except in old pictures. She had no bonnet, and looked as if she had walked straight out of an ancient drawing-room in her evening attire. Of her face, I shall say nothing now. The next instant I met a man on the crossing, who stopped and addressed me. So short-sighted was I that, although I recognised his voice as one I ought to know, I could not identify him until I had put on my spectacles, which I did instinctively in the act of returning his greeting. At the same moment, I glanced over my shoulder after the old lady. She was nowhere to be seen.

"'What are you looking at?' asked James Hetheridge.

"'I was looking after that old lady,' I answered, 'but I can't see her.'

"'What old lady?' said Hetheridge, with just a touch of impatience.

"'You must have seen her,' I returned. 'You were not more than three yards behind her.'

"'Where is she then?'

"'She must have gone down one of the areas, I think. But she looked a lady, though an old-fashioned one.'

"'Have you been dining?' asked James, in a tone of doubtful inquiry.

"'No,' I replied, not suspecting the insinuation; 'I have only just come from the Museum.'

"'Then I advise you to call on your medical man before you go home.'

"'Medical man!' I returned; 'I have no medical man. What do you mean? I never was better in my life.'

"'I mean that there was no old lady. It was an illusion, and that indicates something wrong. Besides, you did not know me when I spoke to you.'

"'That is nothing" I returned. 'I had just taken off my spectacles, and without them I shouldn't know my own father.'

"'How was it you saw the old lady, then?'

"The affair was growing serious under my friend's cross-questioning. I did not at all like the idea of his supposing me subject to hallucinations. So, I answered, with a laugh, 'Ah! to be sure, that explains it. I am so blind without my spectacles, that I shouldn't know an old lady from a big dog.'

"'There was no big dog,' said Hetheridge, shaking his head, as the fact for the first time dawned upon me that, although I had seen the old lady clearly enough to make a sketch of her, even to the features of her care-worn, eager old face, I had not been able to recognise the well-known countenance of James Hetheridge.

"'That's what comes of reading till the optic nerve is weakened," he went on. 'You will cause yourself serious injury if you do not pull up in time. I'll tell you what; I'm going home next week—will you go with me?'

"'You are very kind,' I answered, not altogether rejecting the proposal, for I felt that a little change to the country would be pleasant, and I was quite my own master. For I had unfortunately means equal to my wants, and had no occasion to follow any profession—not a very desirable thing for a young man, I can tell you, Master Harry. I need not keep you over the commonplaces of pressing and yielding. It is enough to say that he pressed and that I yielded. The day was fixed for our departure together; but something or other, I forget what, occurred, to make him advance the date, and it was resolved that I should follow later in the month.

"It was a drizzly afternoon in the beginning of the last week of October when I left the town of Bradford in a post-chaise to drive to Lewton Grange, the property of my friend's father. I had hardly left the town, and the twilight had only begun to deepen, when, glancing from one of the windows of the chaise, I fancied I saw, between me and the hedge, the dim figure of a horse keeping pace with us. I thought, in the first interval of unreason, that it was a shadow from my own horse, but reminded myself the next moment that there could be no shadow where there was no light. When I looked again, I was at the first glance convinced that my eyes had deceived me. At the second, I believed once more that a shadowy something, with the movements of a horse in harness, was keeping pace with us. I turned away again with some discomfort, and not till we had reached an open moorland road, whence a little watery light was visible on the horizon, could I summon up courage enough to look out once more.

"Certainly, then there was nothing to be seen, and I persuaded myself that it had been all a fancy, and lighted a cigar. With my feet on the cushions before me, I had soon lifted myself on the clouds of tobacco far above all the terrors of the night, and believed them banished for ever. But, my cigar coming to an end just as we turned into the avenue that led up to the Grange, I found myself once more glancing nervously out of the window. The moment the trees were about me, there was, if not a shadowy horse out there by the side of the chaise, yet certainly more than half that conviction in here in my consciousness. When I saw my friend, however, standing on the doorstep, dark against the glow of the hall fire, I forgot all about it; and I need not add that I did not make it a subject of conversation when I entered, for I was well aware that it was essential to a man's reputation that his senses should be accurate, though his heart might without prejudice swarm with shadows, and his judgment be a very stable of hobbies.

"I was kindly received. Mrs. Hetheridge had been dead for some years, and Laetitia, the eldest of the family, was at the head of the household. She had two sisters, little more than girls. The father was a burly, yet gentlemanlike Yorkshire squire, who ate well, drank well, looked radiant, and hunted twice a week. In this pastime, his son joined him when in the humour, which happened scarcely so often. I, who had never crossed a horse in my life, took his apology for not being able to mount me very coolly, assuring him that I would rather loiter about with a book than be in at the death of the best-hunted fox in Yorkshire.

"I very soon found myself at home with the Hetheridges; and very soon again I began to find myself not so much at home; for Miss Hetheridge—Laetitia as I soon ventured to call her—was fascinating. I have told you, Katey, that there was an empty place in my heart. Look to the door then, Katey. That was what made me so ready to fall in love with Laetitia. Her figure was graceful, and I think, even now, her face would have been beautiful but for a certain contraction of the skin over the nostrils, suggesting an invisible thumb and forefinger pinching them, which repelled me, although I did not then know what it indicated. I had not been with her one evening before the impression it made on me had vanished, and that so entirely that I could hardly recall the perception of the peculiarity which had occasioned it.

"Her observation was remarkably keen, and her judgment generally correct. She had great confidence in it herself; nor was she devoid of sympathy with some of the forms of human imagination, only they never seemed to possess for her any relation to practical life. That was to be ordered by the judgment alone. I do not mean she ever said so. I am only giving the conclusions I came to afterwards. It is not necessary that you should have any more thorough acquaintance with her mental character. One point in her moral nature, of special consequence to my narrative, will show itself by and by.

"I did all I could to make myself agreeable to her, and the more I succeeded the more delightful she became in my eyes. We walked in the garden and grounds together; we read, or rather I read and she listened;—read poetry, Katey—sometimes till we could not read any more for certain haziness and huskiness which look now, I am afraid, considerably more absurd than they really were, or even ought to look. In short, I considered myself thoroughly in love with her."

"And wasn't she in love with you, uncle?"

"Don't interrupt me, child. I don't know. I hoped so then. I hope the contrary now. She liked me I am sure. That is not much to say. Liking is very pleasant and very cheap. Love is as rare as a star."

"I thought the stars were anything but rare, uncle."

"That's because you never went out to find one for yourself, Katey. They would prove a few miles apart then."

"But it would be big enough when I did find it."

"Right, my dear. That is the way with love.—Laetitia was a good housekeeper. Everything was punctual as clockwork. I use the word advisedly. If her father, who was punctual to one date,—the dinner-hour,—made any remark to the contrary as he took up the carving-knife, Laetitia would instantly send one of her sisters to question the old clock in the hall, and report the time to half a minute. It was sure to be found that, if there was a mistake, the mistake was in the clock. But although it was certainly a virtue to have her household in such perfect order, it was not a virtue to be impatient with every infringement of its rules on the part of others. She was very severe, for instance, upon her two younger sisters if, the moment after the second bell had rung, they were not seated at the dinner-table, washed and aproned.

"Order was a very idol with her. Hence the house was too tidy for any sense of comfort. If you left an open book on the table, you would, on returning to the room a moment after, find it put aside. What the furniture of the drawing-room was like, I never saw; for not even on Christmas Day, which was the last day I spent there, was it uncovered. Everything in it was kept in bibs and pinafores. Even the carpet was covered with a cold and slippery sheet of brown holland. Mr. Hetheridge never entered that room, and therein was wise. James remonstrated once. She answered him quite kindly, even playfully, but no change followed. What was worse, she made very wretched tea. Her father never took tea; neither did James. I was rather fond of it, but I soon gave it up. Everything her father partook of was first-rate. Everything else was somewhat poverty-stricken. My pleasure in Laetitia's society prevented me from making practical deductions from such trifles."

"I shouldn't have thought you knew anything about eating, uncle," said Janet.

"The less a man eats, the more he likes to have it good, Janet. In short,—there can be no harm in saying it now,—Laetitia was so far from being like the name of her baptism,—and most names are so good that they are worth thinking about; no children are named after bad ideas,—Laetitia was so far unlike hers as to be stingy—an abominable fault. But, I repeat, the notion of such a fact was far from me then. And now for my story.

"The first of November was a very lovely day, quite one of the 'halcyon days' of 'St. Martin's summer.' I was sitting in a little arbour I had just discovered, with a book in my hand,—not reading, however, but daydreaming,—when, lifting my eyes from the ground, I was startled to see, through a thin shrub in front of the arbour, what seemed the form of an old lady seated, apparently reading from a book on her knee. The sight instantly recalled the old lady of Russell Square. I started to my feet, and then, clear of the intervening bush, saw only a great stone such as abounded on the moors in the neighbourhood, with a lump of quartz set on the top of it. Some childish taste had put it there for an ornament. Smiling at my own folly, I sat down again, and reopened my book. After reading for a while, I glanced up again, and once more started to my feet, overcome by the fancy that there verily sat the old lady reading. You will say it indicated an excited condition of the brain. Possibly; but I was, as far as I can recall, quite collected and reasonable. I was almost vexed this second time, and sat down once more to my book. Still, every time I looked up, I was startled afresh. I doubt, however, if the trifle is worth mentioning, or has any significance even in relation to what followed.

"After dinner, I strolled out by myself, leaving father and son over their claret. I did not drink wine; and from the lawn I could see the windows of the library, whither Laetitia commonly retired from the dinner-table. It was a very lovely soft night. There was no moon, but the stars looked wider awake than usual. Dew was falling, but the grass was not yet wet, and I wandered about on it for half an hour. The stillness was somehow strange. It had a wonderful feeling in it as if something were expected—as if the quietness were the mould in which some event or other was about to be cast.

"Even then I was a reader of certain sorts of recondite lore. Suddenly I remembered that this was the eve of All Souls. This was the night on which the dead came out of their graves to visit their old homes. 'Poor dead!' I thought with myself; 'have you any place to call a home now? If you have, surely you will not wander back here, where all that you called home has either vanished or given itself to others, to be their home now and yours no more! What an awful doom the old fancy has allotted you! To dwell in your graves all the year, and creep out, this one night, to enter at the midnight door, left open for welcome! A poor welcome truly!—just an open door, a clean-swept floor, and a fire to warm your rain-sodden limbs! The household asleep, and the house-place swarming with the ghosts of ancient times,—the miser, the spendthrift, the profligate, the coquette,—for the good ghosts sleep, and are troubled with no waking like yours! Not one man, sleepless like yourselves, to question you, and be answered after the fashion of the old nursery rhyme—

'hat makes your eyes so holed?
I've lain so long among the mould.
What makes your feet so broad?
I've walked more than ever I rode!

"'Yet who can tell?' I went on to myself. 'It may be your hell to return thus. It may be that only on this one night of all the year you can show yourselves to him who can see you, but that the place where you were wicked is the Hades to which you are doomed for ages.' I thought and thought till I began to feel the air alive about me, and was enveloped in the vapours that dim the eyes of those who strain them for one peep through the dull mica windows that will not open on the world of ghosts. At length I cast my fancies away, and fled from them to the library, where the bodily presence of Laetitia made the world of ghosts appear shadowy indeed.

"'What a reality there is about a bodily presence!' I said to myself, as I took my chamber-candle in my hand. 'But what is there more real in a body?' I said again, as I crossed the hall. 'Surely nothing,' I went on, as I ascended the broad staircase to my room. 'The body must vanish. If there be a spirit, that will remain. A body can but vanish. A ghost can appear.'

"I woke in the morning with a sense of such discomfort as made me spring out of bed at once. My foot lighted upon my spectacles. How they came to be on the floor I could not tell, for I never took them off when I went to bed. When I lifted them, I found they were in two pieces; the bridge was broken. This was awkward. I was so utterly helpless without them! Indeed, before I could lay my hand on my hair-brush I had to peer through one eye of the parted pair. When I looked at my watch after I was dressed, I found I had risen an hour earlier than usual. I groped my way downstairs to spend the hour before breakfast in the library.

"No sooner was I seated with a book than I heard the voice of Laetitia scolding the butler, in no very gentle tones, for leaving the garden door open all night. The moment I heard this, the strange occurrences I am about to relate began to dawn upon my memory. The door had been open the night long between All Saints and All Souls. In the middle of that night I awoke suddenly. I knew it was not the morning by the sensations I had, for the night feels altogether different from the morning. It was quite dark. My heart was beating violently, and I either hardly could or hardly dared breathe. A nameless terror was upon me, and my sense of hearing was, apparently by the force of its expectation, unnaturally roused and keen. There it was—a slight noise in the room!—slight, but clear, and with an unknown significance about it! It was awful to think it would come again.

"I do believe it was only one of those creaks in the timbers which announce the torpid, age-long, sinking flow of every house back to the dust—a motion to which the flow of the glacier is as a torrent, but which is no less inevitable and sure. Day and night, it ceases not; but only in the night, when house and heart are still, do we hear it. No wonder it should sound fearful! for are we not the immortal dwellers in ever-crumbling clay? The clay is so near us, and yet not of us, that its every movement starts a fresh dismay. For what will its final ruin disclose? When it falls from about us, where shall we find that we have existed all the time?

"My skin tingled with the bursting of the moisture from its pores. Something was in the room beside me. A confused, indescribable sense of utter loneliness, and yet awful presence, was upon me, mingled with a dreary, hopeless desolation, as of burnt-out love and aimless life. All at once I found myself sitting up. The terror that a cold hand might be laid upon me, or a cold breath blow on me, or a corpse-like face bend down through the darkness over me, had broken my bonds!—I would meet half-way whatever might be approaching. The moment that my will burst into action the terror began to ebb.

"The room in which I slept was a large one, perfectly dreary with tidiness. I did not know till afterwards that it was Laetitia's room, which she had given up to me rather than prepare another. The furniture, all but one article, was modern and commonplace. I could not help remarking to myself afterwards how utterly void the room was of the nameless charm of feminine occupancy. I had seen nothing to wake a suspicion of its being a lady's room. The article I have excepted was an ancient bureau, elaborate and ornate, which stood on one side of the large bow window. The very morning before, I had seen a bunch of keys hanging from the upper part of it, and had peeped in.

"Finding however, that the pigeon-holes were full of papers, I closed it at once. I should have been glad to use it, but clearly it was not for me. At that bureau, the figure of a woman was now seated in the posture of one writing. A strange dim light was around her, but whence it proceeded I never thought of inquiring. As if I, too, had stepped over the bourne, and was a ghost myself, all fear was now gone. I got out of bed, and softly crossed the room to where she was seated. 'If she should be beautiful!' I thought—for I had often dreamed of a beautiful ghost that made love to me.

"The figure did not move. She was looking at a faded brown paper. 'Some old love-letter,' I thought, and stepped nearer. So cool was I now, that I actually peeped over her shoulder. With mingled surprise and dismay I found that the dim page over which she bent was that of an old account-book. Ancient household records, in rusty ink, held up to the glimpses of the waning moon, which shone through the parting in the curtains, their entries of shillings and pence!—Of pounds there was not one. No doubt pounds and farthings are much the same in the world of thought—the true spirit-world; but in the ghost-world this eagerness over shillings and pence must mean something awful!

"To think that coins which had since been worn smooth in other pockets and purses, which had gone back to the Mint, and been melted down, to come out again and yet again with the heads of new kings and queens,—that dinners, eaten by men and women and children whose bodies had since been eaten by the worms,—that polish for the floors, inches of whose thickness had since been worn away,—that the hundred nameless trifles of a life utterly vanished, should be perplexing, annoying, and worst of all, interesting the soul of a ghost who had been in Hades for centuries! The writing was very old-fashioned, and the words were contracted. I could read nothing but the moneys and one single entry—'Corinths, Vs.'

"Currants for a Christmas pudding, most likely!—Ah, poor lady! the pudding and not the Christmas was her care; not the delight of the children over it, but the beggarly pence which it cost. And she cannot get it out of her head, although her brain was 'powdered all as thin as flour' ages ago in the mortar of Death. 'Alas, poor ghost!' It needs no treasured hoard left behind, no floor stained with the blood of the murdered child, no wickedly hidden parchment of landed rights! An old account-book is enough for the hell of the house-keeping gentlewoman!

"She never lifted her face, or seemed to know that I stood behind her. I left her, and went into the bow window, where I could see her face. I was right. It was the same old lady I had met in Russell Square, walking in front of James Hetheridge. Her withered lips went moving as if they would have uttered words had the breath been commissioned thither; her brow was contracted over her thin nose; and once and again her shining forefinger went up to her temple as if she were pondering some deep problem of humanity. How long I stood gazing at her I do not know, but at last I withdrew to my bed, and left her struggling to solve that which she could never solve thus. It was the symbolic problem of her own life, and she had failed to read it. I remember nothing more. She may be sitting there still, solving at the insolvable.

"I should have felt no inclination, with the broad sun of the squire's face, the keen eyes of James, and the beauty of Laetitia before me at the breakfast table, to say a word about what I had seen, even if I had not been afraid of the doubt concerning my sanity which the story would certainly awaken. What with the memories of the night and the want of my spectacles, I passed a very dreary day, dreading the return of the night, for, cool as I had been in her presence, I could not regard the possible reappearance of the ghost with equanimity. But when the night did come, I slept soundly till the morning.

"The next day, not being able to read with comfort, I went wandering about the place, and at length began to fit the outside and inside of the house together. It was a large and rambling edifice, parts of it very old, parts comparatively modern. I first found my own window, which looked out of the back. Below this window, on one side, there was a door. I wondered whither it led, but found it locked. At the moment James approached from the stables. 'Where does this door lead?' I asked him.

"'I will get the key,' he answered. 'It is rather a queer old place. We used to like it when we were children.'

"'There's a stair, you see,' he said, as he threw the door open. 'It leads up over the kitchen.' I followed him up the stair. 'There's a door into your room,' he said, 'but it's always locked now.—And here's Grannie's room, as they call it, though why, I have not the least idea,' he added, as he pushed open the door of an old-fashioned parlour, smelling very musty. A few old books lay on a side table. A china bowl stood beside them, with some shrivelled, scentless rose-leaves in the bottom of it. The cloth that covered the table was riddled by moths, and the spider-legged chairs were covered with dust.

"A conviction seized me that the old bureau must have belonged to this room, and I soon found the place where I judged it must have stood. But the same moment I caught sight of a portrait on the wall above the spot I had fixed upon. 'By Jove!' I cried, involuntarily, 'that's the very old lady I met in Russell Square!'

"'Nonsense!' said James. 'Old-fashioned ladies are like babies—they all look the same. That's a very old portrait.'

"'So, I see,' I answered. 'It is like a Zucchero.'

"'I don't know whose it is," he answered hurriedly, and I thought he looked a little queer.

"'Is she one of the family?' I asked.

"'They say so; but who or what she was, I don't know. You must ask Letty," he answered.

"'The more I look at it,' I said, 'the more I am convinced it is the same old lady.'

"'Well,' he returned with a laugh, 'my old nurse used to say she was rather restless. But it's all nonsense.'

"'That bureau in my room looks about the same date as this furniture,' I remarked.

"'It used to stand just there,' he answered, pointing to the space under the picture. 'Well I remember with what awe we used to regard it; for they said the old lady kept her accounts at it still. We never dared touch the bundles of yellow papers in the pigeon-holes. I remember thinking Letty a very heroine once when she touched one of them with the tip of her forefinger. She had got yet more courageous by the time she had it moved into her own room.'

"'Then that is your sister's room I am occupying?' I said.

"'Yes.'

"'I am ashamed of keeping her out of it.'

"'Oh! she'll do well enough.'

"'If I were she though,' I added, 'I would send that bureau back to its own place.'

"'What do you mean, Heywood? Do you believe every old wife's tale that ever was told?'

"'She may get a fright someday—that's all!' I replied.

"He smiled with such an evident mixture of pity and contempt that for the moment I almost disliked him; and feeling certain that Laetitia would receive any such hint in a somewhat similar manner, I did not feel inclined to offer her any advice with regard to the bureau.

"Little occurred during the rest of my visit worthy of remark. Somehow or other I did not make much progress with Laetitia. I believe I had begun to see into her character a little, and therefore did not get deeper in love as the days went on. I know I became less absorbed in her society, although I was still anxious to make myself agreeable to her—or perhaps, more properly, to give her a favourable impression of me. I do not know whether she perceived any difference in my behaviour, but I remember that I began again to remark the pinched look of her nose, and to be a little annoyed with her for always putting aside my book. At the same time, I daresay I was provoking, for I never was given to tidiness myself.

"At length Christmas Day arrived. After breakfast, the squire, James, and the two girls arranged to walk to church. Laetitia was not in the room at the moment. I excused myself on the ground of a headache, for I had had a bad night. When they left, I went up to my room, threw myself on the bed, and was soon fast asleep.

"How long I slept I do not know, but I woke again with that indescribable yet well-known sense of not being alone. The feeling was scarcely less terrible in the daylight than it had been in the darkness. With the same sudden effort as before, I sat up in the bed. There was the figure at the open bureau, in precisely the same position as on the former occasion. But I could not see it so distinctly. I rose as gently as I could, and approached it, after the first physical terror. I am not a coward. Just as I got near enough to see the account book open on the folding cover of the bureau, she started up, and, turning, revealed the face of Laetitia. She blushed crimson.

"'I beg your pardon, Mr. Heywood,' she said in great confusion; 'I thought you had gone to church with the rest.'

"'I had lain down with a headache, and gone to sleep,' I replied. 'But,—forgive me, Miss Hetheridge,' I added, for my mind was full of the dreadful coincidence,—'don't you think you would have been better at church than balancing your accounts on Christmas Day?'

"'The better day the better deed,' she said, with a somewhat offended air, and turned to walk from the room.

"'Excuse me, Laetitia,' I resumed, very seriously, 'but I want to tell you something.'

"She looked conscious. It never crossed me, that perhaps she fancied I was going to make a confession. Far other things were then in my mind. For I thought how awful it was, if she too, like the ancestral ghost, should have to do an age-long penance of haunting that bureau and those horrid figures, and I had suddenly resolved to tell her the whole story. She listened with varying complexion and face half turned aside. When I had ended, which I fear I did with something of a personal appeal, she lifted her head and looked me in the face, with just a slight curl on her thin lip, and answered me. 'If I had wanted a sermon, Mr. Heywood, I should have gone to church for it. As for the ghost, I am sorry for you.' So saying she walked out of the room.

"The rest of the day I did not find very merry. I pleaded my headache as an excuse for going to bed early. How I hated the room now! Next morning, immediately after breakfast, I took my leave of Lewton Grange."

"And lost a good wife, perhaps, for the sake of a ghost, uncle!" said Janet.

"If I lost a wife at all, it was a stingy one. I should have been ashamed of her all my life long."

"Better than a spendthrift," said Janet.

"How do you know that?" returned her uncle. "All the difference I see is, that the extravagant ruins the rich, and the stingy robs the poor."

"But perhaps she repented, uncle," said Kate.

"I don't think she did, Katey. Look here."

Uncle Cornelius drew from the breast pocket of his coat a black-edged letter.

"I have kept up my friendship with her brother," he said. "All he knows about the matter is, that either we had a quarrel, or she refused me;—he is not sure which. I must say for Laetitia, that she was no tattler. Well, here's a letter I had from James this very morning. I will read it to you.

"'My Dear Mr. Heywood,—We have had a terrible shock this morning. Letty did not come down to breakfast, and Lizzie went to see if she was ill. We heard her scream, and, rushing up, there was poor Letty, sitting at the old bureau, quite dead. She had fallen forward on the desk, and her housekeeping-book was crumpled up under her. She had been so all night long, we suppose, for she was not undressed, and was quite cold. The doctors say it was disease of the heart.'

"There!" said Uncle Cornie, folding up the letter.

"Do you think the ghost had anything to do with it, uncle?" asked Kate, almost under her breath.

"How should I know, my dear? Possibly."

"It's very sad," said Janet; "but I don't see the good of it all. If the ghost had come to tell that she had hidden away money in some secret place in the old bureau, one would see why she had been permitted to come back. But what was the good of those accounts after they were over and done with? I don't believe in the ghost."

"Ah, Janet, Janet! but those wretched accounts were not over and done with, you see. That is the misery of it."

Uncle Cornelius rose without another word, bade them good-night, and walked out into the wind.

Miss Jéromette and the Clergyman

Wilkie Collins

1

My brother, the clergyman, looked over my shoulder before I was aware of him, and discovered that the volume which completely absorbed my attention was a collection of famous Trials, published in a new edition and in a popular form.

He laid his finger on the Trial which I happened to be reading at the moment. I looked up at him; his face startled me. He had turned pale. His eyes were fixed on the open page of the book with an expression which puzzled and alarmed me.

"My dear fellow," I said, "what in the world is the matter with you?"

He answered in an odd absent manner, still keeping his finger on the open page.

"I had almost forgotten," he said. "And this reminds me."

"Reminds you of what?" I asked. "You don't mean to say you know anything about the Trial?"

"I know this," he said. "The prisoner was guilty."

"Guilty?" I repeated. "Why, the man was acquitted by the jury, with the full approval of the judge! What can you possibly mean?"

"There are circumstances connected with that Trial," my brother answered, "which were never communicated to the judge or the jury—which were never so much as hinted or whispered in court. I know—of my own knowledge, by my own personal experience. They are very sad, very strange, very terrible. I have mentioned them to no mortal creature. I have done my best to forget them. You—quite innocently—have brought them back to my mind. They oppress, they distress me. I wish I had found you reading any book in your library, except that book!"

My curiosity was now strongly excited. I spoke out plainly.

"Surely," I suggested, "you might tell your brother what you are unwilling to mention to persons less nearly related to you. We have followed different professions, and have lived in different countries, since we were boys at school. But you know you can trust me."

He considered a little with himself.

"Yes," he said. "I know I can trust you." He waited a moment; and then he surprised me by a strange question.

"Do you believe," he asked, "that the spirits of the dead can return to earth, and show themselves to the living?"

I answered cautiously—adopting as my own the words of a great English writer, touching the subject of ghosts.

"You ask me a question," I said, "which, after five thousand years, is yet undecided. On that account alone, it is a question not to be trifled with."

My reply seemed to satisfy him.

"Promise me," he resumed, "that you will keep what I tell you a secret as long as I live. After my death I care little what happens. Let the story of my strange experience be added to the published experience of those other men who have seen what I have seen, and who believe what I believe.

"The world will not be the worse, and may be the better, for knowing one day what I am now about to trust to your ear alone."

My brother never again alluded to the narrative which he had confided to me, until the later time when I was sitting by his deathbed. He asked if I still remembered the story of Jéromette. "Tell it to others," he said, "as I have told it to you."

I repeat it after his death—as nearly as I can in his own words.

2

On a fine summer evening, many years since, I left my chambers in the Temple, to meet a fellow-student, who had proposed to me a night's amusement in the public gardens at Cremorne.

You were then on your way to India; and I had taken my degree at Oxford. I had sadly disappointed my father by choosing the Law as my profession, in preference to the Church. At that time, to own the truth, I had no serious intention of following any special vocation. I simply wanted an excuse for enjoying the pleasures of a London life. The study of the Law supplied me with that excuse. And I chose the Law as my profession accordingly.

On reaching the place at which we had arranged to meet, I found that my friend had not kept his appointment. After waiting vainly for ten minutes, my patience gave way and I went into the Gardens by myself.

I took two or three turns round the platform devoted to the dancers without discovering my fellow-student, and without seeing any other person with whom I happened to be acquainted at that time.

For some reason which I cannot now remember, I was not in my usual good spirits that evening. The noisy music jarred on my nerves, the sight of the gaping crowd round the platform irritated me, the blandishments of the painted ladies of the profession of pleasure saddened and disgusted me. I opened my cigar-case, and turned aside into one of the quiet by-walks of the Gardens.

A man who is habitually careful in choosing his cigar has this advantage over a man who is habitually careless. He can always count on smoking the best cigar in his case, down to the last. I was still absorbed in choosing my cigar, when I heard these words behind me—spoken in a foreign accent and in a woman's voice:

"Leave me directly, sir! I wish to have nothing to say to you."

I turned round and discovered a little lady very simply and tastefully dressed, who looked both angry and alarmed as she rapidly passed me on her way to the more frequented part of the Gardens. A man (evidently the worse for the wine he had drunk in the course of the evening) was following her, and was pressing his tipsy attentions on her with the coarsest insolence of speech and manner. She was young and pretty, and she cast one entreating look at me as she went by, which it was not in manhood—perhaps I ought to say, in young-manhood—to resist.

I instantly stepped forward to protect her, careless whether I involved myself in a discreditable quarrel with a blackguard or not. As a matter of course, the fellow resented my interference, and my temper gave way. Fortunately for me, just as I lifted my hand to knock him down, a policeman appeared who had noticed that he was drunk, and who settled the dispute officially by turning him out of the Gardens.

I led her away from the crowd that had collected. She was evidently frightened—I felt her hand trembling on my arm—but she had one great merit; she made no fuss about it.

"If I can sit down for a few minutes," she said in her pretty foreign accent, "I shall soon be myself again, and I shall not trespass any further on your kindness. I thank you very much, sir, for taking care of me."

We sat down on a bench in a retired part of the Gardens, near a little fountain. A row of lighted lamps ran round the outer rim of the basin. I could see her plainly.

I have said that she was "a little lady." I could not have described her more correctly in three words.

Her figure was slight and small: she was a well-made miniature of a woman from head to foot. Her hair and her eyes were both dark. The hair curled naturally; the expression of the eyes was quiet, and rather sad; the complexion, as I then saw it, very pale; the little mouth perfectly charming. I was especially attracted, I remembered, by the carriage of her head; it was strikingly graceful and spirited; it distinguished her, little as she was and quiet as she was, among the thousands of other women in the Gardens, as a creature apart.

Even the one marked defect in her a slight "cast" in the left eye—seemed to add, in some strange way, to the quaint attractiveness of her face. I have already spoken of the tasteful simplicity of her dress. I ought now to add that it was not made of any costly material, and that she wore no jewels or ornaments of any sort. My little lady was not rich; even a man's eye could see that.

She was perfectly unembarrassed and unaffected. We fell as easily into talk as if we had been friends instead of strangers.

I asked how it was that she had no companion to take care of her."You are too young and too pretty," I said in my blunt English way, "to trust yourself alone in such a place as this."

She took no notice of the compliment. She calmly put it away from her as if it had not reached her ears

"I have no friend to take care of me," she said simply. "I was sad and sorry this evening, all by myself, and I thought I would go to the Gardens and hear the music, just to amuse me. It is not much to pay at the gate; only a shilling."

"No friend to take care of you?" I repeated. "Surely there must be one happy man who might have been here with you tonight?"

"What man do you mean?" she asked.

"The man," I answered thoughtlessly, "whom we call, in England, a Sweetheart."

I would have given worlds to have recalled those foolish words the moment they passed my lips. I felt that I had taken a vulgar liberty with her. Her face saddened; her eyes dropped to the ground. I begged her pardon.

"There is no need to beg my pardon," she said. "If you wish to know, sir—yes, I had once a sweetheart, as you call it in England. He has gone away and left me. No more of him, if you please. I am rested now. I will thank you again, and go home."

She rose to leave me.

I was determined not to part with her in that way. I begged to be allowed to see her safely back to her own door. She hesitated. I took a man's unfair advantage of her, by appealing to her fears. I said, "Suppose the blackguard who annoyed you should be waiting outside the gates?" That decided her. She took my arm. We went away together by the bank of the Thames, in the balmy summer night.

A walk of half an hour brought us to the house in which she lodged—a shabby little house in a by-street, inhabited evidently by very poor people.

She held out her hand at the door, and wished me goodnight. I was too much interested in her to consent to leave my little foreign lady without the hope of seeing her again. I asked permission to call on her the next day. We were standing under the light of the street-lamp. She studied my face with a grave and steady attention before she made any reply.

"Yes," she said at last. "I think I do know a gentleman when I see him. You may come, sir, if you please, and call upon me tomorrow."

So we parted. So I entered—doubting nothing, foreboding nothing—on a scene in my life which I now look back on with unfeigned repentance and regret.

3

I am speaking at this later time in the position of a clergyman, and in the character of a man of mature age. Remember that; and you will understand why I pass as rapidly as possible over the events of the next year of my life—why I say as little as I can of the errors and the delusion of my youth.

I called on her the next day. I repeated my visits during the days and weeks that followed, until the shabby little house in the by-street had become a second and (I say it with shame and self-reproach) a dearer home to me.

All of herself and her story which she thought fit to confide to me under these circumstances may be repeated to you in few words.

The name by which letters were addressed to her was "Mademoiselle Jéromette." Among the ignorant people of the house and the small tradesmen of the neighbourhood—who found her name not easy of pronunciation by the average English tongue—she was known by the friendly nickname of "The French Miss." When I knew her, she was resigned to her lonely life among strangers. Some years had elapsed since she had lost her parents, and had left France.

Possessing a small, very small, income of her own, she added to it by colouring miniatures for the photographers. She had relatives still living in France; but she had long since ceased to correspond with them. "Ask me nothing more about my family," she used to say. "I am as good as dead in my own country and among my own people."

This was all—literally all—that she told me of herself, I have never discovered more of her sad story from that day to this.

She never mentioned her family name—never even told me what part of France she came from, or how long she had lived in England. That she was by birth and breeding a lady, I could entertain no doubt; her manners, her accomplishments, her ways of thinking and speaking, all proved it. Looking below the surface, her character showed itself in aspects not common among young women in these days.

In her quiet way, she was an incurable fatalist, and a firm believer in the ghostly reality of apparitions from the dead. Then again in the matter of money, she had strange views of her own. Whenever my purse was in my hand, she held me resolutely at a distance from first to last. She refused to move into better apartments; the shabby little house was clean inside, and the poor people who lived in it were kind to her—and that was enough.

The most expensive present that she ever permitted me to offer her was a little enamelled ring, the plainest and cheapest thing of the kind in the jeweller's shop. In all relations with me she was sincerity itself. On all occasions, and under all circumstances, she spoke her mind (as the phrase is) with the same uncompromising plainness.

"I like you," she said to me; "I respect you; I shall always be faithful to you while you are faithful to me. But my love has gone from me. There is another man who has taken it away with him, I know not where."

Who was the other man?

She refused to tell me. She kept his rank and his name strict secrets from me. I never discovered how he had met with her, or why he had left her, or whether the guilt was his of making of her an exile from her country and her friends. She despised herself for still loving him; but the passion was too strong for her—she owned it and lamented it with the frankness which was so pre-eminently a part of her character.

More than this, she plainly told me, in the early days of our acquaintance, that she believed he would return to her. It might be tomorrow, or it might be years hence. Even if he failed to repent of his own cruel conduct, the man would still miss her, as something lost out of his life; and, sooner or later, he would come back.

"And will you receive him if he does come back?" I asked.

"I shall receive him," she replied, "against my own better judgment—in spite of my own firm persuasion that the day of his return to me will bring with it the darkest days of my life."

I tried to remonstrate with her.

"You have a will of your own," I said. "Exert it if he attempts to return to you."

"I have no will of my own," she answered quietly, "where he is concerned. It is my misfortune to love him." Her eyes rested for a moment on mine, with the utter self-abandonment of despair. "We have said enough about this," she added abruptly. "Let us say no more."

From that time we never spoke again of the unknown man. During the year that followed our first meeting, she heard nothing of him directly or indirectly. He might be living, or he might be dead. There came no word of him, or from him. I was fond enough of her to be satisfied with this—he never disturbed us.

4

The year passed—and the end came. Not the end as you may have anticipated it, or as I might have foreboded it.

You remember the time when your letters from home informed you of the fatal termination of our mother's illness? It is the time of which I am now speaking. A few hours only before she breathed her last, she called me to her bedside, and desired that we might be left together alone. Reminding me that her death was near, she spoke of my prospects in life; she noticed my want of interest in the studies which were then supposed to be engaging my attention, and she ended by entreating me to reconsider my refusal to enter the Church.

"Your father's heart is set upon it," she said. "Do what I ask of you, my dear, and you will help to comfort him when I am gone."

Her strength failed her: she could say no more. Could I refuse the last request she would ever make to me? I knelt at the bedside, and took her wasted hand in mine, and solemnly promised her the respect which a son owes to his mother's last wishes.

Having bound myself by this sacred engagement, I had no choice but to accept the sacrifice which it imperatively exacted from me. The time had come when I must tear myself free from all unworthy associations. No matter what the effort cost me, I must separate myself at once and forever from the unhappy woman who was not, who never could be, my wife.

At the close of a dull foggy day I set forth with a heavy heart to say the words which were to part us forever.

Her lodging was not far from the banks of the Thames. As I drew near the place the darkness was gathering, and the broad surface of the river was hidden from me in a chill white mist. I stood for a while, with my eyes fixed on the vaporous shroud that brooded over the flowing water—I stood and asked myself in despair the one dreary question: "What am I to say to her?"

The mist chilled me to the bones. I turned from the riverbank, and made my way to her lodgings hard by. "It must be done!" I said to myself, as I took out my key and opened the house door.

She was not at her work, as usual, when I entered her little sitting-room. She was standing by the fire, with her head down and with an open letter in her hand.

The instant she turned to meet me, I saw in her face that something was wrong. Her ordinary manner was the manner of an unusually placid and self-restrained person. Her temperament had little of the liveliness which we associate in England with the French nature. She was not ready with her laugh; and in all my previous experience, I had never yet known her to cry. Now, for the first time, I saw the quiet face disturbed; I saw tears in the pretty brown eyes. She ran to meet me, and laid her head on my breast, and burst into a passionate fit of weeping that shook her from head to foot.

Could she by any human possibility have heard of the coming change in my life? Was she aware, before I had opened my lips, of the hard necessity which had brought me to the house?

It was simply impossible; the thing could not be.

I waited until her first burst of emotion had worn itself out. Then I asked—with an uneasy conscience, with a sinking heart—what had happened to distress her.

She drew herself away from me, sighing heavily, and gave me the open letter which I had seen in her hand.

"Read that," she said. "And remember I told you what might happen when we first met."

I read the letter.

It was signed in initials only; but the writer plainly revealed himself as the man who had deserted her. He had repented; he had returned to her. In proof of his penitence he was willing to do her the justice which he had hitherto refused—he was willing to marry her, on the condition that she would engage to keep the marriage a secret, so long as his parents lived.

Submitting this proposal, he waited to know whether she would consent, on her side, to forgive and forget.

I gave her back the letter in silence. This unknown rival had done me the service of paving the way for our separation. In offering her the atonement of marriage, he had made it, on my part, a matter of duty to her, as well as to myself, to say the parting words. I felt this instantly. And yet, I hated him for helping me!

She took my hand, and led me to the sofa. We sat down, side by side. Her face was composed to a sad tranquillity. She was quiet; she was herself again.

"I have refused to see him," she said, "until I had first spoken to you. You have read his letter. What do you say?"

I could make but one answer. It was my duty to tell her what my own position was in the plainest terms. I did my duty—leaving her free to decide on the future for herself. Those sad words said, it was useless to prolong the wretchedness of our separation. I rose, and took her hand for the last time.

I see her again now, at that final moment, as plainly as if it had happened yesterday. She had been suffering from an affection of the throat; and she had a white silk handkerchief tied loosely round her neck. She wore a simple dress of purple merino, with a black silk apron over it. Her face was deadly pale; her fingers felt icily cold as they closed round my hand.

"Promise me one thing," I said, "before I go. While I live, I am your friend—if I am nothing more. If you are ever in trouble, promise that you will let me know it."

She started, and drew back from me as if I had struck her with a sudden terror.

"Strange!" she said, speaking to herself. "He feels as I feel. He is afraid of what may happen to me, in my life to come."

I attempted to reassure her. I tried to tell her what was indeed the truth—that I had only been thinking of the ordinary chances and changes of life, when I spoke.

She paid no heed to me; she came back and put her hands on my shoulders and thoughtfully and sadly looked up in my face.

"My mind is not your mind in this matter," she said. "I once owned to you that I had my forebodings, when we first spoke of this man's return, I may tell you now, more than I told you then. I believe I shall die young, and die miserably. If I am right, have you interest enough still left in me to wish to hear of it?"

She paused, shuddering—and added these startling words:

"You shall hear of it."

The tone of steady conviction in which she spoke alarmed and distressed me. My face showed her how deeply and how painfully I was affected.

"There, there!" she said, returning to her natural manner; "don't take what I say too seriously. A poor girl who has led a lonely life like mine thinks strangely and talks strangely—sometimes. Yes; I give you my promise. If I am ever in trouble, I will let you know it. God bless you—you have been very kind to me—goodbye!"

A tear dropped on my face as she kissed me. The door closed between us. The dark street received me.

It was raining heavily. I looked up at her window, through the drifting shower. The curtains were parted: she was standing in the gap, dimly lit by the lamp on the table behind her, waiting for our last look at each other. Slowly lifting her hand, she waved her farewell at the window, with the unsought native grace which had charmed me on the night when we first met. The curtain fell again—she disappeared—nothing was before me, nothing was round me, but the darkness and the night.

5

In two years from that time, I had redeemed the promise given to my mother on her deathbed. I had entered the Church.

My father's interest made my first step in my new profession an easy one. After serving my preliminary apprenticeship as a curate, I was appointed, before I was thirty years of age, to a living in the West of England.

My new benefice offered me every advantage that I could possibly desire—with the one exception of a sufficient income. Although my wants were few, and although I was still an unmarried man, I found it desirable, on many accounts, to add to my resources. Following the example of other young clergymen in my position, I determined to receive pupils who might stand in need of preparation for a career at the Universities. My relatives exerted themselves; and my good fortune still befriended me.

I obtained two pupils to start with. A third would complete the number which I was at present prepared to receive. In course of time, this third pupil made his appearance, under circumstances sufficiently remarkable to merit being mentioned in detail.

It was the summer vacation; and my two pupils had gone home. Thanks to a neighbouring clergyman, who kindly undertook to perform my duties for me, I too obtained a fortnight's holiday, which I spent at my father's house in London.

During my sojourn in the metropolis, I was offered an opportunity of preaching in a church, made famous by the eloquence of one of the popular pulpit-orators of our time. In accepting the proposal, I felt naturally anxious to do my best, before the unusually large and unusually intelligent congregation which would be assembled to hear me.

At the period of which I am now speaking, all England had been startled by the discovery of a terrible crime, perpetrated under circumstances of extreme provocation. I chose this crime as the main subject of my sermon. Admitting that the best among us were frail mortal creatures, subject to evil promptings and provocations like the worst among us, my object was to show how a Christian man may find his certain refuge from temptation in the safeguards of his religion.

I dwelt minutely on the hardship of the Christian's first struggle to resist the evil influence—on the help which his Christianity inexhaustibly held out to him in the worst relapses of the weaker and viler part of his nature—on the steady and certain gain which was the ultimate reward of his faith and his firmness—and on the blessed sense of peace and happiness which accompanied the final triumph. Preaching to this effect, with the fervent conviction which I really felt, I may say for myself, at least, that I did no discredit to the choice which had placed me in the pulpit. I held the attention of my congregation, from the first word to the last.

While I was resting in the vestry on the conclusion of the service, a note was brought to me written in pencil. A member of my congregation—a gentleman—wished to see me, on a matter of considerable importance to himself. He would call on me at any place, and at any hour, which I might choose to appoint. If I wished to be satisfied of his respectability, he would beg leave to refer me to his father, with whose name I might possibly be acquainted.

The name given in the reference was undoubtedly familiar to me, as the name of a man of some celebrity and influence in the world of London. I sent back my card, appointing an hour for the visit of my correspondent on the afternoon of the next day.

6

The stranger made his appearance punctually. I guessed him to be some two or three years younger than myself. He was undeniably handsome; his manners were the manners of a gentleman—and yet, without knowing why, I felt a strong dislike to him the moment he entered the room.

After the first preliminary words of politeness had been exchanged between us, my visitor informed me as follows of the object which he had in view.

"I believe you live in the country, sir?" he began.

"I live in the West of England," I answered.

"Do you make a long stay in London?"

"No. I go back to my rectory tomorrow."

"May I ask if you take pupils?"

"Yes."

"Have you any vacancy?"

"I have one vacancy."

"Would you object to let me go back with you tomorrow, as your pupil?"

The abruptness of the proposal took me by surprise. I hesitated.

In the first place (as I have already said) I disliked him. In the second place, he was too old to be a fit companion for my other two pupils—both lads in their teens. In the third place, he had asked me to receive him at least three weeks before the vacation came to an end. I had my own pursuits and amusements in prospect during that interval, and saw no reason why I should inconvenience myself by setting them aside.

He noticed my hesitation, and did not conceal from me that I had disappointed him.

"I have it very much at heart," he said, "to repair without delay the time that I have lost. My age is against me, I know. The truth is—I have wasted my opportunities since I left school, and I am anxious, honestly anxious, to mend my ways, before it is too late. I wish to prepare myself for one of the Universities—I wish to show, if I can, that I am not quite unworthy to inherit my father's famous name.

"You are the man to help me, if I can only persuade you to do it. I was struck by your sermon yesterday; and, if I may venture to make the confession in your presence, I took a strong liking to you. Will you see my father, before you decide to say No? He will be able to explain whatever may seem strange in my present application; and he will be happy to see you this afternoon, if you can spare the time. As to the question of terms, I am quite sure it can be settled to your entire satisfaction."

He was evidently in earnest—gravely, vehemently in earnest. I unwillingly consented to see his father.

Our interview was a long one. All my questions were answered fully and frankly.

The young man had led an idle and desultory life. He was weary of it, and ashamed of it. His disposition was a peculiar one. He stood sorely in need of a guide, a teacher, and a friend, in whom he was disposed to confide. If I disappointed the hopes which he had centred in me, he would be discouraged, and he would relapse into the aimless and indolent existence of which he was now ashamed. Any terms for which I might stipulate were at my disposal if I would consent to receive him, for three months to begin with, on trial.

Still hesitating, I consulted my father and my friends.

They were all of opinion (and justly of opinion so far) that the new connection would be an excellent one for me. They all reproached me for taking a purely capricious dislike to a well-born and well-bred young man, and for permitting it to influence me, at the outset of my career, against my own interests. Pressed by these considerations, I allowed myself to be persuaded to give the new pupil a fair trial. He accompanied me, the next day, on my way back to the rectory.

7

Let me be careful to do justice to a man whom I personally disliked. My senior pupil began well: he produced a decidedly favourable impression on the persons attached to my little house hold.

The women, especially, admired his beautiful light hair, his crisply-curling beard, his delicate complexion, his clear blue eyes, and his finely shaped hands and feet. Even the inveterate reserve in his manner, and the downcast, almost sullen, look which had prejudiced me against him, aroused a common feeling of romantic enthusiasm in my servants' hall. It was decided, on the high authority of the housekeeper herself, that "the new gentleman" was in love—and, more interesting still, that he was the victim of an unhappy attachment which had driven him away from his friends and his home.

For myself, I tried hard, and tried vainly, to get over my first dislike to the senior pupil.

I could find no fault with him. All his habits were quiet and regular; and he devoted himself conscientiously to his reading. But, little by little, I became satisfied that his heart was not in his studies. More than this, I had my reasons for suspecting that he was concealing something from me, and that he felt painfully the reserve on his own part which he could not, or dared not, break through. There were moments when I almost doubted whether he had not chosen my remote country rectory as a safe place of refuge from some person or persons of whom he stood in dread.

For example, his ordinary course of proceeding, in the matter of his correspondence, was, to say the least of it, strange.

He received no letters at my house. They waited for him at the village post office. He invariably called for them himself, and invariably forbore to trust any of my servants with his own letters for the post.

Again, when we were out walking together, I more than once caught him looking furtively over his shoulder, as if he suspected some person of following him, for some evil purpose. Being constitutionally a hater of mysteries, I determined, at an early stage of our intercourse, on making an effort to clear matters up. There might be just a chance of my winning the senior pupil's confidence, if I spoke to him while the last days of the summer vacation still left us alone together in the house.

"Excuse me for noticing it," I said to him one morning, while we were engaged over our books—"I cannot help observing that you appear to have some trouble on your mind. Is it indiscreet, on my part, to ask if I can be of any use to you?"

He changed colour—looked up at me quickly looked down again at his book—struggled hard with some secret fear or secret reluctance that was in him and suddenly burst out with this extraordinary question:

"I suppose you were in earnest when you preached that sermon in London?"

"I am astonished that you should doubt it," I replied.

He paused again; struggled with himself again; and startled me by a second outbreak, even stranger than the first.

"I am one of the people you preached at in your sermon," he said.

"That's the true reason why I asked you to take me for your pupil. Don't turn me out! When you talked to your congregation of tortured and tempted people, you talked of Me."

I was so astonished by the confession, that I lost my presence of mind. For the moment, I was unable to answer him,

"Don't turn me out!" he repeated. "Help me against myself. I am telling you the truth. As God is my witness, I am telling you the truth!"

"Tell me the whole truth," I said; "and rely on my consoling and helping you—rely on my being your friend."

In the fervour of the moment, I took his hand. It lay cold and still in mine; it mutely warned me that I had a sullen and a secret nature to deal with.

"There must be no concealment between us," I resumed. "You have entered my house, by your own confession, under false pretences. It is your duty to me, and your duty to yourself, to speak out."

The man's inveterate reserve—cast off for the moment only—renewed its hold on him. He considered, carefully considered, his next words before he permitted them to pass his lips.

"A person is in the way of my prospects in life," he began slowly, with his eyes cast down on his book. "A person provokes me horribly. I feel dreadful temptations (like the man you spoke of in your sermon) when I am in the person's company. Teach me to resist temptation! I am afraid of myself, if I see the person again. You are the only man who can help me. Do it while you can."

He stopped, and passed his handkerchief over his forehead.

"Will that do?" he asked—still with his eyes on his book.

"It will not do," I answered. "You are so far from really opening your heart to me, that you won't even let me know whether it is a man or a woman who stands in the way of your prospects in life. You used the word 'person,' over and over again—rather than say 'he' or 'she' when you speak of the provocation which is trying you. How can I help a man who has so little confidence in me as that?"

My reply evidently found him at the end of his resources. He tried, tried desperately, to say more than he had said yet. No! The words seemed to stick in his throat. Not one of them would pass his lips.

"Give me time," he pleaded piteously. "I can't bring myself to it, all at once. I mean well. Upon my soul, I mean well. But I am slow at this sort of thing. Wait till tomorrow."

Tomorrow came—and again he put it off.

"One more day!" he said. "You don't know how hard it is to speak plainly. I am half afraid; I am half ashamed. Give me one more day."

I had hitherto only disliked him. Try as I might (and did) to make merciful allowance for his reserve, I began to despise him now.

8

The day of the deferred confession came, and brought an event with it, for which both he and I were alike unprepared. Would he really have confided in me but for that event? He must either have done it, or have abandoned the purpose which had led him into my house.

We met as usual at the breakfast-table. My housekeeper brought in my letters of the morning. To my surprise, instead of leaving the room again as usual, she walked round to the other side of the table, and laid a letter before my senior pupil—the first letter, since his residence with me, which had been delivered to him under my roof.

He started, and took up the letter. He looked at the address. A spasm of suppressed fury passed across his face; his breath came quickly; his hand trembled as it held the letter. So far, I said nothing. I waited to see whether he would open the envelope in my presence or not.

He was afraid to open it in my presence. He got on his feet; he said, in tones so low that I could barely hear him: "Please excuse me for a minute"—and left the room.

I waited for half an hour—for a quarter of an hour after that—and then I sent to ask if he had forgotten his breakfast.

In a minute more, I heard his footstep in the hall. He opened the breakfast-room door, and stood on the threshold, with a small travelling-bag in his hand.

"I beg your pardon," he said, still standing at the door. "I must ask for leave of absence for a day or two. Business in London."

"Can I be of any use?" I asked. "I am afraid your letter has brought you bad news?"

"Yes," he said shortly. "Bad news. I have no time for breakfast."

"Wait a few minutes," I urged. "Wait long enough to treat me like your friend—to tell me what your trouble is before you go."

He made no reply. He stepped into the hall and closed the door—then opened it again a little way, without showing himself.

"Business in London," he repeated—as if he thought it highly important to inform me of the nature of his errand. The door closed for the second time. He was gone.

I went into my study, and carefully considered what had happened.

The result of my reflections is easily described. I determined on discontinuing my relations with my senior pupil. In writing to his father (which I did, with all due courtesy and respect, by that day's post), I mentioned as my reason for arriving at this decision:—First, that I had found it impossible to win the confidence of his son. Secondly, that his son had that morning suddenly and mysteriously left my house for London, and that I must decline accepting any further responsibility toward him, as the necessary consequence.

I had put my letter in the postbag, and was beginning to feel a little easier after having written it, when my housekeeper appeared in the study, with a very grave face, and with something hidden apparently in her closed hand.

"Would you please look, sir, at what we have found in the gentleman's bedroom, since he went away this morning?"

I knew the housekeeper to possess a woman's full share of that amiable weakness of the sex which goes by the name of "Curiosity." I had also, in various indirect ways, become aware that my senior pupil's strange departure had largely increased the disposition among the women of my household to regard him as the victim of an unhappy attachment. The time was ripe, as it seemed to me, for checking any further gossip about him, and any renewed attempts at prying into his affairs in his absence.

"Your only business in my pupil's bedroom," I said to the housekeeper, "is to see that it is kept clean, and that it is properly aired. There must be no interference, if you please, with his letters, or his papers, or with anything else that he has left behind him. Put back directly whatever you may have found in his room."

The housekeeper had her full share of a woman's temper as well as of a woman's curiosity. She listened to me with a rising colour, and a just perceptible toss of the head.

"Must I put it back, sir, on the floor, between the bed and the wall?" she inquired, with an ironical assumption of the humblest deference to my wishes. "That's where the girl found it when she was sweeping the room. Anybody can see for themselves," pursued the housekeeper indignantly, "that the poor gentleman has gone away broken-hearted. And there, in my opinion, is the hussy who is the cause of it!"

With those words, she made me a low curtsey, and laid a small photographic portrait on the desk at which I was sitting.

I looked at the photograph.

In an instant, my heart was beating wildly my head turned giddy—the housekeeper, the furniture, the walls of the room, all swayed and whirled round me.

The portrait that had been found in my senior pupil's bedroom was the portrait of Jéromette!

9

I had sent the housekeeper out of my study. I was alone, with the photograph of the Frenchwoman on my desk.

There could surely be little doubt about the discovery that had burst upon rue. The man who had stolen his way into my house, driven by the terror of a temptation that he dared not reveal, and the man who had been my unknown rival in the by-gone time, were one and the same!

Recovering self-possession enough to realize this plain truth, the inferences that followed forced their way into my mind as a matter of course. The unnamed person who was the obstacle to my pupil's prospects in life, the unnamed person in whose company he was assailed by temptations which made him tremble for himself, stood revealed to me now as being, in all human probability, no other than Jéromette. Had she bound him in the fetters of the marriage which he had himself proposed? Had she discovered his place of refuge in my house? And was the letter that had been delivered to him of her writing?

Assuming these questions to be answered in the affirmative, what, in that case, was his "business in London"? I remembered how he had spoken to me of his temptations, I recalled the expression that had crossed his face when he recognized the handwriting on the letter—and the conclusion that followed literally shook me to the soul. Ordering my horse to be saddled, I rode instantly to the railway-station.

The train by which he had travelled to London had reached the terminus nearly an hour since. The one useful course that I could take, by way of quieting the dreadful misgivings crowding one after another on my mind, was to telegraph to Jéromette at the address at which I had last seen her. I sent the subjoined message—prepaying the reply:

> If you are in any trouble, telegraph to me. I will be with you by the first train. Answer, in any case.

There was nothing in the way of the immediate dispatch of my message. And yet the hours passed, and no answer was received. By the advice of the clerk, I sent a second telegram to the London office, requesting an explanation. The reply came back in these terms:

> Improvements in street. Houses pulled down. No trace of per-

son named in telegram.

I mounted my horse, and rode back slowly to the rectory.

"The day of his return to me will bring with it the darkest days of my life."

"I shall die young, and die miserably. Have you interest enough still left in me to wish to hear of it?"

"You shall hear of it."

Those words were in my memory while I rode home in the cloudless moonlight night. They were so vividly present to me that I could hear again her pretty foreign accent, her quiet clear tones, as she spoke them. For the rest, the emotions of that memorable day had worn me out. The answer from the telegraph-office had struck me with a strange and stony despair. My mind was a blank. I had no thoughts. I had no tears.

I was about half-way on my road home, and I had just heard the clock of a village church strike ten, when I became conscious, little by little, of a chilly sensation slowly creeping through and through me to the bones. The warm, balmy air of a summer night was abroad. It was the month of July. In the month of July, was it possible that any living creature (in good health) could feel cold? It was not possible—and yet, the chilly sensation still crept through and through me to the bones.

I looked up. I looked all round me.

My horse was walking along an open high-road. Neither trees nor waters were near me. On either side, the flat fields stretched away bright and broad in the moonlight.

I stopped my horse, and looked round me again.

Yes: I saw it. With my own eyes I saw it. A pillar of white mist—between five and six feet high, as well as I could judge—was moving beside me at the edge of the road, on my left hand. When I stopped, the white mist stopped. When I went on, the white mist went on. I pushed my horse to a trot—the pillar of mist was with me. I urged him to a gallop—the pillar of mist was with me. I stopped him again—the pillar of mist stood still.

The white colour of it was the white colour of the fog which I had seen over the river on the night when I had gone to bid her farewell. And the chill which had then crept through me to the bones was the chill that was creeping through me now.

I went on again slowly. The white mist went on again slowly—with the clear bright night all round it.

I was awed rather than frightened. There was one moment, and one only, when the fear came to me that my reason might be shaken. I caught myself keeping time to the slow tramp of the horse's feet with the slow utterances of these words, repeated over and over again: "Jéromette is dead. Jéromette is dead." But my will was still my own: I was able to control myself, to impose silence on my own muttering lips. And I rode on quietly. And the pillar of mist went quietly with me.

My groom was waiting for my return at the rectory gate. I pointed to the mist, passing through the gate with me.

"Do you see anything there?" I said.

The man looked at me in astonishment.

I entered the rectory. The housekeeper met me in the hall. I pointed to the mist, entering with me.

"Do you see anything at my side?" I asked.

The housekeeper looked at me as the groom had looked at me.

"I am afraid you are not well, sir," she said. "Your colour is all gone—you are shivering. Let me get you a glass of wine."

I went into my study, on the ground-floor, and took the chair at my desk. The photograph still lay where I had left it. The pillar of mist floated round the table, and stopped opposite to me, behind the photograph.

The housekeeper brought in the wine. I put the glass to my lips, and set it down again. The chill of the mist was in the wine. There was no taste, no reviving spirit in it, The presence of the housekeeper oppressed me. My dog had followed her into the room. The presence of the animal oppressed me. I said to the woman: "Leave me by myself, and take the dog with you."

They went out, and left me alone in the room.

I sat looking at the pillar of mist, hovering opposite to me.

It lengthened slowly, until it reached to the ceiling. As it lengthened, it grew bright and luminous. A time passed, and a shadowy appearance showed itself in the centre of the light. Little by little, the shadowy appearance took the outline of a human form. Soft brown eyes, tender and melancholy, looked at me through the unearthly light in the mist.

The head and the rest of the face broke next slowly on my view. Then the figure gradually revealed itself, moment by moment, downward and downward to the feet. She stood before me as I had last seen her, in her purple-merino dress, with the black-silk apron, with the white handkerchief tied loosely round her neck. She stood before me, in the gentle beauty that I remembered so well; and looked at me as she had looked when she gave me her last kiss—when her tears had dropped on my cheek.

I fell on my knees at the table. I stretched out my hands to her imploringly. I said: "Speak to me—O, once again speak to me, Jéromette."

Her eyes rested on me with a divine compassion in them. She lifted her hand, and pointed to the photograph on my desk, with a gesture which bade me turn the card. I turned it. The name of the man who had left my house that morning was inscribed on it, in her own handwriting.

I looked up at her again, when I had read it.

She lifted her hand once more, and pointed to the handkerchief round her neck. As I looked at it, the fair white silk changed horribly in colour—the fair white silk became darkened and drenched in blood.

A moment more—and the vision of her began to grow dim. By slow degrees, the figure, then the face, faded back into the shadowy appearance that I had first seen. The luminous inner light died out in the white mist. The mist itself dropped slowly downward—floated a moment in airy circles on the floor—vanished. Nothing was before me but the familiar wall of the room, and the photograph lying face downward on my desk.

10

The next day, the newspapers reported the discovery of a murder in London. A Frenchwoman was the victim. She had been killed by a wound in the throat. The crime had been discovered between ten and eleven o'clock on the previous night.

I leave you to draw your conclusion from what I have related. My own faith in the reality of the apparition is immovable. I say, and believe, that Jéromette kept her word with me. She died young, and died miserably. And I heard of it from herself.

Take up the Trial again, and look at the circumstances that were revealed during the investigation in court. His motive for murdering her is there.

You will see that she did indeed marry him privately; that they lived together contentedly, until the fatal day when she discovered that his fancy had been caught by another woman; that violent quarrels took place between them, from that time to the time when my sermon showed him his own deadly hatred toward her, reflected in the case of another man; that she discovered his place of retreat in my house, and threatened him by letter with the public assertion of her conjugal rights; lastly, that a man, variously described by different witnesses, was seen leaving the door of her lodgings on the night of the murder.

The Law—advancing no further than this—may have discovered circumstances of suspicion, but no certainty. The Law, in default of direct evidence to convict the prisoner, may have rightly decided in letting him go free.

But I persisted in believing that the man was guilty. I declare that he, and he alone, was the murderer of Jéromette. And now, you know why.

LEONAUR

ALSO FROM LEONAUR

AVAILABLE IN SOFTCOVER OR HARDCOVER WITH DUST JACKET

MR MUKERJI'S GHOSTS *by S. Mukerji*—Supernatural tales from the British Raj period by India's Ghost story collector.

KIPLINGS GHOSTS *by Rudyard Kipling*—Twelve stories of Ghosts, Hauntings, Curses, Werewolves & Magic.

THE COLLECTED SUPERNATURAL AND WEIRD FICTION OF WASHINGTON IRVING: VOLUME 1 *by Washington Irving*—Including one novel 'A History of New York', and nine short stories of the Strange and Unusual.

THE COLLECTED SUPERNATURAL AND WEIRD FICTION OF WASHINGTON IRVING: VOLUME 2 *by Washington Irving*—Including three novelettes 'The Legend of the Sleepy Hollow', 'Dolph Heyliger', 'The Adventure of the Black Fisherman' and thirty-two short stories of the Strange and Unusual.

THE COLLECTED SUPERNATURAL AND WEIRD FICTION OF JOHN KENDRICK BANGS: VOLUME 1 *by John Kendrick Bangs*—Including one novel 'Toppleton's Client or A Spirit in Exile', and ten short stories of the Strange and Unusual.

THE COLLECTED SUPERNATURAL AND WEIRD FICTION OF JOHN KENDRICK BANGS: VOLUME 2 *by John Kendrick Bangs*—Including four novellas 'A House-Boat on the Styx', 'The Pursuit of the House-Boat', 'The Enchanted Typewriter' and 'Mr. Munchausen' of the Strange and Unusual.

THE COLLECTED SUPERNATURAL AND WEIRD FICTION OF JOHN KENDRICK BANGS: VOLUME 3 *by John Kendrick Bangs*—Including twor novellas 'Olympian Nights', 'Roger Camerden: A Strange Story', and ten short stories of the Strange and Unusual.

THE COLLECTED SUPERNATURAL AND WEIRD FICTION OF MARY SHELLEY: VOLUME 1 *by Mary Shelley*—Including one novel 'Frankenstein or the Modern Prometheus', and fourteen short stories of the Strange and Unusual.

THE COLLECTED SUPERNATURAL AND WEIRD FICTION OF MARY SHELLEY: VOLUME 2 *by Mary Shelley*—Including one novel 'The Last Man', and three short stories of the Strange and Unusual.

THE COLLECTED SUPERNATURAL AND WEIRD FICTION OF AMELIA B. EDWARDS *by Amelia B. Edwards*—Contains two novelettes 'Monsieur Maurice', and 'The Discovery of the Treasure Isles', one ballad 'A Legend of Boisguilbert'and seventeen short stories to cill the blood.

www.ingramcontent.com/pod-product-compliance
Lightning Source LLC
Chambersburg PA
CBHW022147010726
47493CB00002B/375
* 9 7 8 1 7 8 2 8 2 6 9 7 2 *